a TROUBLED
an INNOCENT CHILD.
an INEXORABLE fate.

Then the sounds began. Shrieks. Raucous, horrible laughter.
A light flickered beyond the hole he'd made in the floor.
His terror grew as the sounds swelled; the screams echoed,
deafening, and the footfalls pounded angrily on the stones
above. Jon's mind flashed briefly on the threat of the floor
caving in, or his being drawn into the rasping orgy. The
undead spirits would suck the blood from his veins, and the
cloth would absorb what was left, as it had his mother.

The noise stopped.

The chanting stopped.

The breathing stopped.

The truth was swept away by words the man in the shrine
above spoke. "Silver man."

From somewhere deep in the silence above him, Jon felt an
insistent wordless warning. For an instant his terror returned,
but he fought it back. "Father," he whispered and smiled.

**From the acclaimed author of *Mina* and *Nocturne* comes
Tapestry of Dark Souls, the story of a young man who
finds that safety and a future do not lie in a town under
the rule of terrifying evil.**

RAVENLOFT™
the covenant

DEATH OF A DARKLORD
Laurell K. Hamilton

VAMPIRE OF THE MISTS
Christie Golden

I, STRAHD:
THE MEMOIRS OF A VAMPIRE
P. N. Elrod

TO SLEEP WITH EVIL
Andria Cardarelle

TAPESTRY OF DARK SOULS
Elaine Bergstrom

SCHOLAR OF DECAY
Tanya Huff
(October 2007)

ELAINE BERGSTROM

tapestry of DARK SOULS

RAVENLOFT™

the covenant

Ravenloft™
The Covenant
TAPESTRY OF DARK SOULS

©1996 TSR, Inc., ©2007 Wizards of the Coast, Inc.

Cover art by: Erik M. Gist
Original Paperback First Printing: March 1993
First Trade Paperback Printing: June 2007

9 8 7 6 5 4 3 2 1

ISBN: 978-0-7869-4367-8
620-10932740-001-EN

U.S., CANADA,
ASIA, PACIFIC, & LATIN AMERICA
Wizards of the Coast, Inc.
P.O. Box 707
Renton, WA 98057-0707
+1-800-324-6496

EUROPEAN HEADQUARTERS
Hasbro UK Ltd
Caswell Way
Newport, Gwent NP9 0YH
GREAT BRITAIN
Save this address for your records.

Visit our web site at www.wizards.com

Dedicated with love

to Carl,

who let me share his dream.

proLogue

tHe foLLowing taLe is toLd on tHe oLdest scroLL *preserved by the Order of the Guardians. Its edges are charred, though the tale itself is intact.*

Skya, a woman of the Abber nomads in the Nightmare Lands, first saw the meadow-thorns. Her shaman says that the land drew her to them.

She had been fishing with others of her tribe on the Ivlis River, west of their encampment. Their nets had snagged a few fish, enough to tease them with hope that more would follow. They recited ritual thanks to appease the land and reset their snags. Below the narrow gorge where they spread their nets, young children played in the warm, sandy shallows. Older ones, meanwhile, stood guard, their spears ready to pierce any of the gray water snakes and poisonous leeches that hid in the murky Ivlis waters.

The day was hot and deathly still. A charged heaviness hung oppressively in the air, and the few white clouds that dotted the sky were darkening and gathering in a slowly shifting spiral. The hunters knew the danger of these signs and started back to the riverside camp. But the fishermen, intent on their work, their view of the sky obstructed by the sandy cliffs of the river basin, remained at their toil too long.

The sky suddenly blackened. The wind screamed a brief, terrible warning only moments before hail fell from the clouds, covering the dry earth with a steaming coat of ice. The Ivlis, warm and placid only moments before, became a torrent of swollen white-foamed rapids.

Women clutched their children and scrambled up the icy banks to safety as the furious waters clawed at the earth behind them. Skya, burdened by her young son, lost her footing. She managed to toss the child to safety before she slipped down the bank into the center of the rapids and was swept downstream. Filthy water filled her mouth and blinded her, and, more than once, the hungry current pulled her under.

To die between the pounding hand of the river and the rocky ribs of its bottom would make her a slave to the land, a ghost tossed on its tempestuous whim. Determined to escape such an end, Skya ripped off her water-laden skirt and managed a few strong strokes, enough to grasp a scrubby sapling at the river's edge. But the river had already exposed the roots and the trunk broke free, plunging into the raging current.

Skya pulled herself as high as she could onto the narrow trunk. Vapor rose suddenly from the water, thicker than any fog or mist. It closed around her, obscuring her view of the banks. With her arms outspread on the thorny branches, Skya let the river take her where it would.

She should have died from the cold, but the land decreed other-wise. As quickly as the storm grew, it died. The sun shone and the air warmed once more, but the turgid river didn't relent. Unable to reach the shore, Skya traveled for hours, growing more exhausted in her constant struggle to cling to her shifting float.

Then, the fabled Death Mists loomed before her—a pulsing fog. Alive. Eternal. The edge of the world. Skya's tribe had never ventured into their unknown darkness. None would dare. Drowning was preferable to the consuming mists and the emptiness beyond. Fear gave Skya desperate strength, and she twisted toward shore, abandoning the sapling at the first rocks on the river's edge.

Skya crawled onto dry land and kissed the earth beneath her, thanking it for sparing her life. She was far from the encampment, deep in a place of purple sky and whispering insects. But she was Abber, strong enough to survive alone until she came across others of her kind.

The sun was suddenly gone, and the terrain, flat and covered with coarse sand grass and wildflowers, offered no shelter. Skya dug a shallow pit in the sandy soil. She filled it with grasses, burrowed into the center of them and, putting herself at the land's mercy, slept.

Skya woke late the following morning to a meadow vastly changed. The silver-topped grasses were choked by thorn bushes, which bore heavy-scented white flowers. The blossoms, glowing in the brilliant sun, drugged her with their scent. Skya's vision pulsed. A humming in her ears drowned out even the sound of her own voice as she considered aloud what she must do. She had intended to follow the river back to the homelands, but the river had vanished beneath the endless meadow. Reeling with confusion and weariness, Skya returned to her burrow and slept once more.

The next waking brought another change. The glowing blossoms were folding and withering, replaced by a fruit that ripened from pale green to glistening black as she watched.

Famished and thirsty, Skya sampled a handful of the gleaming fruit and found the berries marvelously sweet. Reciting ritual thanks for this gift, she began to eat. The berries stole her hunger and her thirst. The air seemed lighter, the summer sun warmer. The buzzing in her ears quieted. Picking the berries, she walked to the edge of the meadow, but no longer desired to abandon it.

Days later, her tribe discovered her. Her lips and fingers were black from the juice, her eyes vacant.

By now only a few of the cloying white flowers remained on the plants. Nonetheless, the tribe guessed the dangers the land held and refused to walk among the plants or taste the berries. Time meant little to the Abber, living where days and seasons changed by the moment, and so they camped some distance from the meadow and waited. Skya was alive. Perhaps the land would choose to free her.

They didn't have to wait long.

The meadow began to shake, the land to crack.

And from the deep crevasse that formed in its center, a swarm of noisy blue locusts rose and covered the sky. The insects settled on the bushes, stripping the leaves from the plants with the same swift hunger that Skya had known. The insects feasted throughout the day, growing fat and laying eggs on the berries that rotted on the ground. Then the swarm rose in a single dark cloud that disappeared into the black Death Mists at the edge of the world. The eggs hatched that night. The following day the slugs consumed what was left of the fruit, then spun tiny cocoons as soft as the catkins that bloomed after the first snows.

That night, the moon rose and every small cocoon glowed in its light. Skya gathered a handful of them and carried them to the Abber camp.

The tribe craftsmen dumped the cocoons in a clay pot of boiling water, then unrolled the silken threads. The shaman wove a tight chain with his fingers and studied the result. The chain was strong, more elastic than bowstring gut or fishnet fiber. He rolled a cocoon between his thumb and forefinger, unraveling the glowing strands to study the tiny creature inside. But he found nothing, empty air.

"The land has given us a miraculous treasure," he pronounced and ordered a harvest of the cocoons the following day.

At sunrise, the entire tribe descended on the field. There, with the tenacity of the locusts, they gathered each cocoon. Some were used for bowstrings, others for nets. The rest were traded to a traveler from Arbora in Nova Vaasa in exchange for wool cloth and, as a special honor, a necklace of gold for Skya, who had discovered the land's rich gift.

Though the necklace was finer than any worn by another of her tribe, Skya had no use for it and gave it to her eldest daughter. For the rest of her life, Skya treasured only one thing—the iridescent ball of string she kept clutched in her palm. What comfort she took in this reminder of the meadow-thorns, no one ever understood.

In Arbora, a weaver fashioned the fibers into a shimmering gray cloth. Though it was the height and width of three men, the cloth was light as a spiderweb, thinner than the finest silk. Those who saw it felt a strange covetous longing in their hearts, but no one could meet the weaver's price. Men tried to steal it, women to seduce him into parting with it, but the weaver wouldn't, couldn't, let it go. He took to sleeping with it hidden below his pallet, a knife clutched in his hand.

On pain of his life, the weaver finally sold the cloth to a wealthy Nova Vaasan lord for a sum that would support him for two lifetimes. But, like so many others who had touched its shimmering folds, the weaver pined in torment without his marvelous creation. Eventually, he left Arbora, intending, no doubt, to steal the cloth from its new owner. He was never seen again, and the cloth vanished mysteriously into shadow and legend.

part I
Leith

one

after all that has happened during my many months in this desolate place, I am certain the tapestry called me.

My husband Vhar and I had been traveling to an autumn fair in the seaport of Vezprem. I could describe our house, our town, the family that even now must wonder where we have gone, but why dwell on what is lost? The story of the tapestry is all that is important.

I was certain we had missed some turn on the unfamiliar road, but, as Vhar reminded me, "Leith, you have no skill with maps." My repeated suggestion that the ill-repaired road couldn't possibly service the seaport only made him violently angry. No, it was better to keep silent and hope that Vhar would see his mistake in the morning. If we continued on this route, we would never reach Vezprem in time to buy a selling space—one we desperately needed. Even if the port's sales were good, we still faced a winter of privation.

Such reminders only stoked Vhar's anger. His name meant "bristle", and it was most appropriate. Our village called him the "red man"—red hair, ruddy face, and a temper just as fierce. He wasn't well liked, but always respected. Such men usually are. When he courted me, he did so with such single-minded passion that I didn't see how mismatched we were until long after our vows were made. I was as stubborn as he was loud, and if we had devoted half the effort to work that we did to fighting, we would have been wealthy.

At least there were only two of us to feed, I reminded myself as we rode along on that dry and empty road. I tried to take some comfort in the sad fact that we had no family after five years of marriage. Our only child had been stillborn two years before: the one time I ever saw my husband cry. My fingers brushed over the fertility amulet I kept in my pocket. Vhar and I hoped that it might have already been successful, but it would be days before I could be truly sure. As I contemplated this, I heard a warning hiss from Vhar.

The road became rougher and its incline increased. Brown granite cliffs rose to the right of us, baking in the harsh afternoon sun and throwing their dry heat over the steadily narrowing road. To our left, the cliffs fell sharply to a plain covered with dark and twisted trees. A hard wind blew across the plain, pitching the treetops back and forth angrily. And ahead of us towered jagged and forbidding mountains.

I had never heard of this harsh land between our home and the sea, and thought of last night's strange fog as we rode on. Vhar was beginning to doze beneath the wagon's tarp. Though I now knew we were on the wrong road, I didn't disturb him. I wasn't certain we could find our way back, even if we turned around.

In spite of the danger of the rock-strewn road, I shook the reins to hurry the horse along. An odd hunger had awakened in me; I told myself it was from the heat of day or the stark grandeur of the land. But even then, I knew it was something darker, more implacable, drawing me forward. Rounding a steep embankment, I pulled up quickly. A pile of boulders, sheared from the cliffs above, obstructed the road. The wagon couldn't go on. I peered past the obstruction, seeing that soon after it, the road ended at the base of a ruined castle—a castle I had mistaken as a mountain peak before. The fortress's jagged stone battlements stood silhouetted against the brilliant sky.

Crumbling and apparently abandoned, the castle seemed to have perched so many eons on its rocky precipice that it had become one with the earth itself. A great rent cut through its outer wall nearly to the outcropping at its base. Perhaps the place had been prosperous once, perhaps even part of the defense of the scrub plain beneath it. Now it seemed little more than an ancient ruin.

The hunger deepened.

Vhar, now awake, joined me on the seat and stared at the castle with his mouth ajar. "Perhaps we are lost," Vhar whispered to himself. My breath caught short: the fear in Vhar's voice left me cold.

But Vhar's fear meant less than my hunger. Somehow, that castle drew me, inexorably, a passion I've grown only too accustomed to now. A terrible exhilaration took hold of me. Even while I dreaded what I might find, I felt compelled to enter those desolate walls. Jumping off the seat, I climbed over the pile of boulders and started up the path.

"Where are you going?" Vhar called. "Come help me turn the wagon before brigands show up."

I whirled, one hand pointing to the crumbling ruin. "Look at it, Vhar," I called. "No one lives there." I turned and, lifting my skirts with one hand, ran up the path toward the massive wooden doors of the fortress.

Vhar was running behind me now, so I quickened my pace. I remember thinking, perhaps for the first time, that he was a selfish, childish fool, and I wouldn't let him stop me. He called my name, then screamed it. I ignored his cries.

Up ahead, a pair of gray-cloaked figures rushed from the narrow gateway and down the hill toward me. I slowed my steps, sudden fear entering my heart. One of the men carried a rope, and the other pointed beyond me. They rushed past, one hesitating long enough to lay a hand on my arm. "The man will be all right," he said and ran on.

I turned. Vhar had vanished over the edge of the cliff, but I could still hear him alternately calling my name and crying for help. I watched long enough to see the robed pair uncoil the rope and lower it, then spun with odd disregard and continued my climb to the high stone walls. My pace slowed only when I reached the castle's shadow. There I halted, shivering with something more than the sudden chill. I felt, for a moment, paralyzed, and managed only one step forward. Then, as abruptly as it came, the fear lifted, replaced by a hunger too strong to control. I ran through the half-open doors.

Within the courtyard stood a small cluster of stone buildings, made of the same brown stones as the wall without. All but a large two-story hall were missing parts of their roofs. One building had burned and was no more than a gutted shell. I took them in with a single, sweeping glance, my eyes centering on a large, lovely shrine close to the far wall.

The shrine seemed to have been brought to these desert ruins from some more hopeful place, from someplace damp and green. Its walls were built of beautifully matched and mortared red-clay blocks, which didn't resemble the weathered stones of the fortress. Its high-arched windows, now covered with heavy boards, must have been magnificent when they were glazed. Even without glass, the carved stone casings were skillfully worked, and the shrine radiated a feeling of holiness and soothing power. I pictured it, ivy-covered, in the center of some cool and peaceful town. Grass and flowers would surround it; I could almost see the moist green lawn shimmering like a mirage in that desolate courtyard.

I shook my head to clear the vision, then walked forward and laid my hands on the solid iron doors. They bore intricate runes, shadowy in the late sun. An unexpectedly terrible chill flowed into my hand and down my trembling arm. I pulled back quickly, strangely certain that if it reached my heart, I would die. Nonetheless, I slid aside a rusty iron bar and tried the doors, hoping for an instant that they would be locked.

But no, they opened easily. Harsh sunlight fell through the doorway, casting my shadow long and black on the uneven stone floor. If the shrine had ever contained seats or statues, they had long since been removed. I shuffled cautiously toward the altar. As my eyes grew accustomed to the inside light, I saw stubby candles clinging to its dark, stone slab. I paused to find the small flint box I always carried in my skirt pocket and struck a spark.

And in a single flickering flame, through spiraling dust and cobwebs, I saw it—a silvery tapestry that had somehow held its place against theft and time. It hung from ceiling to floor on the wall behind the altar. Breaking a lit candle free from the altar, I studied the tapestry. Woven into it was an intricate pattern: layer upon layer of men and women, all bearing expressions of such terror and evil that the cloth seemed to depict a crowded street in the netherworld.

Yet there was a shimmering majesty to the silk. It was beautiful. A strange power seemed to flow from it, filling me with an incredible mix of awe and fear that I can only describe as sacredness. Though I wanted to run from it, I approached it reverently, falling to my knees before it . . . looking up . . . whispering half-forgotten prayers I had learned from my mother and the stern-faced priests of our town.

I know not how long I knelt there. It seemed an eternity—and a mere moment. But a commotion outside broke the cloth's hold on me. The door swung fully open. A breeze swept through the shrine, and the cloth rippled, producing a sound like fey laughter, as though the souls pictured on the cloth mocked me.

The chapel grew suddenly darker as a gray-robed figure moved into the doorway. "Come out. This isn't a holy place," he said solemnly. I scrambled from my knees and walked hesitantly toward him. His pale face was lined with age, and he hunched over his staff in a way that made him look far shorter than he was. His eyes were bandaged with strips of gauze, and he carried a carved staff to guide his way.

I stammered my apology, then added, "I thought the ruins were deserted." The lie was a weak one, especially since the monks had passed me.

The monk turned to me and spoke so intently that I had the odd feeling he was staring through the gauze. "You did?"

"Well, yes. The shrine looked so beautiful." I flushed. How could I have said that? "I'm sorry. I didn't mean to give offense."

"Offense?" he asked.

"Well, I just mean that . . ."

The sound of others came at the door, and stopping mid-sentence, I tried to move past the monk. He gripped my arm with surprising strength and said, "What you have done was very foolish. Don't you understand the dangers of these lands?"

"Dangers? No, I *don't* understand." I pulled my arm from his grasp and backed slowly toward the open door.

The blind man's expression became thoughtful, then sympathetic. "What is the name of your homeland?" he whispered.

"We are from Morova. We are traveling to Vezprem for the summer fair. . . ." My voice trailed off.

"Was there a fog last night, a strange, sudden fog, darker than a starless night?"

14

"Yes," I said and added, "where are we now?" My voice sounded oddly soft.

"Markovia . . . a land of tyranny and darkness." The words rolled off his tongue like a heavy chant.

The cloth rustled laughingly in another slight draft from the open door. I felt suddenly faint and dropped to one knee to keep from falling. Outside, Vhar called my name, but I didn't answer, not even when, on the edge of my vision, I saw him stagger toward the door of the chapel.

One of his rescuers pulled him back, but it was already too late. Vhar's eyes were fixed on the shimmering fabric; it had bewitched us both. And where were we now? If he had listened to me sooner, we might have found our way back to Morova to face a winter of hardship, rather than of . . . of what? The priests' stories had been as vague as they were terrible. I pushed their memory from my mind. Now I knew the tapestry was enchanted and I suddenly wanted to leave. Turning purposefully from the monk, I walked to the open doors and out into the blasting heat of the afternoon sun. Shading my eyes, I looked at my husband.

Vhar's face and arms were scraped, and he limped, but otherwise he appeared unharmed. "Fool woman. Stop next time when I call you," he grumbled to me.

"These people aren't from this land," the blind monk said to the larger of Vhar's two rescuers, then added more softly, "Perhaps we should see to their safety and offer them shelter tonight."

At this mild suggestion, Vhar's hand fell to the dagger he carried in his belt. "We have a horse and wagon. We can't leave them unguarded," he protested.

"You are right. There are hunters in these hills," the large monk said. "One of us can camp with your horse and provisions tonight. I am Brother Dominic, head of the Order of the

Guardians, and I offer you the protection of these walls."

"And if we choose to leave?" Vhar asked.

"It would hardly be wise. However, you are free to do as you wish."

I tried to catch Vhar's eye, to suggest that we must go, but he was already accepting the invitation, apologizing for his suspicion, letting one of the monks support him as we walked across the yard. The monks took us to the large building that housed the kitchen and meeting hall. When I think of it now, I wonder how the Guardians could have been so foolish as to let us stay. Perhaps, like Vhar and I, they didn't see how they were controlled.

My husband sat on a long stone bench while one of his rescuers, a thin, dark-skinned man with shaking hands, tended his wounds. Brother Dominic waited until Vhar was bandaged before motioning me toward the winding stone stairs at the end of the hall. "Before you leave here, there are things you must know," he said as we began the climb.

two

THE CEILING WAS LOST IN THE SHADOWS ABOVE ME; soot and cobwebs covered the pillars and beams that supported the roof. Nonetheless, the stone stairs beneath my feet were level and solid. Portraits in peeling gilt frames had darkened with the walls, and their subjects stared sullenly at us as we passed. "Did these people once live here?" I asked the monk.

"We believe that they still may," he responded. "At night we sometimes see thin shadows moving along the walls. The wind carries strange howls like the cries of creatures in pain. And there are places in this fortress that even the boldest of us don't visit."

"But they don't harm you, these shadows?"

"I think our presence amuses them," Dominic chuckled. "Or perhaps they are lonely. In any event, they allow us to live here, and we keep them in our prayers."

The steps ended with a wooden door. Swinging it wide, we entered an open tower that overlooked the lands to the north and east. Though the wood floor beneath me seemed sound enough, I stayed away from the tower wall, which was jagged and in ill repair.

"From the land below, these ancient walls look like part of the mountains. We prefer it that way, for we value our isolation. No one visits here. Indeed, we've set a warding spell on the outside walls that prevents anyone who comes from the dread lands about from entering . . . unless they have the calling."

"The calling to join your order?"

"Yes," he responded after a slight pause.

"And the fog your blind companion spoke of?"

"I came into the land through that fog, much as you did," he replied. "I told the others about my passage. That's how Mattas knew to ask about your home." His eyes, as they met mine, were filled with sympathy. At the time, it seemed natural, since he was a holy man. Later I understood how scarce true kindness was in this cursed land.

"And the others?"

"Are from the dread lands around. For some, living here is a sacrifice. For others, the order provides the first real comfort they have ever known."

I looked out at the land around us, the cold plains to the west, the blue rivers and dense forest to the north and east. Below me, the road that had led us here was barely visible as a clear ribbon against the sharp sides of the cliffs.

"This land, Markovia, is an unwise place to linger, as is G'Henna to the west. But if you follow the road back the way you came and stop at the river's edge, you will see a crossing shallow enough for your horse and cart. The road beyond it leads to a town called Linde in the land of Tepest. It is as happy a place as any I have seen. The people living there should tolerate your presence. In time, they may even come to think of you as one of their own."

"I'd rather return to my homeland."

"You cannot," he responded flatly, then his voice softened. "Oh, there are rumored to be ways, but they are few and filled with dangers of their own. Seeking them can take a lifetime and cause far more misery than accepting your fate."

Dominic sat on a bench in the center of the tower.

With difficulty, I pulled my eyes away from the dark landscape and sat beside him, his face in the shadows and mine in the light.

He whispered a few words of a strange language, then asked, "Tell me how you came here."

All my carefully-planned lies were forgotten and I related with as much detail as I could everything that had happened since we left home. Brother Dominic seemed neither surprised nor alarmed by my account. "Two more souls drawn from the outer lands," he said when I had finished.

"Drawn by what? The cloth?"

He shook his head. "You know so much already."

"I will pledge to tell no one that you or the cloth are here," I replied. Though his face was shadowed, I sensed his doubts and knew he had little reason to trust me. We might have spoken further, but a mournful bell tolled, calling us to eat.

The long wood table in the dining hall could easily seat twenty men. There were eight of us at one end of it. These included Vhar and me, and all the Guardians save the youngest, who had carried his evening meal down the path where he would stay and watch over our horse and cart. The meal was a simple one—coarse brown bread and hard cheese flecked with mold on its rind. For sweets, there were early apples and a mush of sweet blackberries picked from the woods below the castle.

Though I was sure Vhar had a hundred questions, and even more suspicions, he was wise enough not to broach them to our hosts. Instead, he wore a thin mask of charm. He told the monks false tales of our family and village, thanked the ones who saved his life, and offered to work to repay his debt.

"I can think of nothing we need done," Dominic replied. "But if you wish, you could leave one of your knives. Our blades are old. They don't hold an edge for long."

"I'll show you what I have and see to sharpening yours as well— but in the morning, please," Vhar said and stifled a yawn.

Dominic lifted a cased candle from the table and escorted us up a weathered outside staircase to a hallway that serviced the second-floor bedchambers. A bottle of wine sat on the table along with two glasses. "The wine is excellent," the monk said, pouring each of us a glass. "It will ease the pain and help you sleep," he said to Vhar and watched while Vhar drank his. I lifted mine, but, though I put the liquid to my lips, I didn't drink. One of us should sleep lightly, I thought. Vhar, with his bruises and pandering lies, seemed far less capable than I.

As soon as the door closed behind our host, Vhar began to mercilessly question me. He asked briefly and distractedly about the land and what I had learned, then turned to the one subject that seemed to have overpowered his mind—the tapestry in the shrine. "I saw it for only a moment, and the light was dim. Yet it seemed to glow, to move, to speak to me," he said. "You were beside it. What did you see?"

"A shimmering gray fabric with an odd, horrible pattern. The fabric looked like silk," I said, hoping he would not press the point.

"It moved. It whispered to me," he insisted.

"The breeze moved it. The folds rustled," I retorted.

My voice had risen, and he clapped an avid hand over my mouth. "What would such a treasure be worth, I wonder?" he asked.

I pushed his hand away. "Since the Guardians seem to value it so greatly, quite possibly our lives," I said and crawled beneath the ragged quilt on the bed. I patted the space beside me. "Come to bed, Vhar. Perhaps you'll be ready to talk about more important matters in the morning."

At any other time, he might have pressed me further, but the monks were filing up the stairs beyond our window. Vhar lay down beside me. As we listened to the Guardians' voices in the hall, Vhar drifted off to sleep.

That night, my mind traveled its own dark paths through the fog to the darkness of the shrine, with its horrible, glowing shroud. The dreams were many and troubling, but only the last and most vivid forced me awake. I saw Vhar strike a silver man with his dagger, but, when he raised his hand to strike again, I had become the victim, and Brother Dominic the attacker. His face was a mask of pity and concern, the tip of his blade biting into my throat.

I sat up in bed, certain that I heard voices and soft footfalls in the hall outside our room. The door was partly open and, when I went to shut it, the whispers became clear enough to understand.

Four men were in the room next to ours. I recognized the voices of two of the speakers, Mattas and Dominic. The others could have been any of the Guardians, for the rest had said very little during the meal. They discussed what should be done with us now that we knew of their existence here and the treasure that they guarded. Dominic spoke of imprisonment; another mentioned spells that would make us forget everything we had seen. With chilling persuasiveness, Mattas argued for murder.

Though it might have seemed the kindest solution, I feared the spells most of all, for I had seen the effects of forgetfulness spells gone awry. Men stripped of their memories often roamed the many summer festivals in our land, searching for someone with a clue to their past. In good years, I would give them coins or food. This year, I only looked away uneasily. I stole back to our bed, sliding in beside Vhar. There I lay quietly for a moment, calming myself before shaking him awake.

"I *thought* they were far too charitable," Vhar said bitterly when I had finally roused him enough to tell him all I had heard. We decided to escape, and dressed ourselves quickly. By the time we entered the corridor, the room next door was silent and dark. But we dared not risk a light. Instead, we used our hands to guide us in the lightless corridor until we reached the outside flight of stairs, which led to the yard below.

There Vhar held me back. "Stay here until you hear me whistle. The exit may be guarded. I'll clear the way," he whispered.

"I have my dagger," I said. "I'd prefer to remain with you."

"You'll be a hindrance if there's a fight," he replied gruffly. "Stay here." With that he was gone, the occasional falling pebble the only sound of his passing.

It seemed that I waited for his signal far too long. I began to expect to hear a cry of alarm from a guard outside, but there was only the distant howl of a wolf, the moaning of the chilling west wind through the cracks in the crumbling battlements above me. I had become certain that Vhar had been overpowered when I heard his familiar whistle. I descended carefully and, recalling the unevenness of the steps, gripped the rotting wooden rail as if it would actually support me.

Just as I passed, a tread gave way. It fell to the ground below with a sound that seemed to boom like thunder in the silent dark. I went more quickly then, less fearful of falling than of being discovered.

I met Vhar outside the wall. "Come," Vhar whispered, and I ran behind him down the path. At the pile of boulders, Vhar went on alone. It always astonished me how, in spite of his stocky build, Vhar could move so silently. His skill served him well that night. When I scrambled over the rocks, I saw the monk lying beside his fire. His blood was black and shining in the firelight. It flowed from his slashed neck into a shallow puddle beside him.

We didn't dare to light a torch to guide our way, so Vhar walked in front of the wagon, leading our horse down the twisting path. The wind picked up and the sky abruptly cleared, unveiling the watchful eye of a nearly full moon.

The sun was rising as we approached the base of the cliffs. Foot-weary, Vhar joined me on the wagon. Below us was a river, winding like a great black snake through the trees. I pointed it out to Vhar and explained what Dominic had told me about the country of Tepest.

"You also said he planned to murder us while we slept. I would hardly call his information reliable," Vhar reminded me, punctuating the statement with a derisive snort.

"I don't see another road," I countered.

The horse rounded a sharp curve and a shadow, huge and dark, rose from the road in front of us. Our horse reared, and the sudden, backward jolt of the wagon nearly threw me over the side. I pulled the knife I always carry. Vhar drew a short sword from beneath the wagon seat as the creature circled silently above us.

Its body was thin and black against the sky. Though I couldn't see its features clearly, it appeared almost human in form. Its wings were huge and leathery, like those of some dark dragon. Where there should have been hands and feet, I saw only talons. A drop of blood fell on my arm and I looked from the terrible creature to the road in front of me. The remnants of the creature's kill covered the road. My breath froze; my heart skipped a beat.

Judging from the shape and size of the limbs and head that remained, the meal had been a human child. I couldn't tell the sex or features from the face, for every shred of soft flesh had been devoured. Only the hair remained on the head, pale copper curls that danced in the wind and glowed in the rising sun.

"Kill it, before it kills us!" I whispered to Vhar.

He nodded irately and jumped from the wagon.

With his sword down, he walked toward the terrible feast. The creature circled lower and shrieked a warning, one that Vhar deliberately ignored. Instead, he fell to one knee beside the remains and reached out, as though he intended to take what was left. The second warning shriek was louder, higher-pitched, filled with rage. The thing rose on the wind, then pressed its wings tightly to its body and dove straight at Vhar.

With eyes fixed on his diving opponent, Vhar raised his sword. Though the creature's taloned arm managed to rip across Vhar's shoulder before veering away, the short sword sliced through one flapping wing. The creature tried to rise for another attack, but its balance was lost, and its wing beat uselessly. Once on the ground, the creature's body was clearly smaller than Vhar's. The long talons, so perfectly suited to airborne battles, provided little balance on the uneven ground. As the bat-thing stumbled back against the hill, seeking an escape, Vhar offered it an obvious opening. The creature, either stupid or unused to fighting a full grown man, lunged at the chance. Vhar's first stroke took one of its arms. Its dark wings beat around Vhar, spattering him with blood, but he stood his ground as the beast moved forward. The black wings circled Vhar, hiding him from my view. I rushed to attack the beast from behind, but saw its dark body stiffen, heard its desperate shriek, and watched it fall.

After noting that Vhar's wound wasn't deep, I walked to where the child's remains lay scattered on the ground. Among the bones lay a small gold ring in the shape of a vine. I thought of my own lost infant, thought of the mother who might be searching frantically for this one. Before Vhar could see what I had discovered, I hid the ring in my pocket. Perhaps I would be able to return it to the family someday.

Vhar moved beside me. "What a mess," he whispered.

"We should bury the body," I said.

"We ought to get out of this infested place before nightfall," he responded in a tone that allowed no argument. He paused only long enough to pick up the monster's severed limb and a portion of its wing, then hid them in our wagon before we continued on.

The area around the monastery had been harsh and scrubby. But, as we approached the river crossing that led to the land Dominic called Tepest, the trees were thicker and towered far above us. The woods were filled with dark shadows and unsettled rustling. Though the day was warm, I was thankful when the road widened enough that the sun beat down on us, as if its heat, like fire, could hold the predators at bay.

three

we traveled only a few miles beyond the crossing before we reached an area where the land had been cleared for grazing. Beyond the fields, a cluster of buildings marked a village. The central buildings were a stone inn—*The Nocturne* by name—and a brick livestock barn with wide plank doors. These were surrounded by a scattering of sturdy cottages and smaller barns. Every wall was whitewashed, and adorned with intricately painted flowers and vines, which garnished the doors. The houses had bright shutters, and flower boxes that overflowed with wildly colorful blooms.

After the emptiness of the land around the fortress, all this beauty was more than just a diversion for my eyes. I believed that the town held peace, and I hoped that Vhar and I could share it. I waved to a pair of children tending a flock of snow geese nearly as tall as they, but instead of waving back, they only eyed me suspiciously. Their copper hair glowed in the noonday sun, reminding me of the dead child we had seen on the road. I gripped the ring in my pocket, holding it like a luck charm as Vhar and I walked through the open door of *The Nocturne*.

The inside was as dark as the outside had been bright. There were deeply stained wooden walls and floors, and black slate tops on the dozen tables and the long bar that faced the door. Behind the bar stood a man, singing in a deep baritone suited to someone far stouter than he. As he sang, he polished an ornate collection of mugs that rested on a pair of stretched wolf skins—one silver, the other white. The wolves had been monstrous in size; even the sight of their pelts was chilling. Wolves also filled murals on every wall: a she-wolf suckling her young, a pack hunting, and, near the door, a winter landscape with a wolf howling at the starry sky.

The man behind the bar could easily have fathered the children outside, his complexion and hair color was so similar. He stopped singing as soon as he saw us. The only patrons, two blond men and a woman—her raven hair all the darker in contrast to the single streak of silver that fell from her widow's peak—were playing cards at a corner table. They stopped in mid-game and watched us as well. I took Vhar's arm as he walked boldly forward, loudly inquiring about food and a room.

"And your coin?" the innkeeper asked, his voice nearly as loud as Vhar's.

Vhar untied the purse from his belt and laid three coins on the counter. They were of a common metal, stamped with the eagle symbol of our land. The innkeeper kept his eyes on the coins as he said, "I could take these as a curiosity, but they've no other value here. I wouldn't show the coins to others, if I were you. I'm used to meeting strangers. Most in Tepest aren't."

Vhar nodded grimly. "Then perhaps a trade of goods?" he suggested, slowly pulling his dagger from its tooled leather sheath and laying it within reach of the man.

The innkeeper's hand brushed the glittering blade then pulled back quickly as if it burned him. The wolf's head pendant he wore around his neck caught the dim light from the doorway and glowed. He picked the dagger up by its wooden handle and tested its balance.

"I have others just as fine," Vhar told him.

"Silver is a rare metal in this land. There are many here who would pay well for a blade such as this," the man commented coldly. "I'm not one of them."

"Could you suggest a shop that might be interested in buying some of these?" Vhar asked.

"Shop?" The man smiled. "You have traveled a long way, I see." He poured us each a glass of ale. I glanced at the card players, noting that they were still watching us. "My name is Andor Merriwite and I own the inn and the barns behind it. If you've a less precious blade, perhaps one better suited to skinning game than an aristocrat's collection, I might be interested in a trade."

"Leith, show him your knife," Vhar said.

I had been fingering the ring in my pocket. As I pulled out my hand, the ring fell, rolling across the floor. I hurried to retrieve it, but I wasn't fast enough. The innkeeper's eyes were sharp. His earlier friendliness vanished. He held out his hand. "May I see that?" he asked.

I set it on the bar beside Vhar's knife. "Where did you get this?" Andor asked, his voice much lower now.

"We found the body of a child on the road. The ring was among the bones."

"The creature left the ring?" Andor asked doubtfully.

"The creature that killed the girl is dead," I replied. "My husband destroyed it with one of his aristocrat's blades. We have proof enough of that in our wagon."

Vhar gripped my arm, painfully indicating that I had told a stranger far too much. He was right. For all we knew, the town had sacrificed the child and Vhar had just destroyed the local deity.

Andor seemed to understand our fear for he quickly allayed it. "We saw her lifted by the darkflyer. We almost reached her in time."

"The foolish child was always running off. At least she had a quick death, far less painful than the beasties might have provided," the woman in the corner commented.

Her coldness stunned me. I frowned and looked more closely at her, staring far longer than was polite. The woman had a vitality that was impossible to ignore. Sensing my scrutiny, she looked my way. I quickly lowered my eyes and pointed to the ring. "I would like to return the ring to the girl's mother," I said.

Surprise glittered in Andor's bright blue eyes. "She'll be thankful," he said. He picked up my knife, running a finger along the fine steel blade. "I will give you a room and your meals tonight and tomorrow for a tool such as this."

"I have a horse and wagon full of goods. Is the brick building your stable?" Vhar asked.

"And the main livestock barn for the town of Linde as well," he said and peered out the door to see the amount of space we would need. "The horse must be kept in the barn tonight," he said, stepping back through the doorway. "There are creatures in these woods that have a taste for any warm flesh."

"Wolves?" I asked, thinking of the pelts on the inn's wall.

"Aye, wolves, but not often. Twice each year, they migrate across the river from the south. Their skins are rare and much prized." He turned to Vhar. "As for your wagon, there's no space for it in the stable. While no one from Tepest would steal your goods, it wouldn't be wise to leave them unprotected. If you pull your wagon to the back of the inn, I'll help you unload your crates into my storage room. It's always locked. I have the only key."

"I can manage to unload, myself," Vhar said and touched my hand in an uncommonly loving gesture, so at odds with his usual ill temper. "We have traveled far. While I unload, Leith should rest."

"Of course." The man led me to the staircase and pointed up it. "You'll have the first room on the right. See that your shutters are latched tonight."

As I climbed the stairs, I listened to the low voices of the card players and the melodic laughter of the woman.

While Vhar worked, I rested on a feather bed far softer than the one we carried for travel. A green quilt, beautifully embroidered with tiny blue flowers, covered me. Thinking myself safe, my trials ended for a time, I slept.

I woke, hot and sticky from a nightmare I couldn't remember. I lay for a moment, listening for Vhar's familiar breathing, but heard nothing. Though it was nearly dark, Vhar hadn't returned. I dressed quickly and went downstairs to look for him.

All the seats at the bar and most of the tables were filled with drinkers and card players. I scanned the outer room for Vhar and, skirting the tables as best I could, looked into the dining hall in the back. No sign of him.

When I turned to go, someone gripped my arm. I flinched, sucking in my breath with an audible hiss of alarm. "Drink with me," the man said, his words slurred. He was a huge man, larger even than my husband, and dressed in brown leather pants and vest. His hair hung in greasy strands around his unshaven face, and he smelled of sweat and stables. I tried to pull away, but his grip tightened, and I cried out with pain. "Drink!" he ordered, pushing his glass into my hand. I sipped the brackish liquid and gagged at the bitterness that assaulted my tongue and throat and rose into my eyes, bringing tears to them. "Another," he ordered, giving my bruised arm a shake.

"Is it a Tepest custom to maul women?" I asked coldly.

Before he could respond, Andor moved beside him. "Leave her alone," Andor said. The man's grip slackened. Though he was much larger than Andor, the innkeeper's eyes were narrow and the grin on his face had a far from friendly look to it.

"No harm," the man said and meekly put his glass on a nearby table. Lifting his grimy outercoat from a hook by the door, he unlatched the door and disappeared into misty twilight. Though no one but Andor seemed to have noticed our exchange a moment earlier, the entire tavern paused when the door opened. Drinks held at the mouth remained there. Cards were left unplayed. Even the dart player halted with his hand raised to throw. They remained that way, frozen, with their eyes fixed on the tavern door until it closed. One of the patrons latched it, and the tension that gripped the room eased.

"Where's Vhar?" I asked, watching the door, half expecting a darkflyer to dive through its thick wood.

"Your husband made a fortune tonight selling his knives . . . and he drank too much . . ." Andor's rich voice fell to a softer tone, "and he talked too much about the fortress in Markovia."

I flushed. Even though we had fled the place, I never would have broken my pledge to Brother Dominic. Vhar had made no such promise, but he wouldn't have invited theft by speaking of treasure—usually. "Where is he now?"

"I sent him off in the company of a half-deaf old townsman who'd once been a village elder and thinks he still is. The man's so senile that Vhar can brag to him all night long and not a word'll be remembered come morning. Considering how much he drank, your husband's probably safely asleep by now, as you should be."

I understood his veiled warning and glanced at the patrons. They were large and strong, and the way they faced each other made me think of gamecocks in a ring, talons ready to strike. The only other woman present was the one I had seen earlier. But she somehow looked more dangerous than the men—the only patron completely and inexplicably at ease.

I didn't want to return to bed; too many evils had transpired when I slept in the wagon or the Guardians' room. But, without Vhar, I needed another protector. This woman had come with no one, her presence challenging every male in the room.

Perhaps she sensed my watching her, for she looked toward me. Her eyes were wide spaced and slanted, making me suspect that she had elvish blood. Though her irises were nearly black, they flickered with the same violet highlights as her raven hair. She was dressed in men's clothing, but with colors more garish than those of the dour men around her—a red blouse slashed nearly to the waist, flowing gold breeches, and a wide, green leather belt. Gold chains circled her neck and gold bracelets her wrists, and her greenstone earrings glittered when her head moved. Her feet were bare, her toenails, like her fingernails, painted blood red.

I found myself speechless as she rose from the table, approached me, and repeated nearly perfectly the innkeeper's words, " . . . and he talked too much about Markovia." She held out her glass for the innkeeper to fill, then asked for wine for me. Andor's eyes met hers for a moment and shifted uneasily away. "She's safe with me," the woman said. "I promise that. But there are things a bard must know."

"Let the poor girl go back to sleep, Maeve," her drinking companion called out. At first glance he seemed an old man—ghastly pallor and wisps of long white hair—but his face had the look of a man in his prime.

"Be quiet, Ivar," the woman ordered, turning to me.

If she heard my words to the landlord, she was close enough now to hear my heart, to listen to me breathe. "He said you two stole the cloth from the order," she whispered.

"He made that up. He's always . . ."

"Look at me," she ordered and I did so. "Are you certain you're telling the truth? Think before you answer."

I did. Vhar hadn't lied to these people; he'd lied to me. I felt a surge of emotion, more anger than fear. Though I didn't answer, my reddening face betrayed me.

"So I thought," Maeve said, her breath warm against my ear. "Did you know that powerful treasures are often guarded by curses for thieves?"

"Yes," I replied softly.

"See that your husband speaks to me tomorrow . . . unless the curse claims him tonight, that is." The woman tossed her head, turned, and strode alone from the tavern. The others paused, but didn't freeze as she left, sensing perhaps that any horror in the darkness would be well-matched in her.

"Things the bards must know . . . ?" I spoke the words aloud, more for Andor's ears than any other's.

"Bards sing of the terrors of our world," Andor said. "Soulless tyrants, warlocks and witches, goblins, hags, vampires, ghosts—the phantom who lives forever in the longings of men. The Gathering Cloth imprisons them all in its burning folds." Andor's voice had acquired a definite cadence. He seemed to chant the last words. "Songs warn the wary, to let them live."

Hearing the innkeeper's words, a drunken man climbed onto one of the tables. "She's not heard the tale of the phantom, then? Let me tell it."

Some of his party nodded. Others called out alternate subjects, but the clamor silenced when a bell clanged insistently outside, impossible to ignore.

Gazing at each other with fearful eyes, the revelers emptied their glasses and left the inn with some haste. Only Andor, the white-haired man—Ivar—and I remained. As soon as they had gone, Andor barred the door and checked each of the windows to be sure the shutters were locked. As he did, a thin, dark-haired woman brought a tray of bread and soup from the kitchen and set it on a table at the back of the room. Our eyes met for a moment, and I sensed the sympathy in her gaze. "We may as well sit together for our dinner," she said, glancing worriedly at the shuttered windows and gesturing for us to join her at the table.

The four of us ate together. Andor and his wife, Dirca, said only a few words during the meal, and, when we had finished, they left me alone with Ivar.

"I heard your husband speaking to Maeve earlier tonight. I assume that he isn't always so foolish," he said with a candor that shocked me. "I think I should tell you plainly what I know of that cloth."

"Plainly?"

"Yes. I didn't speak before the others because they know next to nothing about the cloth, and it's better that way. But you *do* know, enough to be dangerous, but not enough to protect yourself, or your fool husband."

"Go on," I prompted, eyeing him warily.

"I've not lived in Linde for long, but I've heard a great many tales. Some Tepestanis believe that the souls of their dead live on—not in some ghostly other world, but in a physical world with all of the beauty of this one and none of its pain or evil. They believe that all the evil in this other world was miraculously vanquished, leaving a land that is good and pure, a place where a man and a woman can walk beneath the stars without fearing the creatures that hunt the night. Some say the tapestry caused that miraculous cleansing."

"Where did it come from?" I asked in a whisper, then added, "The cloth, I mean."

"The first tales I know of the tapestry claim it fell into the hands of a warlock who used it to steal the souls of his evil enemies. An even more exaggerated tale adds that, though the warlock destroyed the bodies of his enemies, their evil lived on in the tapestry's web. Bitter, hating, the trapped souls wove their own spells, increasing the power of the tapestry until even the warlock found it difficult to resist. It's said that the sorcerer paid a thousand gold pieces for the tapestry, then ten times that to rid himself of it lest he become trapped in its web himself.

"How did the cloth reach the fortr-Markovia?" I asked, my thoughts muddled by the many tales.

"Years ago, before I ever came to this village," the man replied with a nod, watching the door Andor and Dirca had passed through, "three monks came to Linde, carrying a locked box that they kept with them always. One of them was blind, and neither of the others seemed well enough to travel. Yet they stayed here only a night before heading south. Some say these men were of the Order of the Guardians, and that they carried the tapestry in that box."

He suddenly reached for my hand. Knowing what sorcery a touch could unleash, I pulled my arm back and eyed him suspiciously. Shrugging, he went on, "Now there's a legend in these parts, one that tells how our land is peaceful because the cloth is hidden nearby. Few really believe it—but I know it's true." His voice became a hiss. "I've *been* to the fortress where the cloth is kept. I *know* the Guardians and the importance of their work. If your husband's stolen the cloth, he must return it soon. He's got very little time."

"Because of the curse the woman mentioned?"

He shook his head. "Maeve meant to frighten you into telling what you knew. She's always lusted after power." He paused and, as I was about to ask what he meant, he went on, his voice now an ominous whisper. "For all its beauty, what the cloth does best is absorb and magnify evil. And it has other, more terrible, powers as well. It *must* be returned to the shrine before the shadows of the full moon fall, tomorrow night."

I didn't want to believe Ivar, yet I had to. Vhar would never drink too much and leave himself open to theft or worse by bragging about a treasure. And, though he was a cruel man, Vhar would never kill for wealth, not until we found that cursed cloth.

It must have been the tapestry acting through Vhar. It must have been luring us here to unleash its evil.

I was getting dressed the following morning when a wailing—long and desolate—broke the town's silence. I unlocked the shutters and pushed them open. The cries came from a nearby cottage where a woman was kneeling beside a window with splintered shutters. Her hands clutched a blood-soaked scrap of cloth.

I went downstairs. Vhar was nowhere to be seen, but Andor and Ivar were sitting together discussing the killing. "That was the third child taken this month," Ivar told me bitterly after I asked what had happened. "It's time for the men to go hunting again," he added, rising from the table and heading for the door.

A happy place, Dominic had called this. How terrible a sad one must be, I thought.

"I need to get something from the storage room," I told Andor.

Distractedly peering after Ivar, he took the key from the ring on his belt. "You'll find the door outside under the stairs," he said.

The night fog had made the storage door stick in its frame. I had to kick it open, making a bang I was certain carried from one end of town to the other. Though I expected to see Ivar or Maeve coming to take the tapestry, no one stirred on the cobblestone road.

I stood on the threshold, staring into the cluttered, musty room, and held back a sneeze as the dust tickled my nose. The same wave of emotion I had felt in the shrine swept over me again, and I knew the cloth was inside the storage room even before I lit the glass-cased candle and began to search. I stepped around Andor's broken pots and cooking pans, and then my feet were drawn immediately to a box hidden beneath Vhar's felt-wrapped silver daggers. I opened the box.

The cloth was inside.

Why had Vhar stolen it? We were strangers in this land. The sentence for the theft could have been torture or death or worse. As I drew out the shimmering cloth, resting it across my knees, I thought of how poorly I knew my husband and how much I resented him. He didn't love me. I was a useful possession, like the knives in his crates, like this treasure in my lap.

My tears fell onto the folds of fabric and, as I brushed them away, the cloth seemed to console me, telling me it belonged to me, that it was mine to command. I knew it had power, a power that would keep me safe, that would guide me wherever my life would go. I suddenly wanted to drape it over my shoulders, to clothe my body in it and wear it in triumph as I walked out of town, away from Vhar, away from my squalid past forever.

The boldness would be a pleasure, yes. But everyone lusted for the cloth. Vhar would kill for it. If I wished to keep it, and my life, I couldn't risk such a public display. No, I thought, I must be sly and hide the thin fabric beneath my cloak until I was well away from Vhar and his wrath. I was wrapping the cloth in a plain piece of linen when I heard a board creak outside the door. I jumped to my feet and whirled, staring through the sunlit frame.

Ivar and one of the monks stood in the doorway. The monk moved into the cramped storage room, his gray-robed form blocking out the sunlight. He moved forward alone as Ivar stepped away in response to some noise. The monk held out his hand and said in a voice that sounded wise and commanding, "Give the tapestry to me."

"It's mine," I said and backed away from the door, clutching the cloth tightly to my chest.

The monk walked farther into the room. "You don't understand the evil of the thing you have taken," he went on, speaking as a father might to a wayward, well-loved child. "It must go back to the shrine by sundown or its power will destroy you."

I moved to my right. He moved with me. I shied left, but, once again, he stood between me and the door. He was so old I could run right over the top of him, but even with avarice blinding my eyes, I didn't want to hurt the old man. I feinted to one side, then bolted around him on the other.

How could an old man move that fast? How could his hands be so strong? His fingers bruised my wrists. I felt the cloth falling from my arms and struggled to keep from dropping it. Then abruptly, I heard a thud and the old man, crumpling, released me. I fell forward, my face buried in the rich smooth fabric. It smelled of cloying incense, which seemed to suck the air from me. With effort, I forced myself to my knees and looked up.

Vhar stood above me, the old monk lying between us. Perhaps my avarice wouldn't bring me to violence, but Vhar's would.

Despair. All my perfect plans were for nothing. I would never escape Vhar now. Never.

Unless. Unless . . .

Words flowed into my mind, words as sweet as the scent of the cloth, telling me what I must do. I didn't question them. Now, as I write this, I understand fully that I *couldn't* question them. I reached behind me and groped in one of the inn's boxes, my hand closing around the handle of a heavy iron skillet. I held it behind me as Vhar stepped over the body, crooning, "Leith, love, listen to me. Look at the cloth you hold. It's worth a fortune. All the years we struggled together are over once we sell it."

It was Vhar's business to know the value of things, and, I reminded myself, his common sense was one of the reasons I had married him. Still, as I looked down at the gossamer fabric, I knew I couldn't let this treasure be sold for any price. Indeed, I could never think of parting with it, in spite of—or because of—its disturbing luxury.

My confusion must have been obvious, for he knelt in front of me. "Give it to me. You can't protect it."

His hands fell slowly onto the cloth. As they touched it—this treasure I claimed as mine—all the resentments I had buried for so many years exploded into rage, giving me a strength I didn't know I had. I swung the heavy skillet up and sideways against his head. He fell. I hit him again, and again. Then, dropping the skillet, I pounded him with my fists, stopping only when I was too exhausted to continue. Though wounded, he still lived. As I looked at him, his eyes fluttered and opened.

He would follow me if I didn't kill him.

I pulled one of the silver daggers from the crate beside me. As I did, I saw the blood glistening on my hands, Vhar dazed at my feet and, beyond him, the motionless old monk. I'd never killed another soul, but now, my hot and bloody hand was ready to plunge the dagger into my husband and the helpless monk.

With a single cry of anguish and guilt, I grabbed the tapestry—knife still in hand—and started toward the open door. As I neared it, Ivar stumbled into the light. He leaned against the door frame, one of Vhar's knives embedded deep in his shoulder.

"Wait! Listen to me!" he begged, his voice surprisingly strong. I looked at him with fury. I would kill him if I had to. Vhar and the monk were no longer in my way, but this man dared to bar my path. My mind yielded completely to the powers in the cloth. Nothing would stop me from owning this thing.

But Ivar didn't try to call for help. Instead he moved inside and leaned against the wall. His face, ashen with pain, turned sympathetically toward me. "If you won't return the cloth to the shrine, take it out of this land. Travel to G'Henna before the moon rises tonight. The dark priests there can deal with its evil."

"I will leave Tepest gladly," I replied, my voice pitiless, my knife cold and insistent in my hand.

"Maeve," he whispered. I thought of the woman and the power I felt in her and hesitated, listening carefully to his next words. "She may have told . . ." He halted then continued with a different thought. "Don't leave this land by the open road. On the other side of the river crossing you will see a footpath heading west. It leads to some underground passages out of Tepest. The path to the right will take you to the passage to G'Henna. To the left you will see one to Markovia. Go the way you must, but go."

Kill him, something whispered again in my mind. *Kill him or he will follow you.*

The voice was soft, beautiful, compelling. Though Ivar had done me no harm and hardly seemed capable of pursuit, I was compelled to obey the voice. But, as I began to raise my knife for the final, killing stroke, my will stayed my hand. I don't know how long I stood with my arm raised, trapped by the horror of what I still felt I must do. I only know that my indecision was broken by the sound of a low moan behind me. I turned and saw Vhar on hands and knees, trying to find the wits to stand. Though one side of his face was bloody, and his eyes were glazed from pain, I saw the anger in his expression, and the surprise. As I backed away from him, my grip on the cloth slackened for a moment. Before I could turn and run from the room, the tapestry exercised its own terrible power.

Whipped by some internal wind, it broke free of its linen cover and billowed out into the storage room. I held tight to one edge, but the rest flapped out, covering Vhar. He cried my name as the cloth fell, and suddenly his voice grew sad and faraway, as though he were plummeting down a bottomless shaft. I pulled the cloth away too late. Worn planks lay beneath it, but Vhar—husband, adversary, friend—was gone.

Perhaps I screamed—I don't remember. The tapestry seemed to sense my sudden abhorrence for it, for the thin folds twisted, now trying to cover me. With effort, I snatched the flapping edge and drew the cloth resolutely toward me until I held a small, shimmering bundle once more. Certain the fabric would try to escape my hold, I took off my leather belt and tied it tightly around the center of the folds. Then, for the first time, I looked down with clear eyes at this stolen treasure, this abomination I held in my arms.

The horror of the last few minutes shattered the spell cast upon me by the cloth, a spell I was certain had trapped me the moment I first saw the cloth hanging in its shrine.

It was just as Ivar had said. The cloth not only attracted evil, it magnified even the least of it, twisting the smallest annoyance into something dark and lethal. It had used Vhar's avarice to make him a thief. And me? The cloth had used petty resentments from years of marriage to turn me into a murderer! I felt the cloth radiating a false, comforting warmth, making me long to unbind it and caress it, to yield to its dark, seductive power. But I wouldn't be tricked by it, not again. No matter what thoughts entered my head from now until the end of the day, I would fix my mind on one end—returning the cloth to its rightful place in the shrine.

I didn't tell this to Ivar. I didn't have to. He noted the change in my expression, the resolve as I wrapped the cloth in a piece of plain linen and gripped it firmly under one arm. With the silver blade hidden beneath the precious bundle, I ran.

As I crossed the river, I sensed others there with me, watching me. I searched the shadows beneath the thickest stands of trees, expecting to see a gray-robed monk close in and pull this cursed treasure from my grasp.

None came. The cloth seemed to sigh sadly, growing heavier in my arms, slowing my pace. On the opposite side of the river, nearly hidden by the trees, I saw two paths. The left one angled slightly, then paralleled the road.

I started down the narrow path, which ended with the uneven opening of a cavern. A pair of pitch-covered torches were propped inside. I dug the tinder box from my pocket and, with a torch in one hand and the cloth in the other, I entered the open mouth of the cave.

four

THE DARKNESS INSIDE WOULD HAVE BEEN UNBEARABLE
had I not had torches to light my way. I lit one and carried the
other as I started down the path. The damp earth and the darkness
pressed around me, muffling even the ragged sounds of my breathing as I hurried on.

Passages branched out on either side of me. I saw small eyes
glowing in the torchlight, predators watching me silently as I
passed their midnight lairs. Bats rustled on the cavern ceiling,
and small lizards scurried on the slime-coated ground beneath my
resolute feet.

As I traveled in the darkness, I heard whispered promises from
the cloth and saw visions of the life I had always longed to lead. I
saw the fortress as it had once been. I was its lady, a silver-eyed man
its lord, and the stone shrine was an arbor of grapes ripening in the
warm, summer sun.

"Go away!" I cried to all those half-formed dreams, and I quickened my pace.

The cloth seemed lighter now. Perhaps the earlier use of its power
had sapped its strength. Perhaps fear gave me added strength—if I
moved too slowly, the torches would burn out, and I would be lost

in the twisting passages, condemned to die of hunger or thirst or . . . madness.

The first torch began to sputter and die, and I stopped and quickly lit the second. As I did, I heard a brief distant clicking that at first sounded like drops of water falling into some deep underground lake. But the drops moved as I moved, following me as I climbed the path between the sharply narrowing walls.

The cave ceiling grew lower. My raised torch brushed the stalactites, sending bats to flight. Hundreds whirled around me as I crouched with the flame in front of me, protecting my face. The beating of the thousand tiny wings blew out the torch, and there I remained, my head pressed against my bent knees as the creatures swarmed around me. Somewhere in the distance I heard a high-pitched scream of pain, then a steady crunching of teeth on small bones.

I relit the torch and drew my knife. Taking comfort in its weight and the gleam of its silver blade, I went on, waving the torch in front of me until the ceiling grew higher and the swarm of bats thinned.

The torch began to flicker and die. The path twisted. Knowing what would happen if the flame were to go out in the blackness of these caves, I broke into a run. Awkwardly dodging the columns and stalagmites that converged around me, I watched as the flame sputtered and went out. Skidding to a stop, I dug out my flint and steel and tried to relight the torch. Sparks snapped, blue and tiny in that vast blackness, but the torch wouldn't relight. Repeated attempts, each more frantic than the one before, failed.

And I sat, miserable, in the deepening dark.

But, as my eyes adjusted, I saw a faint glow of light in the passage ahead. Rolling to my knees, I squinted to make out what was causing it. It looked like sunlight, dim after descending a great distance through earth. Stumbling slowly forward, I reached a twilit section of the cave and glimpsed its mouth some half-mile away, up a broadening slope. Trudging faster, I followed the rising path to the exit.

Emerging from the cave mouth, I saw the fortress wall loom above me, its stones glowing blood red in the setting sun. The full moon would rise any moment. My eyes found the barren path that snaked up the side of the hill to the fortress. Steep and narrow, it looked far from inviting. But the wider road to the fortress cut farther west, and I had neither the time or the strength to search for it.

I had just reached the first turn in the road when I heard a rustle behind me and a low growl. I turned slowly, keeping my back to the rocky cliffside and had my first real look at the thing that had trailed me through the caverns.

It was a black wolf, well over the size of the ones whose pelts decorated *The Nocturne*'s wall. It crouched behind me with its mouth open, teeth bared, breath hot and cloudy in the damp evening air. I had no protection save the rock wall, and I backed against it, bracing my legs for balance and holding up my knife. The creature eyed the blade with seemingly human apprehension, then skirted to my left, looking for an opening. I felt the cloth twitch, responding to the danger—or the chance for escape. I dropped it between my body and the rock cliff and ignored it, just as I did the pounding of my heart. With my left arm shielding my body and my right hand gripping the knife, I waited for its attack.

When the wolf sprang, I was ready. Though I screamed with pain as its teeth closed over my extended forearm, I managed to sink the silver knife into its shoulder. The beast shook convulsively as I sliced upward as Vhar had taught me. The knife cut through the muscles with far greater ease than I had expected against a monster of that size. The beast's grip on me loosened, and it howled with agony as I twisted the blade, burying it deeper in the animal's shoulder. The creature released me and backed away on three legs.

An even draw for the first round; a far better beginning than I had expected. Exhilaration filled me. I held my bleeding arm in front of me as I had before, but this time I held the knife just behind it, taunting the beast. "Come on!" I cried. "Come and we'll finish this."

The animal's lips curled back, challenging me with its own razor-sharp weapons. I didn't waver. This time I would sink the knife lower, into its stomach. "One more stroke and it's over," I said.

If I had know the true nature of this monster, I would have understood why it hesitated, why it eyed the silver blade with what seemed like human surprise.

I had so little time to spare. Despite my every impulse, I attacked, my knife glancing off one of the beast's ribs. It howled with pain and rolled away from me, off the blade . . . and, unable to recover, over the edge of the cliff.

I didn't look to see how far it had fallen, or to see if it were still alive. I didn't stop to revel in this first, deadly victory of my life. I didn't even look at my wound, though I could feel the warm blood running down my arm and off my fingertips. There was no time. The path to the shrine was steep, the sun had nearly set, and I still had a long way to go.

I remember very little of the climb, save the sheer drops to either side and the sliding rocks underfoot. As I threaded my way along, the tapestry's weight shifted heavily to one end of the roll or the other. I realized with horror that the cloth was trying to throw me off balance. A moment later, it nearly succeeded, pitching me toward the cliff's edge. Flailing, I managed to fall so that only my head and one shoulder hung over the edge, staring down a sheer precipice toward the windswept scrub plains below. Afterward, afraid to carry it any longer, I dragged the cloth behind me.

Ahead, a smoky haze hung over the fortress, as if some fire smoldered underground, about to flare and devour the monks who dwelled there. When I passed through the open gates, the cloth began to tremble, the shimmering folds of fabric working loose from the center of the bundle. But now I knew this was no coincidence, no trick of an unfelt breeze. The cloth feared the shrine as a prisoner fears a solitary cell.

My hands reached out, clutching the fabric, but the thin cloth slipped from between my fingers, twisting out of my tightest grasp. The loose fabric rose in front of me. The eyes of every face in the pattern turned and fixed on me, the rage in their expressions more frightening than any trial I had faced since I had entered this land. I screamed for help. I prayed to all the half-forgotten gods I could recall, prayed that they might aid me in containing this evil.

And someone heard. Through the thickening smoke and the flap-ping folds of cloth, I saw the monks walking toward me, moving between the cloth and the fortress doors. Their eyes were fixed on the tapestry, and their mouths were opened in chants, repeating strange, ancient words over and over. A litany of a single line.

Their chant had power, a power that forced the swirling cloth up from the ground. Trapped in the cloth's moving folds, I was lifted with it. Drifting across the sandy courtyard, the cloth bore me through the open shrine doors and into the candlelit space inside.

I sighed, relieved that my trials were over. But, in the next moment, I discovered that they had just begun. As I clawed myself free of the cloth, I saw that the pattern had begun moving, much as the cloth itself had moved—first slowly, then with increasing agitation. One of the monks, standing just outside the door, reached toward me. Though I tried to grasp his hand, the writhing patterns on the cloth reached out *off* the fabric, and dragged me back. With growing terror, I watched the monk step away from the shrine doors, which slammed shut in front of him, and I heard the outside bars slide into place. Through it all, the monks' chant never wavered.

How could the monks have done this? I thought. How could they lock me in with this hideous thing?

I looked at the cloth and saw what the Guardians feared most. The shapes took on a shadowy life separate from the fabric, spinning away from it one by one, beating at the door like dry winter leaves in a gale. They slowly took on the substance they had possessed before they were trapped. Real hands pinned my arms and legs and ripped at my clothing. Real voices howled with fury at the chanting captors outside. I howled with them—first with fear and later with the terrible certainty that I belonged with them, that this was the punishment I deserved for my part in Vhar's end.

But no! Vhar was alive! I saw his face among the rest. As I opened my mouth to scream his name, all sound in the shrine silenced. A silver-eyed man, the same beautiful creature I had dreamed about, stepped toward me. Silver eyes and silver hair. His cold lips covered mine. His hands, like ice, caressed my sides. More of the whirling souls descended on me, their touch cold as the grave.

I screamed into the silence. I thrashed, but couldn't break free. In the hours that followed, I was helpless to do anything, except imagine escape.

The night's end was as abrupt as its beginning, the doomed souls' final pounding against the windows and doors, their final testing of the bars in futile fury, their sudden, smothering silence as the moon set. And then, all the condemned lay around me, flat and dry as leaves in late winter. Yet their eyes still moved, their empty husks trembled with the last moments of life, quiet only when the doors opened and the rising sun fell on them.

One of the monks came forward, picking up the tapestry that was now an unpatterned shimmering cloth. He dragged it from corner to corner of the shrine, dusting up the dark souls to form a new design, a pattern to hang until the release of the next full moon. My body bled from a thousand bites and scratches, its tissues sore inside and out. I lay unmoving, past all thoughts of modesty, waiting for the monk to bring the cloth and cover me.

But he didn't. Instead he fastened.the tapestry to its place on the wall, then wrapped me in his outer robe and helped me return to the room where I had slept beside Vhar two nights—a lifetime—ago.

I rested for days, eating little, drifting in and out of sleep that gave little respite. Nonetheless, I began to heal. When I grew strong enough to understand his words, Brother Dominic came to my room. He held my hand as he spoke the words I expected, and dreaded.

There were seven in the order when Vhar and I first came here. Now there were five. The old monk Vhar attacked in Linde died. Hektor, the one whose throat he cut outside the monastery, was found quickly and survived. A third, who had been waiting to help me at the river crossing, had been killed. "Judging from the wounds on his body, we assume he was attacked by the same wolf that you fought later that day," Dominic said. His voice was hoarse with sorrow, but held no hint that he blamed me. Nonetheless, I blamed myself and said so.

"You were blinded by the powers trapped in the cloth and by the lust the cloth inspires in all who see it," Dominic responded. "When you understood the dark nature of those powers, you worked to set things right. Had you been less brave and resolute, the evil you saw loosed in the shrine would have been loosed on the world instead."

Brave and resolute. I had never considered myself that way. What I had done seemed nothing more than necessity. "Has that evil ever escaped?" I asked.

He nodded. "Many years ago, before I joined the order, the cloth was worshipped openly in a land far from here. During a full-moon service, the souls trapped on it found the strength to break loose. In the end, the order that worshipped it succeeded in containing the evil, but at a terrible price."

He paused. I saw the anguish in his face, but I didn't ask him to stop the tale. In a moment, he went on.

"All but the three youngest monks of our order were destroyed. Most of our scrolls dealing with the history of the cloth were burned. Only the tapestry remained, untouched by the battle."

"Can the cloth be burned?" I asked.

Dominic smiled ruefully. "Do you think the order has never tried? The cloth cannot be destroyed by ordinary fire. It cannot be shredded or even torn. All spells used against it seem to increase in power and turn on their casters. Perhaps those who founded our order knew the means to destroy it, but they are long since dead, and those that remain have no such knowledge. The only strength we seem to have is in containing its evil, not destroying it. Now, even that will be difficult, for there are so few of us left, and the evil on the cloth is apparently growing in power."

I nodded. It had even managed to send its shadow across the barriers between the worlds to find me.

"There must be some way to destroy it," I said.

"There is a prophecy written on one of our few remaining scrolls. *One day love will corrupt the cloth. One day corruption from within will destroy it.* We don't understand the words, but they give us hope that the future may be less burdensome than the past."

I looked away from him, out the narrow chamber window at the brilliant blue sky. "The future," I repeated, thinking that mine had never seemed so unsure. I thought of how solicitous the monks had been in tending my wounds, how careful in conveying their thanks that I had returned the cloth. It seemed impossible that these were the same men who had coldly discussed my murder on the night I came here. Peering intently into his eyes, I repeated the words Mattas had spoken that night. " 'It would be better if they die quickly at our hands than that our presence here be known to the world.' I heard Mattas say that on the night we escaped."

"You didn't drink your wine that night, did you?" he asked. I shook my head and he went on. "Those who sleep within these walls dream as the powers on the cloth wish them to dream. The potion you were given was the same as the one I drink when I am not guarding the cloth or the fortress. It holds the most vivid dreams back."

"So, in the morning, you would have simply let Vhar and me leave?"

He shook his head. "We would have made you forget what you had seen." He saw my alarm and hastened to explain, "Brother Leo was a wizard's apprentice before he came to us. He learned his lessons well. Nothing he would have done could harm you."

I wasn't so sure, but it hardly seemed important to mention that now. I had harmed them, and now there was only one way to set things right. "If it is allowed," I said, "I wish to remain with the order and share in your work."

"A woman has never had the calling before."

"Nonetheless, I wish to remain." I meant it. As I spoke the words, I sensed how right they sounded, how at peace I suddenly felt.

Dominic looked thoughtful. "Perhaps you do have the calling. We shall have to discuss your request." He hadn't accepted me outright, but I knew I would be allowed to remain. There were too few Guardians left for the work they did.

As soon as my arm had healed, I began taking my turn with the Guardians, watching the shrine, making certain that no one disturbed the tapestry's sleep. Sometimes during those long nights, I would hear the cry of a wolf, the click of claws on the rocky ground outside. The innkeeper in Linde had said that wolves were scarce in this land. I wondered if this was the same one I had wounded.

In a month's time, I stood outside the shrine doors with the others, risking my life and my sanity to keep the awakened souls from entering this already-sorry world. "Return to the darkness," the Guardians chanted in their strange, foreign tongue. And I chanted with them, even though I already sensed that the peace I felt in the fortress was a false one, that the darkness waited for me, as inevitable as the death that comes to all of us.

I was pregnant. That alone was clear enough within a few weeks of my recovery. I tried not to think of who the father might be, but hoped it was Vhar. We had longed for a child of our own for so many years that I wanted some part of him to live on with me. Besides, I had suspected that I was pregnant before that terrible night in the shrine. Even so, I couldn't be certain that I had conceived before then.

Especially since the child growing inside me seemed to have slowly unhinged my mind.

The symptoms began innocently enough. I began to experience blackouts on the nights I guarded the fortress. At first, they lasted only a few moments, and I thought I had nodded off to sleep. I didn't mention it to the others, for it hardly seemed important, and I wanted so much to stay with them.

One night, as I stood at the fortress gates, looking at the jagged shadows the moonlit cliffs threw across the road, a strange longing rose in me. I felt a dread desire to merge with the night, to run free beneath the cloud-swept sky. I thought of the darkflyer and the danger of the cliffs. I thought of terrified travelers and little copper-haired girls with lovely rings on their fingers. I fought the hunger. I hid it, even though it grew ever stronger, ever more insistent.

Brother Leo seemed the one most sensitive to my struggle. As the moon grew fuller, he demanded that I be allowed to rest, to conserve my strength for the long night of struggle. He gave me draughts that forced my body to sleep. After a time, I thought the hunger had vanished, but the truth was far more brutal.

It slept with me.

On the evening of the second full moon since I had joined the order, we Guardians assembled together outside the shrine. The sky lightened as we recited the ritual prayers of preparation and began the chant. With all my concentration focused on the mental bond between me and the other monks, I had no energy remaining to resist the dark forces in me.

The moonlight washed over the land and, as its silver light touched me, the hunger in me woke and roared. The words of the chant fled my mind. I looked at Hektor standing beside me, at his pale hands, his neck. I could see his pulse throbbing in the moonlight, smell the scent of his life, feel the radiating warmth of his flesh. Prey! I was so hungry. And Hektor's blood was hot, fragrant. He and all the others were nothing more than meat for my needs!

My muscles tensed with the desire to attack. My body trembled as what remained of my sanity fought to control this terrible craving. I backed away from the other Guardians, seeking the strength to turn and run.

I couldn't. Through my hunger, I felt another, greater pull. The cloth itself was calling to me, inviting me to come and merge with the souls trapped inside. Though the howls of rage beginning within the shrine made me weak with fear, I took a step toward the barred doors.

A hand gripped my wrist and I looked into Brother Leo's knowing eyes. He lifted his clenched fist toward my face and opened it. A fine sand flowed through his fingers. As it did, he whispered a few quick words in my ear. Darkness closed around me. I felt myself falling against his outstretched arms.

The next morning while the Guardians slept, I sat in the empty dining hall, staring at the patch of sunlight tumbling through the open door. A fine day for travel, I thought, trying to focus on the adventure to come rather than on the sorrow of leaving the monks without even a good-bye. I didn't want to face them, to have to admit that I could never be trusted to guard the cloth again. Wearing only the clothes the Guardians had given me, carrying the knife that had served me so well on the terrible journey here, I stole away from the monastery and down the winding path to Tepest.

five

WHEN I DECIDED TO TAKE THE LONGER, EASIER ROAD rather than the dark passage to Tepest, I hadn't counted on a change in the weather. The sky blackened and the rain, whipped by a frigid wind from G'Henna, beat against my face, blinding me and slowing my descent. The road became slippery, and I stayed close to the cliffside. I had nearly reached the end of the descent when a deafening crack shook the mountain. The air sizzled from the lightning, and a boulder broke loose from the force of the bolt, setting off a landslide directly above me. With a speed I never suspected I possessed, I ran beyond the avalanche of boulders and mud. Stopping was far more difficult. As I tried to slow, my foot slipped into a sinkhole in the road, and I fell hard, slamming my head against a rock.

My ankle throbbed. Consciousness threatened to leave me each time I raised my head. Nonetheless, I had to find shelter or I, and the child in me, would die. Slowly, painfully, I slid down the trail until I reached a stand of trees, which gave some shelter from the biting wind. With my back against an ancient oak, my knees pressed against my chest, and my muddy cloak wrapped tightly around my shivering body, I fell into a wary sleep.

I woke to utter darkness, and a forest filled with noises. First I heard the sound of an animal rustling in the bushes near me, then a sniffing noise from another direction, as if another creature were trying to identify me by scent. With my back protected by the tree, I pulled out my knife and waited.

The creatures moved closer—at least four, perhaps five. I heard panting to my right, a string of gibberish from something a stone's throw in front of me. I waited for the attack, refusing to stab at the darkness in case the unseen hunters had hands to grab my arm or my knife.

The moments stretched out eternally. When at last the beasts came, they did so from all sides. Something caught my hair, pulling my head sideways, while another creature came at me from the front. With my eyes straining to see in the darkness, I stabbed upward, sinking my knife into its flesh. As it shrieked with pain, I kicked it away and sliced into the arm of the one ripping at my neck. My hands, slippery with blood, lost their grip on the knife and it fell, sliding away into the blackness of the night. Even with the knife I knew I would die. "I'm sorry," I whispered to the child in me, knowing that in a moment the battle would end. They would have me.

Teeth bit into my wrist and leg, hands closed around my neck. Flailing to wrench my arm and foot free, I gasped for air. The thrashing sounds of my own limbs and the jabbing pain grew dulled.

On the edge of shock, I sensed something that startled the monstrous pack. They pulled away and scattered, their screams tearing into the damp silence of the night. Their cries were answered by the challenging snarl of a wolf.

The black monster must have come to seek its revenge. So be it. I had defeated it once. I could do so again. My hand groped for my knife. I had just managed to grasp its hilt when the wolf's huge body pressed against me.

+―+―❦―+―+

The world returned in a series of quick, unformed images. A bright ceiling. A white-haired man bending over me. A woman in a red gown sitting beside me. Much later—pale blue walls patterned with interlaced daisy chains. Strands of tinkling brass bells in front of an open window. My silver knife on a table beside me. A copper kettle steaming over a small stone stove. A polished brass mirror over a carved wooden table, its top covered with perfumes and pots of rouge.

And singing . . . beautiful melodic notes that rose to incredible heights like soaring hawks over my homeland. My head was propped up on pillows and turned toward the stove and window. When I tried to move, my body wouldn't obey me. I looked down at my arms, resting on a soft fur coverlet, and saw that they were thickly wrapped in bandages. One of the wounds had bled, leaving a dark red stain on the white gauze.

The song continued, rippling like laughter through my mind. And though the room's pale beauty seemed out of character for the woman, I knew who the singer must be. "Maeve?" I called, my voice creating a strident contrast to her mellow tones.

"So you woke." She came into my range of vision, her orange blouse looking bright in the pale blue room. She carried a cup of tea. Her hands, as they helped me sit farther up in the bed, were delicate, but strong. I tried to speak again, but she covered my lips with one finger, then arranged the pillows behind me and held the cup to my mouth so I could drink. Swallowing was difficult. I gagged and coughed, and my head pounded.

"The blow to your head and the bite on your neck are the worst of your injuries. The rest look far more serious than they are." Maeve smiled at my confusion. "There are reasons for the town's shutters, beyond their pretty looks," she said. "The 'wee beasties' the Tepestanis call them—a far too poetic word for goblins, I think, even those smaller and hairier than most of their perfidious ilk. Goblins have a taste for human flesh. You are lucky I heard your screams."

I looked at her face and arms. Maeve had no marks on her. I commented on her fighting skill.

"I've hunted them before," she said with pride. "Tepestanis have little use for their flesh or their pelts. I agree about the meat, but as to the fur on their bellies . . ." She lifted the cover from my feet so I could see the quilt's handsome sunburst pattern of gold, muted browns, and black.

"They don't value something as beautiful as this?"

"They do when they think it comes from the great cats of Markovia. Since I sell the quilts for six times what they're really worth, I've no real interest in enlightening them."

I smiled, not daring to risk the pain of laughter, and took a few more sips of the tea she offered, saying nothing until a shadow filled the window.

"Ivar!" Maeve whispered, irritation clear in her voice.

He leaned through the window. "I thought you might be awake," he said to me, ignoring the woman. "Dirca sent me to see how you are. Andor said . . ." He paused to walk to the door and knock politely.

Though it clearly galled her to do so, Maeve let him in. He stood at a respectful distance and went on.

"Andor said to tell you that your things are as you left them. He said he has Vhar's money."

"Vhar?" It took a moment to even recall my husband's face.

"It's yours now, of course."

"Mine?"

"After you two disappeared from the inn, we heard that goblins killed both of you. But here you are, escaped from their clutches."

"Vhar wasn't so lucky, tales tell. They say that the goblins wounded you badly and that you camped in a cave just inside the border of Markovia until you were well enough to return to Linde," Maeve added.

"Is that right?"

"Perhaps I was dazed and wandered through Markovia until I found my wandering wits," I said, my smile far from serious.

"No one wanders witless through Markovia and survives to tell of it," Maeve said, watching Ivar warily as she spoke.

I had thought them friends, engaged in friendly banter, until Maeve left us for a moment. As soon as she disappeared, Ivar whispered, "Remember your pledge to the Guardians. The woman lusts for the tapestry, so mind your words well. I will come again tomorrow."

As soon as Ivar had gone, Maeve reappeared and sat by me, her beautiful eyes fixed on mine. "Is your husband really dead?" she asked, and I realized, finally, that she knew nothing but what little she had guessed.

"I don't know where he is," I responded, pleased to be able to tell her the truth, however indirectly.

Maeve didn't press me for details. I sensed that she knew where I had been for all those days.

Perhaps that was even understandable since, as I found out that night and the nights thereafter, Maeve's nighttime hunts ranged for miles. While the other townsfolk locked their shutters and told stories by their fires, Maeve braved the predators that walked the shadows of the moon. She usually returned with pieces of goblin pelts, which she would cure in the rear of her enclosed garden so the stench wouldn't fill the house.

I never spoke of her habits when Ivar came to visit. Instead I told him how attentive she was in caring for me, how much better I felt. Then, on one of the rare moments when we were alone, I asked bluntly why he mistrusted her.

"Her violet eyes, her black hair, her bewitching voice. She's from Kartakass—a fair-haired folk—but she's not fair haired. A Kartakan with black hair comes from bestial stock, no doubt about it. They're a clannish people, Kartakans. She didn't leave that land willingly."

"You're not from Tepest either," I retorted. Maeve had treated me with more kindness than I had ever shown a stranger, and I wouldn't be disloyal.

He paused then, perhaps sensing that if he divulged some of his background, I would be less wary of him. "My wife and infant daughter live in Gundarak. My wife's family means much to her, my daughter's future much to me. In Gundarak, families who have female children are fined, as if being a woman is some sort of crime. The fine is far too large for a land as poor as Gundarak, so I have come here to make enough money for my daughter's ransom. My wife's sister Dirca, Andor, and I own the inn and stables."

"What happens if you can't pay the fine?"

"Sondra will be given to Duke Gundar, the lord of the land. There are as many stories of what becomes of his booty as there are families mourning their losses. All the tales are grim."

"And, which do you believe?"

"I think he eats them. "

Ivar had never seemed anything but sensible. He believed this ludicrous story, and his belief alone convinced me. Throughout the time he sat with me, he told me the strange, sad story of that terrible land. Sometime during his account, Maeve joined us, running a carved bone comb through her midnight hair as she stared at her reflection in a mirror.

"And what of Tepest?" I asked when he had finished.

"The people believe that no one rules the land, but I know better," Ivar replied. "The storm that nearly killed you trapped two young shepherds in the hills. They were found only this morning with their bones picked clean."

"The village should hunt the goblins," Maeve said derisively, speaking for the first time since Ivar had begun the account. "Instead they cower by their fires and pray their families won't be touched, as if their gods listen to cowards."

"You can't change the way people think or what they believe, Maeve," Ivar replied, his tone weary, as if they had discussed this many times before.

"Of course not. I've never tried." She winked at me as she turned away. I thought of her dangerous night hunts. How heroic she seemed to me then.

How little I knew her.

That evening, as she brought me tea and venison stew, I took her hand, pressing it against my cheek. "You are so good to me, Maeve," I said.

"I see my mother in you," she responded and quickly turned away.

She planned on going to the inn that night. I watched as she replaced her daytime working clothes with a shimmering blouse of deep violet, with flowing lavender sleeves, loose breeches in blue suede, and soft black boots that laced to her knees. She darkened her eyelids with kohl, her long lashes brushed her rouged cheeks, and her hair shone with bright feathers. She had a deadly beauty, far from the simpering femininity I had been trained to adopt; the steel blade she carried in her belt was curved and sharp. No one would trouble her. No one would dare.

After she had gone, I pushed myself to my feet and, leaning heavily on the cane Maeve had made for me, walked to her dressing table and sat in front of her mirror. There were circles under my eyes, a sickly pallor to my skin. I lifted her comb and began to slowly run it through my plain, brown hair. I had been in bed far too long. It was time to begin living again.

That night, the moon was full. As I prepared for bed, I sensed its pull, could almost hear the chant of the Guardians standing motionless outside the doors to the stone shrine. If Maeve had been at home, we could have talked or played one of the many card games she had taught me during my convalescence. With her still gone, I had no one to help take my mind off the past.

Later, I could recall pulling back the covers to my bed, but I remembered nothing after that until I woke, shivering and naked, in the courtyard behind Maeve's cottage.

Since Maeve sometimes remained out all night, I had no way of knowing if she had returned yet. I crept through the dark cottage to the solace of my bed and fell asleep. When I woke later, Maeve was home, idly dealing cards by the window. It seemed then that she hadn't noticed I had been gone. Later I discovered she had her own reasons for ignoring my absence.

The next night was a repeat of the last. Early the following morning, I awoke with blood on my hands and the musty smell of some animal on my body. The newly formed scar where the wolf had bitten my arm three months ago throbbed. As I pushed myself to my feet, the world seemed to spin around me. I retched and vomited chunks of raw meat onto the carefully swept stones of Maeve's courtyard.

I couldn't go to bed in such a state. At the very least, I had to wash. Maeve would certainly wake and question me. It was best that I face her, I decided, best that I ask the help of this wise and powerful woman. After all, at that time she seemed my dearest friend, indeed my only real friend in this strange land. Even now, after all that has happened, I still think of her that way. I took a deep breath and went inside.

When I lit a candle, I saw that Maeve wasn't at home.

As the morning brightened, I thought of the danger these night walks of mine must pose to the child within me, and I vowed they would stop. I was no longer the fool I had been when Vhar and I happened into this blighted land. But, until this morning, I had run from the truth. Now I faced it squarely. One by one, I considered and dismissed possible explanations for my memory lapses, my strange walks. In the end, only one explanation remained. The test for it was simple.

I dug into the box where my few possessions were stored and found the silver knife I had carried through so many trials. Gritting my teeth, I pressed the blade against the scar of the wolf bite on my arm.

A searing pain flowed through me, a pain not just from the blade-shaped burn that formed on my arm, but also from the finality of understanding exactly what I had become.

Lycanthrope. Werewolf.

I had hoped for a happier answer. Still, truth was better than ignorance. Later in the day, I walked down the road to the inn. I remembered how Andor had pulled his hand back from my husband's silver blade, and how he wore a silver wolf pendant.

The inn had no customers when I arrived. Andor sat with Dirca at a table near the door. I went to him, laid the knife on the table, and showed him the blade-shaped burn on my arm. "Take her to Ivar," he said to his wife. I picked up the blade and followed Dirca through the kitchen to the family's private quarters. From a small interior room, a staircase descended in a long spiral into the earth. I stayed close to the wall as I tried my best to keep pace with the woman.

At the bottom of the stairs was a narrow passage with a number of dark branches that reminded me of my flight through the cave only weeks before. The main passage led to a long, stone-walled room, which smelled of musty paper and dried herbs. The space was filled with leather-bound books and stacks of scrolls. Two lamps lit the room—one near the door and a second at the rear of it. There, Ivar sat at a plain, wooden table, his long, white hair forming a feathery cowl over his face. As we neared him, I saw that he was making notes in the margins of one of the books. Though he must have heard us approaching, he didn't look up until his thought was finished.

Though I knew him, I felt embarrassed and tongue-tied. But his plain gray eyes were so filled with compassion, his smile so sincere that I smiled in turn and went to sit by his side. Dirca left us, and I told him everything.

"Am I harming my child?" I asked when I had finished.

He paused long enough to open a book and read a few words. With one hand resting on a copper coin on his table, the other on my growing belly, he closed his eyes. A moment later he opened them and shook his head. "Your son has a strong mind. He seems well," Ivar said.

"A son," I repeated, breathless. "Do I harm him when I change?"

"The harm you do to yourself will harm him. That is enough."

"Can you alter what has happened to me?"

"No. But there are other ways to help you. Come."

Opening a long box that lay beside one wall, he produced and unrolled a woolen carpet covered with runes. We sat on it, facing one another, the lit incense burner between us giving off the scent of young grass in spring. He placed an earthen plate beside the burner, and set a small lump of silver in it.

The ritual began.

I had been prepared for pain and terrible visions, for that is what the mage in our village had always inflicted on those unfortunate enough to need his help. Instead, as Ivar's hands moved like pale shadows through the rising green smoke, I felt my soul lighten, the burdens of the past weeks lift. As the rite drew to a close, Ivar's hands curled above the silver nugget, and strands of blue flame arched between them. The light grew, shining cold and blue through the incense-filled room. Then, with a final incantation, he pointed both hands at the silver nugget. Flames flowed from his fingers. The silver melted, glowed, and reformed in the image of a wolf.

When it had cooled, he placed it on a chain and fastened it around my neck. "I haven't altered your life, for that is beyond my power, but I have given you a choice," he said. "As long as you wear this amulet, you can resist the change into beast form."

I didn't ask what would happen if I took the pendant off. I had no intention of ever doing so. "Andor brought me my money. I can pay whatever I owe you," I said, thinking that such a spell wouldn't come cheaply.

"It is my spell that keeps the gate of the Guardians shut against strangers, child. Do you think I feel no guilt that I worded my spell so that 'no one from the dark domains may enter these walls, save those who have the calling'? The dark souls of the tapestry had little use for a greedy craftsman and his wife, save that you might pass my wardings and steal the cloth. I have changed the wards since then, but cannot return you to your land. For that, I owe you what little happiness I can give. Now place your knife on the carpet."

After another incantation, briefer than the last, he returned the blade to me. I felt the warmth of the spell as I grasped it.

"As you change, silver will become more deadly to you. But not this knife. It has served you well in the past. It will continue to do so."

I looked down at it, so heavy and beautiful in my hands, then at Ivar's pale, kind face. "May I?" I muttered and kissed his hands.

As soon as she saw me, Maeve detected the change. I sensed it in the way she watched me when I returned, the sly smile that touched her lips when her eyes met mine, the way she glanced curiously over her shoulder before—dressed in her dark hunter's clothes—she left.

I didn't care. I slept soundly for the first night in many, without even the hint of a nightmare. Ivar had freed me.

Maeve hadn't returned by morning. This absence wasn't unusual, and I was hardly concerned as I went about my work—opening the shutters to let in the morning air and laying the dried dung chips in the stove over last night's banked embers. Soon I had made a pot of tea, toasted biscuits, and spread them with jam. I was carrying my meal outside to eat in the morning sun when Maeve's door flew open.

Viktor, one of the men Maeve sometimes met in the tavern, stood in the doorway, his face livid. "Where is she?" he bellowed. "She was supposed to meet me last night, and she didn't." He looked at her mirror, her pots of rouge, the gold ring beside them—reminders of her. As he stared at them, his rage dissolved into tears that seemed out of place on his coarse face. "Give her this. Tell her that if it isn't me, it will be no man," he said, thrust a box into my already full hands, and left as abruptly as he had arrived.

The teacup tipped, the hot liquid scalding my hands as the cup fell and shattered. The box fell as well, flying open when it hit the floor. A gold ring rolled into the darkness beneath Maeve's bureau. I retrieved the ring first, surprised to see that Viktor's gift was a man's ring with another woman's name engraved inside it. Cleaning up the

tea and the cup, I kept the ring and box in my pocket until Maeve
returned. I laid the box in her hand, then went for her tea, bringing
it to her at her dressing table, never saying a word of reproach.

"I wonder what I should do with it," Maeve commented, as she
looked down at the ring resting in her hand. "Return it to him . . .
or to his wife?"

"You would do that?" Surprise mingled with a thrill in my voice.
She would dare anything!

Maeve turned to me, her violet eyes filled with sorrow. "Do you
think I would be so cruel?"

"I don't know. I don't really know you at all."

"Yes, you do, Leith. You know me well. I am alone in this land.
I have no mate and no family. I live as best I can, and I will allow
no man to threaten me. That is something you must learn as well if
you intend to raise your child unassisted."

She yawned and stretched, then went to take a nap, leaving me to
meditate on her advice. I thought of how I must look to her—my
plain brown hair tied in a tight knot at the nape of my neck, my
simpering and apologetic manners. I went to her dresser, took down
my hair and began to rearrange it in soft ringlets around my face.
I dabbed a bit of her rouge on my cheeks and dusted kohl over my
eyes. They seemed more upturned than they had been, my smile
more wicked. I unhooked the front of my blouse, exposing the
pendant I wore. For all its power, it seemed so plain compared to
Maeve's beautiful jewelry. I held a golden link necklace to my neck
then put it quickly down. Heavy, beautifully formed. What had she
done to earn it?

"Use my blue scarf to tie back your hair," Maeve called from her
bed. Blushing, I complied. When I couldn't tie the bow, she came
and helped me.

Viktor chose that moment to reappear. Maeve purred a soothing welcome. I rehooked my blouse and left them, walking down the dusty road to the inn to purchase bread from Dirca. She had baked trays of sweet buns as well, and I sat with her for awhile, pleased by her compliments on my appearance. "If you think you're ready, Andor would have work for you. We could exchange part of your salary for a room here if you want to leave that woman's house."

Her words told me exactly what she thought of Maeve. I hardly cared. Though I was loath to return home so soon, I did, and found Viktor just leaving, his expression pleasant, his ring back on his finger.

In the days that followed, Maeve's hunting went well. She had gathered more than two dozen beautiful pelts for her designs. As soon as she had finished them, she sold them to a trader bound to Nova Vaasa. "I've made enough money to keep us comfortable for the winter," she said happily. "We're celebrating tonight. This time I won't let you refuse."

She arranged my hair, applied my make-up, and took me to the inn with her. Men from Linde and the small villages to the east were attentive to us both. I found myself teasing them, much as she did. When the banter grew serious, I slipped out the back.

It was near dark and the road was already empty. I had walked nearly halfway to our house when I heard someone following me, closing the distance stealthily. I ran the rest of the way to our cottage and was just opening the door when someone grabbed me. "Let me in," one of the men from the tavern whispered in my ear. He was huge and smelled of ale and sweat. His arms held me so tightly I couldn't breathe. I wondered if someone would come to my aid if I screamed.

But someone already had. "Let her go!" Maeve commanded.

The man spun. "You! Go back to your lovers, I've found mine."

Maeve grabbed his arm, pulling him away from our door. "Go inside and bar the door," she ordered, but I refused. I had my knife.

I didn't need it. Faster than I ever thought a person could move, Maeve pulled her own blade and spun the man around, locking one of his arms behind him, the curved steel at his throat. "Touch her again and you'll never touch another," she told him and kicked him away to land in the dust. He pushed himself up and traveled back down the street, cursing us all the while. "May the goblins devour him," Maeve said and followed me inside. There I fell into a chair and began to cry.

Maeve knelt in front of me and pulled my hands from my face. "I didn't encourage that," I whispered.

"Of course you didn't, but it makes no difference. Evil devours the weak. If you wish to see your child reach adulthood, you must remember that, particularly since the babe you carry will be your only one."

"How can you know?"

She pointed to the pendant I wore. "Nothing can stop the change. Once it is complete, you will be barren. Know that and live accordingly."

"I don't understand."

"Deny your strength, and the land will destroy you and your child. Use it instead, and you will both live, and live well."

She left me. I barred the doors and shutters and sat in the darkness, meditating on all she had told me.

Maeve didn't return for three days. I passed the time doing my usual work—cleaning the cottage, clearing weeds from the herb garden in back, boring holes in the cut goblin hides so that Maeve could sew her patterns with greater ease.

Viktor also disappeared. Though the villagers hunted for him, they did so resignedly and, as they expected, found no trace of him. He was the third man lost that summer. All had been accomplished hunters who should have been safe in the wild, even at night. Though I thought Maeve and Viktor might have left together, I lied to hide her absence. At last she returned, stealing through the garden door, her clothing dirty and torn and a huge bundle of hides beneath one arm. I didn't ask about Viktor. Maeve had been hunting. Now she was safe. Nothing else mattered.

I brought her food and sat with her throughout the afternoon. She told me tales of her travels through southern Tepest and into Markovia.

"I'm so accustomed to the goblins—the way they move and think. They're such an easy hunt," she said. "But the mountains of Markovia held different creatures. They walk on two legs and look almost like men. They even speak the language of men, but their eyes are strange and empty, as if a priest of G'Henna had stolen their souls."

"Enchanted," I suggested, thinking of our village mage and the minds ruined by his forgetfulness spells.

"Perhaps. And vicious." Her hands were clenched into white-knuckled fists. "I have never been attacked so cruelly. I killed eight before I was forced to retreat. They attacked me twice, but I managed to reach the border, and they wouldn't follow me into Tepest. Perhaps they can't. If so, Linde is fortunate. The Guardians must have a hard time with them."

She was testing me, I knew. She had done it before. "You killed eight?" I asked instead.

"I inherited my skills from my mother."

"You said I reminded you of your mother. But I'm hardly a fighter, as you know."

"There are many ways to fight, Leith, as *you* know. Let me rest awhile and tonight I'll tell you of my family."

I sat by the window, boring holes in pelts while she slept. When she stirred, I prepared dinner.

After we had eaten, she poured herself a second cup of tea and began. "My father loved my mother deeply. He thought she was a mortal woman with a bit of elvish blood, but the truth was tragic. She had been infected by a vixen, not long enough before to make her barren, but enough that I was her only child."

"What is a vixen?" I asked.

"The most beautiful of the lycanthropes, and the most charming. Only women are infected, and they assume the shape of a silver fox instead of a wolf. Often their human hair is silver, their features sharp and delicate."

Maeve smiled ruefully and went on. "While my mother carried me, she warded off the change. I was told, however, that even as I emerged from her womb, her features sharpened, and her ears took on an elvish point. She survived my birth, but her will was no longer her own. Instead, she longed constantly for the companionship of the woman who had infected her. She viewed my father not as a husband, but a jailor. When not watched, she left him, wandering Kartakass in search of the vixen who had created her. Like you, she wore an amulet to keep her from changing. She denied the better part of her nature, and, in the end, that denial drove her mad.

"Her fate enraged my father. He prowled the land, seeking the woman who had infected my mother. He killed every silver-haired woman he met, destroying them brutally. He hoped that killing the one who enslaved my mother would release her from her curse. He never found the woman or, if he did, her death made no difference."

Maeve stood and began to pace the room. Tense though the silence was, I chose not to interrupt. When she finally continued, her voice was filled with anguish and hate. "The Kartakans trapped and burned him. They built a pyre around him. I stood with my mad mother and, though I shut my eyes and covered my ears, I couldn't block out his screams.

"My father's brother sheltered us. He came to love Mother with no less devotion and far more sense than Father had shown. But I despised my uncle—he could have stopped my father's death if he had been less cowardly. When old enough, I took what vengeance I could on those who murdered my father, and left Kartakass. I've little desire to return."

The room had grown dark. I lit the oil lamp on the table, filled Maeve's teacup again, and took it to her, standing beside the shuttered window. Tears filled my eyes. Hers were dry. "You wouldn't return even to see your mother?" I asked.

"My mother died soon after I was born. The being that replaced her, even though she made me what I am, was someone I never loved. My father used to speak longingly of her wit and beauty before the change. I think she could have reclaimed it any time she wished, but she was too cowardly to leave him. Instead, she allowed herself to be trapped by him, then by my uncle, and then the town."

"What did you do for vengeance?"

"It happened years ago. I was twenty then. I'm twice that now. The deed is best forgotten."

I had thought her half that age, and said so.

"One benefit of my curse, if it is a curse, is that I don't age. But, sadly, I can never have children." She blew out the candles and opened the shutters. She undressed in the shadows and stepped into the light of the half moon, which flowed like cold water into the room. As I watched, her features melted and changed. Silver fur grew on her long arms and legs. Her ears lengthened, her features shifted into something different, but no less characteristic of Maeve. I had always thought of the *were* as ugly, but Maeve was beautiful; more beautiful than any creature I had ever seen. I walked slowly forward, my hand extended, and rubbed the soft down covering her still-human face.

"Take off the necklace," she said, her violet eyes fixed on mine, her voice elegant.

My hands shook, but I did as she asked, laying the tiny silver wolf on the table beside my bed. My clothes followed and, as I stepped into the moonlight, she took my hands. "Change, but don't forget who you are. Remember before you make your choice," she whispered and shifted form again. In moments, a large silver fox stood before me, its head tilted, its expression expectant.

I did as she asked, stifling a scream as the pain coursed through me. Then, in moments, I released a yip of pleasure at the power of my wolf body. I followed Maeve through the open window into the scented night. The night's shadows whirled past me as I ran, for the first time free of guilt, through Tepest's misty forests.

SIX

I SLIPPED THE AMULET ON AS SOON AS THE NIGHT
ended, then took it off when the sun next set. It became a ritual with
me, and one dusk flowed into another. Maeve and I hunted deer
and goblins in the thick forests of Tepest, climbed the snow-covered
mountains surrounding Lake Kronov, and stole back to our cottage
before the first morning light.

We began ranging farther, beyond the southern border of Tepest.
One night we even reached the mountain where the Guardians kept
their cloth. I tried to turn our path away, but Maeve glimpsed the
castle on its high pinnacle. The following morning, she questioned
me about the fortress. I said I could remember little about it, save
that it held dark secrets and was best left unexplored.

"Legends say the walls are protected and that no one may enter,"
she responded, knowing full well that I had just confessed to having
been inside. "The tapestry's there. That's where you took it, isn't
it?"

I didn't answer her. I suppose there was no need. "I'm going
there," she said.

"It's protected. You won't be able to enter."

She paused in her pacing, her face animated with so many emotions

I couldn't distinguish them. "Answer me one thing. Is that where you were infected?"

"No. A wolf attacked me in the forest on my way to the fortress."

She said nothing, staring instead at my bare arms. The scars confessed clearly how many times I had been bitten. She looked from them to my face, as if seeking some answer in my features.

"We live well, Maeve," I told her. "Do you want that all to end?"

She moved close to me and cupped my chin, forcing me to look into her eyes. "The moon is full tomorrow night. You will go with me to the fortress and you will enter the gates and return with the cloth. I order it, my child, and you will do as I ask."

I was stunned by my need to obey, but my will was still my own. I loved her as I would a sister, well enough that I wouldn't allow her to be destroyed. I said as much, then asked what she would do if she possessed the cloth.

The question seemed natural enough, but it took her some time to reply. When she did, her anger told me the words were genuine. "Shall I tell you how my father's family treated me after he was burned? They beat me for every small display of vanity, as if I were responsible for my parents' fate. Though they knew my vixen nature made marriage abhorrent to me, they forced me to take a husband I barely knew. He was as demanding as they were. Yes, I will have my vengeance on all of them. I will release the creatures on the cloth, charm them as I have the elders of this town. I will lead them to Kartakass and order them to destroy my enemies."

"You'll never get so far. The cloth will destroy you first. It has that power."

"We'll go to the fortress tomorrow."

"You'll go alone."

She glared at me, but my gaze was as strong and as steady as hers. I expected the battle of wills to continue, but, inexplicably, she shrugged and turned away. In the nights that followed, we hunted in the mountains to the east, never crossing the border. She didn't mention the tapestry again.

The child growing inside me began to make me awkward in either form. Nonetheless, I went on hunting with Maeve until the first time the baby kicked. The quiet reminder of the life inside me made me feel guilty and maternal. I put on the amulet and, though Maeve begged me to join her, I refused to remove it. My child was more important than my night pleasures, than Maeve, than even my life.

Maeve took to hunting alone. She stayed away for days while I sat in the shade of our garden, growing heavy and complacent. When she was home, she slept like a cat in a sunny window. I tiptoed around the cottage, trying not to disturb her, or I walked to the inn to share a meal and gossip with Andor or Dirca. I was lonely, but I wouldn't confess it to Maeve. Now that I had shared her world, I understood her needs and would never deny them to her.

One day, when Maeve had been absent for some time, a tinker came to our door. His name was Fian. He had the same raven hair as Maeve, the same violet eyes. I asked if he were Kartakan. "Kartakan and gypsy," he replied. "Accepted by neither, though I have more than my rightful share of gypsy wanderlust."

I gave him work to do. As he did it, he told me tales of Kartakass. By the time he had finished mending two of our pots, the sun was setting. He had no money for the inn and, concerned that he might be killed by the goblins, I said he could sleep in our garden. It seemed natural that I would share supper with him, then share his wine. So sweet it was, so honey-thick, so full of power. I woke with him beside me. Later, I lay in bed and let him fix my morning meal and bring with it another glass of that potent vintage.

When Maeve returned, she sniffed the air in the room. "Someone was here?" she asked.

I nodded.

"Who was it?"

I told her. She reacted with alarm when I told her his name, checking her jewelry to be certain he hadn't stolen any of it, then voicing the concern that he might have been sent from Kartakass to spy on her.

"Am I so ugly that no one would want me for myself?" I asked, bristling at her implied insult.

"No. Actually, you have no idea how beautiful you have become. As for Fian, he sounds like the sort who could charm his way into your arms with no need for any potion. What do you suppose you told him in those hours you cannot recall?" Her anger grew with the last words. She checked it and added more softly, "I have powerful enemies in Kartakass. I am constantly on guard. I will never be able to rest until I find a way to destroy them. I had hoped . . . well, I will question your tinker if he returns."

One winter evening in the middle of my sixth month of pregnancy, Fian reappeared at dusk. I was coming back from the inn when I saw his tall form at our door. Hurrying toward him, I noticed that Maeve was drawing him inside, like a spider into a web. Her questions wouldn't be pleasant, and I decided I would rather not listen to his replies. Instead, I walked to the center of town and sat on a stone bench across from the inn. The shepherds were calling to one another in the hills, and cattle bells clanged peacefully, echoing through the valley as the herds returned to their sturdy barns.

Such a peaceful place, yet Maeve could have no peace, even here. Musing darkly, I tried to push thoughts of Fian from my mind. In time, I decided I should start home. When I was nearly there, I heard Maeve fearfully call my name, and I rushed to meet her, pausing for a moment at the doorway to make sense of the battle inside.

The bureau was overturned, one of the beautifully carved sitting chairs shattered. Maeve, gripped by Fian's strong arms, had tried to shapechange, but each time, he had recited some incantation that prevented it. She was growing weak. I didn't know what Fian intended, but my loyalty was to her, not him. Skirting the pair, I pulled my knife from its hiding place under the bed. Careful not to touch Maeve with the silver blade, I stabbed deeply into Fian's shoulder.

He howled with agony. His grip slackened, and Maeve managed to jerk herself free. Retrieving her own knife from the floor, Maeve advanced on the man.

He retreated toward the far corner of the room. As he did, Maeve dropped her weapon and bounded through the open door. Desperate, she didn't care who might be watching as she ripped at her clothes and ran, changing quickly until, in fox form, she disappeared into the trees. Turning, I saw that Fian had stripped, his body melting into the shape of a huge gray wolf. Leaping through a window, he followed her. There was blood on the floor, but he seemed little wounded by my attack.

Maeve could never outrun him, never defend herself when he caught her without my aid. I tore the amulet from my neck and a moment later—gripping the wooden hilt of my silver blade between my teeth—I ran, four-footed, after them.

So many months without the change had slowed my pace, but not my senses. Though I rapidly lost sight of them, their scent lay heavy on the spongy ground, easy to follow.

Fian was wounded, as likely a kill for the two of us as the animals we routinely hunted. I expected Maeve to rely on me, to turn and make a stand. Instead, she ran east, paralleling the Timori Road before crossing it and continuing along the south shore of Lake Kronov. She undoubtedly intended to tire Fian before their final battle. I hung back, content to follow them and help only if I were needed rather than risk wounding my unborn son.

The forest thickened. The river made a sudden bend away from the road. Some innate animal sense made me pause and flatten to the ground, creeping through the underbrush. The scents of my lover and my friend drew me forward, despite another, unsettling odor. The farther I crept, the more it became dominant, until I knew it was the growing reek of decay. I wanted to turn and run, but I wouldn't abandon Maeve. And so I continued on.

The large, whitewashed cottage that came into view seemed hardly dangerous. It was a cheerless place, darkened by the trees around it. Other than the dense smoke rising from the chimney, no one appeared to be there. Circling around the cottage, I found a pile of goblin bones, boiled clean, pale as a tangled white-oak deadfall. The heads formed a second, smaller pile, the expressions on those that still had skin as disgusting in death as they had been in life. Some were dark, some pale and—I focused more clearly on the stack—some were human. Heads of men, women, and an occasional child were thrown like so much refuse with the rest.

The fur on my neck rose. Fearful that the slayer of the goblins would take note of me, I slowly backed away, then darted into the scant cover of the woods around. An abrupt rustling sound made me freeze. Terrified, I waited; a woman rushed past me and into the clearing.

Maeve! Yet her gait was wrong, the scent of death heavy on her body. It *was* Maeve, and it *wasn't*.

"Fian!" she called, the lilt in her familiar voice teasing, challenging. "Face me as a man, Fian. If you dare!"

Some time passed before Fian responded. In wolf form, he stepped out of the brush, his head moving right and left as he scanned the shadows beneath the trees. Then, with as much fluid grace as he had shown in our cottage, he assumed his man form and moved toward Maeve, his knife pointed upward, ready to strike. I circled slowly about in the foliage, preparing my attack.

Maeve moved toward Fian, her arms held out. In the moment when I thought she intended to surrender, Maeve latched onto his arms and pulled them with inhuman strength out to his sides. As she did, she let out a cry of triumph, which was echoed by two coarser shouts from the cottage itself.

The light around Fian's body shimmered, forming transparent rods of silver that encased him. Though he struggled and tried to pull away, Maeve easily held his arms until the shimmering ended. With a cold laugh, she let him go, stepping away from his magical cage. His arms remained outstretched, pinned between the glowing bars, and, though he strained to move them, he couldn't.

Two horrifying apparitions emerged from the cottage, waddling on their misshapen legs toward the cage and their beautiful captive. One was tall and midnight black with teeth so huge she couldn't close her mouth, not even to swallow. Spittle leaked down her chin, forming long threads of slime that hung on her shapeless gown. The second appeared only half the size of the first. Jaundiced, leprous, she let out a harsh cackle as she approached the cage.

These must have been the hags that Andor spoke of, I thought. I wanted to bolt out and save Maeve, but my hackles prickled at the thought, and my intuition insisted *that is not Maeve.*

Fian tried desperately to pull his hands inside the cage, begging Maeve to free him. Apparently oblivious to the hags converging on her, Maeve seemed for a moment that she might help. She took his hands again and crooned softly to him as she kissed them. My sharp lupine ears heard her whisper, "Will you love me now, husband?"

"I always have," he responded.

As he spoke the words, she laughed. She wouldn't be taken in by false promises, not my Maeve.

At that moment, a second Maeve, with her pointed vixen face and brilliant silver pelt, stepped into the clearing. And the first Maeve shape-shifted into her true form.

The creature was the smallest of the three hags. Though her skin was green as a toad's, her eyes bright orange with reptilian slits, she still held some semblance of what might have been her former beauty. Her feet were dainty and, as she moved around the cage, studying her captive, she walked with some grace. Her curse must have been the worst of all.

"Will you love me?" she asked again in Maeve's musical voice. One hand—thin, lizard-skinned, with black, curved talons— reached for his. A talon from the other opened a cut in his wrist. She lowered her head and drank the thin trickle that flowed from it, motioning the others forward to join her. As she did, the wound on Fian's wrist closed and the short, leprous hag bit deeply into his wrist for her taste. The shiny black hag who had waited until the last took her turn, her huge teeth ripping strips of flesh from Fian's exposed arm.

"It will give us great pleasure to kill someone as beautiful as you, even more when we think of all the time it will take you to die," the smallest one said, still using Maeve's voice. Fian was beyond listening. He screamed, the cries high-pitched, hysterical, insane.

"Little fox," the black monster called when she had finished her meal. Her booming voice grated my sensitive ears. "Come forward and claim your prize." As she said the words, she threw two large bundles of goblin pelts across the clearing. Maeve, still in fox form, retrieved them, dragging them away by their bindings, her tail submissively between her legs.

The hags were intent on their prize, Maeve on her reward. With Fian's screams burning my ears, I retreated. Careful to remain downwind from Maeve, I followed her path toward home.

When she was well away from the house, Maeve stopped and shifted to her human form only long enough to retie the pair of bundles into one large pack and make a collar out of the remaining bindings. Then, with the collar already in place on her neck, she changed again. This time I saw the agony in her expression, heard the pain in her single scream.

And a wolf stood in the clearing. The huge black wolf I knew all too well!

She had picked up the binding and begun to run when I overtook her. Circling in front of her, the blade gripped in my teeth, I growled and stood my ground.

What did I see in those black, feral eyes? Surprise, of course. And sorrow. Then Maeve transformed into her best-known self, a wry smile playing over her rouged lips. "So now you know," she said. "I am Kartakan. I share my father's curse as well as my mother's. I change to whatever form I wish."

I cocked my head. Though I couldn't speak, the question in my expression was clear enough.

"That horrible trio rules this land," Maeve said bitterly. "And they rule me. They have placed a curse on me that leaves me no choice but to obey them. Soon I may be powerful enough to break their spell, free at last. No one will rule me then."

And me? Who ruled me? With a snarl I sprang, knocking her onto her back. I retreated, momentarily, changed to human shape, and attacked again. Her scream rang out as the knife sliced through her flesh.

I would have killed her had I not stopped to look into her eyes one last time. So perfect, so beautiful, so resigned. She wouldn't fight. I could do as I wished. Horrified by the blood-lust within me, I pulled away from her, dropped my blade, and ran.

The forest provided well for me in the days I roamed it in wolf form. I slept beneath the trees, sifting truth from myth. Maeve was my mistress and, like her mother, once I gave birth, Maeve would control me utterly. I already knew what her first order would be.

My choices were few and tragic. I could return to the cottage and destroy her, and my sanity in the process, or I could destroy myself and my unborn son. I couldn't bear the thought of either, so I traveled south and west. With a mountain between me and Linde, Maeve's pull on me would diminish, as, too, would her hot-edged passion to steal the cloth. I knew then what I must do.

The next day, I climbed the steep path to the fortress where the Guardians dwell. And though I am a burden on them, they have treated me kindly, seeing to my every need, giving me and the child within the best of their meager fare. They even took turns sitting with me until I forbade them.

I asked, then, for some means to set down the story of Vhar and me and the cloth. On this scroll, I have written far more than that, but someday you, my son, must understand the reason for what I now do.

You see, I miss Maeve—miss her more than if I had killed her. So when you are born—Vhar's child or the child of that night of horror, what does it matter?—I will give you to the Guardians. Then I will go into the shrine and pull down the tapestry from its place on the wall. I will cover myself with its gossamer folds and feel my life dissolve, my soul, my body, my mind stretch like the others on the fibers of the cloth. And though I will have no peace, I will have the comfort of my husband and the others of my kind. Not damned—I don't think anyone is damned until life ends—but trapped, as I have always been, until the fates judge me.

part II
JONathan

seven

I KNEW THE WOMAN WOULD CONCEIVE; KNEW IT FROM *the moment I touched her trembling body. Ah, delicious! After so many hungry years of half-life in this prison, her fear bubbled through me, fresh and sweet as new wine. How I used her, feasting on her innocence. How I use her still, tormenting her through all her days of self-imposed damnation. Of all the fools who brought this doom upon themselves, she is the greatest, for she alone possessed the power to destroy my dreams, and she abandoned it.*

Scores of empty nights, and then, this unwilling lover from another world gives me hope! I wait for our child—the destined one to come— and he will set me free.

Brother Dominic, head of the Order of the Guardians, sat at a table in the dining hall, his face buried in his open palms. Leith's legacy to her son lay unrolled in front of him. The other four brothers of the order sat around him; they would need to make the decision together.

The Guardians had known Leith's mind was unhinged when she came back to them, but even Ivar, Leo's former teacher, couldn't discern the source of her strange despair. The monks had watched her, hoping her sadness would lift when her babe was born. Instead, she disappeared less than a week after the birth. Now, far too late to help her, the Guardians had found the scroll she had hidden in their library.

Now, they understood.

Though many of their questions had been answered by the scroll of Leith's tragic account, another, far more serious question had been raised. The child.

As usual, Mattas was the most direct and the most ruthless, as if the loss of his sight had somehow taken all compassion from his soul. "The infant is the son of one of the souls trapped on that cloth. Destroy him now and be done with it," the old monk said, chopping the table with his arthritic hands.

Hektor looked down at the baby sleeping in his arms. A huge man in his prime, Hektor had heavy features and a mane of dark, unruly hair. He look more like the brawler he had once been than the gentle giant who had assisted Dominic with Leith's delivery. In the days since Leith had disappeared, he had cared for the child as if it were his own.

Now, the horror in his expression was plain to see. "We are an order that worships peace and harmony," he said. "Mattas would turn us all into murderers."

"Think of the monsters trapped there," Mattas said. "Undead."

"Undead don't sire children," Hektor retorted. "Lycanthropes."

"Not all were are evil, Mattas. Consider Andor. If Andor had the calling, would anyone here argue against admitting him?" Brother Peto asked softly.

"Andor was bitten, not born to it," Mattas replied. "Leith wrote of a silver-haired man from the tapestry." He brushed his fingers over the bindings on his eyes and continued. "I recall that silver-haired man. I recall his face perfectly because it was the last one I saw before my eyes were burned from my skull. He blinded me. He's destroying the order. Now the child has silver hair: how can you deny his parentage?"

"Many children are fair when young. Hair often darkens with age," Hektor responded.

"Is there no test we can perform to give us an answer?" Peto asked.

Dominic noted how Peto's hands trembled, as they did whenever he experienced any strong emotion. On the nights when the souls in the cloth woke, the pale, thin monk would shake like a willow in the wind. Yet Peto never broke the Guardian's circle. Dominic marveled at the depth of the young monk's resolve. He glanced at the others and wondered what had happened to their beliefs, their unity.

"There's a way to know if the child is an ordinary infant. I have the means," Dominic said. "I will call on the god I served before I came to this land. He is the god of the sun and the life it gives. His powers are many. Perhaps he'll provide us an answer."

"And if his answer is that the child is tainted, what will we do then?" Mattas asked.

"I'll agree to destroy him," Dominic replied. He turned to Leo, who sat beside him, listening thoughtfully. "I'll need your assistance in this. And the others need to know how you stand."

"I agree with your decision," Leo replied.

"Leo and I will need time in private to prepare," Dominic said. "We will hold the ceremony here." Rising, he retired to the library. Leo followed and shut the door behind them. Once they were alone, he sat stiffly on the bench across from Dominic. His dark eyes seemed to bore into Dominic's, and his voice, though soft, demanded an answer.

"Your prayers are useless in this land," Leo said. "Why did you lie?"

"Mattas is the only one of us who served in the old days, when our order was large and powerful. Now, with so few left in the order, we must stand together. If we murder the child, as Mattas demands, we will be destroyed from within."

"But what if Mattas is right? What if the boy is son to the wizard who destroyed the first shrine?"

"He is an infant. As with any man, his choice for good or evil will come when he is older."

Leo considered this. "What part in this charade do you want me to play?" he finally asked.

"Cast an aura around the child. Green, I think. When I pass my amulet through the aura, brighten it. That should be convincing enough. Afterward, we'll send the child away."

Leo nodded and pulled his spell book from the library shelf. While Dominic sat, praying that his decision had been the right one, Leo memorized the words and gestures of a simple spell.

At length Leo closed the book, and the pair joined the other Guardians in the dining hall. Hektor reluctantly handed the infant to Leo, who laid him naked on the table in front of Dominic. The child shivered with the cold and seemed to scowl at the indignity, but didn't cry. His eyes, still that deep shade of infant blue, focused on the nearest object—the amulet Dominic held above him.

The circular brass amulet bore a sphere with a line arching above it. Once, in a different world, the symbol stood for the hope of the rising sun. Dominic smiled grimly; even in this world, it was the sunrise that freed them from their labors beneath the full moon.

As Dominic recited his incantation, Leo whispered his, and a halo of light began to form over the infant, a brilliant green aura that grew stronger with each spoken word. When the aura reached its zenith, Dominic passed his amulet through the light. Instead of growing stronger, as Dominic had requested, the amulet reflected the aura, sending bright beams of light across the faces of the monks. The beams illumined Mattas's stoic expression, and glittered on Hektor's tears.

As Dominic pulled the amulet away, the aura pulsed, weakened, and slowly died. "It is finished. He is not a son of evil," Dominic proclaimed. "Now let us take the child outside for his naming ceremony."

They conducted the naming ritual out in the cold wind, in front of the shrine's open doors. If the cloth had any hold on the boy, Dominic hoped it would manifest now. They knelt on the rough stones of the courtyard, the child lying before them. And they chanted words that commended the infant to the path of righteousness.

"I name thee Jonathan," Dominic said when they had finished, repeating the name Leith had chosen. "I commend thy soul to goodness." He reached down to the child's head with an aspergillum, but the chain of his amulet broke. As the heavy brass disc fell, its sharp edge cut the child's cheek, and the disc wedged upright in the stones of the courtyard.

Jonathan turned his face in the direction of the amulet and the edge cut into him again, making a second wound above the first. He let out a single cry, then fell silent as the water dripped onto his forehead to ritually purify his thoughts, his hands to guide his work, his feet to lead him on the path of goodness. As the rite continued, Dominic waited anxiously for some sign. But, the infant lay quietly while the frigid wind shrieked in the fortress walls, and the cloth hung silent, brooding in the darkness of its shrine.

"Jonathan," Dominic repeated and wrapped the child in his blanket. He dismissed the others and carried the babe back to his sleeping room.

Leith had spent so many days composing her life's story—Jonathan's only legacy—that it seemed wrong to deny the boy its knowledge. Nonetheless, the Guardians agreed that knowledge of the boy's possible parentage would devastate him.

Again in the library, Leo placed his hands over the final words of Leith's account. He recited a simple incantation and Leith's words blurred, lightened, and vanished. Taking a pen and imitating her painstaking script, he revised her legacy. Afterward, he read through the account, altering any references to Jonathan's parentage to make him seem clearly Vhar's son. The rest of the account remained as Leith had written it. He placed the scroll in a carved stone box in the library with the other histories of the tapestry, then locked the box with a complex spell he and Dominic alone could undo. None of the other Guardians could read, but surely others, thieves and necromancers, would find the histories a key to power.

In another few months, the child would be old enough to travel. When that time came, they would send him to Kartakass. Leo knew a family there and, with the boy's fair coloring, he would blend in well. Such things mattered to children. Perhaps someday, the child would return to them. When he did, he would have a right to know his mother's fate.

That night, the monks feasted on fresh-killed deer and their last Linde wine, a rare and heady treat. Whether from the wine or ill fortune or fate, Leo tripped as he carried the final vial of dreamless potion from the cupboard. The bottle fell from his hand and landed on the table beside Mattas. The blind monk, groping, caught it and set it upright, after spilling half its contents.

Leo, Dominic, and Peto drank as Mattas and Hektor prepared to guard the shrine and the fortress. But when they separated for the night, Mattas became faint. His face was flushed, and covered with a sheen of sweat that signaled the return of an old illness. Peto willingly took his place that night, but Mattas had no potion to drink. "It has been so long since I dreamed," Mattas said as Dominic helped him to his room. "No matter how terrible the visions, I will welcome them."

"If you need me, call out and I will come, old friend," Dominic replied gravely.

"I'm accustomed to the tricks the cloth's prisoners play. Remember, you may dream as well tonight," Mattas replied and began unwinding the bandage that covered his eyes. Dominic recognized the unspoken request and left the old monk. When he had gone, Mattas removed the last of the bindings and ran his fingers over the empty sockets that had held his eyes, pushing against the scarred tissue, thinking of the night so many years ago when fire had fallen in burning sheets from the angry sky, destroying their shrine, their homes, and so many innocent lives. Mattas had been brave then, rallying the Guardians who were unhurt, focusing their minds on their work until their terror subsided.

In the end, the powers in the cloth had their revenge. They killed all but one of the other Guardians. And they left Mattas with the final, terrible vision of his comrades with blood flowing from cracks in their blackened skin. Even when the fiery bolts struck his eyes, Mattas had managed to continue the chant.

Even then.

Whatever boldness he possessed had vanished with his sight. Endurance, alone, remained. He had won that terrible battle. No new cruelty from the powers on the cloth could exceed what they had already done.

"Come," he whispered as he lay back on the narrow bed. "Come, dark souls, and show me what you will."

As he drifted toward sleep, blood filled his mouth and he coughed, scattering drops of crimson over his pillow. His heart beat faster, fear and weakness combining to make him faint. For a moment, the weakness was so vivid, so real, it couldn't be a dream. Then, he heard a voice calling him to come begin the chant, calling from a long way off, it seemed. And he knew his night of torment had begun.

He tried to rise, but found he couldn't move. He tried to speak, but had no voice.

Darkness closed around him, and from its depths he heard the other Guardians chanting his name, felt the pressure of the bindings as they wrapped his body, heard the beginning of the long, slow dirge for the dead. He felt himself lifted, carried down the stairs from his chamber to his grave, which was already dug beside the shrine. It was the custom of the order: his soul would guard the cloth in life and in death. And they lowered him to the bottom. He felt shovelfuls of earth dropping on him, weighting him down. He heard laughter . . . a cacophany of mirth.

Seductive. Triumphant.

Night fell. When he was alive, Mattas had been old and shrunken with age. The joints in his hands and legs had been swollen and twisted. But the ghost of what he had once been rose from its grave, restored to youth and perfection. Mattas could once again see as he floated to the front of the shrine, to take his place and wait to join in the long night of chanting.

Only two Guardians walked from the hall. He stared at the pair, recognizing Dominic and Leo only with difficulty. They had been terribly altered.

Dominic held a staff, and he leaned heavily on it to take the weight off his weakened legs. His eyes were rheumy, hands white and lined with age. His free arm shook as he stumbled forward to his place before the shrine. Leo stood beside him, also old and weak, but no less resolute. A darkflyer circled above the fortress, throwing a sharp shadow on the courtyard. Others—earthbound beast-men—prowled outside the keep's crumbling walls. As the last of the Guardians began their ritual chant, the beast-men's claws and fur-covered hands broke through the rotted doors. The grotesque band of creatures rushed forward, their mouths open and foaming, hungry for the feast. The lead creature, huge and dark, more bear than man, knocked Leo against the stone wall of the shrine. Its gigantic paws ripped through the plain gray cloak and the aged, white skin beneath.

Starting awake, Mattas calmed his rasping breaths and let his mind again drift toward sleep. As the peaceful darkness of dreamless sleep flowed over Mattas, someone began to whisper in his mind.

Had Mattas pulled himself fully awake, had he eyes to see, he would have spied the gray shadow beside his pallet, the thin-lipped mouth moving. Throughout the night, the shadow stayed with him, invading his unordered dreams, forming words that fixed on the edge of his memory, "Jonathan will do this. Jonathan will destroy you. Jonathan must be sent away."

When Mattas joined the others at the morning meal, he discovered he wasn't the only one who had dreamed of some terrible future. Dominic and Leo had similar dreams, but Leo's contained an admonition that the child be kept close, and Dominic's didn't include Jonathan at all.

"Perhaps these were true dreams," Hektor suggested. "I remember how, in my childhood, my father each morning told us his dreams and interpreted them for living that day. *I'd* like to know my dreams. I drink Leo's potion only because you'd banish me from the order if I didn't."

"And rightfully so," Mattas retorted. "You don't know what our nights were like before Leo came to us and began preparing his potion."

"Mattas's dream has some merit," Peto said. "No one stays here without the calling, not even a child."

"I agree—we should send the child away," Hektor added, his opinion utterly unexpected. "But not so far that we can't have news of him. Not so far that he can't return to us if he has the calling."

"Distance doesn't matter if his vocation is true," Peto responded. "I sailed the mists to reach this order."

"But if we are wrong about the child—if he is evil—it is better that we know the truth when he is young," Hektor went on. "Send the infant to Linde. We can get news of him and if our concerns are groundless and he has the calling, he can return to us."

"I agree with Hektor," Dominic said, joining the debate for the first time. "And if he has a choice, as I believe all creatures must, Andor and Dirca can watch over him and see that he makes the right one."

Peto gave quick support to the proposal. "I vote to send him to Linde," he said and turned to Leo. Before the monk could speak, the familiar cry of the child filled the hall.

Leo looked at Hektor, noting how his friend's expression brightened as he listened to the cry, anxious to go care for the infant. Could he really condemn Hektor to never knowing the fate of the boy? "I agree," he said, though instincts said the words were wrong.

"And I," Dominic said.

Mattas sighed and nodded wearily. The dreams cast doubt and dissension, and he refused to worsen it. As he shuffled up the stairs and walked into the nursery, he prayed that his concerns were nothing more than the foolish caution of an old man.

A shaft of sunlight slanted through a narrow window, brightening the floor and the simple wooden cradle that Peto had crafted for the child. Blankets and changing rags lay folded on a shelf against the wall. Knowing Hektor already stood in the room, Mattas called out his name and followed the younger monk's voice to the bench beside the cradle. Hektor had mixed goat's milk and grain into a thin gruel that the child sucked greedily from the spoon. When he'd finished feeding Jon, Hektor lifted the infant and lay him in Mattas's arms. "You had a family once," Hektor told him. "Did you never sing to your children?"

If he could have cried, Mattas would have now as he crooned an old, never-to-be-forgotten song and thought of his sons, destroyed in the burning of the temple so many years ago. When he had finished, Mattas lowered his face to brush the infant's soft hair, inhaling the sweet scent of new life, new hope.

Dirca had just put the day's bread in the oven to bake when she saw the shadow move across the eastern window of the inn, heard the quick, familiar knock at the rear door. It had been months since Brother Leo had come seeking Ivar, her sister's husband, and Dirca went joyfully to unbolt the door.

As he entered, and they greeted each other warmly, Dirca asked about Leith. Leo shook his head sadly, implying what she assumed had happened. Strength was important in childbirth, though hardly as much as endurance. Leith, so thin, so remote as her time neared, hadn't enough of either.

Ivar had never explained to her or Andor how the woman had become *were*. On the many afternoons she and Leith had spent together, Dirca didn't think it polite to admit that she knew the truth . . . how could she not know when the woman wore the wolf amulet around her neck? Dirca would never suggest that Leith's child might be tainted by her curse. But, in the last days before she disappeared, Leith had grown so fragile she seemed transparent, as if the life growing inside her were a hungry predator, devouring her strength.

Brother Leo placed a basket on a table and Dirca pulled back the blanket and looked at Leith's child. She immediately regretted her thoughts. She ran her fingers through Jonathan's hair, wondering at the softness and the odd silver color. Dirca touched the scar the amulet had left on the infant's cheek and brushed one of the tiny palms. The child closed his delicate hand in a tight grip over her finger.

"Leith came to us seeking peace and solitude. We granted it. But we cannot keep her infant," Leo said. "Jonathan needs a mother, father, other children, companionship, not solitude. We thought of you."

He didn't need to remind her why. Tears came to Dirca's eyes as she nodded. "I'm certain my husband will agree," she said. "You'll find Andor outside, rehanging one of the shutters."

"I'll go ask him as well," Leo said, though Dirca, her finger still held by the infant's hand, hardly seemed to hear his words. Her mind was lost in the past, he decided, and, stooping to kiss the child good-bye, left without disturbing her.

Leo was correct about Dirca's thoughts. The tragedies of her past returned often to haunt her. She had given birth to two girls in Gundarak, a land where female children were taxed. The amount levied brought privation on most families. Torvil, her husband, wasn't willing to pay it or support the girls, who would undoubtedly be taken from him later. So Dirca had done what so many women in the land had done. With her own hands, she carried each babe to the hills and left her to die. Afterward, she sat in her plain stone cottage and listened to the distant howls of the wolves, thankful her daughters had been born in winter, when the cold alone would kill them. When she abandoned the second girl a year after the first, she thought of lying down beside the child and letting the cold claim her as well. All that kept her alive was the knowledge that suicide brought no peace in the afterlife. So she lived and prayed each day that the curse of the land, and of her callous husband, would be lifted.

In her bitterness, she chose a desperate course. During the following spring, the Vistani made their main camp deep in the forest, then set up a second, smaller one on the edge of town. From there, the unaccustomed sound of gypsy music and laughter lured the despondent community into the Vistani's greedy clutches. Torvil had gone with the other men to the camp to buy drink and, perhaps, women. Some of Gundar's enforcers also roamed the gathering, allegedly to maintain order, though the enforcers had no better manner than common thugs. Dirca knew that as an unescorted Gundrakan woman, she would be easier prey than the spirited Vistani wenches with their hot-tempered men. But that night was her only chance to buy the potion she needed. She went alone to their camp, staying well in the shadows, searching for a Vistana likely to help her.

She decided to approach an old gypsy woman who sat behind a wagon at the edge of the camp. The crone tended her own small fire, keeping a pot warmed on the edge of it. From the pot, she poured mugs of a steaming liquid, then sipped it slowly while staring into the fire and stirring its embers. Younger Vistani occasionally brought her meat and bread. Dirca found their respect encouraging, the woman's remote location from the main activities of the camp comforting. Her husband wouldn't discover her there.

Though Dirca was concealed in the shadows, the woman looked at her through the fire; their eyes met. "Step forward, timid child," she called. "I am Madame Avana. Come and tell me what you must."

Dirca did. As she described the birth and death of her two infants, her voice, at first halting, grew bolder. Anger added strength to her words. "Since he won't do his duty to his children, I will no longer do my duty to him. I wish to conceive no more children. That is the curse I place on him."

"And on yourself," the gypsy reminded her gently.

"Aye," Dirca admitted. "Even if there were means to assure boy children, I still prefer none. He deserves this curse. His own mother begged on her knees for the life of his daughters, but he wouldn't relent."

"Strong men have been known to disappear," Madame Avana suggested. "Curse him, not yourself."

"I couldn't ask for that," Dirca responded.

"Even if it were out of your hands?"

"I'm here, am I not! I would be responsible!" Dirca snapped, wanting to banish the temptation.

Madame Avana eyed her with greater respect. "So you are. And your coin?"

Dirca held out five copper pieces, hoping they would be enough. The old woman waited, believing, no doubt, that more would be offered. "It's all I have," Dirca said. "And they're not even mine; my husband's mother gave them to me."

The woman fixed her dark eyes on Dirca's. "To do this?" she asked.

"Yes," Dirca responded. "She knows, and agrees."

The old woman laughed softly. "So you both have that same, unyielding strength. You'll need it tonight." She lifted the coins from Dirca's hand and held out her own drinking mug. "Finish this," she ordered.

Though the liquid was barely warm, it burned as it flowed down Dirca's throat, leaving the taste of herb tea and anise. Dirca coughed. Her eyes watered. Nonetheless, she drank it all. The woman poured her more. "Finish this as well," she said. "I'll mix your potion now." She disappeared into her wagon, the pale orange of her lamp throwing light through cracks in the painted door.

Dirca waited in the shadows, sipping the warm liquid and listening to the music and occasional bursts of laughter from the larger encampment. Her foot tapped in time to the drumbeats, and she wished she were unmarried so that she could go dance with the others. The drink strengthened that longing, as if a part of the gypsy soul was fixed in the bitter brew.

When the old woman returned, she carried a small bottle. "Swallow this once you get home," she said. "If you drink it now, you'd never get home tonight. Don't delay in consuming it, for the drink I gave you will kill some of the pain." She gave a low whistle and one of the young Vistani appeared at her side. "Take the woman home, Alexi, and take care that no one sees you or it will go badly for both of you."

Dirca hid the bottle inside her cloak and turned to leave, but the woman grabbed her arm. "Once done, this cannot be undone."

"I understand," Dirca said, thankful for the honesty.

"Someday," Madame Avana replied in a traditional Gundrakan farewell, given only to respected friends. She watched Dirca disappear into the shadows.

"Someday, daughter," the woman repeated to the darkness and returned to tending her small fire.

As Dirca expected, Torvil wasn't in the wooden cottage when she returned. Most likely, he wouldn't return the entire night. Like many of the homes in their village, Dirca's had a single room with a small stone hearth. A ladder led to a lofted sleeping space warmed by the chimney. Dirca considered going upstairs and drinking the potion, then decided against it. If the liquid made her ill, she'd prefer to be near the door. She uncorked the bottle and tasted the contents.

Though many herbs had been added to the mix to make it more palatable, the base still tasted of blood and decay. Dirca gagged on the first sip, then resolutely downed the rest, swallowing long after she had finished in order to keep the brew inside her. As quickly as the nausea came, it passed. Then the pain began, waves of it, like a bloody, stillborn delivery. Dirca rejoiced in the thought, even as she doubled over, stifling the urge to cry out. She threw the empty bottle into the fire, watching the few remaining drops sizzle and burn with a cold, green light. Her knees pulled tightly to her chest, her jaws clenched to keep from screaming, Dirca felt the pain grow until unconsciousness mercifully claimed her. She lay, senseless, until morning.

The fire had died in the night, and damp had crept through the shutters to fill the little cottage. Dirca woke cramped and shivering. Though pain still lingered, it had subsided enough that she could stoke the fire and prepare some food. The meal revived her, and by midday, Torvil would never detect what she had done.

But, even if she had been unconscious, Torvil wouldn't have noticed. He arrived home on a pallet, carried by four of the villagers. They laid him on his bed and departed, with only a quick word of explanation. Torvil had apparently drunk too much and fallen down the steep riverbank. There he lay unconscious, half his body in the cold, black water, until the rising sun lit the lands. Some of the stragglers from the Vistani camp spied him, a lump on his head, and his legs cold and lifeless. Thanks to them, Torvil lived—and didn't live, seeing and hearing nothing.

"I've seen this before," one of the rescuers said. "He may wake, but he'll never work again. When Duke Gundar's men hear . . ." He stopped a few words too late. His ruddy face grew even redder and he blurted an apology. If her husband couldn't work in the fields, she would be taxed. Like most of the peasant families in Gundarak, she and Torvil were destitute already. Without charity, they would both starve.

Her sister came as soon as she heard the news. Sara, well into her pregnancy, offered to stay and help care for the invalid. Dirca refused her aid. "Your child will be born soon," she said. "You must think of yourself and Ivar."

"You are certain you'll be all right?" Sara asked, sensing dark desperation in her sister's tone.

"I promise it."

"Ivar said he'll help as best he can."

A generous though useless offer, Dirca thought. Ivar's only talent lay in wizardry, but, since he'd come to Gundarak, he dared not recite a single incantation. Duke Gundar had great skill at detecting mages in his land. In spite of Ivar's caution, Gundar had heard rumors of his presence, and his henchmen had been seen prowling the town. If Ivar's skill were discovered, he would be forced to flee or serve the duke. To a man like Ivar, either choice would be unbearable.

"You have troubles enough," Dirca told her sister. "I'm able to take care of this on my own."

"We do have troubles," Sara admitted. She seemed unsettled, about to say something else. But instead, she kissed her sister and left.

As soon as she was alone, Dirca bolted the door, then went to her husband, and removed the blanket covering him. His clothes were damp. She should change him. His lips were slack and blue with cold. She should feed him some broth. Instead, she looked down at him and thought of her babes. Lovingly, she began washing his face, which looked so much like theirs. She combed the leaves and mud out of his hair, the same shade of autumn brown as theirs. Then, she went about her day's work, smiling bitterly, listening to Torvil's half-conscious pleas.

By night, Torvil had fallen silent again. Dirca left the shutters open, let the fire die, and slept in the trapped warmth of the loft. In the morning Torvil was dead. She had just stripped and covered his body when Duke Gundar's men arrived and, rather than collecting a tax for Torvil's lost labor, they found themselves grudgingly paying Dirca a widow's pence instead. Gundar's lieutenant noted the cold hearth and night chill in the room.

"We've little wood to spare for spring fires after you tax us for it," Dirca said when the man questioned her.

"Even to save your husband's life?"

Dirca wanted to laugh. Instead she said nothing, hiding her terror until after the men left. Once alone, though, she gave into her fear and paced, certain the men would return for her. She was young and would make a good slave for Duke Gundar.

Ivar found her in the loft of her little cottage, half hysterical with fear. "Gundar's thugs think I killed him," she whispered to the man, pointing at her husband, but refusing to look in his direction.

Ivar responded with a soft question, "Did you?" Though Dirca had intended to tell no one what she had done, she nodded.

"Gundar can force the truth from you far easier than I. Do you want to leave this land?"

She looked numbly at him. Only a fool would try to flee Gundarak. Sometimes a strange mist would suddenly rise there, confusing the senses, routing refugees into the clutches of the border patrols. Gundar's thugs were far from merciful. Those caught fleeing died as an example to others.

In spite of the danger, Ivar had been determined to go for some time. "Sara will bear a daughter. Once the girl is born, Gundar's men will expect us to flee. I'd hoped Sara would be able to leave now, but she won't risk the babe's life on such a journey, nor drink the Vistani potions I purchased to help us pass the mists."

"You would leave her now?"

"I must. The duke's men have been asking about me. Soon they'll try a more direct approach. If they take Sara . . ." He left the thought unfinished. "But if we go, you and I, Sara can speak the truth. You killed Torvil, then we left together. No one can blame her for our betrayal. She can stay with your mother until the child can travel. Then, I'll return with the money and means to take her and the girl safely away."

"Sara agrees?" Dirca asked, knowing how dependent her sister was on Ivar.

"Sara insists."

Dirca agreed. She said good-bye to no one the night she stole through the fields and into the trees where Ivar was waiting. The pair traveled quickly to the border. Once there, Ivar drank half the Vistani potion and handed her the bottle. "There's no sign of the mist," she whispered. "We hardly need it."

"We may need it yet," he replied. "My spell will attract the duke's attention, but it can't be avoided. I won't leave Sara penniless. Stand guard. Shake me if you hear anyone coming."

At the side of the road stood an oak so ancient that six men with their arms outstretched would barely form a circle around it. There, Ivar dug a narrow hole among the ferns and placed beside it three of the plain copper discs Gundrakan peasants used as coin.

Dirca stood on the opposite side of the huge tree, her eyes and ears fixed on the forest. She listened for the sound of wolves, or Gundar's ruffians, or even a pack of kobolds said to live near the borders.

A light, brighter than the sun, suddenly danced through the treetops and cast the oak's shadow across the ground. "Ivar?" Dirca whispered, shielding her eyes. She heard only the quick muttering of an incantation in reply.

"Ivar?"

He appeared at her side. "Gundar senses my power. Follow me!" he whispered and ran down the narrow path leading to the border. Dirca followed on his heels.

Someday, she thought, using the traditional farewell, then whispered the conclusion every peasant left unsaid, "we will be free."

As Dirca ran, mists rose from the ground beneath her feet, circling her ankles, her legs, her body, like a maelstrom in a swiftly rising pool of water. Though Ivar was only a few feet in front of her, he disappeared. She called his name and felt his walking staff brush her arm. She grabbed it, holding tightly as the swirling clouds covered her face. "Run!" he repeated. She continued forward, though the ground beneath her had already become invisible.

In a place where the mists were thickest, Ivar halted. With one arm around Dirca, the other holding his staff upright in front of him, they stood, silent and waiting, Ivar's incantation the only reality in the terrible, pressing darkness.

Things moved around them . . . small skittering animals that stared at them with huge unblinking eyes; spiders and centipedes larger than any Dirca had ever seen. Then, abruptly, a tall, pale man with eyes that glowed in the dull light held out a hand to her and beckoned her to come. Though she felt the power of his commands, she pressed closer to Ivar and trembled.

She didn't know how long they stood there, only that Ivar muttered a complex incantation. On the final word of it, the mists cleared and the night sky sparkled. All about them, the terrain that had been flat and thick with trees became sloped and grassy.

They stood on a hill, and below them lay the town of Linde.

Ivar had crumpled to the ground at her feet, seemingly as lifeless as Torvil had been. She called the wizard's name, rubbed his cold hands with her own.

"I've done it, Sara," he whispered, staring into Dirca's face, but using his wife's name. "I've done it. I've moved us to a safe home." He lapsed into unconsciousness as she cradled his head in her arms.

He had never attempted that spell before, he told her later when he revived. He wasn't sure he possessed the strength to ever use it again. Leaning heavily on her, they staggered down the forest path, through the cleared fields of grazing cattle, to the comfort of *The Nocturne*, which young Andor Merriwite had just inherited from his father.

She never told Andor why she had fled her homeland, only that she couldn't bear children. Months after they were married, he told of his curse. "My children would've been violent and bestial. When you told me you were barren, I rejoiced, for I'd already come to care for you. I do want children," he confessed, "and surely this hard land makes many orphans."

His words proved false. Linde was composed of extended families. When parents died, their children were taken in by relatives. True orphans never survived long enough to find their way to *The Nocturne*. In the years that followed, Dirca tried to accept her fate.

Now she looked down at Jonathan—the beautiful, pale-haired infant that had been given to her care—lowered her head to the basket, and wept tears of joy.

Her joy was short-lived. As soon as Leo kissed the child good-bye and began his journey back to the monastery, the child's peace ended. Jonathan barely slept and, in the hours he was awake, he screamed. Though his cries were undoubtedly due to hunger, his tiny fists would beat away the skin of goat's milk that Dirca used to nurse him. His body arched and twisted, trying to escape Dirca's loving arms. The scar on his cheek—the "fire sign" Ivar called it—turned an angry red each time anyone approached him.

Ivar did what he could for Dirca and her husband. A simple incantation gave the couple a few hours' rest each night. With effort, the wizard could also calm the infant long enough for Dirca to feed him. "The child has a strong will," Ivar told them. "It's unwise to use sorcery too often on an infant." He looked at Dirca's stricken expression and quickly added, "I will help you for one more week. If Jonathan hasn't accepted you by then . . . well, something must be done."

Dirca and Andor waited and worried, but, if anything, Jon's writhing and screams intensified. Finally, the couple made the only decision left to them, asking Ivar to summon Brother Leo.

Dirca had prayed the monk's arrival would have no effect on the child, that she could demand Ivar's continued help. But she already knew the truth. As soon as Leo arrived, the child's screams ceased. As soon as Leo held him, the child cooed happily and, his head on the monk's shoulder, slept.

"Perhaps the infant already has the calling," Ivar whispered to Leo.

The monk nodded and placed the sleeping child in the same basket that had brought him to *The Nocturne.* The plain woven blanket had been replaced by a colorful blanket of thick wool and a feather pillow for the child's back. Dirca gave him a second bag filled with clothes and gourd rattles and skeins of bright-colored yarn. She thought she could say good-bye, but, when she bent to kiss the child, the tears she had been holding back began to flow.

"Rest awhile before you start back," Ivar suggested to Leo.

Andor offered a meal and he, Leo, and Ivar sat and ate together in the inn. Upstairs, in the whitewashed room Dirca and Andor had given the child, Dirca sat alone, rocking the basket in her lap. She sang to the sleeping infant as though, only in this parting, Jonathan belonged to her at last.

"It's for the best," Andor said after Leo had gone. "We may find another foundling in need of a home."

"Yes," she agreed woodenly, knowing that Andor spoke out of love. She didn't smile as her husband went on trying to cheer her up. A bitter seed had been planted deep within her. No child could ever replace the silver-haired boy she couldn't have.

eight

ONCE, I TEMPTED THEM DIRECTLY, TWISTING THEIR *righteous hopes, destroying their prayers with profane visions. Once, when I was new to this terrible fate and far stronger, I turned their spells back on them, sending down a rain of fire that destroyed nearly all their order, as well as their crude temple. Every battle weakened me; the effects, while pleasing, were hardly worth the effort. Now I draw my strength about me like a shield. The Guardians think my power has waned, for I hide it well and use it only when I must.*

Already, I have sown dissension among them. Now my shadow sits beside my son's bed year after year, murmuring promises to his innocent mind, sensing his power grow, and mine with it.

My son. My only son. The only creature I have ever dared to love. I wait for you.

In the years that followed Leith's disappearance, Jonathan grew into an intelligent, obedient youth. His hair darkened, but kept its silver highlights, and the baby-blue of his eyes transformed to a strange silver shade, which grew more pronounced as he matured. During that time, the five lonely men who cared for him came to forget how stormily the infant had cried, how stubbornly he had demanded to be returned to their home. After so many years with only one another for company, the Guardians considered the boy a ray of light, of hope.

Despite the order's isolation, the Guardians were well equipped to teach Jonathan. When only a few years old, he began learning the history, geography, and ecology of Markovia and the neighboring lands from blind Brother Mattas. The old monk sifted fact from legend, describing the creatures who lived in the mountains and deserts, and beneath the face of the earth. He taught Jon many things, withholding from him only information regarding the tapestry. The brotherhood believed that, to be genuine, Jon's calling should precede any knowledge of the cloth. But all other tales, Mattas told with relish. Unable to see the effect of his stories, the old monk listened for fear in Jonathan's voice, fear that told the old monk his words had been received and understood. "In this land, fear is a virtue," he'd lecture at the end of nearly every lesson.

Mattas might have toned down his stories had he known the effect they had on the boy. Often, Jon would lie awake in his room, his eyes straining to see in the darkness. On some nights, he felt certain a vampire would, at any moment, fly through his window to drain his blood. On others, he expected a wight to stop his heart with a freezing touch. On nights when the terror grew too great, he tiptoed down the hall to Hektor's bed. Claiming he was cold, he would crawl beneath the covers and take comfort in the huge monk's presence beside him. He longed to be grown, to be strong and fearless, as Hektor was.

As soon as he was tall enough to sit at the library table, Jonathan began to learn reading and mathematics from Leo and Dominic. The pair soon discovered that the child possessed an astonishing skill. After reading a passage only once, he had committed it to memory. Often, after the evening meals, Jon would be called upon to recite the tales he had read only hours before. He memorized songs just as easily. Peto taught him to play the harp and, with Peto accompanying on his flute, Jonathan would sing ballads from the monks' homelands. His voice was so clear and beautiful that the others sat and listened rather than joining him and marring the music.

When Jonathan reached his teens, Hektor began teaching him the basics of fighting. The monk pursued his former craft with a joy that Jon found infectious. Hektor started with simple wrestling holds, punching and parrying blows. Later, when Jon was older, the monk began working with staves and wooden swords. Though Jon moved quickly and showed good judgment during their matches, he didn't have the strength or size to be a brawler. A larger man would easily subdue him through weight alone and, Hektor thought sadly, most men would be larger. And the boy took defeat sorely.

"Remember that you have a warrior's courage, a warrior's heart, and the intelligence to know that fighting is usually not the answer," Hektor would tell the boy when his strength failed him.

"Is that as important as strength?" Jon countered.

"More important than strength. Besides, you have other skills far greater than mine."

Jon nodded. Hektor's words were certainly true.

"Where did you learn to fight so well?" Jon finally asked him one day when they were finished with their lesson. Of all the monks, Hektor was the most secretive about his past, even with Jon.

Hektor looked at his pupil, nearly seventeen, full of knowledge yet still so naive. "Come outside the fortress with me," he said. The pair walked to the edge of the road and sat on a pair of rocks overlooking a steep drop. In the distance stretched the harsh wasteland of G'Henna.

"I have spoken to very few about my past," Hektor said. "But you, Jon, I will tell. Others would only scoff at my mistakes; you can learn from them."

Gesturing out to the east, the huge man said, "I was born in the land of Borca. My father was a huge man, over eight feet tall, with arms the size of a normal man's leg. He would brag that he had giant's blood in him and that I had inherited his size and strength. It certainly seems so. When I was just a child, I was half again the weight and height of my peers.

"It was a custom in my village that all males, even small boys, would pair off in shows of strength. The master of the land my father farmed saw me fight for the first time when I was only six. He'd heard my father's bragging and now saw it was true. He bought me from my parents and had me trained as a warrior and later as an assassin. Though I was seven feet tall at your age, I had less skill than you. The training was hard." Hektor paused then added, "I hated it."

"You could have run away," Jon responded.

"My master thought the same, so he devised means to keep me in his service. He was a poisoner, though I didn't find out until later. The potion he put in my food had no taste and no effect. But when I tried to leave him, as he knew I would, the drug faded from my body and pain began, a pain so terrible that all my thoughts centered only on ending its agony.

"I went back to him and begged forgiveness. He put me in irons in the courtyard of his castle. His other slaves, for that is what we truly were, listened to me scream for two days before his potion ended my pain. After that, I believed I could never leave his service."

"How did you escape?"

Hektor laughed. "By being foolish and very lucky. A man owed my master money and left for Dorvinia without paying the debt. I was given a mount and sent after him to collect it or, if he proved stubborn, to make an example of him. But, when I reached his estate near Lechberg, his men ambushed me.

"They beat me senseless and carried me away. Sometime on the journey, I woke. I was in the back of the wagon and when I raised my head all saw around me were barren rocks. A harsh, frigid wind lifted dust into my eyes and, through my tears, I saw that those who guarded me had their faces covered to protect against it. Some time later, the wagon stopped and the guards rolled me off the wagon and left me, bound hand and foot, beneath the midday sun. By the time I managed to free myself, the wagon had disappeared, its tracks destroyed by the incessant wind.

"My master had assumed I would be gone a day or two, no more. That would have been a long enough time to make me uncomfortable, though hardly in any real pain. Instead, I had been abandoned in what I later learned was G'Henna. As the effects of the potion wore off, the torture began."

Hektor looked at the land that had nearly claimed his life as he went on. "In agony, I suffered through that night and the next. On the third day, I found a stream and drank some brackish water. It forestalled my death, but didn't end my pain. Eventually I ran upon a path that led into the hills where there might be some shelter from the wind."

He paused. The boy knew nothing of the cloth. Though Hektor disagreed with the order's belief that Jon's calling must come before his knowledge of the tapestry, he was oath-bound to respect it. Nonetheless, the boy looked at him expectantly, and Hektor went on. "Night was coming when I heard chanting. I headed in the direction of the sound and staggered into the fortress where the Guardians had just begun . . . their evening prayers. They were so caught up in their ceremony that at first they didn't notice me.

"In that moment it seemed that my past was crying out to me. I had a choice—to go or to stay. I moved toward them, shouting one curse after another, anything to get their attention. Leo turned to me. And Dominic. They drew me into their circle. I let myself collapse and, pressed against the ground, I prayed to whatever gods they worshipped that my curse be lifted from me."

"And was it?" Jon asked, his voice filled with awe.

"Not directly. Leo tried to help me, but didn't have the skill. Later, he brought Ivar from Linde. Ivar knew of ways to lessen my agony. It took weeks for the pain to leave me completely, but, when it was gone, I was free for the first time in my life. There were many things I could have done with my life. I chose to remain here with the others. Like the others, I have never regretted it."

"I would like to stay as well."

Jon was only seventeen. So ignorant, Hektor thought. So ready to abandon all the possibilities of a world he had never known. "You should live for a time in the world outside these walls before you decide that," Hektor said.

Hektor was giving support to a suggestion Dominic had already made. "Dominic says I don't have to go far," Jonathan thought aloud. He looked at Hektor and went on. "He spoke of a town called Linde in Tepest."

"Come with me," Hektor stood and gave Jon a hand up. Jon followed him to the opposite side of the fortress and down a footpath that led to a high cliff overlooking Tepest. The land was green and a river ran through the center of it. Hektor pointed to the valley. "Linde is just across the river. How far away do you suppose that is?"

Jon brightened. "Close enough for me to visit."

"Exactly." The huge monk hugged him. "No one would ever close these doors to you."

A bell sounded in the great hall, summoning Jon to help prepare the evening meal. "Thank you," Jon said and ran up the path to the fortress.

Jon thought of Hektor's final words throughout the meal. In spite of his usual nightly sleep potion, Jon lay awake, trying to decide what to do. Moonlight streamed through the cracks in his shutters, throwing strange shadows on his chamber walls. On the edge of sleep, he heard a whisper in the familiar voice that always sounded so much like his own. "Leave the monks. They can teach you nothing anymore."

"Leave," he responded. As always, he was half convinced the thought was entirely his own. Hektor's words blended with the whispered ones.

He was still debating what to do the following morning when he sat with Leo in one of the upstairs rooms, studying as he had for so many years.

He had started learning simple spells from Leo soon after he had been taught to read. At first the lessons were no more than tricks, a way of testing his talent, discretion, and dedication. His natural memorization ability served him well, though the gestures that accompanied the words were as difficult for him to master as they would have been for any novice. However, as time passed, Jon began to show an aptitude for magic well beyond his years.

Nonetheless, Leo doled out his wisdom in small, miserly pieces. Though he would sometimes let Jon light the hearth in the great hall or start the cooking fires with a word and a gesture, he taught Jon only enough to assure his survival in Markovia. "The hills around are filled with enemies. Markov, the beast lord, dwells to the east. He leaves us alone because we live in hiding in a fortress that the beast-men think haunted. Do nothing to draw attention to us."

"What's the use of learning this if I can't use it?" Jon once complained.

"For protection. But if you display your power outside these walls for any reason except to save your life, I'll burn your spellbook. Do you understand?"

After this threat, Jon strove to always be properly respectful. If he assured his teacher of his sincere desire to obey, Leo would continue to allow him to copy the spells he had perfected into his own book. If he was particularly well-behaved, Leo would teach him a new spell or two. But, despite his words, Jon found himself more often than not set to work perfecting a spell he already knew. If he said the slightest word of reproach, his lessons would stop altogether, sometimes for weeks, leaving him frustrated and furious.

Leo's discipline had the opposite effect the monk hoped for. Jonathan knew that he had great native power for magic. As the years passed, his desire to use it grew, rather than diminished. Sometimes he thought he would do anything to acquire the knowledge to wield it.

When Dominic first suggested that he leave, Jonathan was filled with a familiar panic. The farthest he had strayed beyond the fortress was into the scrub around to hunt rabbits. But the more Jon considered the matter, the less panicked he felt. He'd met Ivar a few times and knew he had been Leo's teacher. Perhaps Ivar would teach him as well. The prospect of learning more magic from someone who might encourage his talent might be a compelling enough reason to leave the fortress, Jon thought. He'd hardly mourn leaving Mattas, would actually relish saying good-bye to Leo. He'd miss Peto and Dominic, though. As for Hektor, the thought of leaving the huge gentle man for more than a day or so filled Jonathan with sorrow. Nonetheless, tomorrow he would go to the river to get a glimpse of Linde. By that evening, he hoped to have reached a decision.

The smell of yeast always hung in the air of *The Nocturne*—yeast rising in the bread and bubbling through the ale. The heady scent mixed with the fruity aroma of fermenting Linde wine—a blend of grapes and cloudberries famous through Tepest and Nova Vaasa for its taste and potency. Famous also for its price—paid in lives lost in cloudberry harvests.

The berries grew near water—on the steep hillsides on either side of the river and on the edges of upland bogs in the high valleys above the grazing lands. The berry patches were widely separated, and each yielded only a few pails of berries. Due to the isolation and size of the berry patches, harvesters worked in small groups, which made them vulnerable.

In some harvests, no workers died, but in many others, tragedy struck. Sudden, fierce storms sometimes swept down from northern hills like an invading force, toppling trees onto workers, freezing them in the wilderness, or flinging them from the narrow mountain paths. Others would slip and be dragged into the icy, turgid river, or fall from a sheer face to the valley below. Just as often, people would simply disappear never to be found again

The Tepest goblins were most vicious in the autumn, gathering for winter, so most townsfolk blamed them for the harvest deaths. Others believed that creatures more deadly lay in wait, knowing that when the harvest came, so would their chance for tender meat. No mother would let a young child go to the harvest; the young village children spent the harvest days at the inn. There, they were tended by some of the older girls, who drew lots to decide the privilege of staying behind.

Though she had lived in Linde nearly two years, tomorrow would be Sondra's first year helping with the cloudberry harvest. Even so, she would get little rest tonight. The harvesters would be hungry after their day's work. Since her father and uncle owned the winery, adjoined to the rear of *The Nocturne*, it was the inn's responsibility to provide the workers' food. Sondra had just finished adding flour and honey to her aunt's dough starter when she heard a scratching on the tiles of the roof. A hungry raccoon, lost and starving after last night's storm, had probably smelled the dough, Sondra thought. She thumped the broom handle on the ceiling to scare it off. Something skittered down the roof, and Sondra continued with her work, determined to do everything perfectly this time so that her aunt would have no reason to scold her.

Instead of leaving, the shape on the roof moved stealthily from the tiles above the kitchen to the dense mass of stick and wattle that covered the inn's tavern. The storm had weakened a section of it, and the creature paused there, rooting its flat face in the sticks. With sensitive, pointed ears, it listened to the people moving within.

"You'll not be picking tomorrow, eh Mihal?" Andor called to a drunken patron sitting alone in the corner.

"Nor any day," Mihal replied, his voice slurred. "Someone's got to tend the barn and protect the little ones left behind." The man laid his knife on the table and ran his finger down its long, curved blade. "Besides, I've little use for the wine. Ale's the drink of men, after all."

"Of men without coin, you mean," a patron called to him. His companions, circling the bar, hooted in agreement.

"Of men!" Mihal insisted. "Cheap. Plentiful. I'll take another mug of it, Andor."

"If you're able to come and get it."

"I can come." Mihal managed to push himself to his feet and take a single step before admitting defeat and falling back into his chair. "I guess I'll settle for this," he grumbled and soon after lowered his head to the table and slept, snoring loudly.

The men at the bar were planning how to make this harvest safer than the last. Eventually they grew tired of Mihal's noise and moved their discussion to one of the long tables in the dining hall, leaving Mihal alone in the dimly-lit tavern. After they had been gone for some time, the creature on the roof began digging through the sticks, listening all the while for the footsteps of someone awake and wary.

Sondra had just put the loaves in the oven when she heard a soft whistle coming from the tavern. She paused and listened, then returned to her work until a second, less familiar sound caught her attention. Brushing the flour from her hands, she went to the door beside the bar, stood, and listened.

The sound came again, a sighing as if the room itself were breathing. Sondra felt a cold draft and glanced at the door, surprised to see that it was closed and latched.

"Mihal?" she called, walking to the far corner of the room, where the drunken man lay motionless, his head on the table. "Mihal? Are you all right?"

Her only reply was the breeze curling slowly around her feet like a hungry cat.

She had just stretched out her hand to touch the man when she heard the rustling of the wind in the stick roof above her. She looked up and saw the hole.

"Mihal!" she whispered and shook the man. As she did, he fell sideways out of the chair. The blood from his cut neck had pooled on the table, dripping slowly onto the white bones that were all that remained of his legs. The knife he might have used to defend himself was gone.

A scream caught in Sondra's throat. She gripped her neck, trying to make some sound, trying to see the creatures scurrying through the shadows beneath the tables. She sensed that they were measuring her terror and waiting confidently for her next move. Mute, shaking, certain that if she encountered the things that had devoured Mihal, she would be as easy prey as he had been, she backed toward the kitchen door.

As she turned to bolt for the kitchen, she saw one of them standing in her path. Its hairy arms and legs were a grotesque imitation of human limbs, its flat face expressionless save for a dull, predatory intelligence. Though it was shorter than Sondra, the red-skinned little monster was far more muscular, and it gripped Mihal's knife in one hand. Sondra stepped backward, moving slowly away from it. The creature began scratching at its piecemeal armor and gibbering softly in a harsh and high-pitched voice—sounds impossible for a human throat to produce. Behind her, another of its kind answered, then a third.

Sondra tried to scream again, but the only sounds she could make were strangled grunts of fear. Though she could hear the men talking in the dining hall behind the tavern, her cries attracted no more attention than a pot falling in the kitchen. She wouldn't think of Mihal and how silently the goblins had taken him. No, instead she concentrated on how close the men were, and how the noise of any attack on her would bring them running.

Perhaps the beasts sensed this as well because the two closest to her padded silently to the main door and pulled it open. The well-oiled hinges made scarcely any sound. The third bolted after the pair, pausing to turn and study her a moment longer, its head cocked sideways, its dark, deep-set eyes glowing in the light from the kitchen. Then, as silently as it had arrived, it was gone.

Sondra closed and bolted the door after them, then rushed to the window and, peering through a crack in the shutter, saw the trio race away through the night streets. Checking the lock on the window, Sondra returned, shaken, to the kitchen. No one would know what a coward she was, she vowed as she buried her hands in the dough. The men had heard nothing. Neither had she.

As she worked, Sondra's fear began to grow. How could she go into the forest tomorrow when the beasties would be everywhere? She had thought the tales of harvest deaths were legends designed to frighten children into obedience. Now Sondra knew the truth. And it terrified her.

Her hands shook as she lifted them from the bread, shook as she stirred down another batch of rising dough. The men were filing into the drinking hall. She heard one of them swear, the sound of a chair being overturned as the men rushed toward Mihal's body. A moment later, her uncle ran into the kitchen. "Are you all right?" he asked, hugging her tightly. "Did you see anything? Hear anything?"

She shook her head. "Nothing," she replied, surprised that she could speak at all.

Early the next morning, Sandra stole into the kitchen and tossed all her dolls into the cooking fire. In the two years since she had come to Tepest to live with her father, they had been her only close companions, their tiny wooden bodies and delicately painted features reminding her of mother and home. The dolls' house, a miniature duplicate of the one she had abandoned in Gundarak, was a home she could take with her wherever she went. Her mother had made it in the months before the sad woman had gone away.

Gone away was Sondra's chosen phrase. Even though she had watched her mother slowly languish and die by Gundar's terrible decree, the words meant that her mother might, through some magic of her father's, be restored to life. Sondra dreamed that she might leave her father's cluttered rooms in the rear of *The Nocturne*, walk down the road, and find her mother waiting, her arms outstretched.

Gone away was easier to say than *dead*.

But dead was the real word, and now Sondra decided she must destroy all reminders of the life she had lost. The fire in Aunt Dirca's stove flared and died with each small addition.

When all the dolls had burned to ashes, Sondra put the first of the loaves into the oven. In turn, she drew out the small, fully baked breakfast rolls and filled a bowl with them. After spreading them with butter and jam, she carried them down the narrow, curving stair to her father's study, in the cavern below the inn.

She rarely went into the cavern unless he summoned her. The subterranean darkness frightened her in much the same way that the beasts had. She never quite understood why he chose to work in such secrecy. He had told her once that the powers of Tepest would seek him out if they knew of his existence, but then he had added, in a conspiratorial tone, that Tepest was a far safer home than Gundarak had been. It was true. Here, she could walk through the daylit town alone without fear, and here the word "someday" meant only a vague promise, not a whispered defiance to the lord of the land. Indeed, if her father hadn't told her that someone must rule Tepest, she would have believed that Linde and Viktal and all the other towns were kingdoms unto themselves.

"Are you awake, Father?" she called as she entered the cavern.

"For hours. You didn't have to bring me a meal, I would have come when you rang the bell."

"I wanted to see you."

"And speak of last night?"

"I didn't tell the men the truth," Sondra said.

"I knew that when you came here," he responded.

"I saw the beasties after they killed Mihal. I couldn't do anything, not even cry out. I was such a coward!"

"Coward?" Her father laughed, then added, "I'm not teasing you, child. After surviving years of terror in Gundarak, you can't call yourself anything but brave."

She heard the somber tone of his last words and understood how hard it was to remind her of those days. "But I couldn't even call for help," she added.

"The things you saw are the beasties the Tepestanis fear. They are smaller and hairier than most goblins, but goblins they are. When we fled Gundarak, we were pursued by creatures far more loathesome than they. On that journey, no matter what horrors you glimpsed, you always did as I ordered and kept silent," her father replied. "Perhaps you learned to hold your screams too well. But a coward, Sondra, you could never be."

She kissed him and started toward the stairs. "Everyone will understand if you don't go to the harvest today," Ivar called after her.

Everyone but me, Sondra thought. "I want to go," she said, refusing to look at him lest he see her fear and know that in this, at least, she lied to him as well. Before she reached the kitchen, she paused and wiped away her tears. Though her father hadn't realized it, he'd burrowed right into her. Right to her secrets.

Dirca and Andor were dressed and in the kitchen when Sondra returned to it. "There's an odd smell in the air," her aunt commented, wrinkling her nose in disgust and stirring the embers beneath the oven. "If you vented the stove wrong again, it will ruin the dough. You should have learned by now."

Sondra stiffened more than usual from the rebuke. For the first time, she realized she had no way to explain her missing dolls, or why she had burned them. "Perhaps the beasties blocked the flue?" she suggested. She watched anxiously as her aunt stooped and picked up a scrap of tattered blue lace from the floor, fingering it as if trying to remember where she had seen it before.

"Sondra, did you burn something in . . ." her aunt began, then recalled where she had seen this lace before. "Sondra, where are your dolls?"

Sondra paled and flinched even before her aunt's hand shot out, slapping the side of her face so hard that she fell against the table in the center of the room. Her aunt's hand was raised, ready to strike again when Andor gripped her arm. "Dirca, the dolls were hers to destroy."

"Destroy!" Dirca held the lace in front of his face. "This scrap of lace is all that remains of my mother's wedding gown. Sara wore the same gown when she married Ivar. When the fabric began to rot, Sara used its lace for the doll clothes. She even made the doll with her own features. If Sondra hadn't wanted her mother's gift, she should have given it to me. I would have cherished it. Poor Sara, poor dead Sara, to have such an ungrateful daughter!" She faced Sondra as she finished, her fury clear in her eyes. "Tell me you're sorry," she demanded.

Sondra, her hand on her bruised cheek, said nothing. Dirca reached back to strike her again but, seeing her husband prepared to stop her, walked stiffly from the room instead.

Andor poured a glass of cider and held it out to Sondra. Though she knew he was waiting for some explanation of what she had done, she had nothing to say. She drained the juice quickly, put on the wool coat her aunt had woven for her, and went to join the others already at work on the cloudberry harvest.

It wasn't a task she would have relished, even before last night's terrors. She dreaded the deep forest and the things that dwelt in the shadows beneath the trees. In Gundarak, children weren't allowed to venture near the woods. Those who disobeyed were killed or, worse, simply vanished without a trace, leaving families unwilling to hope and less willing to mourn.

Here things were different, her father said. Even so, the dark woods looked the same as those of Gundarak. The lurid stories the Tepestanis told of the "wee beasties" and the evil spirits that kidnapped the wicked all came back to her with a new, sharper terror. Those were the things she had seen at the inn last night; "beasties" was far too harmless a name for them. Before she left to join the harvesters, she placed a knife in her belt. The goblins might terrify her, but she vowed that she would fight back if attacked.

Because she left the village later than the others, Sondra was told to join a group of three young women harvesting beside the river, just outside of town. As she hurried to reach them, she spotted a flash of white on a narrow footpath leading to the river crossing. The figure was gone as quickly as it had appeared.

"Arlette!" she called, thinking she had seen one of the Linde girls, who always wore undyed skirts. "Arlette! Is that you?"

Arlette returned her call, her voice coming from the riverbank. Nervous, Sondra ran down the path toward the river, slowing her pace before she came into view of the others.

The day was thick and damp. Sondra stripped off her wool outercoat and, as soon as her pails were full of berries, went down to the river and let the cool water run over her wrists and through her hair. She lifted her head, letting the water roll slowly down her back from her dark ringlets. The bells on the cattle pastured nearby added a pleasant clanking to the afternoon's work. The berry-pickers were chattering in the woods behind her, and Arlette began a lecture to two younger girls.

"It's little wonder Mihal was attacked," Arlette told them, her voice loud enough for Sondra to hear. "There's been plenty of beasties in the forest over the last week. They know the harvest is near. They'll pick off stragglers if they can and lick the bones clean. They never touch the face, though. Odd how choosy they are."

The goblins want us to recognize our dead, Sondra thought. Suddenly, the words Arlette spoke seemed less a taunt than an omen. The harvesters should have all been made to view Mihal's body. If they had, they wouldn't be running off alone like the one in white she had noticed on the footpath. Sondra stood up and began to walk toward the others, intending to describe what had happened to Mihal. She reached the wood's edge where the voices had been.

But the other girls had vanished.

"Arlette!" she called softly, lest goblins hear the fear in her voice. No one answered. She listened, but heard only the faint breeze in the treetops, bees drinking the sweet juice from crushed, fallen berries.

Someone giggled near the riverbank.

"Arlette?" Sondra called again, her voice somewhat louder, her body tensed, ready to flee.

Someone giggled again, the laugh far too young to be Arlette's. The girls were playing a trick on her, nothing more. Furious, Sondra picked up her full buckets and headed back toward the inn. After traveling only a few feet into the forest, she saw scattered berries, an overturned pail. Her uncle would have paid good coin for these. None of the girls would have dropped them as a joke.

Something had taken one of the girls.

Sondra grabbed the pail and ran to the clearing. Once there, she called sternly to the younger girls. The pair came out of their hiding place, still giggling until they saw Sondra's shocked expression, the empty pail. "Arlette is missing. We're going back to Linde to get help," Sondra said. When they reached the cleared land at the top of the bank, they were in sight of town. There, Sondra turned and called Arlette's name. The only response was a rustling in the trees that might have been the wind or . . .

Sondra had a sudden vision of Arlette, surrounded by goblins, struck mute by the sight of them as she herself had been the night before. "I'll stay here in case Arlette comes back." .

"You must leave with us," the older of the pair said. "The beasties will take you, too."

Sondra pulled her knife. "I have this. Now run!"

I'll be alone only a little while, Sondra told herself as she called Arlette's name and scanned the woods for some sign of the girl. Unlike poor Mihal, she was sober and prepared. Her knife was sharp, and she knew how to use it. "A little while," she repeated aloud, though the words gave no real comfort.

She thought that if the goblins came, they would take her quickly, as they had Arlette. She didn't anticipate that they already knew her weakness. They knew she couldn't scream.

With a sudden gasp, she realized that they were watching her. Their intense red eyes glowed in the forest and by the bank, in the weeds and behind the bushes. She glanced back fearfully toward the inn, but no one was in sight. She tried to scream, but only a hoarse hiss emerged.

The beasties began moving forward. A half dozen came one by one from the forest to stand around her. Though she couldn't be certain, the last looked like the goblin she had faced in the inn.

Taller and less hairy than the others, he seemed more human. In his dark hands, he held the red and white remnants of a corpse. It was small and delicate, undoubtedly Arlette's. As Sondra's eyes widened with horror, it threw the body on the ground in front of her. The corpse's middle finger was missing. The gold ring that had once shone so beautifully on Arlette's hand now hung on the rope belt the goblin wore, holding a crudely fashioned leather sheath. The goblin pulled a knife from the sheath, holding it before him so Sondra could admire the magnificent carvings on the handle, the sharpness of the curved blade that had once been Mihal's.

She was determined she wouldn't die as easily as Arlette had died, wouldn't feed them as Mihal had fed them. She raised her knife and waited.

In the heartbeats before her final battle, something unexpected happened. Three huge wolves appeared on the edge of the clearing. They stood silently, their attention fixed on the goblins rather than on Sondra, who was trying desperately to be brave. The goblin leader pointed, stammering, toward the wolves, and the others turned. They gasped.

The wolves crouched and prepared to spring. With harsh, high-pitched shrieks, the goblins scattered into the trees, and the wolves bounded after them. Sondra stood, dazed by the suddenness and strangeness of her rescue. A youth about her own age climbed the bank toward her, clawing through the drooping strands of the river willows.

His shirt was white, his breeches pale gray, and his hair shone like silver when the diffuse sunlight struck it. He must have been the pale figure she had seen on the path earlier. She marveled that he would roam the hills alone. "Did you summon the wolves?" she asked. The words sounded foolish when they came forth, but she had heard her father speak of such a spell.

He shrugged. "I was prepared to do far more. Thankfully, more wasn't necessary," he replied. His voice, like his face, was beautiful.

"You aren't from Linde?"

He shook his head.

"Then where do you live?"

He smiled and shook his head again. "I can't tell you."

She wished he would say something more, but men were shouting her name in the woods. With a last look at him, she called to her belated rescuers. As she did, the youth stepped backward into the concealing shadows of the trees.

As always, dinner was served in the inn's dining room. Andor, Dirca, Ivar, and Sondra sat at one end of a long table. The empty seats on the other end always made Sondra feel like guests had failed to come to dinner. Guests or relations. She hated the evening meal. It made her think of her dead mother and the family she had left behind in Gundarak.

Tonight the memory was stronger than usual. Her aunt ate in silence, still fuming about the burned dolls. Andor seemed reluctant to speak to Sondra lest he invite his wife's fury. Her father also looked disappointed about the dolls and—more specifically—Sondra's carelessness in the forest. But he was willing to forgive her, especially after the two tragic deaths so close together.

After they had eaten, Sondra described the youth she had met in the forest and how he had saved her from the attack. "You didn't mention the boy to the men who found you," her uncle commented. "Why?"

"He worked some spell on the animals. He didn't want to be seen, so I kept him secret. I'm only telling you because you might know something about him."

"He's called Jonathan," her father said. As he spoke the name, Dirca rose suddenly, collected the plates, and disappeared into the kitchen. Her uncle's gaze followed his wife with a fearful intensity.

Thinking her aunt disliked the boy, Sondra came to his defense. "He saved my life," she said.

The men waited a moment. When Dirca still didn't return, Sondra's father asked, "Did he say he had summoned the pack?"

"No, not exactly. Maybe he flushed them from the woods."

"Wolves?" Andor asked. Ivar suppressed a smile.

The men questioned her a few more minutes, then began, in stiff and veiled terms, discussing the boy.

Thinking she might hear more from a less conspicuous vantage, Sondra cleared the rest of the dishes from the table. As she carried the dishes into the kitchen, she saw her aunt closing the cupboard where the wine was kept. There were tears in Dirca's eyes, but when she noticed Sondra, her expression hardened. Without a word, she left the room. Even before Sondra burned the dolls, Aunt Dirca had disliked her. Why, Sondra neither knew nor dared ask. But she constantly looked for clues.

Sensing that Jonathan might provide some answers, Sondra took her time wiping the glasses and returning them to the cupboard. The whole time, she stood near enough to the doorway to hear the men talk about him.

" . . . came himself. He asked if there might be work here for the boy," her father was saying. "They believe Jonathan can't stay with them forever, or he'll never have a real choice in his future. They'd like him to come here, if only for a little while."

"What's he able to do?" Andor asked.

"Read . . . write . . ."

Her uncle snorted. "We've little use for those skills in Linde."

" . . . hunt . . . track . . . He's a wild creature himself when alone in the woods."

"We could use a good tracker," Andor admitted, thinking of Arlette and the other children lost at harvest. "But Sondra's story troubles me. The boy didn't admit to summoning the wolves, but if he did work some spell . . . well, I don't want attention drawn to us. Can you assure it?"

"If the boy has talent, and Leo assures me he has, it may be difficult to keep him from practicing it. Nonetheless, he'll have to obey me, or I'll teach him nothing."

"What does he know of the Guardians?"

"Only that they're hermits. The monks believe he can't truly choose to join them if he knows more."

"They're foolish old men!" Andor exclaimed.

"Perhaps. Perhaps not. Remember how I lost Leo so many years ago?"

Her uncle didn't reply. "I'll ask Dirca if she minds him staying here," Andor finally said.

Sondra thought this a good time to tiptoe back to the cupboard and close the door. A moment later, she walked past the men and up the stairs to her room.

The moths and flying white beetles were thick outside. She heard them beating against her shutters as she undressed by the light of a single candle. Blowing it out, she went to bed and pulled the covers around her, thankful the roof above her was made of tile.

She lay awake a long time, thinking of Jonathan and the effect his name had on her aunt. Though Sondra was old enough to be courted and think seriously of marriage, Jonathan seemed far too young to be a suitor. Nonetheless, he attracted her far more than Mishya or the other Linde boys. And she longed, more than anything, to see the silver-haired boy again.

In a room down the hall, Dirca also lay awake, sipping the wine she had brought from the kitchen. She remembered those few weeks so long ago when she thought she had a son. In all the years since, she had always embraced the comforting thought that the boy was nearby, that some day he would return to her.

Then fate gave her a new child; not the child she wanted, but a child, nonetheless. She wished she had remained in Gundarak and helped her sister raise the girl. If she had held Sondra when she was an infant, had watched her grow, she might have felt some affection for the headstrong stranger imposing on her life now. Instead, she looked at Sondra and thought of her own little girls, lost to fate so long ago.

They would have been obedient, beautiful, loved.

It had been months since Dirca had drunk this much of the potent Linde wine. It made her dizzy. Tomorrow, she would carefully add water to the bottle so Andor wouldn't guess how much she'd consumed and, worse, how much the loss of Jonathan still affected her. If he sensed her sorrow, he wouldn't let the boy stay with them.

"But you have Sondra here," she reminded herself once again in a soft, bitter whisper, as if the girl were less her niece than her rival. Both sought the affection of someone neither of them really knew.

NINE

at night, my soul wanders the ancient halls of *the keep, helpless to do anything but observe the Guardians' lives, listen to their concerns. They believe my son may have the calling, as if he would ever stand with them and hold me back from the world.*

My son asks about his father sometimes. When they cannot evade the truth, they lie. I whisper to him that he must be certain to remember that.

That night at dinner, Jonathan told the monks about the goblins and the wolves. He made it clear that, if he hadn't led the wolves to the scene, the girl would've certainly been killed. He hadn't used magic to lead the wolves; they had mysteriously followed him. And he'd managed to obey Leo's admonition despite the urge to see what he could do—to feel the power coursing from his mind to his hands and through them. He could've destroyed the goblins with a few words, a quick gesture. Instead, he held back. Though he'd disobeyed the Guardians' orders when he left the lands around the fortress, he expected some praise for his discretion. Instead, the monks disapproved, Mattas most vocally.

"Have you learned nothing in your years here?" Mattas admonished him. "There are powers in these lands that would take great interest in your existence. Would you like to be a slave of Markov the beast lord? Would you like me to repeat the story of the three flesh-eating crones of Tepest? Evil wields the only real power in these lands. The rest of us survive as best we can, and the wisest men know enough to hide."

"The goblins would've killed the girl," Jon retorted. "They kill many in Tepest."

"Mattas!" Dominic exclaimed. Jon saw the shock in Dominic's expression and heard the resignation as he added, "Jonathan wasn't seen by anyone but the girl. His presence was fortunate."

"And I worked no magic," Jonathan repeated, looking at Leo as he spoke, but seeing no sympathy in the man's expression. Jon had no explanation as to why the wolves were trailing him. Leo no doubt believed that he'd summoned them. There would be no lessons in the morning, probably none for weeks. Jonathan had discovered a spell in one of Leo's books that he thought would make his teacher obey him. He wished he had the courage to try it.

"It's natural that he would want a glimpse of Linde. He may be going there soon enough," Hektor said, gripping the boy's hand in support.

"It seems to me that he's already visited Linde once too often," Mattas grumbled. The others ignored him.

"It's done now," Dominic said levelly, lifting his plate from the table and nodding for Jon to do the same. "It won't happen again, so we need discuss it no further."

That night, the voice was stronger and more insistent. Jon sat up and reached out in the direction of the voice. The shadows in his room merged and acquired the shimmering silhouette of a man. "Who are you?" Jon asked. He received no reply and turned to light the candle beside his bed. The golden light of the candle drove the shadows from the room. Jon was alone.

The following morning, Jonathan sat cross-legged on one of the battlements of the Guardian's fortress, facing a wide crevice in the crumbling outer wall. In the distance, just visible through the trees, lay the green hills of Tepest, cleared for cattle and crops. He thought of the girls he had seen laughing by the river—thought particularly of the one brave girl who'd used her small blade to face down half a dozen goblins.

He pushed himself to his feet. The chores were done and it was scarcely midday. He picked up the sack of fresh bread from the ground beside him and, with all the stealth he could muster, descended the steps to the courtyard. Mattas was dozing against the sunny wall of the shrine. Jon didn't want to wake him and answer the usual questions about where he was going.

When Jon first began roaming the hills around the fortress, he had thought of the beast-people solely as dim-witted and mad. Leo and Mattas had said that the creatures would crush Jon or carry him off to Markov if they caught him. When he was younger, he relied on his sharp senses and intelligence to keep out of their sight. Now, he knew spells to make them regret any attack. So far, he had no reason to use them.

There were two communities of beast-men in the area. The larger group was fierce and well ordered. Guards circled their crude encampment, making Jon's spying attempts difficult. The second community was looser-knit, its members constantly on the move, hunting in packs like the animals they resembled. Jon had observed both groups from a distance, but knew he couldn't approach them without risking capture.

That day, Jon hunted rabbits, not beast-men. Tearing chunks off a loaf of bread, he lured the rabbits into range of his sling and managed to kill five. He would take three to Leo to cure. The two others he took to a shallow valley near the river. Stepping into a small clearing in its thicketed scrub forest, he let out a low whistle. Soon after, a trio of figures—two male and one female—emerged from the trees. They had human faces, but the bodies of unnatural creatures. They were outcasts from the beast tribes, their legs and backs twisted. The smaller of the two men was missing an eye, the socket oozing a yellow pus onto his fur-covered cheeks. Until Jon had discovered the group, they had been starving, surviving on berries and an occasional river fish.

Unlike the large beast tribes, this crippled band had no regular shelter. They were constantly in the open, always on the move. They fled the others of their kind as well as Markov, who, they were certain, would end their miserable lives.

Jon had observed the little band for months. He watched the way they gestured to one another as they rested, the way they cared for one another. Gradually, he came to understand that, though they were deformed and dim-witted, they had once been human, and some of that humanity remained. Could he approach them? Learn to understand them? He only knew he wanted to try.

He began by leaving food for them, whistling each time he dropped a gift, then hiding in the withered trees. Later, he let them glimpse him, moving a bit closer to them after they approached the meat. Eventually, they let him stand near them, let him touch their coarse fur, let him share their simple exchanges.

Last time Jon had met them, there had been two others in the band. One was a tiny woman, who had the sole alterations of a soft, golden-haired pelt that covered her body, and a blank emptiness in her blue eyes. A huge man also accompanied them, his body resembling a bull's, with rear hooves, and horns grafted unevenly to his low forehead.

"Where?" Jon asked, holding his hands out to indicate the two missing members of their party.

The woman tried to explain. Her mouth, hardly more than a thick scar across her scabrous face, couldn't form words. Little remained of her tongue, so her voice had the inflections but none of the syllables of speech. Tears fell from her slitted eyes, and she lowered her head and covered her face to hide her shame.

The one-eyed man touched her arm. His expression grew painful as he sought for some way to explain. Then, silently, he displayed the raw gashes on his side and pointed toward the river, gesturing that Jon would find the answer there. Jon nodded and picked up the sack, holding it out to the crying beast-woman. She took it from his hand and opened it. The three looked inside, eying the feast within. They turned to Jon, bowing effusively in genuine thanks. The smaller of the two men kissed Jon's hand, the larger stroked his silver hair with a huge bear paw that wasn't meant to occupy so thin an arm. The woman tried to smile, then ripped a few pieces from the broken loaf and, holding them delicately between the curved red talons of her fingertips, fed them to a ferret sitting on her shoulder.

Jonathan had often seen the beast-women with pets, but he had never spotted a single child among any of the beast tribes. When Markov created these horrible mutations, he apparently also made them sterile. Jon often wondered if the children would have been human or if they would have been animals. He knew the story of the one who had created them, a man so twisted that the Vistani called him "the master of pain." The Guardians had made certain Jonathan learned of Markov well before he set foot outside the fortress. The stories had given him nightmares of being bound to a table in Markov's estate, the sharp blade of the knife glistening in the firelight as it descended to cut away his human flesh.

"Monster," Dominic had called him. "Twisted genius. He sets himself as far above men as we do above the beasts we use for food."

Jon thought of those words while he watched the trio devour the rabbits he had snared, ripping the limbs from the carcasses, eating the meat raw, wiping the blood from their hands with hunks of bread torn from the loaves. When they had finished their feast, Jon asked them to take him to the place where the others had died.

The pair had been killed at the edge of the swift, rocky river. Their ravaged bodies had been ripped apart, their limbs stripped of their flesh and arranged in a heap on the bank. Near them, untouched and unmoving, lay the creature that had killed them. It was the most lethal beast-creature Jon had ever seen. It had human feet, a human face, human breasts—useless without infants to suckle—and the sleek body and tail of a mountain cat, mutated to monstrous size. Its mouth hung open, the long feline fangs indenting the lower lip. Even dead, the thing made Jon shudder. The thought that there must be more of them hunting the area made him want to run back to the protective walls of the fortress.

"You killed this?" Jonathan asked, pointing to the cat-woman's body, then to the wounded beast-man.

The man nodded. As he did, he let out a long, grunted laugh and proudly beat his chest with an open hand. When the blustering had ended, the beast-man crouched beside the riverbank and pulled a short sword from a hiding place in some deep bushes. He handed it to Jonathan, gestured significantly, and began to shamble away.

"No!" Jon said and laid it back into the beastman's hairy hands. "Keep. Use."

The creature returned it to the thick bushes where it had been hidden. Jon retrieved it and tried to give it to him once more, though he knew it was already hopeless.

The man was shaking his head and Jon was trying to explain that he should keep it when a low snarl came from the brush farther up the bank. As Jon turned toward the sound, he heard a second snarl, and a third.

The woman shrieked and tried to run, but her ruined legs produced only hobbling. Jon rushed after her and pulled her back, motioning for the others to retreat to the river. As soon as their feet touched the frigid water, the trio refused to go any farther. Jon imitated a cat clawing for its prey, but the three still wouldn't move. Exasperated, Jon thrust the sword against the beast-man's chest. "Then fight!" he ordered and reached for his sling. The stones were small, better suited for hunting rabbits and squirrels than the huge cat-men stalking from the trees, forming a half circle around them.

Why didn't they attack? Jon wondered. Their little group was helpless, perfect prey, and yet the catmen waited. In a moment, Jon understood. The thing that followed the pride into the clearing was undoubtedly their leader.

In some perverse joke, Markov had polymorphed mountain cats by giving them human faces, then created a lord of the cats from a human by giving him a cat face. Though he had a human body, his legs were feline, and his human arms ended in huge cat's forepaws. He fixed his orange eyes on Jon, and the others followed his lead. Their gaze dizzied Jon, and he understood. They didn't intend to kill him. Instead, they would charm him into sleep, then kill and devour the others. Once they had feasted, they would take Jon to Markov, who would use his body as he had all the other unfortunate strangers who wandered the land.

Fear gave Jon strength, and he managed to avert his eyes before sleep claimed him. Drawing on all the skill Leo had taught him, Jon prepared the only attack that might destroy the beasts. He spread his legs for balance and dug his heels into the spongy earth of the riverbank. His hands were pressed together as if in prayer. The words formed slowly in his mind. As they did, he poised his fingers and waited.

The cat-men paced on all fours, moving closer as they waited for an order from the orange-eyed creature at the rear of the deadly pride. Ignoring them, Jon concentrated on the power building inside him, trying to harness the flow of energy as Leo had instructed.

He wasn't sure how long the cat-men waited before they made their move, but when they did, Jon was prepared. His hands pointed forward and a sheet of fire moved out from his fingers. One of the attackers, his fur in flames, rushed to the river and was swept away by the rapids. The rest weren't so lucky, for Jon had lowered his hands, setting fire to the grasses around them. Sensing his advantage, the armed beast-man attacked, stabbing his sword into the shrieking cats, disabling them. His companions followed and crushed their heads with rocks.

The power Jon had focused vanished in the single blast of flame, but the battle wasn't finished. The catfaced leader of the attack had merely been singed by the flames. Now he retreated slowly toward the trees, his mouth open, the long feline fangs bared. With a savage cry, Jon pulled the short blade from the beast-man's hands and pursued the leader. Though he was weary and far less powerful than the creature he followed, Jon had to make this a fight to the death. Markov's creation couldn't live to tell his evil master what Jon had done.

The blade Jonathan held seemed far too short and blunt to be of any use against such a deadly foe. He reminded himself of the beast-man who had killed another of these cat-faced monsters. Jon knew the monster had more agility, more skill, and far more power than he. He would disobey no one if he used his magic now. Heartened, Jon slowed his pace and began a second incantation. The terrain grew rougher. Huge boulders covered the ground. As Jon expected, his foe waited on top of one of these. He halted and raised the blade in both hands waiting for the creature to leap.

He saw the dull surprise in the creature's eyes. The illusion Jon had cast made him seem taller than his actual height, though still thin and weak. With a nod of grudging respect for Jon's brave stand, the creature pounced, aiming for Jon's throat.

Perhaps the beast's aim was faulty. Perhaps Jon's illusion had worked. No matter. As the predator's body passed above him, Jon stabbed upward, ripping into the cat's belly, twisting the blade as the beast screeched and fell. The clawed feet lashed out, but Jon was ready. With a single cut, one of its legs dangled, loose and bleeding.

The beast rolled over, thinking only of escape as it pulled itself toward higher ground. Jon hacked at it from the side, playing with its misery as the cat-man would have played with his. Finally, breathing heavily, he knelt above it for the last, killing stroke to the back of the neck. As the tip stabbed deep into the creature's body, the blood spurted out onto Jon's face, into his open mouth. He choked on it and swallowed as the creature quivered and lay still.

He had killed it!

This wasn't some game animal dying meekly to fill the Guardians' hunger but an adversary—powerful and cunning. He had used all his training with a steadiness he never thought he possessed. The blood of this creature seemed suddenly sweeter, the taste something he should savor and remember. He sucked the thick red drops from his hair, licked the backs of his coated hands, reveling in the taste.

It had all been so perfectly done! Jon's laughter flowed like an evening song through the trees. The group he had left by the river-bank heard it and approached him cautiously. Still laughing, he motioned for them to come forward and view his kill.

Markov will never know what I did here, Jon thought with relief. He handed the sword back to the beast-man, went to the river, and washed the blood from his body and clothes. When he left the crippled band, he knew he would likely never see them again. Even so, he didn't look back. His thoughts were on something far more important than these pitiable creatures. He thought instead of his power, his knowledge, and how he could increase both.

At supper that evening, Jon told the others his decision. "If it is no trouble, I would like to go to Tepest as soon as possible . . . before I change my mind," Jon said, trying to look uncertain, though he was determined to go. Dominic, his face grave and his eyes grim, yielded his place at the head of the table. Jon responded to the gesture with pride, sitting as if he belonged in the leader's seat. As he ate, Jon saw the others watching him. Some of them watched him with fearful expressions. Others flashed him brief smiles of hope, as if they considered some future when the fortress would be his rightful home.

The Guardians had taught him so much in his years here, but so little about the purpose of their order. He knew they wished to live apart from the world. They told him the shrine was the house of their god, the center of their faith, and a place that, in their humility, they dared not enter. All the rest was a mystery they couldn't share unless he discovered a calling, a vocation to join their order. Once he had tried to pry more out of them, asking countless questions. Every question was left unanswered or rebuffed. He'd stopped asking long ago.

Though he would be in the fortress only a few more days, he

decided to solve what few mysteries he could. That night, after Jon had prepared for sleep, Leo came to his room to give him the nightly potion that would allow him to rest undisturbed. Jonathan drained the tiny glass, but let most of the drug pool under his tongue when he swallowed. As soon as Leo left, he spit it into his water jug, then rinsed out his mouth—the drug was more bitter than usual. Last night's presence hadn't been a dream. He hoped that tonight he would discover who it might be.

In spite of the little he drank, Jon soon slept. He might not have awakened at all that night, but a touch on his shoulder, light as a breath of wind, roused him. His head ached, his mouth was dry, and the bitter taste of the potion was intense and nauseating.

Jon stood, staggered to his bedroom door, and found it locked. Though he beat on it until his hands were bruised, no one came.

Were the other monks as drugged as he had been? He pushed open the shutters and stared out beyond the fortress, where the long, dark shadows of the towers fell over the moon-drenched land. He had never realized the moon could be so bright. He leaned far out his window until he could see the full, magnificent circle of the moon and the stark gray patterns on its face. As he balanced there, his eyes glowing silver in the light, he heard the Guardians' chanting coming from below, from inside the fortress walls. And with it came a soft, muffled sound—shrieks of pleasure, screams of pain.

These weren't the ghostly howls heard so often in the cracked, windswept walls of the fortress, nor the whisper of his drugged sleep. No, these sounds were more sinister, more alive, yet no less familiar. He had heard these voices before in a monthly dream that went back to his earliest memories.

He listened more carefully. The chant and the frenzied cries were both coming from the area near the shrine. One of the Guardians' secrets. Someday, he vowed, someday he would learn what it was that they guarded with such fervor.

By morning, he'd forgotten how long he had sat by the window, how many times he had tried to force the door. When he woke again, his fists were clenched, bruised, and bleeding. His knees were pressed against his chest, and he shivered, though the morning sun baked his room.

ten

THE AMBITION OF MY CHILD ASTONISHES ME, AS DOES *his power. He has heeded my words, that much is certain. It pleases me to know that I have been heard. I have thought of telling him who he is and how he has been betrayed, but I sense that the time is not yet right. A few more months of prison means little after so many years.*

Two days later, just before noon, Jon and Leo entered Linde. Leo was an occasional visitor to the town, and the villagers recognized him at a distance as one of the Guardian monks. Since he wanted no one to associate the silver-haired boy with the order, this time Leo traveled disguised as a portly missionary. He fell into his role completely, walking piously ahead of Jon as they entered the town. As for Jon, this was the first time he had ever entered a town, and the people around him were the first strangers, other than Ivar and the girls at the river, that he had ever seen. He clutched his single bundle of clothes tightly to his chest, trying not to gape at the tiny painted cottages, the many different flowers that lined the road, or the people, adults as well as children, who paused in their work to stare openly at the boy and the black-robed man.

Even inside the inn, Leo kept the cowl of his robe over his head. He spoke to Andor in a booming voice suited to his apparent calling, managing to tell everyone that he was on his way to preach to the heathens in G'Henna, then asking if Andor would take his son as a servant until he returned. When Andor agreed, Leo slid a small pile of coins across the bar to pay for the first few weeks of the boy's keep.

"Will you stay until tomorrow?" Andor asked.

"My work doesn't allow for such comfort. There are many more hours of daylight. I'd rather travel on," Leo responded.

"Take care to enter G'Henna before nightfall or you'll be wasting your words on the hungry beasties instead," one of the patrons called to him.

"As if he won't be wasting them later. The bloody priests of G'Henna'll eat human flesh and souls," his companion added, with a wicked chuckle.

"They sound like they're jesting," Andor said, continuing the ruse. "But they speak truth. I doubt we'll see you again."

"I've had more than my share of luck before. Still, I wouldn't take my son. As to money, the coins were all I had," Leo responded. He pulled his cowl closer around his face and left Jon with only a single farewell.

Jon watched Leo go, then stood inside the door, his hands shaking. He hid them behind his back and kept his body pressed against the wall. Certain that any words he spoke would only make him look foolish, Jon waited silently. At last, Dirca came for him, leading him up the stairs to the tiny room already prepared for him. Its window faced south, and, in the distance, he could see the hills he loved so well. He looked from them to Dirca, who stood in the doorway, an odd, wistful expression on her face. "I'll bring you something to eat," she said.

"Is Ivar here?" Jon asked, his nervousness making his voice louder than he intended. They were the first words he'd spoken to anyone since he arrived.

"Ivar? No, he's with Andor in the winery, overseeing the pressing. He'll be back tonight. In the meantime, you should rest," she said. Then she turned and left him, brushing something from her face as she went.

Jon unpacked quickly, placing his clothes in the cupboard. Then, he went downstairs again, meeting Dirca in the kitchen, where she was preparing a tray for him. "I'm not tired," he said, explaining his presence, and sat at the table. All the time he ate, he sensed Dirca's watching eyes, but when he looked at her, she fearfully averted her gaze. Perhaps that was how women treated men, he thought, and decided to watch her later in her husband's presence.

Jon had just finished when the girl he had saved in the forest entered the kitchen through the rear door. Her forearms were stained purple, nearly to the elbows. Her ragged smock was covered with spots of the same color and clearly had been used for this work before. She stopped when she saw him, hiding her arms behind her back.

"I think it's a beautiful color," he said, his eyes bright.

She flushed. "They told me you were here," she said. "But I didn't think you would be *here*."

"Jonathan, this is my niece, Sondra."

"We've met," he said and smiled at the girl. "Perhaps I might help in the winery?"

"Jon, you've already walked a long way this morning," Dirca said.

"I'm not an invalid," he replied sharply, then softened his tone. "I'm accustomed to work. I prefer to help."

"There's plenty to do," Sondra said. "You can start by helping me prepare the workers' lunch."

The pair carried the food to the winery, where Andor introduced his new servant to the men working the press. The smell of cloudberry juice filled the room, a sweet cloying scent that hinted at the magnificence of the wine to come. As they ate, the men said little, eyeing Jon suspiciously. In a town surrounded by flesh-eating predators, and steeped in stories of shape-shifting monsters, strangers were never trusted. When the workers finished the meal, Jon helped load the berries into the winepress while Sondra stood beneath it, cleaning the skins and seeds from the narrow spout.

Two men poured the pails of juice into vats while Ivar mixed the beet sugar and honey that would sweeten the wine and add to its potency. The men left as soon as the evening bells rang. Ivar, Sondra, and Jon remained until the pressing was done. Afterward, they ate a late dinner in the kitchen.

When they'd finished, Ivar retired, leaving his daughter and Jon alone. The girl could think of little to say to the silver-haired boy. Then, she remembered the sad story of a relative who once lived in Tepest.

"I had an aunt, a beautiful girl I have heard, who lived in Viktal in Tepest," Sondra began in the settling silence. Jon leaned forward to hear. "When the time came for her to marry, she decided she wanted her own ceremony rather than the group vows taken each spring in Viktal. A week before her wedding day, she vanished. Her betrothed disappeared from his cottage a few days later. No sign was ever found of them. Such things happen often in Viktal and Kellee, but rarely here. My aunt's parents were mad with grief. One night they also disappeared. It's believed that they were lured from the inn by the beasties—the goblins—and devoured," she said.

"Do you believe those creatures are capable of such trickery?" Jonathan asked, trying to allay her fear.

Lifting the lamp, she led him into the drinking hall. There, she pointed with a shaking hand at the repair in the roof. "The beasties entered the inn through there," she said and told him the story of Mihal.

"Your father has magi—means to deal with those beasts. Don't you want to learn?" he asked.

"No," she replied bitterly. "His gift brought only misery to my mother. Because of magic, he was forced to abandon her. He did the best he could for her and left behind a few coins he had changed from copper to gold. But when she tried to spend them, Gundar's men recognized the sorcery that had created them. They took the coins and everything else of value that we possessed. Then, for revenge on my father, they forbade anyone from helping her. Though I was young, I remember too well how she died. She starved." Sondra paused then added, "I don't condemn what Father is, but I couldn't bear the burden of his power, or his conscience."

Her sorrow was so deep and lasting, it seemed Jon could feel it inside him. To lighten her thoughts, he lifted a lute from its hanging place beside the dining hall door. "Do people often play?" he asked as he tuned the strings.

"Never. They say that Maeve, the woman who sheltered your mother while she lived here, once used it. Father ordered her to stay away from the inn before I ever came here. Arlette told me they were once friends, but bad blood developed between them—that he cursed her. Maeve in turn has vowed revenge on anyone who dares bring music into *The Nocturne*. She often sings at the seasonal festivals. I have never heard a lovelier voice. "

"Do you know any songs?"

"A few. I have no voice, though," she said.

"Have you heard this one?" He began a simple melody, singing the familiar, tragic legend of a healer who, driven by pride, placed himself above the gods and gave life to dead flesh. The gods retaliated, destroying everything he loved and leaving him alone, half mad with grief.

The song shifted to an even sadder lament, that of the monster he had created, condemned to live on the edge of humanity, longing forever for the warmth of human love.

Maeve's voice was beautiful, but it didn't touch Sondra's heart as this youth's did. He sang the first part with exquisite clarity, but the last verses displayed the real emotion behind his song.

When he finished, Sondra blurted, "That's the most beautiful song I've ever heard." She touched his face with her fingertips, her hand fluttering like a small wild bird against his cheek.

The song had awakened Andor, and he lay beside his sleeping wife listening with his sensitive ears to the beautifully-sung lament of the monster.

When the lightning flashes, I think of the night I was born.
When the storm strikes, the memories return.
When the winds fade, I long for the death that will not claim me.

Andor found himself thinking of those terrible, destructive years before that fateful night when Ivar arrived at the inn, before the wolf's-head pendants. The cold moonlight leaking through the cracks in the barred shutters roused the beast in Andor—a beast that still thrilled to the exhilarating memories of the old hunts, the magnificent taste of fresh blood.

During the next few days, Ivar and Jonathan worked together in the winery. Jon knew he was being tested and obeyed every order, following instructions without flaw. Finally, on the night the wine was given its final straining and was placed in the aging kegs, Ivar asked the boy to join him in the cave beneath the inn. "And bring your spell book," he added.

Jonathan, nervously holding the book in both hands, followed the white-haired man down the winding stairs. Neither of them spoke as Ivar motioned the boy to a seat across from him at the cavern's only table. A half-dozen candles lit the space, and Jon set the book between them. Before Ivar opened it, he ran his fingers over the leather cover Jon had made for it, examined the braided binding. The boy had done much with his meagre supplies. He clearly loved his chosen craft.

The first pages were filled with the intricate directions and incantations even the simplest spells required. Most dealt with fire, a fact that hardly surprised Ivar. "You have so few pages in your book," Ivar commented. "Did you plan to learn so little?"

"I was afraid . . ." Jon began, his eyes colored amber from the soft glow of the candle flames.

"Afraid?"

"To seem too ambitious or to ask too much of Leo. Each time I did, he would stop teaching me. I thought that if I agreed to come here, you would be my teacher. I want so much to learn."

The boy's voice was even, his eyes glittered, and Ivar wondered if he were about to cry. Though it tore at him to be so harsh with one so talented and to whom he already owed so much, Ivar pressed on. "Did Leo explain why he was reluctant to train you?" he asked without a trace of sympathy in his voice.

"A little. He said that no matter how much I learned, I couldn't use it without endangering myself and those I cared for."

"He's correct. In these lands, the small powers are the easiest to practice. The land twists the great ones to its own evil ends."

"Then what is the use of learning at all?"

"Part of your training will be discretion. Another part will be knowing when to take a risk. I would use my spells to save an innocent's life. And, for the risk you took for Sondra, I owe you a great deal."

"So you will teach me?" The boy sounded hopeful.

Ivar hadn't trained an apprentice since Leo abruptly left him. The temptation was great even though he expected this boy to show the same abrupt signs of the calling as Leo, so many years before. Perhaps that was his function, Ivar thought. Perhaps the Guardians needed the learning he could provide. If so, he should move the boy forward as quickly as possible. "No one in Linde save Andor and his family knows that this cavern exists. Should you reveal the secret to anyone, I will do far more than stop your lessons. This is the first part of our pact."

"I promise," Jon said, his voice rising with expectation.

"Your spellbook will be kept here or hidden in your room. You must show it to no one, give strangers no hint it exists. That's the second part of our pact."

This time Jon nodded, afraid to speak.

"Your spells will be learned here. You may practice them only alone here or in my company outside of these walls. But you never use magic alone unless I give you leave, unless you or another innocent will die if you don't. That is the third part of our pact."

"I agree."

"And finally, you must tell no one outside of our family of my power or your own. Swear to all of it." Jon agreed too quickly, and Ivar spoke sharply, "Swear by your power to do everything I ask."

"I do," the boy said. "By my power, I swear it."

"Good." Ivar smiled tightly and turned the book to face his pupil. "Now show me what you know. Take whatever time you need to prepare."

Jonathan scanned his spellbook, then collected the materials he needed for casting. He had never been able to push his powers to their limits before—Leo seemed to fear them. Now, he set to the task with relish. The small fire on the hearth grew brighter. Its color changed from golden to red to deep blue.

Flames few from Jon's fingertips to light the candles on the table. An ordered breeze extinguished them. The fire in the hearth died. Jon reached for the glowing phosphorus on the table and blew a pinch of it into the wind. Instantly, magical will-o'-the-wisps danced across the darkened floor and flowed into the hearth, starting the fire once more. Jon's form grew taller, shorter, stooped, and aged. At last, exhausted by his display, he closed his book, dropped his hands to the table and stared at Ivar. A smile of delight played across his lips, a smile that grew when he saw that Ivar's expression mirrored his own.

The wizard reached across the table and fingered the scar Dominic's amulet had left on the boy's cheek. "This is a fire sign. It came to you at your naming. In some places, it would be considered an omen."

"Of good?" Jon asked.

"Of power. It will be a pleasure to teach you, and perhaps to one day learn from you."

Later, as Jonathan lay in bed with the promise of many more hours in the cavern, he laughed, muffling the sound with his pillow. He had finally found a teacher who respected him. Now he would learn. Nothing was as important as that.

In the weeks that followed, Ivar and Jon worked in the winery, nursing the vats of purple and amber through the final days of fermentation. At night, they would study together in the cavern. Finally, with the last of the amber wine corked and shipped throughout Tepest and into Nova Vaasa, the deep purple blends sealed in their aging casks, they turned more of their time to Jon's education.

Jon proved a brilliant apprentice. The speed and accuracy with which the boy memorized simple spells made Ivar certain that his pupil could master more difficult ones almost as easily. Nonetheless, the boy was obsessed with light and fire. Any spell dealing with these held his interest. Others, no matter how well he learned them, did not. Yet, Ivar told himself, the boy had managed to summon the wolves, a difficult spell under ordinary circumstances, nearly impossible given the scarcity of the beasts in these lands.

"Tell me the words you used to bring wolves to my daughter's aid," Ivar finally ordered.

Jon hesitated. Ivar sensed that the boy thought of lying, then decided he would be caught. "It wasn't my doing," Jon admitted, refusing to meet his master's eyes. "I'd been wandering the woods when I noticed them trailing me." He described the wolves and went on. "When I heard the girls run by, screaming, I went to the clearing and saw Sondra. The wolves followed. I . . . I spoke to them and they seemed to listen. I honestly don't know if that was a spell."

"Sondra said you summoned them."

"I didn't tell her that, or deny it, either."

"Nor did you deny it to me when I questioned you."

"I knew enough fire spells to destroy the goblins. I would've done so had the wolves not attacked first."

"Do you care for Sondra? Is that why you lied?"

"I'm too young to care for anyone, but when I saw her in the woods, facing those things, I admit . . ." His voice trailed off uneasily.

"She faces danger well, doesn't she?"

Jonathan nodded.

"Most of the young men in Tepest are married by the time they're seventeen. I'd give permission for you to court Sondra, should you choose to ask."

His pupil grew so flustered that Ivar knew his instinct had been correct. Jon answered, "Not yet."

A sensible reply, and one that strangely saddened Ivar, for he longed for one of his own blood to teach. It was said that he had obtained his skills because his father possessed them. Ivar had never known the man. Instead his mother had helped him with his first tentative castings.

Ivar stretched and yawned. "I feel weary," he told the boy, as he prepared to leave. "Go on with your lesson. You're more than able to manage on your own."

Jon remained alone in the cavern, working with little determination to magically erase the words on the parchment in front of him. He saw no use for the spell. It wouldn't protect him, wouldn't give him knowledge, and seemed to subtract rather than add to his power. He suspected that Ivar had required him to learn it as a sort of discipline. He managed to make the letters fade and decided to continue his training the following evening when his mind was sharper.

Closing his book, he laid it beside Ivar's thick tomes and scrolls, doused the fire in the hearth, and blew out the candles. He had climbed the winding stairs to the inn so often that he no longer needed to carry a light.

A narrow passage at the top of the stairs cut behind one of the walls in the dining hall. As Jon walked down it, he heard Ivar and Andor discussing him. The Guardians had their secrets; perhaps this family did as well. Curious, Jon paused and listened.

"Jonathan has to do something besides learn with you," Andor said. "People will start to wonder what he does here. There's already been talk. Maeve started most of it, as if she hasn't caused enough trouble for the boy already."

"Jon told me that he didn't summon the wolves. He said they were following him. Their leader was huge and black."

"Wasn't the mother's life enough for that cursed woman?" Andor commented bitterly.

"Leith chose her course freely. No one forced her."

"Does Jon know what happened to her?"

"He thinks she died giving birth. It's better that way."

What could they mean? Could his mother have been killed? The men had mentioned Maeve, and Jon recalled the fact that she had been banned from *The Nocturne*. His mind swiftly linked his mother and Maeve and, as swiftly, dismissed the thought. That wouldn't have made the Guardians lie.

A second, somehow more troubling, possibility came to mind. Perhaps his mother was still alive. If she were, why hadn't she come for him? Jon stood in the darkness, not daring to breathe lest Ivar discover him standing in the dark passage, tears running down his face. He waited until they had moved to the kitchen, then, composing himself, went to meet them.

"Now that the wine has been bottled we've been wondering what sort of work you would like to do in Linde," Andor said.

Jon feigned surprise. "Hunting," he finally decided. "I've little skill in dealing with people."

Andor smiled, thinking of the village girls who had suddenly begun frequenting the dining hall at odd hours, hoping to glimpse Jonathan or hear him pluck the lute and sing. He thought more grimly of the young men who had begun expressing their dislike of their unassuming rival, especially Mishya, who was furious that Sondra no longer encouraged his company. "You're not unskilled, you're ignorant," he said. "That will pass. Meanwhile, I think one of the hunting parties might be willing to take you on."

Might be willing! Jon had seen how they hunted. They were all fools. The boy's eyes became icy slivers, his mouth a thin white line. "I hunt alone. I always have," he said.

"Not in Tepest. Too many men have been lost in the thick woods."

"Quail, squirrels, rabbits. I could hunt those with a sling in the pastures and still remain close to town."

He fixed his attention on Andor, mentally ordering him to agree, and wasn't entirely surprised when the man did. This persuasive talent, like his charm, was innate. People usually did what he asked, here as in the fortress. He listened restlessly to the warnings Andor gave about hunting alone, but nothing could dissuade him. There were questions that needed answers and he could only find those on his own.

"I'll start tomorrow, in the fields about town," he said when Andor finished.

Ivar shook his head. "You'll begin down there," he said, pointing down to the cavern. "Among my scrolls are two tied with black ribbons. Before you wander these hills alone, read them both."

Jon hardly slept that night and rose well before dawn. As he descended the stairs, a rat skittered away, disappearing into the darkness of one of the unused tunnels. He often marveled that the vermin didn't ruin Ivar's scrolls or devour the food left on the table. Rats had plagued Leo's small library terribly, but Ivar apparently had means of controlling their simple minds. Ivar had set the scrolls out for him, and, after rubbing the sleep from his eyes and lighting the candles on the table, Jon began to read.

The first account regarded the three hags said to live in Tepest. Leo had told him part of the story, but this account was far more detailed. Powerful sorcerers in their own right, the three took on seductive forms of strangers or loved ones, luring unsuspecting wanderers into a deadly trap. The tale only made Jon more resolute, more eager to acquire the power to make himself invincible to their spells.

The second scroll contained information far more interesting. Ivar had already told him about Andor's curse. Now he learned that Andor wasn't the only *were*-creature in this town. Another, the woman named Maeve, was believed to be in league with the hags, supplying them with victims from among her many willing lovers. Ivar had perhaps suggested this scroll so Jon would know to stay well away from her. But one fact particularly amazed Jon; in wolf form, the woman was huge and powerful, with thick black fur. He had met the woman already—leader of the pack that had followed him. He intended to meet her again, soon.

eLeven

tHere is Life of a kind in the days between the full *moons. I sense the passing of the seasons, the sunshine and the storms in the minds of the people around me. The boy's dreams are dark and troubled, and that is good. Darkness will bring him to me. Soon he will be mine.*

Jon's hunting skills easily surpassed those of any other youth in Linde. He had a gift for sitting so still his prey didn't see him until the stone flew, for setting snares so perfect that even the most wary animal didn't notice them. As a result, he didn't have to work very hard to gain Andor's praise. The inn's food became plentiful and cheap and its smokehouse well-stocked for winter.

It was time to harvest the autumn grain. Jon joined the harvesters for a while, but couldn't find the right rhythm for the scythe or the strength to wield it for long. Though the village hunters commented derisively on his weakness, Jon welcomed the banter: the jeers held some friendliness he hadn't detected before.

Linde townsfolk had never harvested so many bushels of grain and hay. Neither had they ever seen such ideal weather for the work, weather that held for the autumn goblin hunt and the harvest festival after.

Tents were erected outside the inn. Like the houses, they were white, bearing intricately-painted flowers and vines on the walls and rain flaps. Brightly colored banners waved from the top of the center poles. Every family brought vases of flowers for the dining tables, their best casseroles and bakery to share, their crafts and weaving to sell. One of the inn's hogs was butchered and roasted whole over a trench of smoking coals and damp herbs. Dirca basted it with onion butter and cloudberry jam until the hide was dark and crackling. Jon, raised by the ascetic Guardians, had never shared in such a bountiful feast.

After the village had eaten, the leftovers were piled on a single table to provide sustenance for the night's revels. The dining tables were cleared from the town square to make room for musicians and dancing.

Jonathan had never danced before, but he couldn't resist joining the others. The magnificent songs, the whirling revelers, and the touch of Sondra's hands were more intoxicating than the Linde wine and cloudberry pies. As the night deepened, the harvest moon rose in the sky, its light competing with the mounted torches, throwing brilliant silver streaks around the golden puddles in the center of the town.

In the middle of the evening, Maeve made her first appearance. Jon had glimpsed her a few times and been startled by her beauty, but never as much as now. The silver streak in her hair was braided through a thin golden chain. The rest fell loose over her shoulders. Her multi-colored skirts were long and gossamer, her blouse tight over her breasts. She had tiny cymbals attached to her fingers and bells on her ankles. As she walked barefooted through the crowd, everyone, women as well as men, paused to look at her. A sudden hush fell over the crowd. Smiling oddly, she motioned them to form a circle in the center of the tent.

"She's going to dance as well! Oh, it's been so long!" one of the girls said to Jon. She didn't look at him. Her gaze, still fixed on Maeve, was adoring.

"Her usual entrance," Sondra said softly, moving forward so she and Jon reached the clearing's edge.

Maeve stamped her foot three times in the dust. She raised her arms above her, the loose folds of her sleeves falling to cover her chest. The cymbals rang gently and, with her face raised to the moon, she began to sing. It was a tune hunters often sang, subtly altered from a hunting song to a wolf's lament for a winter mate, one who would share the cold, dark hours and warm the den until spring.

As she sang, her hands began to twist about, her feet to pad the beat. She circled the clearing, whirling toward the fire pit at its center. Her arms and voice wove patterns in the firelight, patterns Jon felt rather than saw. Sondra moved closer to him, her hand reaching for his. Caught up in the emotion, he didn't hear the singing stop. He raised Sondra's hand to his lips and kissed it, then looked at her. "You look so beautiful," he whispered.

Her lips were open, ready to reply, when he was pulled away from her and into the ring. "Look at you," Maeve said, painfully gripping his arm. "So fair. So perfectly Kartakan. I hear that you can even sing."

He felt numb, speechless, embarrassed.

"Of course you can," she purred. "Come. Give us a song and we'll let you go." Maeve looked from him to Sondra. "A love song perhaps? A betrothal song?"

Mishya took advantage of his rival's absence to move to Sondra's side and whisper in her ear. She pulled away, her eyes fixed on Jon's.

The sight of his rival gave him courage. "Yes!" Jon declared and took a lute from one of the musicians. He began to sing, a simple courting tune that Sondra recently taught him. He played well and his singing—clear as the frigid waters of Lake Kronov—rivaled Maeve's. His voice, compelling and impassioned, brought to each listener longing for his or her heart's desire. The longing brought tears to their eyes and emptiness to their hearts.

Near the end of the song, Mishya moved behind Sondra, pressing his body against hers. "They say that evil's spawn has a pleasing voice," he whispered, his hands moving from her shoulders to her breasts. Pulled from her reverie, she twisted out of his grasp, turned, and, without thinking, slapped him.

Though it was hardly more than she had done before when he had become too forward, Mishya returned the slap, hitting her harder than he expected. She fell backward into the dusty ring. Jon had been singing to Sondra, watching her reaction to the words. As she fell, he threw aside the lute and lunged for his rival.

Since Jon had arrived, he had witnessed a number of tavern fights. He had expected he might one day find himself caught up in one, but he hadn't anticipated how much rage he would feel. When Mishya struck Sondra, something exploded in him, some evil he'd never suspected lurked there. Mishya was a tall, stocky youth, but Jon was quicker, and his years of wrestling Hektor had prepared him well. Mishya's first swing swiped through air, and he lost his balance. Before he could regain it, Jon attacked. He threw all his weight against the tall youth. Mishya fell backward as the silver-haired boy's fists pounded his head. By the time villagers pulled the two apart, Mishya's face was covered with blood from slashes Jon's nails had made.

"Go and wash," one of the elders said to Mishya without sympathy, then turned his attention to Jon. "As for you, cool that fire in your blood, or you'll not be welcome in this town."

Jon, fighting to control his rage, looked for Sondra and saw her running toward the inn. He thought of following her, but the elder announced, "Maeve, it's time for the hunt song and our sacrifice."

The mood of the evening shifted as dramatically as it had when Jon threw aside the lute to attack his rival. Hushed, expectant, the village formed a new circle around the dying embers of the night's feast. The musicians laid aside their lutes and recorders, replacing them with huge standing drums.

Maeve, positioned beside the fire pit, began a rhythmic dance in time to the drumbeats. The slow tempo gradually quickened, the sound increasing until it beat against the chests of the assembly. The drumbeats stopped abruptly. The crowd hardly seemed to breathe as Maeve chanted, "The rye-wolf! The corn-wolf! The wheat-wolf! The barley-wolf! Come!"

Four men stepped forward. Each had cut the last stalks of grain in the fields. Now they wore them bound to their arms and legs. Their hands joined and the drums resumed their heavy beat. The four danced around the edge of the circle, weaving through one another's upraised arms in an accelerating rhythm. As they danced, sweat began to stream down their arms and legs, and their quickening steps grew weary. When exhaustion finally claimed them, they threw their sheaves on the fire, making it flare once more.

"The sacrifice!" Maeve cried, her hands outstretched, beckoning them forward. "Which of you shall be our sacrifice?"

"We all willingly give our lives for the good of the land, but ask that another stand in our place," the four men responded.

The four men went into the nearest game hut, bringing out an iron cage with open bars on all sides. Inside was the red-skinned goblin trapped during the harvest hunt. In the days since its capture, the children of the village had avenged the deaths of their companions by poking sticks at the creature, allowing it little rest. Even so, the creature had enough strength left to tear at the carrying poles, to reach through the bars, trying to grip its foes in powerful hands.

As the creature was carried into the circle, the village elders laid dried sticks on the fire, building the embers to a bright blaze. The elders chanted, "To the spirit of the land, we give this sacrifice. May its pain and its blood make the earth fertile, make the spring seed sprout, make the waters flow."

The villagers repeated the chant. The men held the cage high as they walked on either side of the pit. The fire licked at the soles of the goblin's feet and singed the fur on its legs. The creature shrieked and pounded against the sides of the cage, but the men held it firmly, slowly lowering the cage as the fire died.

"Would they sacrifice one of the cattle if no goblin could be found?" Jon whispered to Andor.

"Cattle aren't acceptable. If there were no beasties, the village would use a criminal under sentence of death. Without either, the men would draw lots," Andor replied. "The solstice festivals are celebrations of sacrifice, the only times of the year the village is thankful for the beasties that overrun our land."

Jon hardly heard his last words, concentrating instead on the high-pitched, goblinoid screams that echoed across the empty hills. "Accept the death of our enemy!" the elders chanted, and again the villagers repeated the words.

Maeve led Arlette's mother forward, tears streaming down the woman's face. Her body shook with grief for her child, killed by the goblins during the cloudberry harvest. With Maeve beside her to support her, she circled the pit, pouring fat on the fire. Together, they watched the goblin writhe in the center of the rising, hungry light.

"May our winter hunts be fruitful. May the land grant our needs," the elders cried, and the village repeated the words.

Jon noted Andor's savage expression as he stared at the creature, his fingers idly moving over the wolf pendant he wore. Jon returned his gaze to the goblin. Some dark pleasure was churning in him as well, the savagery of the sacrifice arousing a hunger he could scarcely understand. His eyes burned from the flames as he watched Maeve kick the cage to the edge of the fire pit. She raised her knife.

"May the flesh of our enemy make us strong," she called out as she sliced a strip of meat from the goblin's charred carcass. Though the inside was nearly raw, she didn't seem to notice as, caught up in the rapture of the ceremony, she put part of it in her mouth and handed the rest to Arlette's mother, who did the same.

The village pressed forward while Maeve sliced the body, filling eager, outstretched hands with meat. Jon joined them and the taste, as foul as he expected, held all the satisfaction of victory after a long, bloody war.

The feast had ended. The villagers began returning to their homes. Maeve moved close to Jon and took his hand, pulling him into a copse of trees between the road and the river. "You are welcome to come and see me any time you wish," she whispered and kissed him. He tried to pull away, but her grip was too strong and the emotions she touched in him were as potent as his rage had been. "There are things you ought to know, child," she said and laughed as, freed of her grasp, he headed quickly toward the road and the welcome light streaming from the inn. Inside, men were singing festival songs in voices far less harmonious than before.

Mishya, along with his friends Alden and Josef, waited for Jon just outside the inn's doorway. The trio blocked his way inside, challenging him to cry out for help. Jon didn't. Instead, he let himself be pushed away from the square of light, into the trees around the village square. His hands were clenched into tight fists, holding back the power he felt rising in them. A word, a gesture, and these men would trouble him no more.

"I saw you watching the moon tonight," Mishya whispered. "Was our festival as wild as the ones of your past?"

Jon didn't understand the taunt.

"Were the beast-women as passionate as the girl you stole from me?"

This time there was no mistaking the intent of the insult. Jon had been held back once tonight. Now no one could stop the fight. He sprang at Mishya, but the youth's companions caught his arms and dragged him farther into the woods as Mishya rolled back his sleeves. It was a coward's act and a coward's fight. In the beginning, Mishya's fists fell in places where the bruises wouldn't show. Later, after Jon's well-aimed kick caught him in the midsection, the brute was less particular.

"Take him to the river," Mishya told the others. "Tie him there and let the beasties gnaw his flesh."

"You're not coming?" Alden asked.

"I'll be missed," Mishya whispered. "Remember who rid you of Vladish when he came collecting."

Barely conscious, Jon didn't call out as he was dragged farther into the woods. He had the means to save his life. He needed no other assistance.

"After the festival tonight, the beasties will be thick here, ready for revenge," Josef said, scanning the brush anxiously.

As if replying to his fear, the bushes near the river rustled. "Leave the bait!" Alden cried. They dropped Jon and ran.

Josef felt hands close around his ankles. As he fell, he twisted onto his back, intending to fight. Some creature, larger and darker than any of the Tepest goblins, covered him. Clawed hands and feet tore at his limbs while the muzzle forced his head up and ripped the scream from his throat.

Jon crawled to the top of the bank, then turned to see the creature that had come to his aid. The thing sat beside Josef, its wolf head digging into the flesh of the dead boy's neck, its human hands with their brightly painted nails undoing the laces of the shirt.

"Maeve?" Jon called softly.

The werewolf turned, her head cocked, acknowledging her name for just a moment before turning her attention to her kill.

Alden ran to the center of town before he realized he was alone. The cottage doors were all barred. The shutters were latched. The only light came from the inn, the only sounds festival songs sung by late-night revelers.

"Josef?" he whispered into the darkness.

No reply.

He should go home, sleep, pretend he didn't know what had happened, but he knew that no one would believe him. He and Josef had been together all night. They'd been seen by everyone.

"Josef?"

"Alden," someone whispered back. Alden whirled.

Jonathan, bruised and bleeding, stumbled forward. In spite of the beating, his words were spoken evenly in a whisper so low that Alden had to strain to hear them. "Josef's hurt. I left him by the river. I thought you'd prefer to help me than have me go to the inn, take the others back, and explain what happened."

Jonathan was the last person Alden should trust. He knew it, but the knowledge was buried well below his fear. He shook his head, trying to clear it, to focus on what he should do.

"I know about Vladish," Jon whispered.

The threat hardly concerned him, Alden decided.

After he found Josef, he'd make sure Jon never passed his knowledge on to anyone. Nodding silently, he followed the silver-haired boy.

Jonathan stopped on the edge of the festival fire pit and pointed to the blackened bones of the caged goblin. The creature seemed more human now, stripped of flesh, its small, skeletal hand clutching the bars of the cage. Jon looked at it a moment, then said, "The beasties are prowling the edge of town. Fire will keep them at bay."

"Fire," Alden repeated emptily. Some niggling voice in his mind told him the silver-haired boy had placed the word on his tongue, that Jon was directing his thoughts. But he couldn't resist the suggestion. He pulled a pair of pitch-covered torches from the stack beside the fire and lit them in the embers. Holding them high, he followed Jon into the dark forest, starting at every flickering shadow around him.

"Josef?" Alden called, his voice soft with fear.

Soon, Jon pointed at the ground beside him.

Alden raised the torch and stepped forward. At the base of a tree, he saw part of one hand, half a face, the other bones stripped and stacked into a small, circular pile. His face white, the torch shaking in his hands, Alden looked from the remains to Jon.

"You knew!" he said.

Jon nodded but didn't speak. His face was rigid with concentration.

"I'll tell them you knew!" Alden said.

"Will you?" Jon asked. The torches Alden held grew hot, burning his hands. He flung them down in front of him. As he did,

Jonathan's hands pointed outward, streams of flames shooting from his fingers.

The tendrils circled Alden, pulling like yarn circling a skein. Alden froze, fearing the flames would catch his clothes. He measured the length of his life in heartbeats, yet couldn't find the breath to scream.

Alden's eyelashes were singed, the burning hair on his arms leaving needle-pricks of pain on his skin. Jonathan pulled his hands apart, tightening the deadly knot around Alden's body. In agony, Alden breathed in the flames, letting out his last breath with a long hiss that might have been the beginning of a scream.

Two were dead. One other still lived. Dry-eyed and furious, Jon returned to the inn to plot his revenge. He entered through the back door, meeting Sondra in the kitchen.

"Where were you?" she asked then, noticing his bloody lip and the cuts on his face. Her concern turned to anger. "Was it Mishya?" she asked. "It wouldn't be the first time that thug—"

"It wasn't Mishya," he replied coldly.

"Sit down. I'll get a basin and some warm water," she said, trying to sidestep Jon's strange anger.

She had just begun dabbing at the worst of Jon's cuts when the front doors to the inn slammed inward. An elder whose house was close to the river stood in the doorway, his two sons behind him holding torches.

"Beasties!" an elder cried, his words echoed by his sons. "Beasties killed someone at the river." Whatever words followed were drowned by the sounds of men running from the inn, following the torch bearers to the riverbank.

Mishya was among the last to go. With an odd smile, he stood to follow the others. Then he noticed Sondra at the kitchen door, and Jon standing behind her. Sondra sensed his sudden fear and, when she looked over her shoulder, saw hatred smolder like cold fire in Jon's eyes. Whatever she glimpsed there dissipated in a moment though. Mishya ran after the others.

Jon returned to the table. "Mishya beat me while the others held me," he told her. "Afterward, he ordered Alden and Josef to drag me to the river. They were going to tie me there for the goblins. Before they could, the goblins came. I ran."

"And people call the goblins beasts," she whispered. She looked away, stunned by what she had just said, then cleaned his cuts as quickly as she was able. "Come upstairs," she said. "The men mustn't see you, not with the way your face looks now."

Outside his door, she paused, "I was the only one in the kitchen tonight. If I am questioned, I'll say you were with me for the last hour." Her hand brushed the bruise on his forehead. "The hour after Mishya attacked you."

"I don't need your lie."

"I'll lie anyway," she said and kissed him. He intended to respond with a chaste show of affection, but the emotions that night had roused in him were too new, too strong. He ground his lips against hers, unaware of her panic until she used all her strength to shove him away. He knew what he had done only from the fear in her expression as she wiped his blood from her lips with the back of her hand.

"I'm sorry," he said. The words held no sincerity. When she didn't reply, he went into his room and closed his door.

Jon had seen Maeve's secluded cottage before, but the morning following the festival was the first time he'd really noticed it. Whatever charm it once held had faded like the paint on its shutters. The shutters were cracked, the roof in need of repair. Vines had claimed the garden wall, and the garden gate was missing one of its hinges. The place was the ghost of a happier past, of abandoned dreams.

As Jon lay belly-down in the brush near the river, wondering if he dared accept the woman's invitation, the cottage door opened and one of the village elders came out. Maeve followed, her bright orange gown glowing in the morning sun. Her parting kiss was as deep as the one she had given Jon last night, though her eyes were open, and she stared over the elder's shoulder at the place where Jon was hidden. A small, private smile danced lightly on her lips as the man said good-bye. After her visitor left, Maeve went inside, leaving the door open behind her.

What can I hope to discover here besides more shame? Jon wondered. Nonetheless, the woman had hinted that she had information for him. He followed her in.

Maeve didn't turn to meet him. Instead she sat at her cluttered dressing table, combing out her tangled hair in front of the gilt-edged mirror. "I expected you last night, if only to thank me," she said, her eyes fixed on her reflection.

"And when I didn't come, you found another to take my place?"

"I had my choice of any man at the festival. Perhaps I'll choose Mishya next. Would you like that?"

He sensed danger in her response and glanced at the open door. "I'll take care of him in my own good time. Now tell me about my mother."

"Very well." Hair arranged, she began slipping thin golden bracelets on her wrists. "She stayed with me. I was her friend."

"You destroyed her."

She faced him for the first time, her violet eyes wide but far from innocent. They held a blaze deep inside them that spoke less of passion than insanity. Her laugh convinced him of it. "Did they tell you that, those Guardians of the cloth? Oh, don't look so surprised that I know of them. The tales are clear enough that I can recognize one of them in the flesh. I even know their names—Leo, Dominic, Hektor . . ."

"No one told me," Jon interrupted.

She laughed again. "Well, perhaps my kiss convinced you. Was my passion so terrible?"

"Did you destroy my mother?"

"I cared for her. I wanted her to be with me always, like a beloved sister. I don't think that was so wrong. If she had stayed, you would have been raised here with us, instead of in that dreary fortress with those foolish men. The pair of us would have seen to your education. Wouldn't you have preferred that?" She stood and walked toward him, challenging him to deny it. He didn't move until she tried to touch him. Then he backed away, not out of fear but loathing.

"They ruined you," she said bitterly. "Just as they ruined your mother, filling your mind with guilt as they did hers. Tell me, do you deny your power as she did?"

"Power? I have no power."

"No? I know that you work with Ivar at night, there in his smoke-filled cave beneath the inn. I know what you do there as well. And I know what is kept there, just as I know what is kept in the fortress from which you come." She must have seen the amazement in his eyes, for she waited for his question. When it didn't come, she frowned and supplied a cryptic answer. "Knowledge," she said. "And power. All you have to do is take it."

"Why do you tell me any of this?"

"So you know you can trust me, if the need arises. Though Ivar's a fool, we have a kinship of sorts; we are both outcasts from our lands, both more than we appear to be. Tell him what I told you, if you wish. It's of no concern to me. But if you're wise, you'll keep silent, for your own sake."

She turned back to face the mirror, looking once more at her reflection. A dismissal, Jon realized, and left her. She appeared to take little notice of his departure.

Winter came so early to the land that year that the townsfolk spoke of having two seasons rather than four. The snows came only days after the festival, smothering the grazing hills with thick gray drifts indistinguishable from the cloud-swept sky. Winter was a desolate emptiness into which only the bravest hunters dared venture. Some returned with game. Others were lost, frozen, devoured flesh-and-bone by winter-starved goblins.

And in the darkness of winter, the stories began. Part of a hand, half a face—enough for a father to identify his son. While most believed that Josef's death had been nothing more than the beasties retaliating for the festival sacrifice, others recalled that Jon's face had been battered and cut on that same night. Sondra reported seeing wolves in the forest when Arlette had been killed, and there were wolf prints in the river mud on the morning after the festival.

Connections enough for conjectures at the Linde hearth-fires. Few took the rumors seriously. The most vocal opponents noted that Mishya, who had lost his chosen mate to Jonathan, started most of them. Others noted, as honestly, that Sondra had found a far better mate. Nonetheless, the stories continued, fueled by boredom and isolation.

A small group of townsmen kept the inn alive. With no travelers on the road, the inn served few meals, rented no rooms, washed and polished only occasionally. The regulars still requested Jonathan to sing, but otherwise, his days were idle.

Jonathan used his free time to increase his knowledge of the arcane, spending hours alone in Ivar's cavern, memorizing spells he was forbidden to use, not even on dark nights far from the curious eyes of Linde townsfolk. While fire spells fascinated him most, he began learning more subtle incantations, spells that no one would notice, not even Ivar.

With a quick word, a quicker gesture, Jon could set Andor and Dirca to quarreling. As their argument grew more bitter, Jon reversed the spell, and found the couple hugging one another a few moments later, Andor whispering loving words as he stroked her hair. The inn's patrons asked Jon to sing more frequently, laughing at the happy words, crying at the sad, tipping him graciously for each song. He hoarded the coins he received, along with those left by his mother.

As the days passed, Jonathan thought of Maeve's words more frequently. He considered visiting her, but the desire he felt for her held him back. The guilt that desire aroused made him more attentive to Sondra than he otherwise might have been.

As for Sondra, she glowed in Jonathan's presence. One night, after they had spent hours together, shoveling snow off the covered porch and stick roof, he looked at her, standing with the snowflakes glittering in her dark hair. He took her hands and blurted words he had often thought of saying. "I love you. Will you marry me?"

She laughed, kissed him, and was about to reply when she remembered that such an open acceptance was hardly considered proper. "You must ask my father first," she said.

"Come with me," he said and pulled her inside the drinking hall where Ivar was mopping puddles from the melting snow on the roof. "I want to marry your daughter," Jon told him, pleased by the sudden happiness he saw in Ivar's expression.

"Nothing would please me more," Ivar said. "Announce your betrothal immediately, if you wish. There's still time to make a

gown for vow-taking with the other couples at the winter festival."
Ivar pulled wine goblets from the glass-doored case behind the bar
and poured four glasses of cloudberry wine. "Go get your aunt," he
told Sondra, "for the toast."

Sondra found her aunt upstairs mending sheets and happily
told her what had happened. "Since you are my closest female
relative, would you take my mother's place at the toast and give
your blessing?"

Dirca's reply was cold. "The boy was raised by old men. What
does he know of women? What does he know of children and
responsibility? You've moved too fast, girl. It'll bring you grief in
the end."

Sondra scowled. She wanted to remind Dirca that her own first
marriage had hardly been a happy one. Instead, she went downstairs, preparing an excuse for her aunt's absence from the traditional
betrothal toast. Before she could give it, Dirca followed her into the
hall and lifted one of the glasses. Her aunt's mouth was set in a grim,
resigned line, her eyes fixed on Jonathan as she gave her approval
to the match.

Jonathan's studies had progressed at an astonishing pace. Unlike
Leo, who had always been frightened by his pupil's ability, Ivar was
pleased, though a bit puzzled by Jon's incredible talent. Finally,
admitting he had nothing more to teach Jonathan, he encouraged
the boy to begin working alone in the cavern.

Jon usually laid a fire in the hearth for warmth, but the light came
from cold, glowing balls that floated above his shoulders, illuminat-
ing the scrolls he read. Sometimes he sensed a presence in the cavern,
as if some airy creature struggled to make itself heard or seen. When
he focused on it, the presence faded.

One night, when Jonathan was placing his most recent reading back on the shelves, a shadow touched a scroll near the bottom of the pile. Jon moved his hand over the spot, but the shadow remained. As he crouched to study the odd trick of the light, the shadow flowed into a narrow crack in the cavern wall. Jon heard a whisper coming from the darkness beyond, soft as a breath of air, and as indistinct.

"Who's doing this?" Jon called, scanning the cavern, seeking the intruder. "Ivar . . . ?" he added, then cut off the thought. Ivar wouldn't try to frighten him with such a childish display. No, the shadow was something else, a spirit that perhaps sought contact. His attention returned to the crack. Kneeling in front of the opening, he directed one of his luminescent balls of light into the space.

A scroll was hidden there. Jon had never read any of the scrolls Ivar forbade him to touch, but this wasn't one of them. Perhaps Ivar hid this one before Jon came, then forgot about it. He pulled it out and noted that its edges were yellowed and brittle. He untied the twine and unrolled it. With the lights dancing above his shoulders, he began to read, struggling to comprehend the strange dialect, the faded, trembling scrawl of its creator.

We came here together, fleeing one evil for another, wandering at last into the southern regions where only the dead dwelt. There, we built the temple, each doing his part. When we finished, we sealed the walls in the old way and kept the doors closed and locked, save on the nights of the ritual. Through our prayers and vigilance, the treasure within cleansed the village, freeing us from the evil around. But we should have expected our peace to be short-lived; we had never known real peace before.

Evil came in the comely guise of a white-haired youth who entered our village one morning. Visitors always came in the evening, always remained with us through the hours of darkness and left at dawn; the dead in the land were jealous of the living and would slay those who traveled by night. We didn't ask the white-haired stranger how he had traveled by night. Instead the village fed him, let him eat our simple food and drink our water, watched to learn what kind of creature he might be.

He commented on the beauty of our hills and town, on the carefree life of doors left open, children free to roam. And he loved our magnificent shrine. His words were as fair as his form, but we knew their deceit.

We learned he was the young ward recently taken by the lord of our homeland. Some said he had been sold by his parents for an incredible sum. Others believed his parents had been murdered and the child taken. All rumors agreed. The youth had power, not only the sorcerous power of his master, but an innate power to see into human hearts, to twist desires.

Though the stranger had shown no sign of this power, the whispers still flew through the village. He had come to learn our secret. He had come the morning before the full moon. Despite the danger, the ritual would have to take place. We told the man that we had no shelter that night and insisted he leave.

I saw the anger flash in his pale eyes. He sensed his betrayal, for until that moment, we had been perfectly kind. I didn't approve of what the others did, approved even less of the blood they would have spilled had he refused to go. But he left that night, with only a few words of reproach. Our hearts were troubled by what we had done; if he were truly a traveler, we had condemned him to a terrible end. We watched him disappear into the evening mists, then turned to prepare the ritual.

At the height of the ceremony, the stranger returned and entered our shrine through the open doors. I don't know how long he stood there, watching our ritual, listening to our chants. But suddenly he was singing, singing in a voice louder and purer than our combined tones. His words profaned the holiness of our shrine and mocked our gods. And, when we looked at him, we saw his form change, his features transmute to resemble those of our gods.

Rage rose in me as I rushed toward him, part of the mob ready to destroy him. As we reached for him, the air in our shrine exploded into a shimmering cloud, a cloud of sparks spiraling in frenzied orbits around us. We were frozen in place. Some wizard's trick, I thought, for I could breathe and see, though the sting of the burning sparks maddened me. Paralyzed, unable to scream, I watched him walk through the glowing shrine to the altar where the cloth hung.

Despite my agony, I heard the beauty of his laugh as he ripped the cloth from its holy place. "You would condemn a stranger to death to protect this? This!" His hands grabbed an edge and pulled, as if to rip the tapestry in two.

It was the last act his living body committed. The cloth lashed out, covered him, smothered him, absorbed his life. The cloud of sparks vanished as the man did, until not even a trace of heat remained.

That night, we buried our dead and set about trying to forget. How naive we were to think that no power could challenge the Gathering Cloth.

Next evening, we discovered our mistake. As the moon rose full once more, the trapped souls also rose. The town died that night. Even small children were destroyed in fiery agony as the priests' spells were twisted against us. In the end, High Priest Wolgar chanted a different incantation, one meant to contain the evil rather than destroy it. With his last breath, he finished the liturgy. The few of us left repeated it, drawing the souls out of the town, back into the shrine. And, somehow, we pushed the shrine doors shut with our burned and bleeding hands.

But the dead of our village didn't rest. Like the poor condemned souls in the land around us, they rose, clamoring with charred lips for a revenge we couldn't grant, and for the sleep of death.

Only three of us, the least powerful of our order, escaped the terrible wrath of the evil trapped in the tapestry. Nearly all our order's scrolls were destroyed; the spell that contains the dark souls on the cloth is known through memory alone.

Though one of us is badly wounded and another blind, we three will leave here tomorrow and search for a new hidden resting place for the tapestry. I set down these words so that others may take warning of the power of the dark souls trapped in its web.

The account ended as abruptly as it had begun. Jonathan sat and stared at the writing. He recalled Maeve's mention of the tapestry and knew he had discovered the secret the order guarded. "Thank you," he whispered to the shadow that had guided him to the scroll. As he returned the scroll to the ledge on which it had been hidden, his attention was drawn to the crevice beyond its resting place.

With a single command, Jon shrank the balls of light, intensified them, and sent them rolling through the narrow opening into a larger passage beyond. Heedless of the fear prickling his spine, Jon polymorphed into a mouse, squeezed through the opening and, with his lights to guide him, crawled forward.

The passage grew larger. In just a few feet, Jon was able to resume his true form and stand. A cold wind struck his face, giving hints of an exit somewhere ahead. Jon thought of the goblins and the other creatures Mattas said lived underground, but he took comfort in his lights and the fire at his control. The passage headed eastward, twisted, and began to rise. Glowing phosphorus veined the walls, and tiny blue lizards skittered from beneath Jon's feet as he pressed on. Traveling almost a quarter mile, he reached a cavern more vast than the one Ivar had claimed as his own.

The balls of light couldn't touch all the corners of the room. Jon sent them rising. They spiraled upward until they reached the milky stalactites hanging far above him, stalactites that dripped cloudy water into the shallow pools that patterned the cavern floor. In the pools he saw fat, glowing leeches and striped green fish that darted through the water. They fled his shadow and the balls of light he had brought with him.

He thought of the research he could perform in this vast cave, more deeply hidden than Ivar's. Heartened, Jon went on, looking for an outside entrance. He discovered it after a long though easy climb. Like the opening from Ivar's chamber, it was hardly more than a crevice in the rock, just wide enough for him to slip through. It had apparently been overlooked even by the goblins. He stood on the icy precipice of the entrance, his hair whipped by the bitter wind. He smelled the smoke of distant Linde and saw in the valley below the shadowy outline of Maeve's cottage.

Close yet hidden. Even Ivar couldn't complain about the work he would do here. Nonetheless, Jon decided this place would be his secret. Thinking his absence might have been discovered, he turned and rushed back through the cavern and passage to the familiar comfort of Ivar's chamber.

In the weeks that followed, Jonathan retreated from the world above the caverns. With precise care, he copied in a second spellbook every incantation he had learned. He added many he had ignored because they couldn't be worked in the close confines of Ivar's chamber, and he was forbidden to cast them outside.

He also set about transforming the vast cavern into his own. Fire quickly warmed the frigid waters in the pools. The leeches died, the fish starved, and the lizards retreated to less-traveled passages. Colored lights brightened the emptiness, dancing like an aurora trapped in stone.

Jon studied with stolen time. He returned to the inn through the underground passages when possible and walked back above ground when it wasn't. Only once was his absence noted, and then he rattled off a prepared excuse. If it hadn't been for Sondra, he would have left the town altogether, living like a hermit in his bone-white cave.

One morning, a few weeks after he'd begun working in his cavern, Jon took leave of his work to sit in Ivar's cavern and write a new song. On festival night, he would sing the story of the three hags, idealizing their fall from beauty and grace so that they wouldn't be insulted should they hear. But he also included enough truth that the verses would serve as a warning to the town. As he recited the poetry aloud, he heard the whisper once again. The indistinct words came in front of him, behind him, in the dark shadows of the caverns around him. Jon mouthed a few words and thrust out his arms. The glowing balls that lit the room exploded into a light that would rival the sun's.

The shadow of a man stood beside him, the features almost clear. As Jon stared, the form shimmered and vanished, leaving only the emptiness of a memory, the weariness of power spent.

The vision left only a final parting word. As much thought as sound, as familiar as the dreams Jon had dreamed in the isolated, wind-swept fortress, the word rolled through the cave.

"Home."

"Soon," Jon whispered lovingly to the empty room. If he wanted to know the secrets of the fortress, he had best acquire the means to learn them. He worked for hours, studying spells that detected magic, unlocked doors, would make even a wary man sleep.

In the afternoon, as he always did, he went upstairs to eat and spend the next few hours with his betrothed. The sun warmed the air as they walked outside, holding hands.

Sondra looked at him sadly. In spite of the attention he lavished on her in the last few weeks, in spite of how lovingly he held her hand, he rarely spoke to her. Today, she decided to break through his silence. "You've been absent from the inn so often lately. Are you learning as much as you hoped?" she asked, her voice as light as she could make it.

"Yes," he replied.

"Could you share some of it with me?" she went on.

"I thought you had no desire to learn," he said, looking at her coldly.

Even Mishya would be preferable to this! Sondra pulled her hand out of his and began walking back to the inn alone. Jon hesitated, then followed, tugging at the sleeve of her coat until she stopped and faced him. "I'm sorry. Please don't go," he said.

Sondra glanced at the boys in the festival square, who had stopped building snow forts to watch the couple. She looked longer at Jon, seeing how much he wanted her to stay, and seeing something more—a strange satisfaction, as if her anger made him proud.

She thought of the shy boy she'd first seen in the woods, and she wondered what had happened to him in this month since they had decided to marry—how sad, how remote, how secretive he had become.

Magic required great energy and intense concentration. Hadn't her father told her that often enough? She was Ivar's daughter, she ought to understand her betrothed's preoccupation. She stepped closer to him and laid a gloved hand on his cheek. He would share whatever troubled him in good time. Like the good wife she would soon be, she decided to be patient now, ready to listen when he finally talked of his work, ready to support him.

The thought stayed with her the rest of the day and grew more sour as the sun dipped low. That night, despite misgivings, she went down to Ivar's cavern.

Had she come a few moments earlier, she would have found an empty room. Instead, she discovered that her betrothed was somewhat dirty, a bit out of breath, as if his work exhausted him.

"Is something wrong?" he asked, noticing that her feet were bare and she wore only a thin night shift under her cloak. He thought perhaps the goblins had attacked. His fingers tingled as he prepared a spell to defend his betrothed's family.

She shook her head and went to him. Wrapping her arms around him, she kissed him deeply, trying to return the passion of his kiss from the festival night.

He pulled away, almost angered by her forwardness. "Is this right?" he asked.

"You didn't know?" She smiled at his naïveté. "Once a couple announces their betrothal and is certain of the marriage, in matters of . . . intimacy they are already married. In most families it is even encouraged. As to our marriage, *I* am certain. Are *you*?" She took his hands and lifted them to the cord that held her cloak together.

Sondra's trust humbled Jon. "Come, I will share a secret with you," he said and led her in mouse form through the narrow passage to his private place. She marveled at the pools, the white stalactites hanging above her, the sprays of colors his magic made on the pale rock walls. As globes of light danced above them, they consummated what they had agreed on months ago when she had first seen him standing in the shadows of the trees.

"I would do anything for you," she said, no longer concerned about the wall of secrets he had built around himself, thankful only that she was inside it with him.

twelve

ODD HOW THE PAST BECOMES CLEAR WHEN IT NO *longer matters. Though I cannot recall my name, I know that people worshipped me once as they never did my master. I was sent not to destroy but to be destroyed. It is frustrating to dwell on the past when so little of it can be recalled, but I can hope that someday . . .*

On the night of the next full moon, the creatures of the cloth rested. The Guardians, apprehensive of this odd peace, continued their night chant, and, in the pauses between the words, heard a rustling sound within the shrine, like the tumble of dry leaves in an autumn breeze. Occasionally before, they had sensed decreases in the power of the creatures trapped on the cloth, but never this strange quiet. It was a portent, and they waited anxiously for what the future would bring.

One night flowed into the next, and little changed save that a brief winter thaw brought Jon to visit. He gave the Guardians sweet bread from Dirca, a jug of cloudberry wine from Andor, and potions from Ivar to treat winter colds and Mattas's arthritic pain. The monks sat with Jonathan in the great hall, listening to his stories of Linde. After their evening meal, they drank the wine while Jonathan played his songs for them. Then he spoke of his affection for the people of Linde and, more importantly, of his upcoming marriage.

He expected congratulations. Instead, the revelation was greeted with stunned silence. "Are you so certain this is the future you wish?" Dominic finally asked.

"I am. I was certain the first day I saw her."

"Then a toast to Jonathan and Sondra!" Hektor said, raising his glass. The others joined in the toast, but only Hektor appeared truly happy. The others seemed disappointed, as if they had planned something different for him. He was tempted to remind them that *they* had suggested he leave the fortress—*they* had wanted his future to be his own choice. But it hardly seemed right to mention that now. Besides, he'd come here to look for secrets. He'd hardly be able to do that if he weren't on good terms with the monks.

That night, he only pretended to drink the potion Leo brought him. Afterward, he lay with his eyes open, watching the candle cast dancing shadows through the room, waiting for the whispers, the solid shadow, the shimmering figure of the man. An hour passed. The monks in the rooms around him slept dreamlessly, but the figure didn't come to Jon.

Nonetheless, he decided to act.

Pulling on a hooded black cloak, he padded silently on bare feet down the dark hallway, down the narrow stairs, and through the great hall into the stone-walled chamber Dominic and Leo used as their library. The room was small and narrow, the ceiling lost in the shadows above. The wooden table, which took up much of the space, had nothing resting on it. Jon thought of how cluttered the table had been when he'd been studying in this room, and felt a pang of guilt for what he intended to do.

If he were discovered here, he would repeat the conversation he had overheard at the inn and insist that he had a right to know what had happened to his parents. In a way, he hoped he would be discovered so that the matter could be brought into the open once and for all. Perhaps the Guardians would only tell him lies and hide the truth, but he was certain he would find the truth here. He left the matter to the fates, risking a light so that someone might see, moving slowly and softly so no one would hear.

In the past, he had been allowed to read the scrolls kept in the polished chest of drawers that covered one wall. He would find no secrets there, he knew. Instead, he began moving his fingers over the stones on the wall, then over the worn timbers of the floor until he encountered a loose one.

Dirt had settled in the cracks around it, and Jon could only lift the long board with difficulty. But when he had, he knew he'd found what he sought. He became even more certain when he was unable to open the unlocked black marble box.

He'd spent weeks preparing for this moment. He attempted the most powerful spell he knew for opening locks. It took a number of minutes before he finally got it right. At last, the stone lid shook and settled more naturally on the box. It lifted easily then. Inside were scrolls written in Leo and Ivar's familiar hands. He ignored those, seeking one whose parchment seemed newer, whose small script was unfamiliar.

. . . *I am certain the tapestry called me.* . . .

By the time Jon finished his mother's account, his hands were clenched into fists, white knuckles showing the emotion the rest of him hid. He rolled the scroll, tied it, and returned it to its box. He didn't attempt to reseal the box; he didn't care if the Guardians discovered what he had done. Everything seemed clear to him now, as if a voice from the darkness had revealed the truth.

The Guardians had lied.

He heard voices in the great hall beyond, and the sound of doors opening as the Guardians filed out to begin their morning prayers—prayers he finally understood. Fearful he would be discovered, he waited in the library, scarcely breathing and forbidding himself to cry. He waited with one of the common scrolls unrolled on the table before him until the Guardians began their chant. Then he hurried out to his room. There he lay, awake on his soft, narrow bed in the room Mattas had given up for him because it was warmed by the flue of the hearth below. He bundled beneath the feather quilt Peto had sewn for him and looked out the window, which had been enlarged when the monks made the room his nursery.

No, he didn't think of all they had done for him or how much they loved him—only that they had lied. As he meditated on this, the heat of anger moved through him, quietly invading every tissue. He no longer had to hide the emotion, it was simply there, like his hands or his feet. Accepted. As much a part of him as his past.

He thought nothing of his mother any longer. She had tried to murder his father. She had abandoned him. Her family meant nothing to her, nothing at all, and so he would leave her to her fate.

But his father, his father was alive, trapped on the cloth, and no one had tried to free him!

Throughout the day, Jon considered confronting the Guardians and demanding an explanation. But he held back. The Guardians had lied to him for seventeen years. They wouldn't tell the truth now.

By evening, his false contentment had worn thin. Hektor asked him to walk outside the fortress for awhile. They stopped at the bluff overlooking Tepest. "Is something wrong?" Hektor asked. "You've been so quiet tonight."

"I was wish I knew some spell to split my soul in two. I love Sondra and want to stay with her, but I miss you all so much."

"There'll be other visits," Hektor responded. "You made the right choice. Your mother would agree."

Jon sensed that Hektor was inviting him to ask about his family. He had many questions, but chose the most innocent one. "Hektor, do I resemble her?"

"Not in looks," Hektor said. "But in temperament, yes. When you were only hours old, she noticed it."

"I thought she died during my birth."

"Soon after," Hektor said.

At least, Jon thought, Hektor told the truth. "The sun has set," he commented. "We ought to go back." As soon as they joined the others, he said good-night.

That night, as Jon expected, the presence he had felt so many times in his life returned as a pale shadow in the darkness. Jon followed the shadow down the hall and through an empty sleeping room to a passage that cut behind the shrine. Though centipedes brushed his bare feet and thick spiderwebs covered his face and hair, he didn't dare conjure light.

Cautiously, he felt his way down a set of dark stairs and through a narrow inner passage littered with rocks that had fallen from above. As he went on, he felt shattered bones and rusted remnants of armor beneath his feet. Jonathan had heard accounts of the ancient custom, and now he walked across the result. These were once warriors, most likely the greatest heroes of the people who had built this fortress centuries before the Guardians claimed it as their own. They had been entombed here to give their strength to the walls.

Were these dead condemned to haunt the fortress in ghostly form, reliving the last hours of their lives? Was it their moaning the Guardians heard at night or only the sound of wind blowing through the cracks? Though Jon quaked with fear, the shadow moved insistently forward. In a few more yards the passage ended with no apparent means of escape.

He was deep enough now.

Conjure a light.

Had he heard the words, or was it his own idea?

No matter. A few words, a simple gesture, and a small golden ball glowed brightly in the darkness. Jonathan searched for the exit and saw a hollow beneath his feet, partially blocked by a rusty shield. He knelt and, working as quietly as possible, cleared the debris from the hole dug in the base of the fortress wall. When he'd finished, he examined the earth beneath it.

The soil seemed soft, yielding, as if someone had dug a tunnel there long ago. Perhaps the warriors hadn't gone to their deaths so willingly. If so, they had become confused about direction, for they had been tunneling into the fortress rather than out. He thought of their despair when they realized their mistake. Nonetheless, he rejoiced as he began shoveling loose dirt from the hole. If his reckoning was correct, the tunnel should lead into the back of the shrine.

The farther he dug, the more dank and putrid the soil smelled, as if the earth he dug was the remnant of corpses. His globe of light was useless in the close confines of the tunnel, so he worked in darkness and steeled himself against screaming if his hands touched bone or rotting flesh. He felt nothing but soft earth until his fist closed around a piece of mortar.

Gripping it, he slid out of his hole to examine the find. When he did, he saw streaks of pale morning light behind the cracks in the wall. He also heard the Guardians at the front of the shrine, standing together, softly chanting their morning prayer. Weary, he thought he should return now, undetected, during the chant. He dropped the mortar and headed back through the wall.

The chanting stopped. Jon was too late. Soon the Guardians would file into the great hall, and someone would go to Jon's room to wake him. Since he wouldn't be there, his only chance was to be found somewhere else. He retreated down the passage to a crumbling section of the outer wall and climbed one of the cracks until he found a crevice he could force his body through.

With hands scraped and bleeding, feet cut by the bones and stones and armor, cloak hanging in rags over him, he descended the outer wall to an ice-covered cliff, scarcely wide enough to support him. The wind hammered his body against the stone wall as he worked his way toward the road and entrance.

His hands were growing numb, and his feet had already lost most of their feeling when the ledge ended near the corner of the wall. It had been designed that way to keep enemies from scaling it. In the years since the fortress had been built, the rocks beneath it had weathered, providing toeholds farther down. Jon began the dangerous descent, cursing his impetuous stupidity, mumbling pleas to the shadow and the Guardians' gods to save him.

A wider ledge cut into the rocks, giving him temporary shelter from the biting wind. As he sat for a moment, catching his breath and rubbing his frostbitten feet, he heard Hektor calling his name. Death waited for him if he attempted to scale these rocks alone and he returned the call, his cry holding no more substance than a whisper in the brutal wind.

He longed to remain where he was, to sleep, to become part of the ghostly band of dead in the fortress. He might have, but for his anger. Pushing himself as far over the cliff as he could, Jon gripped the rocks and screamed Hektor's name.

The wind stole his voice. He didn't hear a reply, didn't feel his hands losing their grip, didn't notice his body sagging, until Leo pulled him upright. A rope circled his waist. Dangling over an impossible drop, he felt himself raised into Hektor's waiting arms. A moment later, Hektor pulled Leo to safety.

Jon felt nothing but the warmth of Hektor's body, pressed against his until he woke. He was swaddled in coverlets and lying beside a fire in the great hall. Leo and Dominic were speaking of him in quiet tones. "I've examined him carefully," Leo said. "He's only scraped. No signs of bites, just scrapes and bruises. He'll heal."

"And thaw," Jon said, more softly than he intended.

They moved to his side, their joy so sincere that his next words set heavy on his conscience. "I heard a screaming in the night like a woman in pain. I went outside to help. I must have fallen. The wind made it impossible to climb."

"You were foolish," Dominic said, his tone like that used to lecture a far younger Jon. Then he noticed the silver eyes watching him belonged to an adult, not a child. "Well, you're alive, and that's most important," he concluded and left Jon alone with his old teacher.

"I've been remiss in your education, I see," Leo said in a tone that tried to sound light.

"Not remiss. I fell so quickly I never had a chance to save myself. No spell could have helped me avoid the rock my head hit or the cold that drained me."

"Be more careful. We'd hate to lose you."

Jon's eyes were bright with tears. A rush of thanks and love, Leo thought, not realizing they were remorse for his deceit.

Jon's recovery took far longer than the Guardians expected. Two nights later, after spending the entire day in bed, he returned to the tunnel.

This time he came prepared for the work he would do. He changed into a set of old clothing and slipped into an excavation that seemed to have grown larger in the nights he had been away. He no longer noticed the smell of decay, only that the soft earth felt moist and warm and safe. He worked ceaselessly, immune to fatigue and oblivious to the passing of time.

When he finally extended his tunnel beneath the shrine, he didn't dare use a hammer on the floor stones. Instead, he scraped and pried away the mortar until he pulled out a single small stone. Pleased with his victory, he sent a globe of light into the shrine. All he could see was a large stone slab rising vertically in front of the hole. Probably the altar. The hole was in a shadowed place, less likely to be noticed should the Guardians go inside. Nonetheless, he fit the stone back in place and piled a hill of dirt beneath it to hold it there. Heartened, he slipped from his hole, changed his clothes, and returned to his room to spend another day in bed.

Two nights passed, two productive nights in which he widened the hole enough that he could poke his head through it, though no more.

He wanted to see the cloth exactly as his mother had seen it so many years ago. He lit the candle he had brought and placed it on the floor outside the hole, then maneuvered his head through and saw . . .

And saw . . . !

His mother's words couldn't prepare him for this sight. The horror and beauty of it were as inseparably linked as the souls were linked to the weave of the cloth. The rush of emotion he felt made him want to run, to hide. He even began to pull his head back when he remembered his purpose in coming and softly called his father's name.

"Vhar."

For a moment, it seemed the cloth stirred. Perhaps it was only the flicker of the candle, or perhaps the cloth's growing power. He called again. "Vhar?"

The response was stronger, the cloth moving as if it were touched by a breeze.

"Father, I've come to help you," Jon whispered.

The breeze grew. It blew out Jon's candle and swirled the dust on the shrine floor. Jon shut his eyes to protect them and whispered, "No matter what the power of the cloth, I'll save you. The moon is full tomorrow. When you wake, I'll come for you."

Though it was no later than midnight, his work was finished. He returned to bed and slept.

As he had occasionally done, Jon joined the Guardians for their morning prayer in front of the shrine. Now that he knew what lay inside, he understood the monks' short, sincere call for strength. Though only Mattas was truly old, they all looked pale, as if some draining sickness had touched them all. The guard changed after the prayer; Mattas replaced Hektor for the daytime watch at the fortress gate. Jon watched the stooped old man walk across the courtyard and settle onto a stone bench bathed in morning sun. He suddenly felt no guilt for what he would do.

His father was no wizard, no evil creature worth condemning to an eternal prison. Vhar had been a tradesman, greedy perhaps, but not guilty enough to warrant his sentence. Jonathan saw no harm in what he planned to do. One insignificant soul among all the others on the cloth would hardly be missed.

Jon rested through most of the day. He picked at his evening meal, telling the others that the chills of his accident had returned, that his legs ached. He retired early, pretending to drink the potion Leo gave him, but spitting it out as soon as he reached his room. Some time later, when Hektor came upstairs to check on him, Jon was in bed, apparently drugged but far too awake for him to bolt the door. Later, when Hektor passed Jon's room again, he saw what he thought was Jon sleeping, wrapped tightly in the blankets. He locked the door and went on his way.

By then, Jon had already descended the hidden stairs. As the monks gathered at the front of the shrine, saying the first of many evening prayers, Jon entered the tunnel, sliding the length of it until his head was only a foot or so from the hole he'd made in the floor.

The tunnel seemed to breathe—a draft moving in and out as if some huge creature inhaled and exhaled in the shrine above. The air shifted over him, damp and cool, palpably alive. Inhale—scents of cold fresh winter air. Exhale—scents of mustiness, darkness, decay.

When the chanting started, it seemed distant, muffled by the earth and the chapel above him. Certainly, it wasn't as loud as the breathing, which had grown louder even than the beat of his heart. He heard a rustling in the shrine above, steps on the floor.

Then the sounds began. Shrieks. Raucous, horrible laughter. A light flickered beyond the hole he'd made in the floor. His terror grew as the sounds swelled; the screams echoed, deafening, and the footfalls pounded angrily on the stones above. Jon's mind flashed briefly on the threat of the floor caving in, or his being drawn into the rasping orgy. The undead spirits would suck the blood from his veins, and the cloth would absorb what was left, as it had his mother.

As he stared at the hole he'd made, his plan seemed ill conceived. Even if he could find his father, the man would never fit through this. If Vhar somehow did get through, where would they go?

But another voice in Jon's head told him he had worked too hard to abandon hope. He twisted around onto his back and slowly inched toward the hole. The pounding continued above him, bits of stone and earth falling on his face and into his eyes. He shut them, letting the tears flow and moved forward again.

The noise stopped.

The chanting stopped.

The breathing stopped.

The things in the chapel waited for release.

Jon's face was bathed in sudden light, brilliant and white like winter sun on fresh snow. He opened his eyes and saw that his face was exactly below the hole, where the light came from. Though he saw nothing more than the brightness above him, he sensed eyes watching him, weighing the resolve in his soul.

Time seemed to pass too slowly. His legs and arms felt numb. The rest of his body seemed frozen. A face appeared above his hole—a dark, masculine silhouette. Then it moved back, and Jon could discern the features. The face was triangular, with high cheekbones and wide-spaced silver eyes framed with thin, white hair. When Jon was older, these would be his features. It must be his father, and yet . . . Leith described him differently. She called him the . . .

The truth was swept away by words the man in the shrine above spoke. "Silver man."

From somewhere deep in the silence above him, Jon felt an insistent wordless warning. For an instant his terror returned, but he fought it back. "Father," he whispered and smiled.

"Take my hand." The voice, so like his own voice, spoke the words clearly now. He obeyed, and they touched, the man's hand trembling with emotion, yes, but cold and lifeless even so.

"The night will end soon. For us there will be others. Do not let me go."

In response, Jon squeezed his father's fingers. Though something clawed at them, trying to break their hold, Jon held fast until the light disappeared. Air hissed through the tunnel, around Jon, and into the shrine. Jon, feeling his father pull away from him, gripped the hand harder, wedging his knees on either side of the hole to keep from being sucked into the maelstrom above. His skin tingled from the final, terrible roar as the creatures whirled and screamed and beat their last defiance against the doors and walls of their prison.

And then they were still.

The hand Jon held became dry and light as if the substance of life had drained, leaving only a flat, empty shell. "Father?" he whispered and felt an answering tremor. Without being told, Jon drew what was left of his father carefully through the hole, fearful of tearing him on the sharp-edged stones. When he'd finished, he propped the floor slab back in place and slid backward through the tunnel, carrying the lifeless husk of his father draped over one arm.

Near the foot of the stairs, he found a shallow opening, and laid the body in it. Only its shape looked human, only its eyes moved, and they were filled with gratitude. Jon couldn't take his father to his room, so he left the body there, protected by his spell. Before he left, he whispering a promise to return after dark.

He waited in an empty sleeping room until Leo unlocked his door, then stole down the hall. He pulled the pile of clothes from beneath the blanket and slept. He was aware of the others looking in on him, of Leo's hand brushing his forehead, but no one tried to wake him until the midday meal. When he joined them, he dressed warmly, his walk stiff. "As soon as I'm able, I'll go back to Linde," he said. "I doubt I'll be able to return here for quite some time."

"Before you leave, there's something we need to discuss," Dominic said.

Jon would have asked to speak with him immediately, but he felt far too weary. "Tomorrow," he said and returned to his bed.

He slept far longer than he expected. Food sat on the table beside him, along with the potion that would drug him back to sleep. His door was unlocked—in fact open—and, in the distance, the chanting rose up again.

Did they expect him to go to the shrine, to see the ceremony? Would they answer his questions afterward? Most likely they would, but, before he went to them, he had to see to his father. He dressed quickly and followed the passage to where his father waited.

The body looked thicker now, the coloring of the face, while pale, seemed natural. "Vhar," Jon whispered, not daring to touch the form. "Father?"

The eyes opened and fixed on his. The thin lips curved upward in a bitter smile. His father sat up and gripped Jon's hand. The touch was strong, alive. "There is sorcery in these walls. I tried to go to your room, but couldn't. I tried to go into the tunnel to . . . give comfort to the others. I cannot. Perhaps . . . when I am stronger."

"We will leave here. We will go tomorrow."

"I feel a change inside me, caused by those years on the cloth. I cannot move during the light of day."

"I can carry you."

"My body would burn like tinder if sunlight should touch it. We must go tonight."

Jon considered this. He wanted to hear what Dominic would tell him, but if the ritual were as his mother described, there would be no better time to go. "If you can't pass through these walls, how can we leave?" Jon asked.

"Take my hand and draw me through, as you did from the shrine."

"Then come."

Jon left a note in his room. It was rambling and disjointed, and spoke of his passion for Sondra, his need for her if he were to recover. He wrote eloquently of torn desires. He thought they would understand.

Afterward, black cloaks covering their faces and hands, he and his father stood in the great hall, watching the monks chanting at the door of the silent shrine. His father whispered a single word. The cloth woke. The screams of the doomed masked the soft footsteps stealing through the fortress gates and into the moonlit night.

They went, father and son, hand in hand, their silver hair and pale faces whitened by the cold moonlight.

Part III
SILVERLORD

thirteen

HIS DAYS HAD ONCE BEEN CONTROLLED BY THE WAXING
and waning of the moon. Now time quickened to a faster pace of
sleep and waking—night when he walked and spoke and learned
from his son; day when he slept in the cavern prepared for him, only
the dried shell of his body visible to Jonathan lying beside him.

His memory returned in disconnected pieces. He saw his reflection in the cave's pool of milky water and recalled children playing
beside a fountain in a village square, a dog howling in warning as
he passed them.

His voice brought death, his hands fire—that much he remembered clearly. He felt the heat, heard the screams. These things he
wisely wouldn't share with his son. "Not yet," he whispered.

"Did you speak to me, Father?" Jonathan asked. He shook his
head and laid a loving hand on the boy's shoulder, willing him to
return to sleep. The boy's breaths grew regular, and the man went
outside.

Only a fool would think the stars could change in the years since
he had seen them with his own eyes. Yet everything seemed clearer,
newer—voraciously alive. Even the soft winter pine needles that
brushed his bare legs as he descended the hillside felt impossibly

sensual, like a loved one's first chaste kiss.

Once, he had fed his hunger in many ways. Dining at a noonday table with his master's guests, he could hide his nature well. Even on his night walks, when he fed the immortal demands within him by draining the blood of mortals, the darkest side of his nature still slept. During the years of imprisonment on the cloth, though, his body had altered, and only the most terrible aspect of his nature remained.

But he was alive, aware, free! His son had given him this gift. His son! He threw back his head, and a peal of brilliant laughter flowed over the frozen land.

In the last few nights, he had hunted the goblins, feeling his power grow with each life he claimed. Now he was ready for richer fare. He moved silently toward Linde, where a feast waited for him.

Men had dug fishing holes in the ice-covered river. Now they sat in small groups in wooden huts that sheltered them from the bitter wind, each waiting for a catch and a chance to go home. Their emotions, dull and hungry, didn't interest him. Neither did the vague dreams of the sleeping townsfolk.

Instead he found one who was awake, her sorrow magnificently deep and alive. The woman sat alone on a bed in a second-floor room of a house near the edge of town. Her thoughts were focused on a memory that she wouldn't abandon, the memory of her son. How could he have died? How could he have died?

The wind curled around the house, beating at the shutters like a demanding child. She unlatched them and looked out at the snow-covered landscape. Her eyes traced down the dark, tree-lined path leading to the river where they said Alden had been killed.

How could the men have known those charred bones were Alden? Shouldn't a mother be able to recognize the body of her son? Perhaps the beasties had left another body beside Josef's, had taken her son away to serve as one more slave in their underground kingdom— starved and beaten, utterly alone.

A shadow, darker than the night, moved on the edge of the charred clearing. "Alden," she whispered, and, as the shadow moved closer to the river, her son's face formed in her mind.

Her husband was fishing with the others, he couldn't stop her from seeking Alden now! She ran through the empty house, dragging a coverlet from the chair at the hearth, wrapping it around her. She ran barefoot out into the town, her footfalls soft on new fallen snow.

Her dark hair whipped in the wind as she ran toward the place where the burned body had been found.

When she was younger, the shadow thought, she must have been beautiful. But now her only beauty lay in her pain, in the tears frozen on her cheeks as she stopped in the clearing, looking for her son.

The figure moved close behind her, close enough to feel the heat of her body, to clothe himself in her memories. Alden's cloak brushed her shoulder. She turned, stifling a cry of delight as she looked up at his face. "Alden! They were never certain the body was yours!" She wanted to call to her husband fishing with the others, but a rush of emotion choked her. She stood, her hands reaching out to touch her son's face, to brush back the wisps of hair, black as her own.

He caught her wrists, his hands as frigid as the snow. "Alden is dead," he whispered. "But you, you are so perfectly alive."

His touch drained the heat from her arms, her shoulders. "Wh-wha-what are you?" she stammered.

"Something that once lived. Something that will live again," Alden's voice said.

Fear shook the visions from her eyes. Though she still saw Alden's face, she knew this was not, had never been, her son. "Who are you?" she whispered tightly.

He wanted to use the name his son called him; he remembered no other. But as the question formed on her lips, he discovered a more correct response, buried with so many other memories. "Morgoth," he replied and pulled her against him, wrapping his cloak around her. She trembled for a moment, then succumbed to his power, lying silent in his arms as his cold hands drew every pulse of life from her.

He dropped the body slowly, cherishing the life coursing through him, cherishing the woman who had returned to him the power of his name. For when he remembered it, he remembered the rest as well.

"Morgoth," he whispered and raised his head to the starry sky. Memory brought power. He felt it, hot as the life that coursed through him now, dark as the despair of understanding! He had taken a human life—a mere whetting of the appetite. The cloth must have altered him, condemning him to hunt like this forever—seeking life, taking life, never sated.

The scent of the fishermen had drawn the beasties from their subterranean lairs. Morgoth heard them moving in the bushes on the edge of the river, sniffing toward the corpse at his feet, and the huddled shacks.

He would have preferred to leave the townsfolk alive; he had always welcomed the adoration of the weak. Such mercy was no longer possible. Still, the townsfolk were *his* cattle, for his hunger alone; he wouldn't share them with these loathesome creatures.

Confident of his memory, Morgoth raised his hands to each side and bowed his head. His body thinned, floating insubstantial as mist, his mind seeking the goblins' simple ones. In moments, he trapped the goblins in his mental net and sent a bolt of fear through them. They scattered. Some made for distant caves in the hills. Others, shrieking with fear, raced in terror across the frozen ice of the river. Men rushed from their fishing shacks, their cudgels and knives ready.

A score of beasties were killed. The men, frustrated from a long night of waiting, set skinning knives eagerly to the task. They carved the flesh into long strips to mix with the livestock grain. But the men's exuberance was short-lived. When a pair of fishermen followed the goblin tracks back to the riverbank, they discovered Alden's mother, lying on her back with her cloak untied, her flesh blue from the cold. She lay on the spot her son had been found. A second set of footprints led to the site, then vanished.

By midday, whispers of sorcery drifted like snow through the winter-bound town.

"The cloth will not wake now that I am gone," Morgoth told his son as they sat together in the milky cave later that night.

Jon hadn't returned to the town. He sat on a blanket on the stone floor, roasting a fish over a small, open fire. He frowned. "It did before you were trapped."

"No, it didn't. I'm the one that empowers the souls." Morgoth looked sharply at his son. "I'm the pale man that destroyed the Guardians' shrine," he added; the boy had already told him of the scroll he had read. Jonathan pulled the fish from the fire and began stripping the flesh from the narrow carcass, eating it slowly as he listened, saying nothing. "Does this make a difference to you?" Morgoth asked.

"No . . . that is . . ." Jon shook his head. Though he didn't look at the man beside him, he said more firmly, "Why did you wish to destroy the shrine?"

Morgoth stood and began to pace, his long, silver robe brushing the stone floor as he walked, its folds shimmering in the soft colored lights of the cavern. "It's time for you to know my part of the story. Like the monk, Hektor, I was sold by my parents. I like to think they sold me unwillingly, especially since my master was cold and powerful. When I didn't learn as swiftly as he wished, he showed me pain. In the end, he taught me too well, and grew to fear me. What else could explain the impossible task he set for me?

"The people of our land came to worship me as they never did my master. He knew I was a rival and decided to make use of me before the end. I was sent to destroy the cloth, for it threatened to draw in my master, imprisoning him. If I failed to destroy the cloth, I would be destroyed in its place."

"Why did you go alone?" Jon asked.

"He commanded me to—facing the cloth was the final test of my power. I thought the task would be simple. A burning spell—you know how simple those are with powers such as ours. But my fireballs returned back on me, charring my flesh. So I rushed up to the cloth, an unfamiliar fear filling me. The screams of my enemies rang triumphant in my ears as I ripped the cloth from its place of honor. As that cursed thing covered me, I tried to pull it away, but found I couldn't. My skin, my flesh, my bones, my power dissolved." He paused and rested a hand on his son's shoulder, as if the touch of living human flesh could remind him of the years before the cloth claimed him. Jon looked up at him with sympathy.

"I even thought death would find me. Something far more terrible happened. Instead of oblivion, my soul was caught in an unbreakable web of faith and power. I lay numb, stretched across it. As the next day passed, I sensed the dull, trapped minds of the creatures that shared my prison. I thought back to my early knowledge and sought a means to break the spell.

"I found it. On the second night, the moon shone, round as the sun. I drew on its power and freed the prisoners from the cloth. In the terrible destruction that followed, the Guardians tried to destroy the cloth, but discovered that spells cast against it turn back on their caster. Despite my efforts, and those of the other desperate souls, we couldn't break the Guardians' spell on the temple walls.

"So I began drawing people to me, people filled with hate and desire. As the cloth gathered more prisoners, my powers grew. No Guardian guessed my strength."

"Until you pulled my mother into Markovia?"

Morgoth nodded. "And planted my seed in her. Now I sense your power, power so great that, like my master, I tremble to think of what you will become."

"And you'll teach me . . . Father?"

"As quickly as you can learn." Morgoth moved to the center of the cavern, to a higher spot surrounded by the pool of water. "Perhaps it's time to tempt you," he said, closed his eyes, and raised his arms.

As Jon watched and listened, his father began a complex incantation, seemingly a call for wisdom. A crystalline sphere as large as Hektor's head began to form above his father. As the incantation continued, the sphere solidified and pressed down on his father's hands. The inside of it filled with glowing white smoke. More words, a slight shake of Morgoth's head, and the smoke gradually assumed the shape of a closed book. Its gold cover was decorated with intricate, overlapping circles and runes. As Jon intently listened to the words of the spell, he saw the pattern grow more ornate with each moment. Finally, his father lowered the sphere to his chest and whispered a final word. The sphere vanished and the book opened to a central page.

Morgoth read the words aloud, the same words he had used to

conjure the book. In only moments, he had memorized the spell once more. He walked to Jon and laid the heavy tome in his hands.

"Look at it," Morgoth said.

Jon did. The pages contained small, precise handwriting. Fire spells. Freezing spells. Spells to summon monsters, to make creatures do the caster's bidding. "The first spell you will learn will be one to improve your concentration," Morgoth said. "Your training must begin with subtlety. Even so, you will learn faster than even I learned, I think," Morgoth said and laughed again, louder. Jon's head automatically turned toward the passage to Ivar's cavern.

"And I promise you, Jonathan; I will love you as a son, in the way I was never loved."

"I promise to love you as a father. To learn . . . never betray you. Will you, in return, bless me?"

"How so?"

"I am betrothed. Soon I will be formally married to the daughter of my teacher."

"Ivar's daughter?"

"Yes."

"He has true power. Of course I bless the wedding. Why be surprised? Life is precious to me. Children are precious, too, especially those who inherit my gifts."

Jon smiled. He took his father's hand. The intense cold of it startled him, but the feeling vanished as quickly as it had come, replaced by a rush of love and warmth that pushed Jon to unaccustomed honesty. "Ivar's scrolls and spell books are in a cavern joined to ours." He pointed to the passage. "The path between them is short. I'm afraid if he hears you, he'll come to harm you. Please, seal the passage—for his sake."

Beneath the child's respect, Morgoth sensed fear. He looked at the narrow crack, gestured and spoke a word Jon didn't understand.

"It is done. We may pass. Others may not, unless you or I will it."

"Thank you, Father." Jon hesitated, clearly pained to go on. Even so, he added, "And I can't spend nights here any longer. My visit to the fortress was to have been short. If I'm gone too long, there'll be questions."

"Those will come anyway. The Guardians possess little skill, but they aren't fools. They'll sense what you've done and will send word to their allies. Their messenger will come in daylight, when you alone can stop him. That will be the first test of your loyalty."

"Is there anything you need, Father?"

"No. Come at midnight tomorrow. We'll begin your education then."

Jonathan went through the outside passage, descended the hill and walked toward town. In a stand of trees near Maeve's cottage, he paused to brush the dirt off his pants and stare at the morning sky, at quick-moving clouds fleeing the rising sun. There, hidden by the trees, he let silent sobs of betrayal flow from him. He thought of the words that Leith had written, the uneven scrawl of her hand.

Her account had made it seem certain that he was Vhar's child, conceived well before her night of terror in the shrine. Now he knew that wasn't true, that he was Morgoth's child. Would his mother have taken so much time to put down her story only to lie to him at the end? He knew she wouldn't. Someone had changed her words, magically erased and reformed them in his mother's hand. He'd learned the very spell from Ivar.

He wouldn't try to understand the Guardians' deceit; wouldn't forgive it, wouldn't feel guilt for its result. It mattered little if his father was Vhar or some creature far older. He, Jon, was still himself—adept, powerful, brilliant. . . . He was his father's son.

When Jon entered the inn through the back door, he smelled bread baking in the oven, saw rolls ready to follow. Though he could pass unseen through the empty kitchen, there were men in the dining hall. Too many questions would be asked if he were seen returning alone at such an early hour, so he slipped into the secret passage behind the hall. It was unusual for the inn to have visitors so early in the day, and he eavesdropped on the men's conversation.

"Alden's mother? Odd that her body'd be found lying where Alden'd died," one of the men was saying.

Jon didn't recognize the voice, but the second was Andor's, and he was fearful. "The men were fishing close to the bank. If she had called out, they would have heard."

"I found her," the first man replied. "Both sets of footprints were fresh, but her body was frozen."

"More than the beasties are responsible for this, I tell you," the voice of Mishya added.

"Sondra, we need more tea," Andor called. Jon heard her footsteps move close to the wall and through the kitchen door. She must have seen the water from his feet on the floor, must have smelled the fresh outside air, for as soon as she had served them, the hidden door to the passage opened. She slipped silently into his arms.

Her warmth comforted him, but the trembling of her body and her words did not. "Three deaths in town this winter. I'm so glad you're safe!" she whispered.

"Nothing can happen to me, and I'll allow no harm to come to you. I promise," he replied.

He felt her nod and relax, secure in the protection of his power. He wanted to take her below, to hold her, to confess what he had done, but she pulled away. "I must go or I'll be missed," she said and left him.

It was pointless to eavesdrop on the men's talk any longer. He had heard enough. Jon descended the stairway to Ivar's cavern to wait for a more opportune time to reappear in town.

The sleep he had taken at his father's side hadn't refreshed him. His dreams had been filled with loneliness and despair. As he lay between the furs in front of Ivar's cold hearth, he thought of the words his mother had written in her legacy. *It had used Vhar's avarice to make him a thief. And me? The cloth had used petty resentments from years of marriage to Vhar to turn me into a murderer!*

And what of himself? Since he first set eyes on the cloth, he had felt lust growing in him—lust for power, for adoration. He had seen his own dream of being united with his father twisted in a way he'd never suspected. Now that his deed was done and his pledge to serve Morgoth made, he could only hope his father would keep his promise, wouldn't use his deadly touch to destroy those Jon loved. He was young, confident. He didn't realize the soul Morgoth needed to destroy most was his. Jon had no gods to pray to anymore. And so, with only sparks of hope for comfort, he slept.

He woke suddenly, knowing he was not alone.

"Who's there?" he whispered into the dark, certain that Ivar knew his secret, that the Guardians had come, that his father sensed his doubt and came to kill him.

"I am," Sondra said and crawled beneath the furs, "your betrothed."

"My wife," he replied.

As he held her, the presence he had sensed remained. Perhaps it was merely the weight of his conscience. Perhaps his father was here, watching them, savoring their passion.

"I won't betray you," he said, so soft that even Sondra, in his arms, didn't hear. The presence withdrew. Alone with his lover, Jon slept in her arms.

In the kitchen, Dirca began pulling the last of the loaves from the oven. Where had the girl gone? This was her duty. If Dirca hadn't happened to pause to take a cup of tea, the bread would've burned.

Sondra was useless, a romantic fool with eyes so blurred by dreams she couldn't concentrate on work. Dirca thought of her own lost girls. If they had lived, they wouldn't have been so foolish. When the time came to marry, they would've taken their mother's advice and not chosen someone as young and naïve as Jon.

As for Jon, he had no experience with women. He could hardly be blamed for his choice.

A sigh that might have been only her imagination drew her attention to the hidden door that led to the caverns. She cracked it open and listened.

Though layers of rock lay between her and the couple, Dirca thought she heard their breathing, their heartbeats, the murmur of Jon's voice as he spoke passionately of his love. Also hearing Andor's boots heading for the kitchen, Dirca closed the passage door and ran to the wood stove. When Andor entered the kitchen, she was pouring tea.

"Sondra told me Jon has returned," Andor said. "She went to him. I came to check the loaves."

"They would've burned," Dirca answered petulantly. "The baking is Sondra's duty. She's shirking her work."

Andor laughed. "Work! Dirca, the girl is in love! Don't you remember how it was with you and me?" He cupped her chin and raised it, intending to kiss her.

His words stung. He saw the hate in her eyes, the jealousy. "He isn't a child, Dirca. He doesn't belong to you. Remember that," he said, his voice low and even as he struggled to resist slapping her.

He hadn't been this angry since he learned to control his lycan-thropy. With the wolf's pendant heavy around his neck, he turned and stalked from the suddenly stifling room.

He didn't dare join the others at the table, so he stood near the kitchen door. Ivar noticed his expression and joined him. "Is something wrong?" he asked.

Andor shook his head. "Just a quarrel with Dirca. Nothing serious, but you know my temper." His hand brushed the pendant as the spoke the last words.

At the table, Mishya's voice rose above the whispers of the others. "I tell you, these deaths weren't natural. Something more than beasties is involved, something new. We should spy on the strangers among us."

Andor bristled. "I'll shut him up if you won't," he whispered to Ivar.

"Anything you say will only make the rumors worse. Let Mishya talk. Everyone knows Jon took the girl he wanted. No one has taken him seriously."

"They do now," Andor countered. He saw it in the grudging nods of the men at the table, felt it even in himself. He watched as Ivar went to the table and soothed the men's fears with a few well-chosen words. Soon after, the men left. Only Mishya remained.Mishya sat uncomfortably at the table. "Bring me ale," he called to Andor.

Andor shook his head. "Not so early," he responded.

"You must have some work to do," Ivar added.

Mishya took a deep breath. "Not until I talk to you," he told Ivar. "Come and sit with me . . . please." Ivar reluctantly did, and Mishya plunged into his confession. "I've always loved your daughter. You knew it. How could you let her marry a stranger?"

Ivar had endured enough of Mishya's self-pity, enough of his gossip about Jon's past. "If you loved her, you wouldn't have struck her on festival night. If you loved her, you would've worked harder and saved for your family instead of spending everything on ale."

"Is that it? Because I'm poor?"

"You call Jon a stranger, but remember, Sondra and I weren't born here. We came from a harder land than this, Mishya. I know real poverty. I also know the kind you brought on yourself, and how you thought to end it. Even if Jon hadn't come here, I wouldn't have let you marry her."

Mishya lurched to his feet, leaning toward Ivar, who sat so calmly across from him. "How dare you—"

"Speak the truth? Because you asked."

With white-knuckled fists, Mishya slammed the table aside. Before he could strike, Andor moved behind him. "Touch him and you'll never be allowed in this place again," Andor whispered.

Mishya turned and looked into Andor's blue eyes, fixed evenly on him, then at Ivar, who hadn't moved from his seat. Both men were smaller than he. This could've been a well-matched fight, but Andor seemed to be waiting for a chance to rip him apart, and Ivar displayed only curiosity. It was as if he had moved beyond the concerns of fragile flesh, as if he possessed a multitude of lethal powers to defend himself.

Andor opened the door.

Mishya didn't need a verbal dismissal. It took all his courage to keep from running.

In the days that followed, Mishya made good use of his own small gifts. He started more gossip and watched it grow. Ivar was a stranger here. And Dirca. And Sondra. There were secrets in that inn, secrets from before Jonathan. The silver-haired man was the catalyst, the one who triggered the killings. Who else could it be? Who else was new to the town?

Though business didn't slacken at *The Nocturne*, many patrons came out of morbid curiosity. Instead of the usual banter between Andor and the townsmen, the men would sit at tables, speaking to one another in hushed tones. Though they still asked Jonathan to sing, they didn't seem as moved by his voice as they had been before. Instead, they appeared to pass judgment on whether a youth so fair, with a voice so sweet, could be murderer.

fourteen

THOUGH HE HAD STARTED THE RUMORS ABOUT Jonathan, Mishya believed few of them. Ivar's words had stung him all the harder for their truth, but now that he had revenge, he found little satisfaction in it. Every time he went to the inn, his attention strayed to the kitchen, hoping to catch some glimpse of Sondra. But she stayed out of sight unless Jonathan was singing. And Mishya found himself paying his rival to play just so Sondra would stand in the doorway to listen.

Most of his friends had announced their betrothals. Their intentions would be formally sealed at the winter festival. He should stand beside them with Sondra, but another suitor would take his place.

Mishya was poor, Ivar had told him. And indolent. The last wasn't true. Mishya worked as hard as anyone, but he lived with his mother and little needed what he earned. They had a cottage, food, a warm hearth. True, they had few luxuries, but they hardly needed them. Besides, his mother never asked for anything.

If it had been summer, he might have hunted more, might have proven his worth by selling beaver and fox pelts to the Nova Vaasan traders. In winter coin grew scarce. Coin! The thought of gold nagged him, driving out all other concerns.

Money was his only hope for winning Sondra.

Andor and Ivar had money, but no one else except Maeve. No one in Linde owned as much as she. Men took her gifts and drank wine she bought with gold!

Gold!

Mishya had never been inside her cottage, but he'd heard enough from those who had. They spoke of gems, jewels—a treasure that would easily satisfy Ivar. He could buy his love.

Mishya spent days in the forest above her house, crouched in a concealing stand of trees, waiting for her to leave. On the third afternoon visit, he was lucky. With the hood of her black cloak pulled tightly around her face, Maeve began walking toward town. Mishya waited until she had disappeared among the distant cottages. Then, keeping to the shadows, he stole down the hill to her garden door. Lifting the broken latch, he moved easily inside the courtyard walls. He ripped the shutters from their casings, and crawled inside.

The house was dark and empty, smelling of musky incense and exotic perfume. In the dim winter light that leaked through the broken shutters, he saw silk scarves hanging from hooks beside the door, crystal goblets on the table, a bottle of expensive cloudberry wine beside them.

He drank it now, drank it right from the bottle, letting the sticky purple wine drip down his chin. Carrying the bottle in one hand, he began digging through the boxes on Maeve's dressing table. Yes, there were coins among the jewelry. He dropped them into the sack he had brought, then gleefully took the jewelry as well.

Wedding gifts, he thought, and laughed. As he lifted the bottle for a parting drink, a shadow covered his light. He turned and saw Maeve at the window.

"Where did you think you could sell those things, thief?" she asked as she stepped inside. He started to answer, but she slammed him against the wall, shaking the cottage. The bottle shattered on the stone floor. Though she frightened him as much as Andor did, she was a woman and no match for his strength. With a growl of rage, he lunged, knocking her backward and landing with his body atop hers.

His hands pounded her, but she fought fiercely back. He reached for the neck of the broken bottle and stabbed at her face, slicing one violet eye, ripping open her mouth. In response, she clawed him all the more ferociously. He slashed again, but her wounds healed behind the jagged glass. Though he kept up his attack, the very frenzy of it weakened him until, with a single heave of her body, Maeve tossed him off her.

The piece of bottle fell from Mishya's hand. He landed hard and lay panting, watching the woman stand and stagger toward him, the last cuts he made vanishing from her face as she reached him.

"Rob me? I should have known you would be useless for anything but prey. It's been a harsh winter. The goblins will welcome my leavings." Her voice was so musical that her threat sounded like singing.

He could say nothing, lying propped on his elbows, catching his breath, his eyes fixed on the inexplicable perfection of her face.

"My slaves tell me of your gossip, of the foolish things you say about the people at the inn. Perhaps Ivar will even let me enter there again, when he hears how I dealt with you."

She gripped him under the arms and pulled him effortlessly to his feet. "Did anyone see you come?"

He shook his head fearfully. With a husky laugh, she pointed to a chair. "Sit," she said, as if to a dog.

Mishya did as she asked, certain any attempt to escape would mean his death.

"Do you know what I am, Mishya?"

The question was one Mishya dared not consider. He shook his head.

"Soon I will show you."

He looked dully at her, expecting some revelation. Instead, she moistened a cloth and began cleaning the drops of blood from her face. Then she sat, facing him, her expression savage and ravenous.

When the gleam in her eyes grew too intense, he finally spoke. "What are we doing?"

"Waiting for night," she replied and ran one delicate fingertip down his trembling arm.

He tried to smile. "That's hours away," he said. "Is there any wine?"

"On the floor." She tossed her long hair over her shoulder and began picking up the shards of broken glass. He kicked, catching her in the chin. As she fell backward, Mishya bolted frantically for the door. Her hand closed around his ankle and he fell heavily. The neck of the bottle pressed against the side of his face.

"Go back to your seat, Mishya. Try to escape again and I'll take out your eyes."

He obeyed, watching the small square of daylight from the window fade, and his hopes with it. At last, she lit a lamp. The wakening light showed that she held an hourglass in one hand and a knife in the other. "We will play a game, Mishya. You will leave here, running not toward town, but away from it. When the sands have run through the glass, I will follow."

"And if I refuse?"

"This is my hunt, Mishya. You play, or die now, painfully. The moon later tonight will give you light. If you run well and fast and do as I ask, I'll kill you quickly. You might even escape, though I doubt it."

She turned the glass, opened the door and held out the knife, handle first. Mishya grabbed it and bolted out the door. Maeve stood in her doorway and watched him run. He reached the Timori Road, hesitated, then turned and headed straight toward town.

Maeve expected as much. She laughed with delight, threw back her head and gave a low, mournful howl, a howl answered a moment later by two of her pack. Her bargain with Mishya was off. She lifted her hands to her face and inhaled his scent, pungent with fear. The torture will be pleasant, she thought as she disrobed.

She had first noticed Mishya watching the cottage days ago. Though she knew a word whispered to him at the right moment would have sent him off to seek an easier target for his avarice, she'd let him come. The winter had been long and lonely, and her desire for the taste of human flesh had grown. It had been so long since she had dared to hunt a man that even the hags couldn't deny her this one night of sport.

The sand stopped flowing. Moments later, a huge silver fox padded from the house and sniffed the air.

+ ✦ +

Though Mishya often braved walking by himself through Linde at night, he had never been alone in the thick woods after dark. All the lies he had told to scare children returned and added to his terror as he fled Maeve's cottage. He glimpsed shadows beside him, in front of him. Only when they stopped did he see two huge wolves, their teeth bared, ready to attack.

He tried to skirt around them, but they cut him off again. His mother's tiny cottage was in sight, the inn lights bright in his eyes. His opened his mouth to scream. As he did, the wolves moved closer. With a cry of terror, he turned and fled into the hills east of town. The wolves flanked him at a distance.

He had expected tribes of goblins to find him before Maeve. Instead the woods were strangely silent as if every creature knew of the hunt and had decided to stay away. Still, he had his knife—if Maeve caught him, the blade would make him a good match for her. He refused to wonder what form she would take when she caught him. In any form, she was only a woman—powerful, but only a woman.

In time, he could no longer hear the wolves follow him. He even began to convince himself he had escaped. Then he heard the sound of a single pursuer. If it were Maeve, he didn't want to be winded when he faced her. He turned and, with his back to a pile of boulders, waited for her to attack.

A fox padded through the shadows. Just a fox. It sat below him on the hillside, its head cocked, its expression intelligent. Mishya let out a relieved sigh and took a closer look at the magnificent animal. What a price that silver pelt would bring. Perhaps enough . . .

His heart pounded faster than it had through all the hours of his flight. The fox's claws were red in the moonlight, and as he watched the paws lengthened and curved into red-nailed human hands!

"Maeve?" he whispered.

She attacked, ripping the knife from his hand, sinking her still-canine teeth once into his wrist, then backing off. She let him run until, out of breath, he stopped to make another stand.

The quarter moon rose to its zenith and began to set before Maeve wearied of the game. One of Mishya's wrists was broken and bleeding, three fingers were missing from his other hand. When he fell on the ice, as he did often, he would shriek with pain, scramble to his feet, and run a few yards before, dizzied by fear and loss of blood, he would fall again.

In an exposed, moon-drenched clearing, she faced him and rose to her hind feet. The shape of her limbs shifted into something almost human, though her face remained a fox's face; her body clothed in silver fur. He didn't struggle as she came to him and lifted his bleeding hands above his head. Her long, pointed muzzle pushed beneath his chin. Her hot breath brushed his neck.

"Maeve, let me live. Let me serve you."

In response, her teeth cut into his neck and he fell backward with her above him.

A pale mist in the woods covered the face of the moon, distracting her for a moment from the kill. She raised her head and saw the mist coalesce in a glowing funnel beside her, one that slowly solidified into human form. As it did, Maeve felt her own power drain. Though she didn't will it, her vixen shape faded until she crouched naked and shivering in the biting wind.

Silver hair, pale eyes glowing silver in the light. "Jonathan?" she asked, though she knew this creature was too mature to be the youth.

"I felt his fear and his pain. You have need of the flesh, I of the life. We will share," the silver man said, kneeling beside Mishya, who lay with his eyes wide, his mouth a small circle of fear. His hands covered Mishya's eyes. "Feast," he told her and pressed his lips against Mishya's forehead.

Maeve's power returned as quickly as it had faded.

Her shape changed once more. She straddled her prey, her human hands pushing up the front of his tunic, her vixen teeth ripping into the soft flesh of his belly.

She didn't need to be told to kill slowly, to inflict pain as she devoured her enemy. The Silverlord was sampling her handiwork and, for the first time in years, she wished to do whatever she could to please another. She didn't question the reason; his power was reason enough.

The body grew cold beneath her. She raised her head and moved away, watching the apparition claim the final shreds of Mishya's life.

She expected praise, but the man—if this were his true form—only raised his head, glanced coldly at her, and whispered, "Take the body where it will be found."

"And then . . . ?" she asked, but the Silverlord had already begun to melt, and in a moment he dissipated into the moonlit night.

Maeve sniffed the air and detected a sweet, cloying smell that was strong on Mishya's forehead. If the apparition had a scent, it was no bodiless spectre, but a physical creature with a power beyond any in Tepest save, perhaps, the hags. She would find and charm him. It would be difficult on one so powerful, she knew, but her tricks had never failed her before.

But first there was work to be done. Lifting the body's feet, Maeve dragged it down the hills and dropped it near the front door of the inn.

The moon scarcely touched the trees. Maeve had hours until dawn and decided to avoid letting the Silverlord's trail grow old. With one last look at the body, she departed, bounding up the hill to the place where she had seen the man.

In the shelter his son had provided, Morgoth sat, his body tingling with life, savoring the evening's discovery. This land held powers, powers he could twist to his own ends. The woman was only the first of many he would find and use as minions until the souls on the cloth were released. What a find the vixen had been! Beautiful. Intelligent. Filled with a ravenous thirst for lifeblood almost equal to his own. She would come to him tonight, he knew that much. And, as he waited, he thought of all the ways she would serve him.

He wasn't disappointed. She found him even more quickly than he had expected, padding four-footed through the narrow entrance in the rocks.

"Woman," he said, and her form became human. She didn't try to rise, but sat back on her heels, marveling at the beauty of the cavern, at the light that filled it, a light that seemed to come from the air itself.

And him.

He held out his hand and spoke his name. She came forward on her knees and kissed his fingers. "I have done as you asked," she said. Her voice, as Morgoth expected, was as beautiful as her body.

"And if I ask more?"

"I will do whatever you wish." She kissed his hand again and laid the back of it against her cheek, thankful he didn't pull it away.

"Tell me of the powers in this land," he ordered.

Though she had come to learn from him, she spoke of the hags, the goblins, the men she had charmed then turned into *were* to serve her. When she had finished, he smiled. "Sleep here with me through the day," he said. "Tomorrow night we will find your pack and hunt together."

Taking his words as an invitation, she laughed seductively and moved closer, rubbing tapered fingers down his leg. He asked, "You are barren, are you not?"

"Yes," she replied.

In the past, those words had proven useful to Maeve. Not now. He pushed her away and lay down, his knees against his chest on the narrow ledge. A word, a gesture and a transparent crystalline cylinder formed around him. As Maeve watched, Morgoth's body deflated until it was nothing more than a dry, withered husk waiting for the next sunset to animate. Stunned more by his rejection than the change she had just witnessed, Maeve tried to leave the cavern.

But she found the passage magically sealed. She faced Morgoth's form. "May I go and return at sunset?"

He seemed to smile. The withered hand rustled as it moved. "Go . . . beautiful fox," he whispered, his eyes following her as she padded from the room.

Were. The bites on Mishya's neck and stomach made the nature of the killer plain enough. The almost-human footprints in the snow made it even plainer. Even so, the body was frozen, like the last, though the wounds were apparently fresh. The beasties hadn't touched it. Indeed, the beasties were strangely absent from the land. In happier times, Linde would see this as reason to rejoice. Not now.

After Mishya's body was found, many townsfolk recalled Jonathan's violent attack and the rivalry between them and blamed Jon. But, when a third victim was discovered, and a fourth, both with their flesh in ragged strips, their bodies blue with cold, the townsfolk recalled that on those nights Jonathan had been singing at the inn. Their suspicion immediately abandoned Jon, seeking something far more fearful, some twisted creature, darker than any of legend.

Each night the public rooms of the inn were crowded. Men came to discuss the latest rumors about the killings, but they brought their wives and children as well. To leave them at home seemed too dangerous. The companionship and music of the inn was their only respite from the constant, pervasive fear.

People often asked Jonathan to sing. His voice was soothing, his songs so beautiful they brought tears to the listeners' eyes. Even though they paid him well for his talent, Jon would have avoided the crowded rooms had Ivar not told him that it would be unwise to stay away. The boy endured the duty with the same obedient attentiveness he gave to all his tasks, but Andor noted the fear in his eyes as he listened to the rumors, the whimpers of the children, the frightened whispers of the women. Andor hardly blamed him for his reluctance to sing.

A fifth body. A sixth. Two of the elders were also suddenly missing from the town. Suspicions about their disappearance turned to Maeve; she had often been seen with the pair in the past. Some of the men went to her house to question her, but found the place empty, fresh boot tracks in the snow outside. The next day they returned, but she was still absent. Most expected her body to be the next one found. Others thought her somehow responsible for the killings.

Andor knew the truth. He had discovered Mishya's body and had seen the vixen's tracks in the snow. She had left them deliberately, a sign that only he and Ivar would understand. He had brushed them away before anyone else noticed, less out of loyalty to her than out of sympathy for the curse that united them. Besides, he knew there were other *were* in Linde. Like him, they controlled their curse. He wouldn't see them hunted down and destroyed by Linde's fear.

Though Andor had never known Maeve to kill a man before, he knew she often hunted for food in fox form. Andor didn't blame her for such forays any more than he blamed her for trying to end her loneliness by taking Leith for a companion. He understood loneliness, especially now that Dirca was so petulantly jealous.

Since he and Ivar had banished Maeve from the inn, she never spoke to them in public. Yet, on the infrequent occasions when Andor had encountered her alone, she had been as friendly toward him as before. After the inn had emptied and the rest of the household had gone to sleep, he visited her cottage, bearing loaves of fresh-baked bread, and many questions.

She wasn't home, but her door was open. He went inside and sat among her treasures. Would she tell the truth or lie? Worse yet, his amulet diminished his power. While he wore it, she could charm him with a look, with the sound of her voice. Betraying the promise he had made to himself years before, he unhooked the silver wolf's head and dropped it in his pocket. Immediately, the lycanthropic strength filled him, bringing with it the lust for the hunt. Once he had controlled the curse without Ivar's trinket. He thought he could control it now, despite the desire, which was so much stronger than he remembered.

At last, she entered the house in human form. After laying a hand on his shoulder in a gesture of kinship, she lit the lamp. Her dark blue cape and fur-lined boots were loose, easily discarded. He had worn such clothes once. The sight of them, and her, brought back memories with an astonishing stab of regret.

"So many people have died," he said.

She sat in a chair facing him, her long fingers tracing the carvings on its arms, her gaze fixed on the open door as if she waited for someone else to arrive.

"I saw your tracks beside Mishya's body," he added.

"It took you a long time to come," she replied.

"Why did you want me to come at all?"

"There are so few of us in this land, and we are isolated from one another. It isn't right, Andor."

"Since when does a vixen crave the company of a wolf?" he asked. Though they shared similar powers, their natures were utterly different. Wolves ran in packs; foxes were solitary, utterly self-absorbed.

"I inherited the form of a wolf from my father," she reminded him. "In that way, we are kin."

"After so many years of restraint, why do you kill?"

He sensed the desperation in her eyes, the lie behind her reply.

"You've felt the change in the air, the urge to surrender to desire. You wouldn't have removed the amulet otherwise. You want to be tempted. You want to yield to your power, don't you?"

"Why do you think you are immune to danger?"

She still looked at the door instead of him. "I'm protected, even from the hags. I'm free to use my power. No one can stop me any longer."

"The winter festival isn't so far away, Maeve. The goblins seem to have abandoned this land. The town will need a sacrifice for the winter festival. Indeed, they already seek one."

"I am protected," she repeated then added, "wolf."

The word called to the beast within him. His skin tingled with the desire to respond, but he fought it down. Struggling, he reached for the amulet in his pocket. As he did, a mist rolled into the room through the open door. Maeve's hand gripped his wrist, pulling his fingers away from the wolf pendant. Fur-covered now, her hand had all the strength of her vixen form. Her claws cut into him.

The smell of his own blood aroused him. The pain of her attack aroused him. His anger broke what was left of his will. He tore at his clothes as the pressing agony coursed through him, the change reforming his limbs and features.

She fled through the open door. He followed, but once outside, his anger dissipated in the wind that brushed the fur on his back, the crystalline snow that glowed in the moonlight, the score of inviting scents laughing in the air.

Andor stifled a howl and padded after Maeve.

fifteeN

ON NIGHtS WHEN tHE MOON WASN'T fULL, tHE CLOtH
sometimes had exuded a brooding presence that hung over the
fortress itself. It had seemed to watch the Guardians, test them,
seek the means to drain each of his will. The presence had never
been seen, only occasionally felt. In the fortnight after Jon left, the
Guardians began to suspect the presence had left them. Mattas
was the first to voice his suspicion. He did so reluctantly, surprised
when the others quickly agreed. Each had noted a lightening of
the burden.

"It was the boy," Mattas said. "Someone taught him some trick
to use to drain the power from the cloth." The words were heavy
with reproach, directed primarily at Leo though he spoke to the
others as well.

"The power cannot be stolen so easily," Leo countered as gently
as he could.

"But everyone believes that something has changed," Dominic
said. "We must discover what it is." His hand circled his amulet,
and the others looked fearfully at him, already guessing what had
to be done.

That night, while the others stood outside, Hektor and Dominic entered the shrine alone. Hektor carried the torch. Dominic clutched his amulet in one hand. The other Guardians barred the doors after them and began a quiet prayer for strength, for success, for the life of the pair. Dominic intended to call out to the souls on the cloth. This rite was recorded in their history. Though it had been done often when the order was large and powerful, it had never been attempted by any of the remaining Guardians.

The pattern of the cloth always shifted, yet the features of each trapped soul remained the same. Some were more noticeable than others. The Guardians often saw Vhar, the one they began to call "the red man" after reading Leith's legacy, or Leith herself with her flowing chestnut hair. The pack of *were* that had invaded the town where the cloth had once been always clung together, as inseparable in their prison as they had been in life. The stronger powers hid more carefully. The Silverlord, who had brought so much sorrow to their order, appeared in corners, behind others, or spread out across the length and breadth of the tapestry with features so pale they could hardly be seen. He hid best of all. But every name was recorded, and Dominic had memorized them all.

He gripped one lower corner of the hanging cloth, Hektor the other. They spread the folds so Dominic could study each part of the pattern. With a steadying breath that revealed little of the fear Hektor was certain the priest must feel, Dominic began the call.

As each name was spoken, Dominic paused and waited for some effect. The cloth would shift in their hands as the soul named struggled to respond.

Dominic recited the names slowly, receiving a faint response after each until he came to the name of their most fearsome adversary, a name that hadn't been spoken aloud since the destruction of their temple so many years before.

"Morgoth."

No response. The cloth might have been any cloth, the shrine a pile of stones.

"I command you to show yourself, Morgoth."

Command, Hektor thought fearfully. He expected a rain of fire, a lightning bolt directed from the cloth to the amulet Dominic wore. That would be like Morgoth. Instead the Silverlord did nothing.

Dominic wondered if the sorcerer's name had been recorded correctly. He tried variations of it with no better result, then went on with his list. At the end, he spoke the saddest name of all, "Leith." He said it gently, as if afraid there might be pain in the waking.

A breeze brushed Hektor's cheek. The torch flame danced. As he turned to find the source of the draft, his foot dislodged the loose stone slab behind him.

He dropped the cloth, handed the torch to Dominic, and lifted the section of floor.

"Open the doors!" Dominic cried to the others waiting anxiously outside. "Come and see what Hektor has discovered!"

Peto, the smallest of the Guardians, followed the tunnel to its source. Leo went into the library and discovered the unsealed box containing Leith's legacy to her son. Though it was difficult to be certain, he believed that the seal had been broken for some time.

"You should've shown him his mother's scroll years ago," Mattas said. "The boy never had the calling."

"Was your life full-formed at his age?" Dominic asked him.

Mattas frowned. The fire that took his eyes had destroyed parts of his memory as well. "I can't remember," he admitted.

"I remember," Hektor said. "I thought if I escaped my master, I'd marry and raise a dozen children. Instead, I came here and raised only one. Whatever Jonathan did, he did out of ignorance."

"Or out of the cloth's influence," Mattas added.

"Out of ignorance!" Hektor repeated, trying to control his fury.

Hektor had raised the boy, and he wouldn't let him be unjustly condemned. "If I'm correct, it's not too late to set things right."

"There's a greater reason to find him than that," Leo said. "The
shrine is protected on all sides. If Jonathan was able to enter it,
even through the floor, he *must* have the calling. There's no other
explanation."

"Impossible!" Mattas snorted.

"Leo's right," Dominic said. "One of us must find Jon and tell
him. Who will it be?"

Dominic wielded the spells that kept the souls entrapped. Mattas
couldn't travel. Peto was far too small. Hektor's bias toward the boy
disallowed him. Leo was the only one suited to the journey, and his
spells would protect him if Jon were truly dangerous. The mountain
trails were icy, the wind harsh and bitter. Hektor accompanied Leo
halfway through the passage to Tepest. "Don't condemn Jon too
harshly when you find him," he said as he took his leave.

"I must reach Andor and Ivar and tell them what's happened. As
for Jonathan . . . " Leo sighed. "I'll do my best to bring him back
with me."

Though the tunnel that led to Tepest offered a welcome respite
from the frigid G'Henna wind, it had a putrid scent, as if some huge
beast had crawled inside to die. As Leo traveled the winding path
through it, he heard rustling that wasn't from the bats clinging to
the ceiling above or the spiders in their thick, sticky webs.

The smell became more distinct. The rustling grew louder. Leo
recognized the signs for what they were.

Goblins.

Having lived in Tepest before joining the order, Leo knew to
respect goblin cunning. But in all the years he had lived in the fortress, goblins had never been seen in these passages or in Markovia,
for they feared Markov's beast-men.

Only one passage led outside. They would undoubtedly be in it and would have heard him by now. Leo lit the second torch before the first was fully extinguished. The blade of the short sword he carried pressed coldly against his side, giving him as much comfort as his spells as he went on.

As he advanced, the goblins retreated. He could hear them moving ahead of him, speaking their crude tongue in the passage just beyond the torchlight. Though he couldn't determine their numbers, he knew there were more than enough to take him down. He couldn't retreat—fear would bring the attack. He pulled his cloak tightly around him, quickened his pace, and mumbled the beginning of a fire spell.

The end of the cavern lay directly ahead. The goblins were clustered in the shadows just inside the cave's mouth, gibbering with fear and indecision. Leo judged their number at well over thirty. The creatures loathed the sun, yet they seemed more interested in running from him than in attacking.

Leo moved closer, so close the stench of their bodies made his eyes water. As the torchlight fell on them, he noted that most of the goblins were young, or females clutching infants. Their expressions were as frightened and uncertain as that of any human mother's. Even the few males held their crude weapons at their sides, not wanting to break this strange truce.

"Let me pass and I won't harm you," Leo said. Though he doubted that the goblins understood his words, they parted as he raised his torches high. He passed between them into the sunlight. As he began the descent to the river crossing, he could hear them fleeing deeper into the tunnel.

Something had terrified the goblins with such awesome force that they didn't care that Leo was alone and, to all appearances, barely armed. They had lost all will to fight him. He suspected that, even if Peto had come in his place, they would have feared him. Whatever spooked the goblins was out here. He paused long enough to sense a change in the valley—a disquiet similar to the one the presence aroused in the fortress, a disquiet that the warm sunlight melting the winter snow could do nothing to dispel.

The path curved near a stand of trees on the Tepest border, where a black-hooded person sat by the path. As Leo approached, the person stood and pulled back the cowl. Familiar silver eyes, pale skin. "Jon!" Leo called, the joy in his voice sincere, but the wariness in his stance equally so.

"I thought they'd send you," Jonathan said, then added a warning. "Go back to the fortress."

"I must speak with you and Ivar. There's troubling news. I believe you already know of it."

"You cannot pass. If you value your life, turn back."

"My life?" Leo smiled bitterly. "I taught you, remember? Your powers may have grown, Jonathan, but I doubt you are stronger than I." He reached into his pocket, fingering the fine sand he had brought for just this moment. As he did, he whispered the simple spell that would put the boy to sleep.

Though the spell had worked on Jonathan when he was young, it had no effect now.

Leo hid his alarm. Instead, he began walking toward Jonathan, speaking softly as if he were trying to soothe some wild creature, wounded and trembling. "Come with me," he said. "We will go to Ivar and speak to him together."

"No!" It was a harsh cry of denial, of despair.

Leo continued moving forward. In a moment, he would grab the boy. He was larger, stronger. He could win a physical fight, then drag Jonathan to Ivar. "Jon, we don't condemn you. We care for you. Let us—" Only when Leo had almost touched Jon did he see the desperate resolve in those silver eyes, the quick, final gesture of a fire spell readied before his arrival.

A wall of flames broke over him. His last words became a single shriek of agony that gurgled as his body melted and crumbled to ashes.

Jon stood over the charred remains. "Liars," he whispered, and, as he said the words, the past welled up bitter within him. Tears blinded him. Grief closed his throat as he tried to recite one of the Guardian's prayers. "May the bright powers of dawn that banish the darkness . . ." The words fled his mind, as if the deed had made him incapable of recalling them. "Liars," he repeated, but he continued to kneel and weep.

When the tears ran dry, he buried the grief deep inside himself and walked across the river toward Linde. In the distance, he spied Sondra in her blue cloak standing in the door of the inn. Seeing him, she ran to meet him, to hold his arm, to kiss him affectionately. "Jon, I was so worried about you."

"Worried? Whatever for?" he asked, his voice deceptively light.

"There have been so many killings. Please, tell me when you're leaving. I worry. I can't help it." She pulled him through the door of the inn as if the stone and wattle walls could protect them from the evil.

He'd done Morgoth's bidding. Now Sondra was safe from his father's power. Nothing else mattered.

Maeve stood by the window of her cottage, watching mist rise from the sun-warmed hills as night fell. She'd often dreamed of escaping servitude to the disgusting hags, but had never dared test their curse until now. Morgoth had promised that, after the next full moon when his legions were freed from the cloth, he would destroy the hags and free her from their curse.

Like her, he was beautiful and vain, and their goals were much the same. They were kindred spirits, so much so that she risked serving him willingly.

It was nearly dark. Her pack would be arriving soon. She disrobed and changed to vixen form. Lasos, her most recent conquest, arrived first. Then Marc and the village elder, Zapoli. Even in wolf form, they all seemed so uncertain of their actions, so unsure of the new master they served, that she longed to laugh and taunt them. After she had led Fian into the clutches of the hags, they had used him for so many months of twisted pleasure that they had demanded that her offerings have the healing powers of the lycanthropic change. If Morgoth hadn't come to this land, Marc and Lasos would have been in the hags' forcecage by spring, slowly devoured through the summer, dead by the time the first leaves fell.

She waited a while longer, lost in her thoughts. As she expected, Andor didn't join them. She didn't blame him. He wasn't controlled by her, and his presence at the inn would certainly be missed tonight.

She led her pack into the woods above the town. They hunted well into the night, tearing apart a small band of goblins that hadn't fled the land. They padded silently through the shuttered town, past the inn, past empty cottages, to a cabin where a family had decided to make a foolish, lonely stand.

The wolves' bodies pounded against the cottage door. The wife held a pair of burning faggots, the husband the silver knife and a short sword purchased from the red-haired stranger so many years before.

Outside, fur-covered hands pulled the vixen's body onto their roof, fur-covered hands pried open the second-floor shutters, and the vixen crawled inside.

An infant lay on a carved wooden bed beneath a coverlet embroidered with the same vine and grape pattern on the ruined shutters.

The infant's sister lay on a bed near the crib. Neither stirred as the wood cracked, as the cold draft of air and silver mist rolled into their room.

Maeve lifted the infant from its crib and raised it into the glowing mist swirling above her. She felt the terrible cold as it swiftly drained the life from the infant. Then she threw its body out the window to the hungry pack below. The growls of the wolves woke the girl. She slid backward across the bed, her knees pressed to her chest as the vixen approached. A beautiful child, Maeve thought, admiring the girl's strawberry hair and thin, well-formed limbs. Young. Easily made to forget her past. Easily turned.

Maeve's hands gripped the girl's bare arms, lifting her protectively. For a moment, her shape altered enough that she could speak to the Silverlord shimmering beside the bed. "May I have this one for my own?" she asked.

In response, a tendril of mist brushed the child's face, sending a shudder through the tiny body.

The bedroom door banged open. With a cry of rage, the father lunged, sinking the silver sword deep into Maeve's shoulder. Still gripping the child, Maeve bit his wrist, forcing him to let go of the blade. Screaming at the burn the silver made on her hand, she pulled the blade loose. "Mama!" the girl screamed and held out her arms to the woman standing, stunned, in the doorway. With a low growl, Maeve turned and leaped with the girl through the window.

Her pack had only been somewhat sated by the infant. Nonetheless, they did as Maeve ordered and circled the terrified child, moving closer, their claws ripping at her bare ankles. The girl's whimpers became screams of terror. The cottage door opened and her mother ran outside, a flaming brand in one hand, the silver sword in the other. Whipping the flames before her, she moved into the center of the pack and began edging her daughter toward the cottage door.

Strands of mist curled around the woman, mist with enough substance to wrench the torch and blade from the woman's hand, leaving her helpless. She frantically clutched her screaming daughter as the wolves circled them. Then the mist touched her face, pulling the life from her body as the pack would soon pull the flesh from her bones. As she fell, the child grabbed the torch and thrust it into the face of the wolf standing between her and the door, then bolted for the cottage.

The pack, concentrating on the woman's body, had little time for the child, scarcely noticing when the vixen shut the door behind the girl. A crowd of men ran from the inn through the streets. They held torches high, answering the girl's terrified screams. The pack abandoned their kill and scattered into the woods.

The mist remained for some time longer, floating insubstantial as a breeze above the oncoming men, touching their fear, their horror and magnifying it before dissipating into the darkness of the trees.

Blood covered the snow outside the cottage. When the villagers examined the woman, they saw that crystals of ice had formed in the rents in her flesh. Her tears were frozen on her cheeks, her open eyes glazed with frost. The village had seen this bizarre death often enough, but this was the first time they had a witness to the crime.

Inside the cottage, a line of blood marked the father's torturous descent from the children's room in the loft and pooled beneath the bite on his wrist, a bite so deep and powerful that the end of the bone showed through his mangled flesh. His face was ashen from shock and loss of blood, yet he was still conscious, still struggling to rise.

One of the men pulled the girl off him so the village healer could dress the wound. When he saw the depth of the bite, the healer avoided touching it, asking the man, "Kezi, what did this to you?"

"A person dressed in silver fur and a silver cloud," the girl replied for her father.

"Wolves," Kezi corrected.

The healer hurriedly wiped the blood from his hands and backed away. "Then I can do only one thing to help you," he said to Kezi as he lifted the silver blade from the floor.

"Take the child to the inn. She shouldn't see this," someone said.

Though the sentiment was kind, the words triggered fear. "No!" the girl cried. "I want to stay with Papa!"

Ivar had seen the terrified mood of such crowds often enough. They were willing to destroy the man before knowing the details of the attack, as if there would be some protection in ignorance. Ivar had spent all his life hiding his power, but, as he had told Jon, part of a wizard's ability lay in knowing when to reveal it. He proceeded with caution. "Wolfsbane can cure the disease," he said.

"On a bite so deep, never!" the healer countered.

"The curse can be removed," Ivar said. "I've seen it."

"Removed? Who knows how to lift a curse?"

Ivar breathed deeply, weighed the consequences of his answer one final time, and said, "I do."

With those two soft words, the man that oversaw the winery, made the best roasted quail, and had the greatest luck at dice of anyone in Linde revealed himself as something far more than a neighbor and trusted friend. His voice, his stance, his air of confidence inspired respect. The terror of the last few days made even the doubters believe his power.

"Take Kezi to the inn," Ivar said and led the way outside. There Andor was crouched, staring at the carnage, lost in thought.

"Do you think they will attack again tonight?" Ivar asked him in a voice so low no one else could hear.

Andor shook his head. "They're gone," he said.

"Those who aren't staying at the inn should go home now," Ivar called to the crowd.

Kezi screamed with pain as he was lifted and carried through the streets. At the inn, Ivar ground a poultice of wolfsbane and wine while the healer washed the wound and set the arm. "Find Jonathan," Ivar whispered to Andor as he placed the poultice. "I'll need his help."

Andor started toward the door, then hesitated, waiting for Ivar to finish. When the poultice was set, he motioned for the wizard to join him. "Why did you never lift the curse from me?" Andor whispered bitterly.

"Because I don't possess the power to do so. Nor can I lift it from our poor friend, either. But Kezi is a good man with a child to raise. I'll give him the same choice I gave you and hope he has your self-control."

"Then why do you need Jon?"

Ivar smiled ruefully. "The people are terrified, their minds set on blood. They won't believe the curse is lifted if we don't give them the best possible show."

Ivar listened to Andor climb the stairs, heard his footsteps going from room to room on the upper floors where Jon often took refuge when the crowd in the inn became too large and noisy.

Sondra came into the kitchen. Ivar asked her, "Have you seen Jonathan?"

"He went below," she replied. "I just told Andor that."

Yet Andor hadn't come down. The long night had already drained Ivar's strength, and Andor and Jon were proving more hindrance than help. Ivar went downstairs. Jon wasn't there.

Ivar opened his spell book and refreshed his memory of a spell any apprentice could cast. He had hoped for something more dramatic.

But the dancing spheres of color, the light that would flow from his fingers to cover the wound on Kezi's wrist should evidence his power to lift the curse, even if the words that followed were merely a distraction and a sham.

Later, after the "healed" Kezi had fallen into a deep slumber, Ivar went to his cavern to wait for Jonathan. The events of the past hours had sapped his strength and, in spite of his best intentions, he slept. Sometime in the night, the boy passed by him. Ivar never woke.

In the morning, so early that even Dirca wasn't at her place in the kitchen, Ivar packed his books into a cloth bag, took his staff from the cavern, and began the walk to the fortress. He suspected the Guardians possessed many of the answers concerning the deaths that had plagued the town.

While Ivar tended Kezi, Maeve dismissed her wolf pack and limped home. By the time she reached her cottage, her wound had begun to throb. Once inside, she willed her human form and lit a lamp. Soon after, carrying a basin of lye soap and hot water toward her dressing table, she glimpsed her reflection in a mirror. Her hands trembled and she set the basin down hard, spilling the water over the pile of scarves and feathers.

The blade had been silver, that much was certain from the pain of the wound, but even silver couldn't do such damage. As she wiped away the dried blood that covered the deep gash on her shoulder, she saw white pustules and sickly yellow skin around them. Without thinking, she drew her hair back from her face. Immediately, three white boils appeared on her forehead. She looked down at her hands and saw that the burns the silver had made on her fingers were covered with the same white sores.

249

Leticia, the sea hag, had cursed her. If she didn't serve them, she would become as they were.

She returned to fox shape. In this form, there was the single stab wound, but no sores. A moment later, human once more, she looked at her face in the mirror and screamed, a sound so loud and terrified that families in the center of Linde heard it and prayed for the life they thought had been taken. The sores had spread. The yellow skin covered most of her forehead.

She fled, first on two legs then on four. There were hours left before sunrise, more than enough time for Morgoth to use his power and lift the curse.

Outside Morgoth's cavern, she paused and listened, swearing softly to herself when she heard Jonathan's melodic voice. If she weren't so desperate, she'd wait until Morgoth was alone before facing him.

What a conquest Jonathan would have made! A conquest so powerful he might have challenged the hags themselves. Instead, she now served his father and found herself likewise subservient to the son. Until now she had managed to avoid Jon. As she padded inside, she could only hope he would forget her mockery and recall that they were allies.

In the cavern, she saw Jonathan sitting cross-legged on the edge of the pool, a heavy book covering his knees, his brow furrowed with concentration. His hands and lips moved slowly, and he looked like a musician trying to master a particularly difficult harmony. She lay back on her haunches and, with muzzle between her paws, watched as faint sparks formed near his fingertips. He seemed disappointed at the result. In human form, she might not have stifled the laugh.

"Skill will come in time," Morgoth said, his voice coming from the shadows at the rear of the cavern. Maeve padded over to him.

"Little fox," Morgoth whispered affectionately, laying his hand on the side of her neck, rubbing her fine fur between his fingers. "Woman."

Maeve began to change, but fought his command, forcing him to repeat it. In human form, she knelt before him, her face toward the ground, her hands pressed to the stone floor. Spheres of light moved close to her, bathing her in a pool of yellow and rose. She batted at the spheres. They burned her hand, but didn't move. "Help me," she begged and received no reply. "Help me," she repeated and looked into his face while cloudy, yellow tears oozed from her violet eyes.

"The hags did this?" he asked, staring at her wounds with such intensity that he seemed to find them beautiful.

"The hags said I'd become like them if I betrayed them. This curse proves my loyalty to you. End it."

"I can do nothing," he said.

"You haven't tried."

"I cannot expend my power on such a trivial thing," Morgoth said coldly.

"Then release me. Let me beg the hags' mercy." Morgoth shook his head.

"I control the pack," she reminded him.

"Only as long as I will it. Since you wish to test my power, I no longer will it. They won't come at your call, not tomorrow night nor any night."

The loss hardly mattered to Maeve. The pack were merely trained dogs fattened for the hags' feast. She cared for none of them. However, Morgoth's betrayal stung. "I've served you well," she reminded him.

"You served your own interests."

"What am I to do?" she moaned.

"You make a magnificent fox," Jonathan broke in, a twisted smile of triumph on his pale face.

"Serve us both in that form," Morgoth said.

She shifted, turned, and fled the cavern. As she ran, brilliant peals of Jonathan's laughter followed her.

The hags had never been so ungrateful or so demanding. Of course she was a magnificent fox—she had never seen another vixen with her perfect beauty—but the fox shape was hardly made for wearing the finery she loved and collected, for charming men to use as slaves, for songs and dances, for what made her years in Tepest so pleasant.

Morgoth would've helped her if the boy had only asked. The boy hadn't. If this was war, so be it.

She went home and examined herself again. The pustules had grown, the wound itself had lengthened. She dressed quickly and, clutching the bloodstained cloth she had used to clean herself, followed the narrow path from her cottage to the edge of town where she lay in human form, arms forward as if she had been clawing the ground.

She was found by three hunters just before dawn. They took her to the inn where the healer, who was spending the night to care for Kezi, was the only one awake. They placed Maeve on a bench near the door. Concerned that she might be sick rather than wounded, they backed away from her and moved closer to the hearth, where Kezi lay wrapped in furs before a hot fire. The healer examined her sores and forced wine into her mouth. When her eyes fluttered open, he asked what had happened.

"I was attacked," she replied.

"By wolves?"

"By a man whose breath destroyed my skin, whose hands clawed at my flesh . . . he infected me with a sorcerer's illness. We all know him." Her voice still held its power. Her rescuers listened intently as she said the name. "It was Jonathan."

"Did anyone see Jon last night?" the healer asked.

The men shook their head. One of them looked down at Kezi and commented, "His daughter spoke of a silver cloud. Do you suppose—?" He stopped speaking as Sondra came down to begin her morning work. Her eyes were puffy and her clothes disheveled. When she saw the visitors, she smoothed back her hair and pulled her loose work shift more evenly on her shoulders.

"Is something wrong?" she asked when she noticed their serious expressions.

"Where's Jonathan?" the healer asked, and added less seriously. "We need his help with Kezi."

"He'll be down in a few minutes, but I can go get him for you."

"That won't be necessary. Which room is his?"

"To the right, at the end of the hall."

Maeve lay back, feigning weakness, laughing with hidden delight as she watched the men climbing the stairs, whispering to one another. She heard Jon's startled cry when he met them in the hall, heard the brief scuffle that followed.

They'd underestimated the youth, she thought as she heard their terrified screams. A moment later they ran down the stairs, tripping over one another as they fled the balls of flame that rolled after them. Andor rushed from his room into the drinking hall. Eyes wide, he retreated, returning with a blanket to beat out the fires. By the time the blaze was out, Jonathan had fled.

Maeve had watched him go. "Ah, yes. I am a magnificent fox," she mouthed, a yellowed finger brushing back her still-beautiful hair.

As Jonathan sat in the cave, waiting for his father to wake, he thought of the burning *Nocturne*, thought of Andor and his blanket. It occurred to Jon that the spells he had learned were all lethal. That had been his choice; he could've learned others. And now, he was struggling to master a lightning spell. The force he hoped to control frightened him. If his concentration faltered or the spell was chanted incorrectly, the lightning could destroy him. This was the dangerous time, when a wizard had to trust his talent enough to override instinct.

That night, Morgoth noticed the scent of smoke in Jonathan's clothing, the burn on the boy's arm. Jon related what he had done, then added bitterly, "I shouldn't have run. I should've said Maeve lied. Ivar and Andor would've defended me."

"Instead, you attacked them."

Jon nodded. "Now I can never return to Linde. I was such a fool," he admitted.

His father smiled. He raised his hand, paused a moment, then brushed away a smudge of soot on Jon's cheek. "You had to see what your spells could do. It was only natural," he said gently. "As for returning to Linde, you'll do more than return. One day you will rule the town and all of the land around it. When my legions are freed from the cloth, you'll lead them. No powers in this land equal you and I together."

"How can you be so certain that those trapped on the cloth will follow us?" Jon asked.

"They've pledged themselves to serve me. I must free them." Noticing Jon's doubtful expression, Morgoth added, "Your mother is trapped there. So is Vhar. There are others like them, decent people enslaved forever for some small infraction. Don't you think there is honor in releasing them?"

Jon nodded. "Yes," he said, hiding his doubt. He watched his father open his gold-covered spellbook, noting with pride the ones Jonathan had already mastered.

sixteen

"Leo's dead," ivar told dominic as he sat with the Guardians in the great hall.

"I guessed as much when I saw you walking toward the fortress. We were fools to let him go alone," Dominic replied bitterly.

"I saw the cinders that were left of his body, his shadow on the ground. Had you sent two, you would have lost two."

"Who killed Leo?" Dominic asked, the despair in his voice indicating that he already knew.

"Jonathan. It could have only been Jonathan. Now that I have said the worst, let me tell you of the other terrible events in Linde."

"How many wolves attacked the family?" Dominic asked when Ivar had finished.

"The girl saw three. The father was bitten. From his description, I would say Maeve was among them."

"That's hardly a vixen's way. She's making other *were* for a purpose . . . and the purpose hangs in our shrine," Dominic said. "Next full moon, they'll attack. Jon will be with them, and the creature he has freed."

"Why should they wait?" Ivar asked.

"Because with our minds focused on the cloth, we are far more vulnerable than at any other time."

"And for vengeance," Mattas added. "For the souls to be released on us is Morgoth's ultimate revenge."

Ivar thought of Sondra. The boy loved her, of that Ivar was certain. Whatever other atrocities Jon might commit, Ivar doubted he would harm her. But the battle fought here would determine the future of Linde. "The moon is nearly full. I'll stay and help you," Ivar said and laid a reassuring hand on Dominic's shoulder.

For the next two days, Ivar rested, exerting himself only to strengthen the power of the Guardians' vestments, staves, and knives, and to seal the doors of the fortress. He added a second spell to strengthen the ancient fortress doors, hoping that, should the locking spell that surrounded the fortress be broken, the doors would provide time to cast another.

On the night of the full moon, a mist surrounded the fortress, pressing against the stone wall, rising above it, enclosing the cliffs above and below the road in silver isolation. As the four remaining Guardians assembled in the stony courtyard, Ivar stood in the tower on the platform from which Leith had once looked out at Tepest and G'Henna. He wore one of the Guardians' gray cloaks and carried his staff and the materials he would need for the spells he had learned. As he waited, he thought of the bodies of Morgoth's dead, their blue skin, their frozen flesh. What would he face tonight? How long before his adversary drained his life as well?

The Guardians had begun their chant before the still-quiet shrine. They seemed oblivious to the profound silence that surrounded the fortress, like a deadly storm waiting to break. The incessant winter wind had ceased to blow, and moans that normally came from the fortress walls had ceased as well. The glowing mist thickened against the cliffs. Ivar gazed across the narrow, moonlit

ribbon of a road, and he saw the werewolves run, silent and graceful, toward them.

Kezi and his daughter had spoken of three wolves. This time there
were four. And Jonathan was among them. Some sorcery allowed
him to pace them, his grace and speed equal to the pack's. Tendrils
of mist floated above them, moving as they moved.

Ivar had so little time! He rushed to the courtyard and stood just
behind the barred doors of the fortress. He fingered the wide belt he
wore. Hanging from it was a length of rope, a glass rod encased in
fur, a pouch of sulphur, another of phosphorus, and a white feather.
The spells he had memorized seemed weak and too few. He was
no match, even for the boy. His heart beat faster. He pulled back
the hood of his cloak and raised his staff, preparing a valiant stand
before he died.

He glanced at the four monks standing behind him, their backs
to him, their attention resolutely fixed on the shrine. Mattas led
this hour of the chant. His outstretched arms trembled. His voice
seemed far softer than Ivar had ever heard it. The responses of the
others were equally subdued.

Something sensed their fear and doubt, and magnified it.
Knowing the doubt was being forced on him by his adversary, Ivar
struggled to shake it off. He stood straighter, and his resolve deepened as he reminded himself of who he was.

The attack came in a sudden burst of power, a force felt rather
than heard, rolling like silent thunder across the walls of stone and
mist. A booming pounded the fortress doors once, then again,
steady as a confident heartbeat. The wood bowed inward with the
force of each pulse and the power of the creature directing it. Ivar
cast a spell, strengthening the ancient wood. Only then did he sense
a second power working to undo the wards on the shrine. He needed
Dominic's help.

As he turned to summon him, the cloth woke. Never had the creatures on it been so furious, so full of hope. They beat at the doors and the stone walls until the entire shrine shook. The doors held, bound by the force of the Guardians' faith and their concentration, a force somehow increased rather than diminished from the attack.

So many years of vigilance prepared them for this night. Ivar tried to emulate their confidence amid the palpable booms on the door, the frenzied screams of the dark souls imprisoned in the shrine. He thought of the *were*, the undead, the human thieves and rogues and murderers that dwelt in the half-life of the cloth. Then he thought of Leith. Could others like her be trapped, impotent islands of goodness surrounded by evil? He felt a stab of pity for her and for her son and what fate had done to both of them.

The first attack ended with the same speed with which it began. The despair lifted. The booming ceased, the creatures in the shrine fell silent, but the Guardians didn't relax. Instead they waited, more anxious in the quiet than in the assault, awaiting the next display of Morgoth's terrible power.

This time the attack was a silent one. Ivar felt a shift in the spell sealing the walls, and a wave of fire broke over the fortress. Though the spell kept the flames arched well above them, the heat made Ivar's skin tingle, made concentration difficult. The fire descended, and the protective force shifted once again. The door bowed inward, but this time no force beat against it. Instead, a relentless, steady pressure distorted it. Wood began to splinter near the center. In another a moment the ancient doors would burst.

Ivar responded with a magic thrust of his own that forced the fortress doors to straighten. Instantaneously, the pressure outside vanished. The doors exploded outward. One of the werewolves howled with pain as the flames receded.

Though the spell still held the attackers at bay, Ivar now saw them for the first time. The silvery man had features much like Jonathan's, though more mature. He exuded a harsh, overwhelming confidence as he stared down the weary Ivar. Stiffening his lip, Ivar wiped his mind of doubt and concentrated on the words and gestures of protection.

Behind him, the Guardians continued their chant. In front of him, Morgoth began his own. With each word the mist surrounding the walls pulsated.

Ivar hadn't even a sliver of Morgoth's power. Until the wards on the fortress walls were broken, any words against the silver man wouldn't cross the barrier and reach him. Ivar therefore began the words of a spell to send bolts of flame against his enemy, then waited for the proper moment to finish it.

It would be soon. The wards were breaking. The forms of the wolves and men looked distorted, as if they stood behind a shifting wall of water. Tendrils of Morgoth's silver mist oozed through cracks in the magical barrier.

The gap at the ruined doors widened, and Ivar saw with horror that Morgoth had pulled Jonathan in front of him, and thrust the boy forward. Ivar's intent faltered; he loved Jonathan, even now. If his first spell killed the youth, how could goodness prevail?

Ivar cut off the words that would end his apprentice's life and unhooked the rope from his belt, beginning a chant to close the gap. In that moment the souls in the shrine attacked once more, their fury deadlier than before. Peto cried out; Mattas faltered over the words. Ivar whirled and saw the shaking shrine doors. "Hold!" he ordered and pulled the rope tight, using the incantation to lock the shrine instead of the fortress doors.

He spun back around. The werewolves were advancing through the widening gap. Ivar rubbed the glass rod against the fur of its pouch and pointed a finger at the nearest werewolf. Lightning streamed from his hand, bright and glowing as quicksilver. Held in the white-hot cords, the creature howled, shifted, screamed. Another bolt followed, catching the second wolf as it entered the fortress. The foul smell of singed fur and flesh filled the courtyard. The third wolf leaped past Ivar, breaking into the Guardians' circle. His massive jaws ripped at Hektor's arms. Peto turned, grappling for the beast's muzzle. It released Hektor and tore off one of Peto's hands. Caught in the struggle, Mattas fell backward against the wall of the shrine.

With the shrine secure for the moment under Ivar's spell, Dominic abandoned the chant and thrust himself between the werewolf and Mattas. With his amulet held in one hand, his other outstretched toward the werewolf, he uttered a single command, "Go!"

The lycanthrope howled and paused, but the priest's powerful command couldn't override the creature's fear of the new master blocking the gate. His head and tail low with despair, he closed in on Dominic.

Dominic expected a speedy attack. Instead the werebeast moved slowly, as if suddenly drained of strength. Dominic took the advantage. Using his silver-tipped staff like a lance, he stabbed the animal in the breastbone and impaled him.

The fourth and largest of the werewolves paced the fortress. The blood-lust, too long denied, was strong in him and made even stronger by the power of his new master. Nonetheless, he didn't attack until Morgoth commanded him to do so. Confused, enraged, he lunged for Ivar's throat.

Ivar expected the attack. Lightning had begun moving from his fingers, but Jon cried out with a single word, "No!" He gestured, and a magical wall came down between Ivar and the werewolf. The force of the wall stunned the werebeast, and sent Ivar reeling back against the stone side of the shrine. Regaining his feet, Ivar looked more closely at the beast. As the spell wall dissolved, he knelt beside the beast and called out "Andor." The wolf form slowly altered. "Andor," he repeated more gently, and the wounded man relaxed in his arms.

Ivar pulled Andor close to the doors of the shrine where the Guardians had taken refuge within the protection of his spell. His eyes scanned the fortress, looking for Jonathan. The boy had fled and, as Ivar focused on Morgoth, the creature's form spread, stretched and dissolved away. As it did, the mist closed around the fortress, sealing the Guardians inside.

Blood covered the fortress ground. The smell of blood and burning lay heavy in the air. The battle had been won, but at a terrible price. Peto was near death, Mattas unconscious and barely breathing, Hektor pale from blood loss. Only one Guardian was untouched, and the night had hardly begun. Uncertain if this were merely a lull or the end of the battle, Ivar tended to the Guardians' wounds while Dominic stood alone in front of the shrine, reciting the prayers he knew so well. They stayed that way until dawn. Dominic's chanting and the occasional whimper of the wounded were the only sounds in the night.

At dawn, Dominic and Ivar carried the wounded into the dining hall, laying them close to the fire. Peto and Mattas were still unconscious, Hektor in a great deal of pain. Dominic was exhausted, but he stayed with Ivar and helped tend the others. When they'd done what they could, the two men listened as Andor described how he had fallen under Morgoth's power.

Ivar had never seen Andor so defeated, so wracked with guilt. Tears ran down his face; his hands shook as he described how Maeve had tricked him on the first night, how in the nights that followed he had been called unwillingly from his bed to serve the Silverlord. "Once I removed the amulet, Morgoth owned my soul. Even when

I wore the amulet, it didn't give me the strength it once did. The hunger wouldn't relent."

"Why didn't you tell me?" Ivar asked.

"I should've been stronger. I should have been able to resist his power on my own."

"Resist that thing?" Ivar asked gently.

"The first night that I hunted in wolf form, we killed only goblins. It seemed to me then that Maeve was lonely and that my change served only her needs, her vanity and nothing else." Andor paused, then added bitterly, "Later, when it was too late, I knew the truth." He looked at the men sitting beside him—Dominic with a wooden expression masking his grief; Ivar, weary and resigned to fighting on. "I had a part in the killing," Andor said. "I want to stay with you. To help you as long as you need me."

"Come with me," Dominic said and led Andor across the dawn-lit courtyard to the now-silent shrine. Ivar had already lifted the spell that held the doors. Dominic threw them open and walked inside. Andor, recalling the night's horrors, hung back as Dominic dusted the cloth over the floor, claiming the shells of those who had tried to escape its hold. "Come inside," Dominic told him when the cloth hung on the wall once more.

Andor took a reluctant step forward, but at the portal, he hesitated. Drawing a deep breath, he walked inside. Only after he entered did Dominic hold out his arms and draw Andor into them. "Welcome, Brother," he said, his tears of joy moistening Andor's shoulder.

Dominic's words were muffled, absorbed by the evil trapped there. Andor looked once at the cloth and went outside at a pace just shy of a run. Only when the morning sun beat down on him again did he understand why he had bolted. In all the time he had been in the shrine, he hadn't taken a single breath.

Jonathan knew his shift in allegiance endangered them all, but Sondra most of all. He entered Linde through his cave and hid in Ivar's cavern until the inn was quiet. He collected the spellbooks, and a bit of money. It was all he really needed, he thought, as he sat and rememorized the spells from earlier that night. When the inn had emptied and everyone had gone to bed, he climbed the stairs to Sondra's room.

A lit candle stood beside her bed. Though she slept, her hands were folded as if she had been praying, and tears wet the corners of her eyes. He'd left her with so many questions, been gone for so many days without word. How could he expect her to trust him now?

Nonetheless, he woke her, slowly so she wouldn't cry out. As soon as she saw him, her arms circled his neck. He pushed her gently away, but took her hand, refusing to let her go as they sat together. Her love astonished him as she sat, listening to his account of everything that had happened since he freed his father from the shrine. He left out only Leo's murder. That was a guilt he'd carry privately within him forever.

"I want you to leave here with me," he said when he had finished.

"Now? The road is being watched. We'll have to travel through the woods."

She feared the dark, he knew, and the things that walked in the dark. "I'm more than able to defend us," he said.

"I know. I helped put out your fires," she replied and dressed quickly. Following him down the stairs, she paused in the kitchen to steal a knife and a second bag of the inn's coins, then followed him into the night.

She gripped his hand, holding it tightly in fear. They waited until the moon was hidden by one of the few clouds in the sky, then crossed the Timori Road. They traveled past locked barns and glittering, ice-coated fields. If they kept a quick pace, they would likely reach Viktal by midday. Once there, Jon hoped they would be safe. The town was large, and near the forest where the hags lived. His father wouldn't be foolish enough to seek him so close to their lair.

On the edge of the forest, he saw the first faint tendrils of silver mist, reaching like ghostly fingers through the bare trees. He pushed Sondra behind him and slowly retreated. The mist followed, keeping its distance, driving them back toward town. "Why doesn't he attack?" Sondra asked in a tense whisper.

Jon shook his head. He had no answer until they reached the road. As their shadows crossed it, they heard the sound of flint being struck. Torches suddenly flared, blinding his eyes. He heard voices, men rushing toward them, their boots crunching on the ice-coated snow. "Run before they see you!" Jon told Sondra.

"Never!" Sondra cried and moved beside him, her knife gripped in her hand.

The men carried ropes and a cage. Though Jonathan had the power to destroy them, he wouldn't use it. He'd had enough of burning and death.

"Protect yourself," Sondra cried, holding her knife in front of her.

There was still a way out for both of them. Jon began the same incantation he had used to hold Andor and Ivar apart. Once he'd finished it, they could run for the trees. Midway through the casting, though, the mist thickened and encircled him. He cried out, not in pain but in amazement; Morgoth's frozen touch stole the words to his spells. "I take back the power I have given you," Morgoth's voice whispered. The bundle of spellbooks was ripped from Jon's belt and disappeared into the glowing fog.

Jonathan reached for his knife. Before he could raise it, the men were on him. He fought fiercely, wounding two before, by weight alone, they brought him down.

Once subdued, Jon didn't struggle. Nonetheless, they beat him to near senselessness before they tied him and wedged his body into the goblin-size cage. Only when he was securely held did one of the men finally ask, "Are you the one who did the killing?"

"I was responsible," Jon answered and shut his eyes. He knew what they planned to do to him. It was less than he deserved.

Dirca worked alone through the evening, waiting for Andor and Ivar to return. At last, she slammed the doors to the dining hall, dropped into a seat beside the huge wooden table in the kitchen, and tried to plan how she could face tomorrow and the days to come. Not so long ago, she had been a carefree, generous woman. Now she was a bitter, despairing crone.

Perhaps it was because she had little control over anything else. Andor and Ivar had gone. Sondra, locked in a room upstairs, was half insane with grief. And Jon, the only one she truly cared for, was to be executed. Dirca saw no way to save him; judging from the story he'd told, he saw no way either.

And what would become of her? She couldn't manage the inn alone. She was old, barren, joyless. Aside from her wealth, who would want her now?

The latch on the kitchen shutters rattled. As she refastened it, she thought she saw a pale shape flickering in the dark moon-shadows. Through the wind that cracked the frozen trees, she heard a man call her—a sound sharp and empty, a hopeless cry for help.

"Dirrrrrca."

The sound tugged at her will. She began walking to the outer door, where she saw her reflection in one of the glass cupboard doors. She turned and backed slowly toward the barred doors, toward the hall where the men were assembled.

"Dirrrrrca."

He could see her! Even through the walls, he could see her! She blew out the candles and stood in the center of the room, frightened, but somehow charmed by the voice.

"Dirrrrrca."

The darkness didn't hide her. Instead, it magnified the sound of her name, the painful need in his voice. Dirca moved slowly through the darkness to the door and pulled it open. A rush of cold air flowed past her, bringing with it a heaviness, a promise of death.

A glowing figure waiting there.

"Dirca." The man smiled, and stepped inside.

She moved back. He followed, saying in a voice so soft he hardly seemed to speak at all, "I can give you everything you desire. All you need do is promise to serve me, to do whatever I ask."

"Everything?" She looked into his eyes, and doubt vanished.

"Even Vistani curses are simple to undo," he said and smiled. When he did, he looked much like Jon, but stronger and more beautiful. She tilted her head up and blinked coyly as he pulled her body against his. He pressed his lips against hers, sucking her breath in, pushing his own into her.

What was he doing! It seemed to Dirca that his breath filled her body with the promise of life. She went limp, letting his arms support her, letting him control her as no man ever had. When he finally released her and began to give her instructions for the following night, she didn't protest. She had never felt more beautiful, less alone. When he left her, the feeling remained, as real as the promise he had made to her.

On the table beside her, he left a tiny vial of clear thin liquid. She hid it in the rear of the cupboard to wait until tomorrow evening. Now it was nearly dawn. Time to sleep. She laughed as she climbed the stairs, hoping that she would dream of him.

The men put Jonathan in the same small barn where they had kept the beasties for sacrifice. His cage was so small he was forced to lie sideways with his knees pressed against his chest, his hands chained. Though he was guarded, no one approached him. They feared him, he thought, and even now their fear gave him a surge of pleasure that sickened him. In two nights he would be burned. It was better that way.

Maeve came to see him soon after he was taken. He heard her outside, imperiously ordering the guards to leave so she could talk to him in private. He'd expected her visit; now that she had achieved her triumph, she would naturally gloat.

"A beautiful fox, you called me," she purred from the darkness outside. "Am I not beautiful still?"

Maeve stepped into the lamplight. She had melted some of her jewelry to create a golden mask studded with lapis and polished gems, a mask that hid the top half of her face. Her hands were encased in black-tooled leather, with only the delicate fingertips and brightly painted nails exposed. They seemed as graceful as ever, but he detected the lumps, molded flat by the tightly fitting leather. She wore flowing and colorful clothes, with a high neck and long sleeves. Jewels hung over the fabric, laying unevenly over the shoulder that had been stabbed.

"Does the town pity you?" he asked.

"Yes. But your death will prove my faithfulness to the hags, and they will lift my curse. I'm sure of it."

"Then you will go on providing sacrifices to them?"

She frowned, wondering no doubt how he knew the truth about her. But she didn't ask. Instead, she turned to a new taunt. "Perhaps I'll go to Sondra and offer to free you if she will come and stay with me, love me as your mother did, change as your mother did." She laughed at his silent fury, then added, "Tell the town what you wish. The fools will never believe you."

He enjoyed the small victory he received from the uneasiness in her voice. As he watched her go, it seemed her legs had become uneven, her posture slouched and stiff.

seventeen

DURING the struggle on the road, Sondra had wounded two of the men before they wrenched the knife from her hand and dragged her, screaming every curse she could recall, back to Linde. Once she was locked in a room in the inn, with a guard sitting outside her door, she lay across the bed, silent at last, mourning everything that had been lost. In spite of her grief, she wouldn't admit defeat. As long as Jonathan still lived, there was hope.

In the evening Dirca brought her a sumptuous meal—leek soup, some of the smoked duck they had been saving for what should have been a midwinter feast to celebrate her marriage, sweet carrots, and fresh rolls. Most precious of all was the small carafe of cloudberry wine, enough for two glasses. The meat had been cut, the rolls already spread with butter and honey. The only utensil on her tray was a large soup spoon. "They don't trust me, do they?" she asked.

"You fought as best you could," Dirca told her in a voice soothing, gentle, unlike any tone she had ever used with Sondra before. "You've had a tragic day. I know you've never liked the taste of wine, but drink it anyway. It will dull the pain and help you rest."

Sondra reached for her aunt's hand, nearly upsetting the tray in an effort to take it. Dirca grabbed the carafe, holding it steady.

"Dirca! Isn't there any way you can help me leave here? Perhaps together . . ."

"I'll try to think of one, child."

"Oh, please! We must do something. We both love him so much!"

"Aye, we do," Dirca agreed.

Sondra poured a glass of the wine and sipped it. "Odd how much better it tastes than before," she said.

"I'll come back for the tray. Perhaps by then one of us will have devised some escape," Dirca responded and left without saying good-night.

As soon as Dirca had gone, Sondra drank all the water in the pitcher beside her bed and doubled over her chamber pot with her fingers down her throat, heaving long after her stomach was empty.

She wouldn't have tasted the poison in the wine if she hadn't noticed the change in her aunt when she mentioned Jon—a coldness in Dirca's tone, a resolve in her expression that reminded Sondra of how Mishya looked in the days before he died, the way Andor seemed before he vanished. The creature—Jon's father, Sondra reminded herself—had awakened some evil in her aunt as well.

A flash of insight told her exactly what her aunt had planned, and what she must do now. She tiptoed to the door and listened, hearing only the harsh breathing of the man sitting in the hall. She knocked on the door.

"Stand away!" the man called. When she replied from the opposite side of the room, he slid back the bolt and came inside. "What is it?" he grumbled.

"The wine. I've never liked the taste, and in the open carafe it'll spoil by morning. Would you like it?"

"Trying to bribe me, eh?"

"I couldn't help him even if I were free."

He nodded. "That's the best way to think, girl. There's three men guarding your lover night and day and nothing you can do about it."

She looked sad. He patted her arm as he took the glass and carafe. "There's nothing I can do either," he said, "except to say a prayer that the gods are kinder to him than the village elders have been."

"Thank you," she said and looked at her feet, dabbing her eyes with her napkin.

After he had locked her in once more, she sat on the floor with her head resting on the door, listening to his breathing slow to the pace of sleep. The snores grew softer, ever softer until they abruptly stopped.

She picked up her spoon; the wooden shutters were soft enough that the hinges could be easily removed. With no guard to hear her, she set to work. At last, one of the shutters was free.

She opened them only a little way and looked out on the night. Torches were burning at the center of the festival ground. There, men worked to enlarge the fire pit and clear away the ice-coated snow for a place to dance. How many would sing the festival songs, she wondered? How many would dance? The town was like a family, and many villagers had been Jon's friends. How would they feel when they burned Jon, slowly as they had the goblin? Would they believe his pain and screams would please the resting earth? Morgoth would delight in what they felt.

The covered porch was beneath her, its sloped roof coated with ice. Once she was out the window, her feet would dangle over the edge. An uncontrolled fall would be dangerous, but she had nothing from which to fashion a rope. They hadn't even given her a blanket, and she certainly needed her clothes. Wedging the spoon between the shutters to hold them closed, she went to her straw mattress. With only her teeth for a tool, she gnawed a hole in the ticking so she could rip the heavy fabric into strips of cloth. Then, as silently as she could, she slid the bed beneath the window.

It took hours for the men outside to finish their work and leave. The town lay silent beneath its shroud of snow when Sondra finally attempted her escape.

The ice broke beneath her feet, slipping off the roof in a single sheet that made a dull sound as it struck the snow. Icicles followed. Most fell into the snowbank, but some knocked against the carved porch rail, loud as the rapping of an insistent guest. It seemed useless to be quiet—far better to be quick—and, drawing up the slack, Sondra estimated the distance, gripped the rope, and let her body slide over the edge. The rotted ticking broke under her weight, and she fell hard into the snowdrift. The sharp end of an icicle stabbed into her thigh. She stifled a scream as she pulled at it, and it broke off in her hand. The shards inside the wound would melt from the heat of her body soon enough.

She had done it, she was free!

Keeping close to the ground, she began moving toward the side of the inn. The front door opened and two men came out, their torches held high to light their way home. The ragged end of the broken rope swayed in the wind. The icicles and her footsteps were plain in the snow. One of them paused and pointed at the rope. As Sondra ran for the rear of the inn, their cries of alarm echoed with the clanging bell in the town square. Soon the entire village would be searching for her.

Sondra's leg throbbed. She knew she could never outrun the men. Her only hope was that someone had left the inn's rear door open and that the kitchen was empty. She cut to the well-packed path that led to the door, slipped inside, and locked it. Wiping the water from her feet with her cloak, she moved through the dark kitchen to the hidden doorway to Ivar's cavern.

The only light in the passage came from a few narrow cracks in the dining hall wall. Once the curved staircase began, there was only darkness rising to meet her. With her back against the stone wall, Sondra descended—good leg first, wounded second. She had intended to stop at the first turn and sit and wait for the men to give up their hunt when she sensed someone following her—someone who knew the way as well as she. There was a creak on a stair above her, the nearly inaudible sound of stealthy, even breathing.

"Who's there?" she whispered. No reply.

If there was to be a struggle, Sondra wanted it to be well out of earshot of the men in the rooms above her. She went down another turn. Without pausing in her nearly silent descent, she twisted her cape into a thick spiral of cloth, laid it across the stair behind her and went on. . . . one step. Another. Another . . .

Behind her, a woman cried out and fell. Before Sondra could get a firm hold on the stone wall, a body slammed against her, bringing her down. They slid together down the steps to the next wide landing.

"Dirca, is that you?" Sondra whispered. The only reply was a shift in the air as a hand brushed against her hair, metal glancing off the stone wall beside her head. Sondra kicked her attacker away, and, rolling onto her side, she slid farther down the stairs.

Sondra couldn't hide her labored breaths any longer, but neither could her attacker. She couldn't see who pursued her, but was also protected by the utter darkness. Sondra quickened her pace down the stairs until she reached a wide step that sided a sheer drop to the cavern below. With her back against the opposite wall, her knees against her chest, she listened to the creak of the stairs. Fabric brushed her bare legs, and a knife blade cut her calf. She kicked out, shoving her attacker sideways over the edge.

It wasn't a lethal fall, though from that height it might have been.

When Sondra reached the bottom of the stairs and lit a torch, she saw Dirca lying dazed on the stones, her knife well out of reach. Sondra placed the blade in her belt and, retrieving her cloak from the stairs, wet the hem in the pitcher of water Ivar kept on hand. She returned and dabbed at the wound on her aunt's head.

When Dirca's eyes finally opened, she didn't recognize where she was until she saw Sondra kneeling above her. She tried to rise, moaned, and lay still.

"You are my mother's sister. We are both alone," Sondra said, the simple words asking all the questions she had no time for.

"I was forced to kill my infants," Dirca responded, her words broken by the pain. "I should have loved you like . . . the daughter I could never have. . . . Instead I let bitterness grow until I tried to kill you . . ."

"Shhh. Morgoth did this to you. Now, we must hide until the men stop their search, then we'll save Jon."

"Child, you don't understand. Morgoth wanted you alive. He intended the poison for the guard, but I gave it to you instead. He wanted me to bring you here. I disobeyed. Now he'll come for me and for you."

"Then we'll leave here together. If we're caught, we'll tell the village elders everything we know."

"They won't believe us."

"We can try. Can you walk?"

Dirca tried to sit up, but cried out and lay still. "I can't move my legs!" she said.

"Then I'll go and bring the men here."

"Morgoth's coming. I can sense him. Listen. Feel." Sondra heard nothing. The sudden sense of dread she felt seemed only an echo of her aunt's fear until it began to grow, taking on a life of its own within her. She sucked in her breath and looked down at her aunt.

"Even if I survive, I won't live long like this. I don't want to sit and helplessly wait for him to come. You don't know what he's like, child. What he'll do to me. If you care for me at all, you will—" Dirca began, her breathing ragged from terror and agony.

" . . . do what must be done," Sondra finished for her.

As Sondra lifted the knife and prepared the quick, killing stab to the throat, Dirca whispered, "I'm sorry."

"Someday," Sondra replied. But before her blade could strike, the air around them shimmered. Something lifted the knife from her hands and threw her away from her aunt. An intense, sudden cold flowed through Sondra's body until she was certain it would freeze her heart.

"Morgoth!" Sondra said in a whisper. His body formed before her. His robe was white, loose and flowing. The front was open, showing his chest, the black iron amulet he wore. It was shaped like a thin skull, and the yellow gems in its sockets seemed to stare at her. Morgoth's silver hair and pale skin glowed with their own cold light and his eyes glittered with the flame of the torch. The resemblance between him and Jonathan was strong. As he smiled and called her name, Sondra longed to go to him. Instead, she skittered away toward the stairs.

"Morgoth." Dirca echoed her niece's cry. She screamed as his arms circled her waist, lifting her from the floor with brutal force.

"You disobeyed me."

"Let Sondra go, Morgoth. The girl is useless to you."

"Silence! She is the betrothed of my son!"

"You can have another son. You said as much. You promised me your child."

A hand crushed Dirca's spine, and her legs danced in agony. She opened her mouth to scream, but he cut off the sound with his lips. Though he kissed Dirca as he had before, this time he inhaled her life with slow, deliberate cruelty. When she lay limp in his arms, he let her fall and straddled her, his hands moving over her body, drawing every spark of heat from it.

Morgoth lifted his head and looked at Sondra. His expression seemed happy, his need sated. "Daughter," he said and held out a hand. "Come with me."

Sondra shook her head and tried to call for help, but a muttered word and wave of his hand silenced her voice. Morgoth's eyes, bright like his son's, narrowed. "I have been kind for his sake. Now come." As he reached for her, she kicked the side of his face and heard him grunt. The sound told her that he was real, and he could feel pain. Heartened, she kicked and clawed as he pulled her toward him. With one swift fist he knocked her unconscious.

She didn't feel him drag her, transformed, over the sharp granite of the path through Ivar's cavern, through the low passage to his milky-white home where the glowing lights danced. When she opened her eyes again, Morgoth sat on a ledge beside the lake, and she lay on her back over his knees. He was bathing her wounded leg and arms with the water, dabbing at the blood with strips he had torn from her now-ragged cloak.

He saw that she was awake and buried his hand in her dark hair, holding her head tightly, forcing her to look at him. "You were going to the Guardians, weren't you? Did you think those tired old men would do anything to free my son?"

She said nothing. She didn't know.

"When the time comes, I will be the one to rescue him. Until then, you will stay with me. As my son told me, you are beautiful, and you carry the future within your body. Your son will have great power."

"Your grandson?" she managed to ask.

He didn't answer, only looked at her with his pale, metallic eyes.

She thought of Jon's mother and how he had been conceived, and she felt suddenly cold.

He guessed her thoughts. His smile held no reassurance.

The day after Jonathan was captured, the guards were doubled around the barn. He sensed renewed fear in their faces, doubt in the hushed way they spoke to one another, pity in their eyes.

Morgoth, his father, had struck again.

One of his guards spoke of a dark force that Jon could call on to rescue him. The other two said the disappearances meant that two more lives had been taken by the monster—possibly even the creature Jon had described.

"Who is gone?" he asked.

"Sondra and Dirca, both vanished from the inn."

Jon turned his face to the ground to hide the grief he didn't dare reveal. "I'm responsible," he mumbled.

Someone reached a hand through the bars, grabbing his hair, forcing him to look at them. "See his tears," the man said gruffly. "You know he loved her. That thing is still out there just like he said, I tell you, out there and waiting to claim another of us."

"Even if the boy is the killer, burning him won't end it. Evil lives on," someone else commented.

"Not after it's reduced to ashes," a third man said. "Don't look so sorry for him. I've seen tears like this before. Tears of guilt, they are."

"Maeve's the only witness. I don't trust her."

"What of Kezi's girl? She spoke of silver fur, a silver mist. Look at his eyes and tell me it wasn't him."

The debate continued among the guards. But their doubts wouldn't stop the ceremony—not when someone else would have to be sacrificed in his place.

Through the long final day before the celebration, the guards left the outer doors open so Jon could watch the preparations—the tables arranged for the supper, the wood and dung chips laid for the cooking fire, a stack of carefully seasoned split logs waiting for the climactic final burn. Jonathan dug his fingers through the open bars beneath him, burying them deep in the soft straw and earth of the barn and prayed that his father wouldn't come for him tonight. If he did, surely everyone was doomed, himself most of all.

As the sun began to set, a hushed expectation filled the valley, a mood more suited to a sultry summer afternoon than the frozen air of winter. By dark, it reached such intensity that Jon became convinced the entire town must have already been ensorceled. They gave no indication that they sensed it, that they were already trapped in the eye of a deadly storm.

As he lay in his cage listening to the sounds of music and revelry, he thought of the autumn festival and Sondra. How full of hope he had been; how invincible. Now, whether he lived or died made little difference to those he loved. Sondra was undoubtedly dead, destroyed by his father. Ivar and the remaining Guardians would die soon. For all their fates, he was indeed responsible.

The guards were relieved by others midway through the night so that all would have a chance to attend the festival. As soon as the new ones took their place, he heard a girl laughing outside, saw her silhouette move between the door and the torches, kissing each guard in turn before slipping inside.

The girl stepped sideways out of the light and pulled the hood off her face. Jon saw that she was Willa, one of Sondra's friends—a girl to be married tonight. She stood anxiously for a moment, waiting for him to speak. When he didn't, Willa called his name, apologizing if she had awakened him. She spoke quickly, hardly pausing to breathe. "We . . . some of the other girls and I . . . we remember how you saved Sondra from the beasties. We know you wouldn't hurt her. We don't think you killed anyone. We wanted you to have this." She drew a wineskin from beneath her cape and held it up. "The wine is from the festival. We mixed a potion in it. Drink a little and you won't feel the pain. Drink it all and you'll die now."

When he didn't answer, she placed the skin inside the bars, in a place where he could reach it with his mouth. "You can decide later," she said. "We wanted you to know some of us don't agree with the elders."

Willa looked away from him in the direction of the light. He was surprised by the bitterness in her tone, the tears in her eyes. For the first time, he saw a tragedy that he could prevent. "Don't stay and watch the burning," he said. "Leave before the ceremony. Take anyone that's willing to go." He paused to give a silent apology to Ivar for breaking their pact, and told the girl of the secret passage, the spiral staircase, the cavern beneath the inn. It was hardly a safe place, joined to Morgoth's lair, but he could think of no other. "Go to the base of the stairs and hide until morning. The destruction that's coming may not find you there."

The festival music had stopped, replaced by the insistent pounding of a drum. "They're calling the couples for the betrothal ceremony. I must go before someone sees me." Willa started for the door.

"Wait! You must believe me!"

"I do. Once the weddings are over, I'll go and take whoever I can." She moved back to his cage, stooped over it and brushed the side of his face with her fingertips before she left him.

The elder shouted out the words to the marriage ceremony so all could hear. As Jon watched the couples step forward for the formal bonding, he thought of Sondra. Could his father have let her live?

The thought held more horror than her death. He prayed for the passage of her soul to a happier place and the mercy of the fates that he might join her.

The wineskin had begun to leak on his arm. The cloying scent of the wine mixed with the sharper odor of the poison. A painless death tempted him. He shifted his weight as quickly as he could and watched the wineskin fall well out of reach. His time wasn't over, not yet. When it was, he should die by fire.

The ceremony ended and the singing began once more, but the crowd didn't join in with the same exuberance as at the harvest festival. Terror gnawed at their strength, and the night's killing unnerved them.

In spite of the agony in his back, Jon forced himself into an even tighter ball and twisted his head sideways. In that position, he could see the path that led to the inn, count the ones who were leaving; twelve, hardly enough to atone for his wrongs. He strained, hoping to see more, but the huge drums began their steady booming and the men came for him.

They carried the cage out as Maeve chanted and the villagers offered their guilty response. "To the spirit of our land, we give this sacrifice. May his pain and blood make the winter short, make the spring rain plentiful, make the new seed sprout."

Tonight Maeve didn't wear the ceremonial skirts with their bright ribbon trim. Instead she kept her legs covered with flowing pantaloons, tucked into high leather boots. The tiny cymbals on her fingers were muted by the leather of her gloves, making a sound as uneasy as the whispered chant of the crowd. The mask she wore now covered her entire face. Crystals lay like tears in the corners of the eye holes, and the lips curved upward in a perpetual knowing smile. Feathers had been attached to the top and sides, and what hair still fell over her shoulders was thin—drab gray rather than violet-black. Her voice, though beautiful, was strained.

The fire was no larger than the one they had used to burn the goblin. They wouldn't admit their doubt by showing mercy, a point that became all too clear to Jonathan as they lifted the cage well above the hungry flames, then slowly began to lower it.

He wouldn't struggle, wouldn't give them or the land the satisfaction of his screams. But, as the flames brushed his side, the agony flowed through him, a steady searing pain that throbbed in time to the pounding of his heart. For the moment he could endure it in silence. But the moment, like his resolve, would pass. As he raised his head, seeking one final breath of clear air, he saw the silver mist swirling above him. It coalesced for a moment into the face of Sondra, her expression frozen in fear and awe.

"She lives," Jon whispered through clenched teeth.

"She lives," his father replied.

Jonathan beat his body against the bars of his cage and screamed her name.

The mist folded in upon itself, fell into the space between Maeve and the cage, and reshaped into the form of Morgoth. He was dressed in white flowing robes, his skin as smooth as well-worked metal. His thin hair framed a face whose features were given form to meet each person's desires. Some saw Morgoth as male, others as female, but each saw a different face. As the people stopped their chanting, as Maeve began to turn to see what had distracted them, Morgoth said a single, damning word in a loud voice.

"Vixen."

A shudder passed through Maeve. She cried out in rage, in pain. An instant later, she ripped the mask from her face and the gloves from her hands, revealing the hideousness of her curse. The crowd recoiled from her thickened, yellow skin, her oozing sores, her swollen slash of a mouth, her bony, twisted fingers. Morgoth's word overpowered her. The change began.

The skin on her face smoothed, and for a moment all her perfect beauty returned. An instant later, her nose and mouth began to lengthen, her teeth and claws to grow. As she pulled the clothes from her body, fine silver hair sprouted on it, rippling in silver waves as it grew and covered her.

From her place near the front of the crowd, Kezi's daughter screamed and pointed at Maeve. Kezi pushed the girl behind him. He ripped Ivar's amulet from his neck and lunged forward, intending to tear the vixen apart. Other men followed his lead, and Maeve, betrayed and outnumbered, bounded from the circle and disappeared into the black night. As the others stood, stunned by the sudden revelation, Kezi tore at his clothes and began his own lycanthropic transformation. He fell to all fours and pursued.

As soon as Maeve had begun to change, the men holding Jon's cage tried to move it from the fire, but all their strength couldn't budge it. They released the hot bars, but it didn't fall. They took branches to scatter the fire from beneath it, but some force, felt rather than seen, surrounded the pit and repelled their jabs. Panicked, they bolted from the open circle to the dubious protection of the crowd.

With only himself and Jon left in the ceremonial circle, Morgoth turned toward his son, hanging in agony above the flames. "You may choose to die if you wish, but then I will take your beloved and use her as I did your mother. I will create another son."

Though waves of heat washed over him, though his body was in agony, Jon didn't reply.

"Your death will prevent nothing. I will annihilate this town, the cloth, the old men who raised you. With or without you, my legions will be freed."

The flames rose higher around him. Jonathan had never imagined such pain. Yet his flesh blistered no further, his hair didn't ignite. His father was begging him to live, to serve him willingly. If Jon didn't, some shell of what he had once been would continue on—drained of will and sanity, possessing only hollow power and slavish obedience.

"I do what I must," Morgoth told him. "You do what you must. If you choose to be my ally, show me you are still my son. Use your power. free yourself."

With his words, the flames rose, circling Jon's wrists. The chains melted. His hands were free. He felt the spells return to his mind, felt the power coursing through him, bringing with it the old hunger.

"Show me!"

Ivar and Andor were with the Guardians. Sondra was trapped. Would Morgoth's legions share his terrible desires? Would they drain the town for sustenance? Jon looked through the rising flames directly into his father's eyes. He recited the incantation that diminished the flames, another spell that concentrated the heat on melting the lock. Morgoth released his hold on the cage and lowered it to the ground. Jon pushed it open and stretched his body on the frozen earth. Never had cold felt so magnificently soothing before.

"Vengeance," Morgoth whispered.

Jon looked up. In spite of his display of power, the townsfolk had retained the ceremonial circle, their expressions joyous, expectant. Morgoth moved to the edge of the crowd. A mother smiled and held out her infant as if Morgoth were a priest who might bless it.

He touched the babe's forehead. The child shuddered and died without a whimper, laying frozen in its mother's arms. The woman looked from her dead child to Morgoth. He kissed her forehead, and she died as quickly as her child had, hitting the ground so hard that Jon heard her frozen flesh crack. Though they had watched the death, the townsfolk didn't move.

After the first death, Morgoth killed quickly, claiming one enraptured victim after another. Jon wished to scream his defiance, to try some spell to end the silent slaughter. But Morgoth held him in a mental bond so potent that escape was impossible. As his father moved from one person to the next, the bond between him and Jonathan strengthened. Jon sensed energy flowing from his father into him, each life adding to it. When the killing was over, they would both be omnipotent. Jon doubted that even the hags could control them then.

The power tempted Jon. He saw himself as a ruler, Sondra dressed in satins and gold on a throne beside him, the beauty of the land they could create.

As the tenth victim died, Morgoth returned his hand to the victim's forehead. The cold flesh thawed, the limbs twitched, and the body stood, its glazed eyes following Morgoth as he moved to the next in line. No breath from the body clouded the frigid air. The man was his father's slave now.

Morgoth would do this with all of them, Jon realized, then lead the animated corpses to the fortress. "No!" Jon cried, "The village must be destroyed, all trace ended. I claim the right to my revenge!"

Morgoth turned to face his son. The Silverlord's eyes glowed red from the life force coursing in him. He said nothing, but released his son to destroy the village.

Jon pointed his fingers toward the embers in the fire pit. The dying fire roared and rolled inward. He spread his fingers and angled them toward the crowd. A single word and the flames shot outward, the bodies flaring in their heat. As Morgoth turned to him, Jon hid his disgust behind a howl of triumph.

He felt his father's wrath and expected to die for the servants he had immolated. Instead Morgoth reined in his anger and looked from the devastation around him to Jonathan. His face showed satisfaction. Jon felt the first glimmer of hope—the realization that, though his emotions were plain to Morgoth, his motives were veiled. He knew his father was beginning another, more powerful, incantation, but he didn't have the endurance to see its result. The use of his power had exhausted him, and he fell mercifully unconscious.

The ceremony had just begun when Willa led the thirty people who had joined her through the deserted inn to the hidden passage and staircase Jon had described. Aran, her husband, carried their single lamp, holding it high to light their way. At the bottom of the stairs, they discovered Dirca, her body as frozen as the others had been. "We were right about Jonathan," Willa said. "And look!" She took the lamp and held it close to the passage, where thin lines of blood marked the trail to the narrow passage beyond.

"Sondra?" she whispered, more frightened of an answer than of the pressing silence of the earth. "Sondra."

A sound so soft and distant that it might have been imagined came from a narrow crack between the walls; a broken, feeble whimper of despair. Willa moved closer to the wall. "Sondra," she repeated. Taking the lamp, she reached into the crack. It seemed as if the air within had changed into a clear membrane, yielding but far too strong to break. With effort, Willa forced her hand into it and found herself held as securely as an animal in a trap.

Her fingers tingled. Her hand grew numb. Bewildered, she cried out. Aran took hold of her wrist, pulling desperately, watching as her hand became blackened from blood seeping through the tissue.

The hand wouldn't move. Aran opened the lamp and held the flame against the barrier. The wall exploded, spitting him and Willa away from the crack. Aran crashed against the others. Willa fell atop him, screaming as, in the light of the lantern, she looked in horror at the charred stump of her wrist.

The others tended her, and her screams subsided. Once again, they heard the despondent whimper, as if the walls themselves cried for the town.

eighteen

Lights danced, mischievous glowing sprites that played on the shadowy ceiling of his cave. Jon lay groggy on the stone floor, and Sondra knelt beside him. Her bruises had begun to heal, but her face was still swollen and her eyes held no expression, not even relief that he was finally conscious. When he reached for her, she flinched as if he had tried to strike her.

"Sondra?"

A shriek pierced the silence of the cavern.

Stunned, Sondra held her hands over her ears. Tears leaked from the corners of her tightly shut eyes. A second, louder shriek trailed into pitiful sobs.

"No!" Sondra screamed at the emptiness around them. "No, leave them alone!"

"Sondra, what is it?" Jon reached for her hand. His own, though stiffened by the tight new skin that had replaced his burned flesh, was nearly healed. He looked down in wonder as Sondra brushed his face.

"When Morgoth brought you here, I couldn't believe you could still live," Sondra whispered. "He ordered me to bathe you in the pool, to keep your wounds wet. Now you're nearly healed."

"How long have I been here?" he asked.

"Days? Weeks? It's always dark here." She spoke woodenly, emotionless.

"He sleeps during the day. How often has he slept?"

"I don't know. He doesn't stay here. He's used his sorcery to make this my prison. I can't leave. I've tried and failed. I tried to attack him, but he touched me here." She showed him the deep burns on her wrists. "The pool's waters haven't helped me."

"He promised he wouldn't harm you."

"I don't think he meant to. He let me go as soon as his hands did this. He told me the people of Linde are all dead. He drained them. I think he was hungry when he touched me—his body tried to drain me."

Jon looked down at her wrists, and kissed the wounds. "Go on," he said.

"He found others hiding in my father's cavern. Then the real horror began," Sondra said, shuddering at her own words. "He dares not kill them—they're all the life he has left. He doesn't drain the women, for they alone can bear children to feed him. So he inflicts pain on the men and feasts on their agony. He's in there now. There'll be more screams before he leaves them."

"Where does he go?"

"He hunts. I think he searches for Maeve. When he visits you, I hear him muttering her name. He's furious."

"At least her defiance shows he's not omnipotent," Jon noted grimly. "How do you survive?"

"He brings me wine, bread, charred meat." She pointed toward a pile of bones in the corner—long arm and leg bones, and curving bones like human ribs. "This is all he brings me." Sondra said. "At first I wouldn't eat, so he forced me. Now I think more of the hunger than the meat."

He had no hope to give her, no strength to keep her safe, and so he held her and told her he loved her.

When the screams stopped, they rose and tried to leave the cave. Jonathan could walk right through the mouth, but a mystic force stopped Sondra.

"Leave me. Go. Find help," she said.

"Would you abandon me?" he asked.

"Not if I could avoid it."

He smiled, the same confident smile that first attracted her. Striding to the passage to Ivar's cavern, he said, "I'm not saying good-bye." Then he disappeared into the dark crevice.

Ivar's cavern was utterly black and silent, save for the soft breathing of the prisoners who slept and the whimpers of those recently drained. Jon moved slowly among the bodies, pausing often to gauge where they lay. At the foot of the stairs, he felt the barrier his father had conjured to keep his cattle in their pen. It took only a few simple words to break the spell, then Jon passed through and climbed to the inn.

The drinking and dining halls were dark and empty. The front doors hung open, and a biting wind made small snow drifts in the corners. The mugs on the shelf behind the bar were shattered, and kegs of ale intended for the late-night revelers had frozen and split.

Jon stepped outside. He saw the stars and a nearly full moon shining down on the snow, so smooth and unmarred that it might have never held people at all. The beautifully painted cottages had disappeared. The barn and winery were also gone. Piles of stones marked former chimneys, and an occasional charred timber poked through the drifts of snow. The only landmark that was still identifiable was the narrow road that wound through the trees toward Viktal.

The lute he had played so often lay on the porch beneath a dusting of snow. Without picking it up, he ran his hand over the strings. The wood had grown warped, the strings out of tune. Even if it could have been played, no songs remained for him, not even a dirge for the deaths he had caused. He brushed the snow from it and placed it on the hook beside the door.

Something Dominic had told him years ago came to him: "True evil cannot exist in a man unless, given the choice to do good, he rejects it."

He'd made his choice, he realized. He'd made it during the attack on the shrine. Now he needed to discover the means to end the terror of Sondra and the townsfolk. Perhaps the secret lay in the inn or the caverns below. More likely, it lay in his own mind. He glanced at the moon again. He had less than two days to find it.

As dawn broke, he returned to Ivar's cavern. He took his teacher's remaining spellbooks from their hiding places and carried them back to the milky cavern. There, with Sondra sleeping nearby, he began to read.

Hours passed as he memorized spells for his final battle. He thought often of the prophecy mentioned in his mother's legacy— *One day love will corrupt the cloth. One day corruption from within will destroy it.* Jon felt that his father stirred, somewhere deep in the earth. Night had fallen. He closed the book and waited anxiously for Morgoth to come to him.

When Morgoth joined him, Jon immediately noticed the change in his father. Morgoth seemed stronger, confident to the point of euphoria. As Jon sat, his emotions carefully veiled, his father paced the length of the cavern. Morgoth's robe shimmered in the colored light, and the amulet on his neck glowed with its own terrible fire. Morgoth held his spell book in one hand. His other hand clenched and relaxed as if exercising for the struggle to come. "When my legions are free, we will rebuild Linde. We have the seeds in the cavern below the inn. They're all young and strong. There'll be children in this town soon enough."

"And what of the lives you need to live?" Jon asked.

"We'll move east and conquer Viktal. Then we'll take Kellee as well. The towns are large, filled with life and wealth. You and I will rule Tepest together, Jonathan. Nothing will stop us."

"Together," Jon echoed and smiled happily. He pointed to the spellbooks. "I'm studying everything Ivar has learned. I only wish I were less tired."

Morgoth laughed. Sondra stirred in her sleep, but didn't wake. "I can help with that," he said, and rested his hands on Jon's shoulders. Jon felt energy course through him, renewing his strength, his concentration. He recalled the source of that energy and squelched a shudder.

"Father, I need to speak about what happened at the fortress," Jon began. "I had difficulty destroying those men, especially Hektor. They raised me. And Ivar was my teacher. Before I found you, he taught me much."

"Did he?" Jon had expected his father to be furious. Instead Morgoth looked thoughtful. "Do you think those two men would serve you?" Morgoth asked.

"I don't know," Jon answered truthfully. "I think not."

"If you wish, we could spare them."

"You would do that?" Jon asked. His intention had been to explain why he'd acted as he did in the fortress, to voice his regret and promise he wouldn't fail again. He hardly expected his father to make such an offer.

"Mercy is one of the few gifts we can give," his father replied.

Jon looked at his father in amazement. He wondered what sort of man Morgoth might have become had he been raised by men such as Ivar and Hektor and Dominic. Instead of saddening Jon, the insight gave him hope. His own fate hadn't been set at birth. The choice was still his to make. He prayed that, when the time came, he could defeat his father. "We have so little time to prepare," Jon said. "I doubt we can undo the spell on the shrine doors."

Morgoth laughed. "You don't have to undo it," he said. "In the days since our last assault, I've considered the matter. Jonathan, you have the calling."

"Impossible!" Jon exclaimed.

Morgoth smiled. "You don't know it yet, but it is true. You entered the shrine. You can do it again tomorrow night when the moon is full. You will help free the legions, and they will serve you as willingly as they do me."

"Are you certain? Completely certain?" Jon asked.

"There is a way to be certain. Go to the shrine." He shook his head and chuckled. "Ivar is no match for you. Those old men can't stop you." He laid his spellbook in front of Jon and opened it. "Read this, then go to the fortress," he said and left Jon staring numbly at the page.

By morning, Jon had the spell memorized. He pulled a feather from the box on the table and held it in his palm. With his mind firmly fixed on the fortress gates, he recited the incantation and blew the feather from his hand. The room faded around him. The air roared.

Dominic and Ivar were guarding the fortress gates the following morning when Jonathan appeared.

Ever since the previous battle, the fortress had been surrounded by Morgoth's impenetrable mist. The monks had prayed Jon would appear and help in their escape. Now, arriving on the day before the full moon, they eyed him with suspicion.

Ivar joined him outside the fortress walls. Dominic waited just inside the ruined doors in the protected sphere of Ivar's spell. Both men listened carefully as Jon related the tragedies that had occurred since he'd fled the fortress a month ago. "I have come to see if what my father tells me is correct," Jon concluded. "He believes I have the calling."

Neither man looked surprised.

"So you knew as well," Jon said.

"Will you stand with us tonight?" Dominic asked. Jon shook his head. "I must enter the shrine again and speak to the souls in the cloth."

"We can't allow that," Dominic said.

"Can't?" Jonathan walked past Ivar and through the fortress doors, barely pausing when he crossed the boundary of Ivar's spell. "You have no choice," he said and continued toward the shrine.

Dominic rushed forward to stop him, but Ivar saw an unfamiliar strength in Jon's eyes and held the monk back. "The spell on the shrine has always tested the calling. If he can enter, he is a Guardian," he said. They watched as Jonathan lifted the bars from the shrine doors and effortlessly stepped inside.

The air in the shrine was dry and pressed heavily against Jonathan, draining his resolve. With effort, he walked forward until only the stone altar separated him from the cloth. The folds seemed to watch him, waiting for him to pass judgment on himself.

He wouldn't do so, not yet. Instead he lit a candle and, with a single gesture, magically closed the shrine doors. Then he faced the cloth, concealed in the darkness beyond the stone slab.

"Corruption from within," he whispered, and, his voice filled with reverence, he spoke his mother's name for the first time. "Leith."

No answer. He called again more forcefully, concentrating this time, much as Ivar had taught him to focus on a spell, channeling his power and will toward her. He sensed a tentative touch, no more.

"Free her," he called to the dark souls on the cloth. "Free her and let her come to me, or I won't free you."

The terrible surface of the cloth shifted. A presence flowed through him, bringing with it a wave of love more intense than any he had ever felt. "Let me see you, Mother," he said. When the presence didn't retreat, he lifted the candle from the altar and moved its flame closer to the cloth.

A woman's face formed out of the countless figures, a face unlike his own. Yet he saw something, some sadness in the eyes, that told him they shared a similar temperament. He thought of how quickly Leith had chosen death over her curse, of how many times he had contemplated the same sad fate. They were alike: vacillating, fragile, unsuited to this dark and savage land.

Haltingly, fearful that he would dispel her tenuous presence, he confessed to everything he had done, told her of all the evil his father had brought to the land. And, when he finished, he asked her what he must do.

The answer came to him as water to thirst, food to starvation— wordless flashes of insight telling him he already held much of the truth inside him, and that his main difficulty would be accepting the terrible sacrifice he would have to make.

He would have teleported from the shrine, but he sensed any spells he worked would have no effect in these protected walls. When he stepped into the light of the courtyard, he looked with dismay at how low the sun had fallen.

"Will you stand with us tonight?" Dominic asked.

Jonathan shook his head. As Dominic walked toward him, Jonathan whispered. "I've no time to discuss what must be done." A second feather fell from his hand, and he disappeared as Dominic's hand reached for him.

With regret, Ivar watched him vanish. Ivar was the Guardians' only protection through the coming night. But Jonathan's magic and his calling made Ivar's spells insignificant. Even so, Ivar recast the spell that protected the fortress walls—some protection was better than none. He spent the next few hours memorizing other incantations he thought would be most useful—spells that burned, that froze, that drained an adversary's strength and will and memory.

He spent the last hours of daylight considering Morgoth's nature and the sounds he had heard coming from the shrine during the last release. Morgoth's minions would likely be as voracious as their master.

Ivar determined then if Morgoth victored, neither he nor any Guardian would live to feed the souls. He reserved his last spell for the Guardians and himself.

Ivar stood inside the ruined fortress doors, looking at the swirling mists just outside the walls as they glowed in the setting sun. He wasn't surprised to find himself thinking of Jonathan, the boy's growing power, and the terrible choices they would both have to make tonight.

"You were right about everything, Father," Jonathan said when Morgoth joined him in the white cavern just after sunset. "I can break Ivar's spell with a single word. And I have the calling. I can enter the shrine."

"The calling gives you a choice," Morgoth replied, staring at Sondra as he spoke. "How will you stand?"

"With you. I told your legion we will come for them tonight.

They wait," Jon replied with no hesitation, letting his father's crystalline laughter fill the cavern before echoing it with his own. Sondra shook her head and backed away from him, but Jon did nothing more than glance her way.

"We must go soon," Morgoth said to his son. "Before we do I must replenish my power. Seven men remain. Bring me two."

"Here?" Jonathan glanced at Sondra. She revealed no emotion save contempt.

"Here. I can go to them, but I wish to see this sign of your loyalty," Morgoth said, then looked from his son to Sondra and laughed. "Don't worry. There are spells to make her love you . . . and to obey."

Jon moved toward the passage.

"Wait!" Sondra called. "Jon, you mustn't do this."

"My father saved my life when this town would destroy me. I'm hardly concerned about the deaths of his slaves. As for you, watch your words. My spells could steal your memory and your speech." He rested a hand on the side of her face. She slapped it away. He laughed and went for the slaves.

Jon knew words to make men docile. He used them on the pair he chose before leading them to his father. Morgoth chose the more stoic victim first. As he moved toward his first kill, the man cursed him. In response, Morgoth touched the man's lips. They slackened, the jaw opened, and Morgoth reached inside the man's mouth and rested his fingers on the tongue.

A shudder passed through the man as the cold flowed down his throat, freezing his lungs, slowing the beating of his heart. He struggled to breathe, and his frozen ribs cracked. As his legs gave way, Morgoth laid him on the stone floor and brushed his hands over the man's limbs, coming last to the face where the victim's eyes still moved, looking for some rescue.

The second victim had no courage left. He fell at Morgoth's bare feet. Too frightened to touch the Silverlord, he instead kissed the ground in front of him, begging to be allowed to serve him.

"Do you pledge your life to me?" Morgoth asked.

"Yes!"

"Then rise and come to me."

The man saw Morgoth's outstretched arms, the gluttonous anticipation in his pale eyes. As he scrambled backward, Morgoth touched him. He died quickly, his body tossed over the other. "Come," Morgoth said to his son and turned to go. When Jonathan didn't follow, he watched in amusement as Jon said his good-bye to Sondra.

"Listen," Jon told her. "Judge me as you wish, but I'm no different than when you agreed to be my wife."

"Then I have never known you at all," Sondra replied coldly, her eyes focused on the corpses.

Morgoth looked from his son to the men he had killed. "Let us leave your beloved in peace," he whispered and raised his hand, pointing toward the bodies on the ground. A carefully spoken word, a languid gesture, and the bodies were surrounded by a force that glowed and gave off a heat of such intensity that Sondra retreated to a shadowed corner and Jonathan fought the instinctive urge to join her.

The frozen flesh of the corpses thawed. The limbs began to move, pushing the bodies upright. "Come," Morgoth commanded them, his voice nearly inaudible beneath Sondra's extended scream of terror.

"We'll go into Linde first," Morgoth said and took Jon's hand. Jon looked over his shoulder at the faithful dead.

They went quickly to the center of town. There, Morgoth stopped in the center of the ceremonial circle and raised his arms. A luminous sphere formed in the sorcerer's hands. The light inside it grew brighter and shot from its container in glowing beams that played over the charred bodies on the ground. As Jon watched, fascination turned to horror.

The limbs of the dead thawed. Hands and feet twitched. Bodies sat up. Those with legs rose. A terrible keening came from their throats, a wail of protest at being disturbed, of acknowledgment to Morgoth's terrible power.

"I am the ruler of all of you," Morgoth cried. "Of all that live in my land. Of all that died by my hand. Follow me!" Morgoth turned and led Jonathan toward the river and the path to the fortress, while the dead walked behind.

NINETEEN

SINCE THE MOMENT SHE fLED THE CEREMONIAL circle, Maeve hadn't dared to change from fox form. During the day, when Morgoth slept, she stole into Linde, gnawing on the remains of the cattle and the bodies left in the ruins of the town. During the night, she was constantly on the move, using her powers to their fullest, her silver form vanishing in one snow-covered stand of trees after another.

She might have gone to the hags to confess, but she sensed they would be even less likely to remove her curse than Morgoth. Her only hope was to defeat the Silverlord before facing them. She had no idea how.

On the night of the ceremony, she stood on a hill overlooking the village and watched her neighbors and town fall by Morgoth's hand. Though she most grieved the treasures lost in the burning, she also heard Kezi's anguished howl and thought of his daughter with pity.

During the weeks that followed the burning, Kezi pursued her. Savaged by the strength of his first change and maddened by his loss, he wouldn't be charmed. So Maeve used him as a pawn. She ran from him, but kept him always in sight so that, if she and Morgoth met, Morgoth would find an easier feast.

Two weeks after the festival, a storm roared into the valley. It began with sleet, followed by snow so thick it blinded Maeve. She had no choice but to shelter in a low cave in the hills near Morgoth's lair. At the height of the storm, she heard a howling more desolate than the wind, and knew Kezi had somehow managed to find her. Since the cave had only one escape, she slowly made her way outside.

The storm abated somewhat, enough that Maeve could see the wolf waiting for her on nearby rocks. Keeping close to the ground so that her silver fur would blend with the crystalline snow, Maeve inched her way toward him. She was within striking distance when she saw the silver cloud form above Kezi's head.

Though it took all her resolve, she didn't move, didn't tremble when the mist took shape beside Kezi. Seeing the Silverlord, Kezi lunged. Morgoth dodged like a trained dancer, brushing one of Kezi's rear legs. The leg froze, dragging as Kezi attacked again.

The effect was the same. The Silverlord's hand lashed out, freezing the other rear limb. Kezi fell, waiting for Morgoth to drain his life. Instead, Morgoth, with a sly smile, let the werewolf heal and attack again. "We have hours until dawn, foolish beast," Morgoth said and laughed, the sound blown away by the incessant bitter wind.

She watched Morgoth at his sport while the blowing snow covered her. Finally, Morgoth seemed to tire of the game. He raised his arm and plucked a silver sword from the swirling snow, lowered it, and waited for Kezi's next attack. Kezi should run, Maeve thought, but the werewolf was too furious or stupid to save himself. A leap, a deft sidestep, and Kezi fell with the blade through his back. Maeve didn't stay to watch Kezi die. As Morgoth began to pull the final sparks of life from Kezi's body, she backed stealthily away.

At sunrise, she returned to Kezi's body. He had reverted to

human form. Now he lay coated with frost. Maeve dug deep inside him to where the blood had pooled, warm and thick, and feasted. Afterward, she sat and thought of the pain she had sensed in Kezi's final howls and how much more terrible her own pain would be when Morgoth caught her. He was hoarding his power, unwilling to use it fully to find her. Once he had triumphed, though, there would be no place for her to hide, neither here nor anywhere in Tepest.

She knew he coveted the cloth and intended to attack the fortress at full moon. On the afternoon before it, she padded up the mountain path as far as she could. When the mist grew too thick for travel, she found a crevasse in which to hide. Tonight would be the final clash. Tonight she would ally herself with the winning side and find peace, even if it were only the peace of slavery or death. With her body hidden in the snow, with her head between her paws, she watched the mists swirl above the road.

At dusk, the mist thinned. She heard the distant sound of the Guardians' chant. Some ineffable power drew her from her hiding place to the open fortress gates. Weak, unable to resist, she moved forward until she struck Ivar's spell. There she halted, unable to retreat or move forward.

Ivar stood just inside the fortress walls. He wore the simple gray robe of the Guardians. His thin white hair was whipped by the steady winter wind, and he carried a carved staff in one hand.

Ivar saw her, and his staff rose to point in her direction, to destroy what he must see as one of Morgoth's servants. She had no way to tell him otherwise; pride forbade her to reveal the horror of the hags' curse. She would rather die than see his pity, so she watched the sparks grow on the tip of his staff and waited for the fire to destroy her.

Before he could complete the last, lethal gesture, she felt the approach of another power, nearly equal to that of the cloth. Her body trembled piteously as she turned and saw Jonathan approach, followed by Morgoth and a terrible army: the burned dead of Linde.

Animated by some dread sorcery, they walked stiffly in a tight group. Their bodies were blackened from the burnt shreds of charred cloth and leather stuck to their flesh. Those with eyes led; those who were blind followed. Their limbs had been savaged, some by her, others by Morgoth to feed his living slaves. None seemed capable of holding a weapon, but were horrific enough with their bony talons.

Howling in terror, Maeve fought to break free from the pull of the cloth. Ivar stepped away from the fortress doors. Maeve saw him tremble. His arms hung limp at his side, as if he had lost the will to raise them.

The wind around the fortress increased, causing a chill screech in the crumbling fortress walls. Amid the screams, a low voice, confident and sure, spoke. "The dead cannot pass these fortress walls. He knows."

Who had spoken? The voice sounded like Leith's, but Leith had died long ago. The words seemed to renew Ivar's confidence. He raised his staff once more, pointed it beyond Maeve, and finished his incantation.

Flames flew from the tip of his staff. They did no damage to Morgoth or Jonathan, flowing over the pair to flame those already burned. The first ranks of the mindless band dropped, writhing silently in the flames, animated still by Morgoth's despicable power. Those in the rear had been shielded, but halted, unable to move forward without eyes or voice to guide them.

The diversion of the flame gave Maeve a chance to escape. With her body pressed to the ground, her muzzle between her paws, she used what power she possessed to fight the terrible pull of the cloth.

She began a slow, steady retreat from the entrance. A pile of rocks near the edge of the road gave her some protection. She lay flat behind it and watched the battle begin.

His father had raised the dead!

The supreme confidence Jon had gained in the shrine faltered under the weight of his father's power. The sight of the burned corpses rising from their resting places around the ceremonial circle, the sight of the cage where he had spent so many despondent hours, the agony of the flames themselves weakened his resolve. As Ivar's wall of fire flowed around him, he trembled and shrank back, then steadied himself. He possessed the power, he possessed the skill—he wouldn't let fear defeat him.

His father's hand squeezed his shoulder in a gesture of filial support. "This is our night of triumph," Morgoth said. "When it's over, we will rule this land together."

"Together," Jonathan repeated. The horror of that promise bolstered his resolve. He moved forward through flames that couldn't touch him.

He and Morgoth halted outside the fortress arch. "Peto! Hektor! Dominic! Mattas! Andor, my friend, your alliance has shifted!" Morgoth called to the chanting Guardians. "Enjoy the last moments of your calling."

The chant didn't waver. Andor, his concentration broken for a moment, glanced once over his shoulder, then quickly looked back to the shrine.

Morgoth laughed. Tonight, Jonathan couldn't echo the sound. He stood stiffly at his father's side, staring at Ivar with a twisted smile on his face. He and Ivar had studied together for months, he was betrothed to Ivar's daughter. If the wizard didn't trust him, so be it. Jonathan needed no help to do what must be done. No matter how the night ended, he wouldn't waver again.

He and his father had planned this moment carefully. The cloth wouldn't release its prisoners without Morgoth's call. Morgoth would wait to do so until Jonathan had entered the shrine and brought the tapestry outside. That would be Morgoth's victory. The Guardians wouldn't have a chance, Jonathan thought, as he said the words that destroyed the magical barrier Ivar had erected and walked through the gates.

Before Morgoth followed, he turned to the dead. "Come!" he ordered. They shuffled toward their master's voice but, at the fortress gates, halted. The terrible keening from the fortress walls seemed to hold them back, the sound mimicked by the harsh, mournful moans from their throats.

With a disdainful backward glance, Morgoth went on alone into the courtyard, where Jonathan already faced his old teacher.

No amount of courage could make up for Ivar's lack of power. A word from Morgoth, and Ivar and the Guardians became motionless—silent, trapped, conscious-unable to do anything except wait for death. As Jonathan moved through them toward the barred doors of the shrine, Ivar broke Morgoth's hold long enough to grip Jonathan's arm and whisper a single command, "Forget." Though Jonathan jerked away as soon he felt the touch, Ivar's spell had already done its work. The carefully worded incantation of destruction shattered in his mind. He cried out in anger, and his father responded.

Ivar was suddenly circled by a ring of fire Jonathan knew all too well. He thought of Alden as he watched the ropes of flame slowly tighten to destroy his teacher, the father of his betrothed. "No!" Jon screamed. "No! Father, remember your promise!"

It seemed, for a moment, that Morgoth increased Ivar's agony.

Then, as suddenly as the ropes of flame had formed, they vanished and Ivar crumpled to the ground. "Stop!" Ivar called, but Jon ignored him and lifted the bars on the shrine door.

Then Jon turned to his old teacher, crouching over the place where he lay. "Those who hide their powers survive in this land. That's what you told me once. Remember the words as you watch me do what I must," he said and stepped inside the shrine.

The power of the cloth had never seemed so great! Jonathan had been responsible for so many deaths, so much destruction, he could scarcely resist the temptation to step forward, admit his guilt, and merge with the folds. He still had a choice, he knew. He resisted and stepped forward, ripping the tapestry from its place on the wall. The folds twisted in his hands, struggling to break free, to claim his soul, a soul that belonged in the tapestry's dread web.

"Soon," he whispered and turned slowly toward the door, struggling more than he needed to, seeking the time necessary to recall the words that would save them all.

A few steps from the door, he stopped, crying out.

"I cannot pass. I need your help, Father."

"You have the calling," Morgoth replied.

"The calling allowed me to enter, but now I cannot leave. This is some trick of Ivar's. His body will break the spell. Send him to me."

Morgoth's eyes narrowed to icy slivers as he looked from the boy to the wizard he had ensorceled.

Jonathan understood Morgoth's doubt, but held his ground. He had been a dutiful son, supporting his father in everything, even in torture and death. He bowed his head and gave in to the terror he felt. As he appeared to fight the motions of the cloth, he began whispering the first few words of the incantation that would send the souls trapped on it to the judgment of the fates.

"Free him!" Jonathan called to Morgoth when he could go no further with the incantation. "Send him to me before the cloth claims me as it did my mother."

Morgoth laughed as he released Ivar and gripped his shoulder with an icy hand, pushing him toward the shrine door. Jon waited inside. He reached out, gripped Ivar's arm and pulled him through.

The spell guarding the shrine weighed heavily on his teacher. "Jonathan," Ivar called, gripping him tightly. "I can't see. I can scarcely breathe. Please. Let me go!"

Instead of responding, Jon painfully tried to reform the words of his incantation. As he did, Ivar reached for him, his hand brushing Jon's, his fingers feeling the glass rod encased in fur. "You're reciting the lightning spell I taught you," Ivar whispered.

"Yes, but I've forgotten the words. Help me!" Jonathan whispered. His voice was ragged, frantic. If he begged more openly, his father would surely hear and stop them.

Jon gripped the cloth tighter, burying his face in the folds, whispering words loud enough for Ivar to hear.

"Mother . . . Leith . . . Mother . . . help us."

The weight of the shrine's terrible spell lightened.

Ivar rubbed his eyes and cupped Jonathan's chin. As they looked at one another, as they recited the words together, Morgoth watched, still uncertain whether Jon acted of his own will, or as a tool of Ivar's.

"Jonathan!" Morgoth screamed. "Son! Bring the cloth out to me!"

Jonathan obeyed, moving toward the doorway. "No!" Ivar screamed, but Jon ignored him and walked stiffly toward the door, drawn by his father's power as the souls were drawn by the cloth. Ivar grabbed Jonathan's arm and was pulled forward as well.

In the courtyard, Jonathan unfurled the cloth before his father.

As Morgoth began to speak the words that would call the souls from their prison, the pattern on the cloth began to whirl. Jon took a deep breath, recited a quick prayer for his soul and released his grip on the edges of the cloth. The cloth covered him, draining his strength. He fell to his knees as the tapestry began its terrible work.

Ivar struggled to pull him free. Jonathan fought to remain. "Corruption from within," Jon whispered. "Join me. It's the only way to destroy those trapped here."

"A martyr's death," Ivar whispered and gripped the boy's hand, rubbing the glass and fur, as together they recited the words of the incantation, words drowned by screams from the cloth.

They finished. As the souls spun free, bolts of lightning flowed from Ivar's hand, destroying each of them with sorcery and fire.

"Father!" Jonathan shrieked. "Father, help me!"

Morgoth saw the boy on his knees, Ivar gripping him tightly, the cloth stealing the life of his only son. With a shriek of fury, Morgoth rushed forward. His arms flailed, trying to brush Ivar aside, trying to pull the cloth off his son. Jonathan gripped his father's hands. "Don't let go," he cried, his voice pleading.

But he couldn't hide his moment of triumph. Morgoth frowned and wrenched his hands out of his son's grasp. As he reeled backward, his expression showed that he knew now how his son had used his own love to betray him.

"Foolish child," he said. "Don't think I'd let your power die so easily. Now you will serve me forever." He pointed at his son and began a new incantation.

A flash of white streaked through the fortress arch. Maeve struck silently, all four paws landing on Morgoth's back. The weight of her charge pushed him into his son's arms. As the sorcerer fell, Ivar loosed the last lightning bolt at the cloth that covered them.

The cloth reacted as it always did, repelling the spell, turning it against the one who cast it, the one now absorbed in the cloth. Jonathan, Morgoth, and Ivar descended into a maelstrom of fire and agony, a storm Jonathan increased with the last of his power, ensuring that none of them, nor the cloth itself, would escape.

As Morgoth died, his power died. The Guardians fell flat against the ground, shielding their eyes from the burning radiance. But Dominic, braver than the others, raised his head and, through the whirling flames, saw Jonathan kneeling in the center of the storm. He controlled the flames as Leith stood behind him, supporting him with her arms, her face buried in his fiery hair.

epilogue

LONG after JONATHAN HAD Left WITH HIS father,
Sondra realized what his final words had meant. "Come back to
me," she whispered then spent the next hours praying for some
miracle to save them both. But her words had been hollow, filled
with despair.

When the spell that surrounded the cave lifted, Sondra left, rushing to release the others from Ivar's cavern. After climbing the steps,
they stood in the ruined drinking hall, gazing bleary-eyed at the
emptiness where their houses had once been, where their families
had once dwelt.

And they mourned.

The group settled at the sprawling inn. The five couples who had
been betrothed celebrated their marriage in a small, sad feast in the
dining hall. The others toasted them with cloudberry wine from the
storeroom, then they all dined on ham from the ruined smokehouse.
None spoke of the past; they spoke of spring when they would take
the remaining wine to Viktal, trading it for goats to graze their
fields. They spoke of rebuilding their homes, of the children they
would have. Sondra thought of herself and Jon and did her best to
hide her tears.

Dominic, Andor, Hektor, Mattas, and Peto joined them a few days later. After so many years of single purpose, Dominic seemed bewildered, out of place. He took on the task of rebuilding the stone winery, working alone when the weather allowed it. Peto, younger and far more able to adapt, found himself drawn to Willa, whose new husband had been the last man killed by Morgoth. He comforted her with gentle patience, and Sondra suspected they'd soon recite their own vows.

As for her uncle, Andor settled into his old duties. Though he didn't laugh as he once had, he seemed content in the emptiness of the halls. All that ended when Maeve walked through the inn doors, as if she had been there only yesterday. Her beauty was restored, her clothes as colorful as in years past. She glanced defiantly at Sondra, then took a lute from the case on her back and began to play.

The villagers clustered around her, asking for songs, for news of Kellee and Viktal, for still more songs. When the rest went back to their duties, Raesa, one of the younger girls, stayed. Sondra watched the pair speaking together, Maeve's long fingers brushing back a wayward lock of Raesa's dark hair.

"Will you say something to warn Raesa?" Sondra asked her uncle.

Andor looked at the pair. "Maeve's music is beautiful," he said as if that settled everything. In the days that followed, he seemed happier. Some balance necessary to his nature had been restored.

As for Sondra, she couldn't share the optimism of her friends. If only she and Jonathan had said a proper good-bye, she might have opened her soul to another. But instead, she felt empty, alone.

When the first spring thaw came, Sondra left the inn, following the path to the fortress where her love had defeated the evil of his past and paid for it with his life. There, in a pile of blackened stones that had once been the shrine, she sat and waited for his spirit to touch her.

Sections of the fortress had crumbled in the final deadly clash of power. The jagged walls threw broken shadows across the courtyard, shadows that lengthened and merged as night fell. Still Sondra sat, heedless of the darkness and the things that lived in it. She had never felt more safe.

A dim glow appeared in the fortress dining hall. She went to it and saw that, as in Jonathan's cavern, the light seemed to come from the air itself. The table had been laid with a simple meal—coarse brown bread, a few slices of cheese, fresh water for her thirst.

As she took the place that had been prepared for her, she began to speak, as if she and Jonathan shared the meal together. She told him about Linde and the ones who had survived, about Andor and Dominic. At the end, she spoke the words that should have been said at their parting.

"I know you did what you had to. I loved you then, Jonathan. I love you now. I always will."

The light grew and split, the halves forming human shapes, features Sondra could almost see. "Leith," she whispered, then, "Husband."

Silver hands touched her face and she laughed.